PENGUIN BOOKS

THE OH MY GOD DELUSION

The Oh My God Delusion

ROSS O'CARROLL-KELLY
(as told to Paul Howard)

Illustrated by
ALAN CLARKE

PENGUIN BOOKS

PENGUIN BOOKS

Published by the Penguin Group
Penguin Books Ltd, 80 Strand, London WC2R ORL, England
Penguin Group (USA) Inc., 375 Hudson Street, New York, New York 10014, USA
Penguin Group (Canada), 90 Eglinton Avenue East, Suite 700, Toronto, Ontario, Canada M4P 2Y3
(a division of Pearson Penguin Canada Inc.)
Penguin Ireland, 25 St Stephen's Green, Dublin 2, Ireland (a division of Penguin Books Ltd)
Penguin Group (Australia), 250 Camberwell Road, Camberwell, Victoria 3124, Australia
(a division of Pearson Australia Group Pty Ltd)
Penguin Books India Pvt Ltd, 11 Community Centre, Panchsheel Park, New Delhi – 110 017, India
Penguin Group (NZ), 67 Apollo Drive, Rosedale, Auckland 0632, New Zealand
(a division of Pearson New Zealand Ltd)
Penguin Books (South Africa) (Pty) Ltd, 24 Sturdee Avenue, Rosebank, Johannesburg 2196, South Africa

Penguin Books Ltd, Registered Offices: 80 Strand, London WC2R ORL, England

www.penguin.com

First published by Penguin Ireland 2010
Published in Penguin Books 2011
004

Text copyright © Paul Howard, 2010
Illustrations copyright © Alan Clarke, 2010
All rights reserved

'Make Me Smile (Come Up and See Me)', words and music by Steve Harley © 1975
RAK Publishing Ltd. Licensed courtesy of RAK Publishing Ltd

Penguin Ireland thanks O'Brien Press for its agreement to Penguin Ireland
using the same design approach and typography, and the same artist,
as O'Brien Press used in the first four Ross O'Carroll-Kelly titles

The moral right of the author and of the illustrator has been asserted

Typeset by Palimpsest Book Production Limited, Falkirk, Stirlingshire
Printed in Great Britain by Clays Ltd, St Ives plc

ISBN: 978-1-844-88176-5

www.greenpenguin.co.uk

Penguin Books is committed to a sustainable
future for our business, our readers and our planet.
This book is made from Forest Stewardship
Council™ certified paper.

ALWAYS LEARNING   **PEARSON**

You spoilt the game,
No matter what you say,
For only metal,
What a bore.

– 'Make Me Smile (Come Up and See Me)',
Steve Harley and Cockney Rebel

Contents

Prologue

So I check the time. It's, like, eight o'clock in the morning? I peel back the duvet – slowly, roysh, so as not to wake her. I swing the legs out of the bed, again gently, then stort gathering up the old threads, like Hansel and Gretel, following the trail to the living room, where it all kicked off last night.

One of my better one-night stands, it has to be said. Breege. A lady Gorda, of all things, the spits of Vida Guerra, and that's not just me trying to cover over the fact that she's from, like, Mullingor.

I throw on the old Apple Crumble, step into my chinos and my Cole Haans, then fix my hair in the mirror.

Cheeky focker on the door of Copper's, by the way. See, I actually met the bird in, like, Kehoe's? The usual. Gave her one or two of my lines and it turned out Horcourt Street was where she was headed.

Well, I wasn't going to break up the porty.

Of course the bouncers in there know me and they know my MO. 'Bringing a bogger *to* Copper Face Jacks,' one of them went. 'That's a new one for you, Ross. We probably should charge you corkage.'

It *was* a good line, though, and I decided to be the better man and just laughed.

I tiptoe back out to the hall, passing the bedroom, where she's still spitting zeds. Out of the game. I'm not bragging but bulled groggy.

I try the handle of the front door. Except it's locked. It's like, fock!

Not to worry. It's far from a new situation for me.

I tip back into the living room and, using my, you'd have to say, vast experience, start looking for a key. I check practically everywhere. On top of the bookshelves. Under the sofa cushions. In the Nigella Lawson Living Kitchen bread bin in beech and blue.

I literally turn the place over but it's no good. I can't find one.

I *do* find her bag, though, and I have a quick mooch in there. No keys, just her Wolfe Tone. I whip it out and scroll down through her contacts, just out of curiosity. I find my number, then delete it. I can't believe I gave it to her. Getting slack in my old age.

I tip over to the door that leads out on to the balcony and it's like, jackpot!

It's one of those, like, sliding doors – the same as mine – that you open by just, like, flicking the catch?

So I *flick* the catch and then I'm suddenly out on the balcony. It turns out we're a lot of storeys up. It's incredible, roysh, given the number of times I've done this over the years, that I've never developed, like, a head for heights.

I'm suddenly like a monkey sizing up a tree. I'm thinking, if I can climb over the railing there, then hang down, off the edge of the balcony, I could step down on to the rail of the balcony below. Then do the same again, then again, then again. I'll be back on terra whatever-the-actual-phrase-is in sixty seconds, then in a taxi home.

I swing one leg over the balustrade, then the other. Then I take, like, a deep breath and try to, I suppose, *gather* myself? It must be, like, a seventy-foot drop. The obvious crosses my mind. The big question. Is it worth risking my life just to avoid an awkward goodbye?

And the answer – as always – is probably yes.

I take another deep breath. Then for some reason I look back up. And I end up nearly having a hort attack.

Breege is standing on the balcony in front of me, staring at me like she can't believe what she's *actually* seeing?

I feel automatically bad. 'I just didn't want to wake you,' I try to explain. 'No offence but I only wanted it to be, like, a one-night thing?'

She's, like, 'What?' obviously pretty pissed off.

I'm thinking, hey – hate the game, baby, not the player. 'Look, it's nothing personal,' I go. 'I've just never been one for, like, post-match chat?'

And her reply, I have to admit, causes me to nearly lose my grip on the rail.

'Ross,' she goes, 'we're in The Grange. This is where *you* live.'

1. A New Career in a New Town

Rosa Parks, if you can believe the bumf, is a development of highly prestigious aportments in the rapidly maturing South Dublin suburb of Ticknock. Just like the Mother of the Modern-Day Civil Rights Movement – with whom it shares its magical name – this stunning, well-appointed development is, at once, elegant, stylish, intelligent and creative. But, unlike her, it's no trouble at all when it comes to public transport.

'Jesus,' I go, 'who writes this stuff?'

JP takes his eyes off the road for a second and cops the brochure on my lap. He laughs. 'Back in the day,' he goes, 'you and I did.'

I laugh then?

'No,' I end up having to admit, 'I never came up with anything like this. I mean, this is, like, genius.'

I'm staring at, like, the centre spread, which is a photograph – not of what the aportments actually *look* like? It's not even a dude putting on cufflinks or a couple sharing a hilarious joke over a glass of freshly squeezed orange juice at the breakfast bor. No, it's a photo of a proud, smiling – and I have to say it even though it's racist – *black* woman, who could actually be Vivica Fox's more sensible older sister.

Then beside it – you've got to take your hat off to these fockers – it's, like, 'The original Rosa, honoured by this stunning development of 1,736 cleverly crafted homes, became a leading champion of African-American rights after refusing to give up her seat to a white passenger on a Montgomery City, Alabama, bus. And, in that same spirit, we're not asking

you to give up anything either – this resplendent collection of homes combines the pulse of the town with the sedate pace of the countryside . . .'

JP's suddenly lost in thought. We're sat at the Leopardstown roundabout, waiting for a break in the traffic. He shakes his head and says that people would have literally eaten shit back in the day if you'd put enough sugar on it.

I'm there, 'Who are you telling?' because he needs the odd reminder that I was, like, a way better estate agent than *he* ever was?

We get a break in the traffic and he floors it.

I tell him I have to admire him, though – as in, honestly admire him? When Hook, Lyon and Sinker went A over T, a lot of us thought he'd go mental dental oriental again – like the time he joined the priesthood.

'I do get sad,' he goes, 'especially when I pass the old office.'

I'm there, 'Me too – it's real, I don't know, nostalgia-ish, if that's an actual word?'

He nods – which means it must be – then he takes the ramp down on to the M50.

'It's when I think of all the years my old man spent building the business up,' he goes. 'You've heard what's in there now, have you?'

An all-you-can-eat Chinese buffet.

I'm there, 'Hey, don't do it to yourself, Dude. You've got to let go of the past. You and your old man are doing *this* now. And who's to say you're not going to end up loving it as much as you did using your gift of the gab to sell people into a lifetime of debt?'

He doesn't seem convinced, even though he used to love my pep talks, back when we played rugby. He takes exit thirteen, then a few minutes later we're taking the turn into Rosa Parks.

We get out of the cor. He's driving his old dear's Renault Mégane these days – talk about changed times.

The place is deserted and it looks like an actual building site. There's, like, no roads, roysh, only dirt tracks, and there's big mounds of, like, earth everywhere. Only four of the ten blocks were ever finished, according to JP. A couple of them still have the scaffolding on them and there's, like, two or three cranes that have just been left there, basically abandoned.

I notice they've still got the billboard up. It's, like, a police mugshot of the same bird as in the brochure – except in fairness she doesn't look *quite* as hot? – and she's holding up a number, we're talking 7053, then underneath it, in humungous block capitals, it's like, BECAUSE COURTEOUS LIVING IS A CIVIL RIGHT.

'That 7053,' I go, 'I wonder is that how many gaffs are still unsold,' which immediately puts the smile back on his face.

He takes the sledgehammer from the boot and throws it over his shoulder.

Originally, roysh, we're talking back when this was still all formland and they were selling these gaffs off the plans, they were going to have, like, a concierge, sitting in the lobby of each block – like in Manhattan? – tipping his hat to you as you go in and out. That's obviously had to be scaled back a bit, what with the current economic blahdy blah. So instead of Alfred out of *Batman* or someone like that, they've ended up with some total schnack, who's carrying out extensive excavation work on his nose when we walk through the door.

'Pick any winners?' is the first line out of my mouth. I'm actually on *fire* today?

JP hands him the paperwork and tells him why we're here. The goy just shrugs, like he's only paid to sit there, not to read shit.

9

We head for the lift slash elevator, whatever you want to call it. JP punches the button for the top floor.

I've got my nose in the brochure again. Another line leaps out at me. 'The anti-segregation theme is very much in evidence in the combined kitchen-and-dining area . . .'

Fock, the whole Celtic Tiger thing seems like such a long time ago now. 'Can I hang on to this?' I go. 'As, like, a souvenir?'

He's there, 'It's yours. I only brought it so I could see the layout of the place.'

I stick it in my back pocket and ask him if he's, like, nervous. He says no and I don't think he's lying. The lift pings and the doors suddenly open.

We tip down the hallway – pretty nice, it has to be said – and find aportment 273. We knock twice, maybe three times, leaving a good thirty seconds between each.

'The dude must be at work,' I end up going and JP looks at me like he can't believe how actually *stupid* I am?

'Work?' he goes, then he sort of, like, indicates the sledgehammer to me. 'Ross, why do you think we're repossessing his TV?'

I hadn't actually thought about it like that.

He tells me then to suddenly stand back. He grips hord on the handle of the hammer, then swings the head of it over his shoulder, closes his eyes and takes a deep breath, like he's building up to it or some shit?

I get this sudden memory of him at Funderland – fourteen, maybe fifteen years of age – somehow managing to ring the bell on the strongman game, despite being a weedy focker, and winning a Buzz Lightyear for Radha Neilan from Holy Child Killiney, who he was madly in love with at the time and possibly still is to this day? I know *she* still has it in her bedroom – at least she did the last time I put her over the jumps.

He suddenly opens his eyes, then swings the hammer and

it's, like, BOOM! The door immediately gives way and we walk in.

'The bank are in the process of repossessing the place,' he goes, although I don't know why the fock he's whispering. 'The dude's supposed to be back living with his parents. Or his wife's parents.'

We find the sitting room. Doesn't take long. The gaff's *actually* tiny. In fact, the TV covers pretty much one entire wall?

Cleverly crafted is focking right.

JP bends down and unplugs the thing.

I'm there, 'Do you think, I don't know, *God* would approve of what we're doing here?'

I don't *know* why I ask that question? It's just, he might not be studying for the priesthood any more, but I know he's still a major fan.

He laughs. '*The Lord who commands armies told me this,*' he goes, checking out the brackets fixing the TV to the wall. '*Many houses will become desolate. Large, impressive houses will have no one living in them . . . Men will be humiliated . . . The proud will be brought low . . .*'

See what I mean?

'Okay, which one is that?' I go.

He says it's Isaiah and I'm not going to argue with him.

'I'd love a focking TV this size,' I go, as we each take one end and lift it off the actual wall.

He goes, 'I'm sure the finance company are prepared to listen to offers.'

I'm like, 'Yeah, it might make a nice present for Ro, even though I hate to sound like a vulture and shit?'

The thing weighs an actual tonne and I can see why he needed me now. We hulk it out to the lift and he uses his elbow to hit the down button. The doors immediately open and we step in. That's when I decide to bring up the whole Oisinn thing.

'I'm going to try and find him,' I go.

He looks at me, Scooby Dubious. 'He could be anywhere in the world, Ross – literally.'

'Well, then, I'll just have to search the entire world – literally. We need to find him and bring him home.'

I can tell from his reaction that he doesn't actually agree.

'Whoa,' I go, 'out with it, Dude.'

He's like, 'Ross, do you not think he's better off wherever he is?'

I'm there, 'How can you stand there and actually say that?'

'Did you see yesterday's *Irish Independent*? They're saying he has debts of, like, seventy-five million?'

'So?'

'*So?* Do you really think he *wants* to be found?'

I don't say anything because I'm a bit annoyed at his reaction. The lift doors ping again and we wrestle the TV out to the cor. He has to put the back seats down and push the front seats forward about six inches to fit it actually *in*.

'I'm just saying,' I go, 'if I was, like, seventy-whatever million it is in debt, I'd want my friends around me – friends who'd soldiered with me through good times and bad. Jesus, we played rugby together. Does that count for nothing?'

He goes, 'Friends who'd want to bring you back to this?' and he flicks his thumb at one of the half-finished blocks, except he's not just talking about Rosa Parks, of course. He's talking about the banking crisis and Renords supposedly in trouble and Dell pulling out of Limerick and Town Bor and Grill going into supposedly examinership and the end of the construction boom and Subway outlets suddenly focking everywhere.

'The best thing we can do for Oisinn,' he goes, 'is to hope he's happy, wherever he's gone.'

I decide to let it rest for now. I just ask him where we're

headed next. He says we're going to drop this off first, then we've an Alfresia stainless-steel six-burner gas grill to collect from the Beacon South Quarter, Cube One. Then he laughs. 'It sounds like something George Orwell might have dreamt up, doesn't it?'

I laugh as well, even though I neither know nor care who George Orwell is.

He goes back into the building again to bring down the sledgehammer. I climb into the front-passenger seat and sit there just staring through the front windscreen.

There's, like, two dudes up on ladders, I notice, painting over the COURTEOUS LIVING IS A CIVIL RIGHT sign and I'm wondering is that what you'd consider a metaphor.

Ronan rings and I ask him where he is. He says he's in Tiffany's on Grafton Street and it says a lot about my son and the company he keeps that I'm picturing him not in the shop but in the focking vault.

'What are you doing in there?' I go, except what I really mean is how did he get through the door of BTs.

'Ine wit Bla,' he goes, which explains it. What security gord is going to turn away a twelve-year-old – albeit skobie – kid pushing his girlfriend in a wheelchair?

'Her toorteent boortday's coming up,' he goes. 'She's arthur seein a cheerm bracelit she likes . . .'

I'm there, 'Let me guess – you want me to give you the moo to buy it for her?'

Mount Anville girls are expensive to keep. I can tell you that from painful experience.

'No,' he goes, 'I took your credit card from your wallet thudder day. But this fooken sham here says he can only process poorchases made be the owner of the card.'

I laugh. I'm there, 'I'm on my way.'

I hear Blathin go, 'Don't forget to ask him, Ro!'

Ronan, all embarrassed, goes, 'Eh, she's havin a peerty in her gaff. In a couple of weeks. In anyhow, you're invirit.'

Amy Huberman's wearing the Elie Tahari cork wedges that Sorcha was going to get – as in, the Liana purple suede ones? – and I go, 'Oh,' somehow managing to sound interested. She says she has *such* a girl-crush on Amy Huberman.

She looks up from her *Irish Tatler* and lets a sudden roar out of her, loud enough to pretty much shatter the front window of the shop.

'Nooo!'

I spin around and it's basically nothing, except that Honor's got herself tangled up in a dress hanging on the New Arrivals rack. I tell Sorcha I'll sort it, then I get down on my, I suppose you'd have to say, hunkers, then slowly twist the dress until our daughter finally pops out.

'Boo!' I go and Honor storts laughing, pretty much uncontrollably.

Her mother unfortunately doesn't see the funny side of it. 'That's a Lilly Pulitzer,' she tells her – like an actual three-and-a-half-year-old's going to know what the fock that is.

Honor's there, 'I'm sorry, Mommy!' which I don't think she should even *have* to say?

I tell her she was only playing – I don't mention the mucky carob prints she's put all over it – but *I* end up getting the evils from Sorcha then. I'm wondering is she, like, snookered behind the red this week.

The shop *is* quiet today. There's, like, one bird having a mooch around in here, while not one has walked into Circa, her new vintage section, in the hour that I've been hanging around.

And this is, like, lunchtime we're talking?

She asks me how me and Erika are getting on, which is a good question. We storted going on these, I don't know, platonic dates for a little while, to try to – as Erika called it – reimagine our relationship, except then we gave up. To be honest, I think it still weirds her out that we had basically sex twice before we found out we were, like, brother and sister.

'She's too busy getting to know *him*,' I go, meaning the old man. *Our* old man. '*He's* no focking time for me either.'

'I'm sure that's not true, Ross. You were in Cardiff with him for the Grand Slam, weren't you?'

I laugh. 'That's, what, ten days ago? I haven't seen him since.'

'Well, he and Helen are trying to make a real go of the cheesemonger's,' she tries to go. 'Why don't *you* call to see *him*?'

'Because I couldn't be orsed basically.'

'Well,' she goes, 'suit yourself – he probably has enough on his plate anyway, helping Erika with her case.'

This is, like, totally out of the blue.

I'm there, 'What case?' because I genuinely have no idea what she's talking about. Sorcha goes suddenly red. She can't hold her piss, see.

'Er, *what* case?' I go again.

Of course she ends up telling me because she knows I won't leave the shop until I know.

'She's been named as a co-respondent in a divorce,' she goes, slapping a price sticker on a black Rachel Comey dress while she's dropping this bombshell.

'A co-respondent? As in?'

'A co-respondent as in the other woman. Look, there's a chance it's going to be in all the papers, so I might as well tell you – it's Toddy Rathfriland?'

I end up just shrugging. 'The only Toddy Rathfriland I know is the dude who owns all the restaurants that are supposed to be in trouble . . .'

She just continues stickering shit.

'You are pulling my focking chain!' I go. '*Him?*'

'Yes . . .'

'He's . . . He's focking ancient!'

'He's sixty-three, Ross. And stop shouting, you're frightening Honor.'

'We *are* talking about the same dude, are we? Fat little focker? Hair dyed off his head?'

'There's no proof of that, Ross. And anyway, he's actually a *young* sixty-three?'

'Sixty-three is sixty-three, Babes. When *was* all this?'

She sighs, trying to make me feel childish for asking. 'It happened about six months ago. His marriage has been as good as over for years.'

I laugh.

'Well,' I go, 'she's definitely let her standards slip. This is the girl who knocked me back, er, *how* many times before I finally sealed the deal?'

'Ross, that's your sister you're talking about?'

'Half-sister – and it doesn't count as incest, before you say it, because at the time we didn't know. One thing I'll say for me, though, is at least my hair and eyebrows match.'

'According to Erika,' she goes, 'he's very charming.'

'Very loaded, more like. I can't wait to see her again. I'm going to rip the piss in a major way.'

'Ross, please don't say anything!'

'No, no, hopefully this will have taken her down a peg or two . . .'

'That is *such* a beautiful item,' Sorcha suddenly says over my shoulder, then she makes an immediate beeline for her one lunchtime customer, whose eye just happened to linger for more than two seconds on a Catherine Malandrino white cotton bolero with bead trim. 'It'd go amazing over a tunic blouse,' she storts giving it, 'with maybe, like, a grey woollen pleated skirt? Very Betty from *Mad Men*. Do you have patent Jimmy Choos? Or even Alexander McQueens? *Oh* my God, *so* Betty Draper!'

I can't put a name to the bird but something tells me I've woken up beneath her once or twice. She's not *that* unlike Jessica Szohr. It's only when she opens her mouth to ask where the changing rooms are that I cop the gap between her Yasmine Bleeth and realize straight away that it's Keelyn Errity, a bird I knew from UCD back in the day. Not only knew her either. I stallioned her senseless on more than one occasion as well.

'Oh, hi, Ross,' she goes, clearly delighted to see me, and I'm obviously there, 'Hey, Keelyn – how the hell *are* you?' laying it on like subsidized butter.

Fock, those teeth, though. She gave me a lovebite one night and it looked like I'd been stabbed in the neck with a focking barbecue fork.

The look that passes between us doesn't escape Sorcha's attention, and the second Keelyn pulls across the curtain on the changing room she takes Honor out of my orms and goes, 'While we're on the subject of divorce, is Hennessy still handling your side of things?'

I'm there, 'There we were getting on fine – why have you suddenly brought that up?'

'Er, because we're actually *getting* one, Ross?'

'I know we're getting one. But I was thinking we might, I don't know, put it off for a little while. I just thought, er, hello? There's *enough* doom and gloom about the place at the moment?'

She asks me what I'm talking about and I tell her obviously the whole, you'd have to say, recession thing. She sort of, like, stares into the distance, suddenly sad, and says she can't believe that Tesco are selling the same Denby collection that we paid *how* much for in BTs?

She shakes her head and says sometimes she wishes she'd

stayed in the States, even though everyone's saying that things are just as bad there.

Then she suddenly perks up again. 'It really is the quintessential take-anywhere piece,' she goes in the general direction of the changing room, even though she's copped that me and Keelyn have history.

See, she's nothing if not professional.

'It's formal – but it's also fun and flirty? Which means it's wearable if it's just, like, drinks and dinner, but also if it's, like, oh my God, a wedding!'

The curtain goes back and out walks Keelyn, staring at the label with a look of, like, total confusion on her face. 'Is this right?' she goes.

Sorcha dumps Honor in my orms again. It'll be a focking miracle if she grows up without issues. 'You did say a size eight, didn't you?'

Keelyn's there, 'Yeah, no, I'm talking about the *price*? It says, like, twelve hundred euros here?'

Sorcha smiles at her, you'd have to say patiently. The Society of the Sacred Heart teaches its daughters well. 'It *is* a Catherine Malandrino,' she goes. 'You know she did *Project Runway* a couple of years ago?'

This obviously means fock-all to Keelyn. 'Well,' she goes, checking herself out in the long mirror, 'I was only really looking for something cheap and cheerful – just to go over, like, a dress I bought?'

Cheap and cheerful? Sorcha stares into the changing room and cops the H&M shopping bags she walked in with. Even though she's still smiling, you can tell she suddenly wants to rip her focking hair out by the roots. I'm wondering should I offer to take Honor to Stephen's Green.

'Well, I'm sure I don't need to tell you,' Sorcha goes, 'that this is a very – oh my God – *very* exclusive item.'

'*Hmmm*,' Keelyn goes, still not convinced, checking it out now with one hand on her hip and – for all the focking difference it makes – her head cocked to one side. 'It's just, you know, I wasn't expecting to spend anything *like* that amount?'

This is even *though* her old pair live on Appian Way.

Sorcha's there, 'Well, the other beauty of this item is that, because it's cut so high, it accentuates a slim, natural waist like yours.'

Keelyn doesn't fall for her shit. '*Hmmm*,' she goes again, then she tries it with her cheekbones sucked in, but she's still not John B.

What happens next is unbelievable. She goes, 'So what's your recession price?'

It's out of her mouth without any, like, pre-warning?

'My *what*?' Sorcha goes. She actually pins her shoulders back as she says it.

I'm there, 'I think me and Honor might take a stroll up to see the ducks.'

'Ducks!' Honor goes. 'Let's go to the ducks, Daddy!'

'*Stay* where you are!' Sorcha goes, without even looking at us. Then to Keelyn, she's like, 'My *what* price?'

It's obvious, roysh, that Keelyn doesn't know how bang out of order she's being here? 'Well,' she goes, 'everyone's saying it, aren't they? During the Celtic Tiger, we all became price-insensitive . . .'

I'm, like, subtly shaking my head, trying to tell her to shut the fock up, quit while she's ahead. Except on she goes. 'Everything in Dublin is at least twenty percent overpriced – that's a well-known fact.'

'Oh, it is?' Sorcha goes, except she's actually being sarcastic?

'Er, *yeah*? And I don't know why you're giving me this attitude. You *work* in retail. You're going to have to get used to people asking you what your best price is.'

Sorcha turns to me then. For some reason – possibly instinct – I immediately know to block Honor's ears. 'Cheap,' she goes. 'Exactly your type, Ross.'

See, I *knew* Sorcha recognized her. I remember now trying to explain the hickey away at Sorcha's granny's seventy-fifth birthday porty – it was in, like, Sandycove Tennis Club?

Keelyn's there, '*Excuse* me?' and Sorcha ends up just losing it with her, we're talking nought to menstrual in two point five seconds.

'My best price? What do you think this is, a *focking* souk?' she goes. 'Get out of my shop now before I call security . . .'

Keelyn just laughs at her. She has the courage of Lassie, I'll give her that. But then she also has the teeth to back it up. 'You can't have me thrown out,' she goes, 'just because I asked for a discount.'

'Oh, can't I?' Sorcha goes. 'Er, this is still the Powerscourt Townhouse Centre, can I just remind you?'

Keelyn looks at *me* then, presumably for back-up, but I end up just nodding, knowing from painful experience not to, like, cross Sorcha when she's in this kind of form.

I'll ring the girl later to apologize.

Keelyn reefs off the bolero, not giving a fock if it rips, then practically throws it at Sorcha.

She goes, 'Er, *good* luck staying in business with that attitude?'

Then off she focks.

It's only when she's gone, roysh, that I realize how much shit Sorcha's shop must be actually *in*? Because she suddenly bursts into tears and says she wishes she'd taken that job that Stella McCortney offered her. 'But no,' she goes, 'I had to come back here. And all because I wanted Honor to have the same magical childhood that I did – junior dressage, classical piano, Cumann Gaelach debates . . .'

I throw my free orm – the one that's not holding our daughter – around her and I sort of, like, rub her back and tell her that everything's going to work out, even though I know fockall about, I suppose, economics and blahdy blahdy blah.

She looks at me – her mascara sliding down her face now like a focking oil spill – and says she's been trying *so* hord. She's storted opening the shop at 9.45 instead of 10.00, then closing at 5.30 instead of the old 5.15.

I thought she looked wrecked all right.

I can understand *why* she's worried? She's already borrowed two hundred Ks from the bank to restyle the place on Kitson in Hollywood, after seeing Shenae Grimes walking out of there in some magazine or other, laden down with bags and the paparazzi chasing her skinny orse up Robertson Boulevard.

I'm all of a sudden wondering could she be bringing in enough to make the loan repayments. I mean, even Morgan's gone wallop. It's unbelievable how quickly the world is changing. So I go, 'Do you mind me asking, what have you sold today?'

She takes, like, a deep breath and goes, 'Nothing.'

I'm like, 'Nothing? What about yesterday?' meaning Wednesday.

She shakes her head.

I'm there, 'Are you serious?'

She says all she's sold in the past week was a Gypsy 05 Paloma purple rainbow silk maxidress and a Tt Collection romper, both of which the girl returned the following morning. 'No reason,' she goes, 'except that she checked her credit cord balance and got the big-time guilts.'

I shake my head. 'God, when I think back to what April *used* to be like in here . . .'

She pulls away from me and wipes her eyes with her open

palm. She says she has to pop out and she asks me if I'll look after the place for an hour. Not that she needs me to. She could leave the focking door wide open and the flies wouldn't come in out of curiosity.

I'm there going, 'Yeah, I'm pretty sure I know how to work the till,' humouring her more than anything.

She says it's not the till – she's expecting a delivery. 'Will you sign for it?'

I just happen to go, 'Er, what kind of delivery are we talking?'

'Two boxes of Olivia Morris pumps,' she goes. 'The amazing patterned silk ones that Celia Birtwell created?'

She kisses Honor on the top of her head and tells her to be good for her daddy.

Of course I'm more than a little bit taken aback by this. I'm there, 'You're ordering in new stock?'

She shakes her head and tells me not to stort – they're going to be huge this year. I ask her shouldn't she, I don't know, maybe try to sell the shit she's already got first?

'They're saying even people like us are going to have to stort tightening our belts,' I go. 'I mean, a year ago, who would have seen Habitat being gone from Suffolk Street?'

I tell her she has to possibly stort facing reality, except she says she has to go, because she's booked into La Stampa for a Mint-Chocolate Body Scrub.

'Good morning,' the voice goes. 'The Plaza. *How* may I direct your call?'

She has one of those voices that has me picturing her as Chelsea Staub. I tell her that I'm looking to speak to an Oisinn Wallace.

She asks if he's a guest there at the hotel and I tell her that's what *I'm* wondering. All I know is that it's his favourite hotel

22

in the actual world. It was where he stayed anytime he was in, like, New York.

She says that's nice, then I hear her, like, tapping away on her obviously keyboard. 'I'm sorry,' she eventually goes, 'we have no guest staying by the name of Wallace. Do you know *when* he might have checked in?'

I'm there, 'See, the point is, I don't? This is a goy who's, like, one of my best friends. Long story, roysh, but a few months back, he left his cor at Dublin Aiport and basically disappeared . . .'

'Disappeared?'

'Well, pegged it is probably more the case. Keys still in the ignition, blah blah blah.'

'Oh, dear.'

'Yeah, no, there's actually a lot of it going on. Park and Hide, they call it over here.'

'I see.'

'Yeah, I'm the one trying to find him. Hey, you probably even know him – he's stayed there loads.'

She sort of, like, laughs.

'Sir, we have hundreds of rooms here.'

'He's, like, a big stocky dude? Irish, obviously. He actually invented, like, a scent for women, which is how he made his money.'

'The perfume guy?' she suddenly goes. See, I knew she'd know him. The dude's like me – Charmin focking Ultra. I hear her turn to the bird beside her and go, 'This gentleman's a friend of Oh Sheen – you remember the perfume guy?'

The bird beside her goes, 'Oh! My God!' and she says it in, like, a good way? '*Eau d'Affluence*. I only wore it, like, *two* days ago!'

The two of them are suddenly having a good old, I don't know, *reminisce*, if that's a word.

'Do you remember his medal?' I hear the Chelsea Staub bird go. 'He used to ask us to put it in the hotel safe.'

'Yeah, that would have been his Leinster Schools Senior Cup medal,' I cut in. 'See, he was always kacking it – case he got mugged.'

'It was made of, like, tin,' I hear the other bird go. 'It was, like, totally worthless?'

She wouldn't focking say that if she'd been there to see him win it.

'So,' Chelsea goes, 'how is he?'

I'm there, 'Er, not great, I'd imagine. He owes, like, seventy-something million. Seventy-five – that's according to the *Indo*.'

As I'm saying it, I'm thinking, that possibly explains why he's *not* staying at the Plaza?

'Well, sir, if you manage to find him, tell him that the girls at the front desk send their best wishes.'

Erika looks incredible – although obviously not in *that* way? But talk about people doing shit you never thought they'd end up doing. At first, roysh, I think, *her* working in a cheesemonger's? Come to think of it, her working at all.

But when I walk into the shop, she's in, like, mid conversation with one of those middle-aged women who's not exactly hot but not exactly a gruffalo *either*? The woman's asking what the difference is between the Mimolette and the Manchego. And of course that's when I realize I'm wrong.

'Do I *look* like I work here?' Erika goes.

'Well, yes,' the woman goes, not unreasonably either; 'you're standing on that side of the counter and you're wearing a long white coat with Cheeses Merrion Joseph written on it . . .'

Which would have been my exact point.

'I'm standing this side of the counter,' Erika goes, 'because I'm here to see my father. And I'm wearing this coat because

I don't want to end up smelling like a focking nursing home. Is that okay with you?'

The woman reacts, roysh, as if she's been shot – no one expects to be spoken to like that, especially not in the Merrion Shopping Centre. She turns around to me, looking for obvious back-up, except she's so in shock that she can't think of anything to say, except that in future she'll be buying her cheese in Superquinn – as if Erika even cares – then she turns around and focks off.

I laugh.

'It's good to see the old Erika back,' I go. 'For a while there, a few of us thought you were going soft.'

She looks at me like I'm a focking yeast infection. 'What do *you* want?' she goes.

I'm there, 'I'm just as entitled to be here as you are. He's my old man as well, even though *he* seems to have forgotten that basic fact.'

'Charles and I are going for lunch,' she goes. 'And before you ask, Ross, no, you can't join us.'

I act all casual while she's saying this, arranging the shrink-wrapped wedges of Caerphilly into a perfect – you'd have to say – wheel.

I'm there, 'I, er . . . heard about Toddy Rathfriland.'

She suddenly goes – I'm not exaggerating – white.

I'm like, 'You've dropped your standards, do you mind me saying?'

It's, like, rare that you find Erika stuck for words. I have a little chuckle to myself then. 'Toddy Rathfriland, though! I can see why you kept that one quiet. I used to always see him in Renords, throwing his money away, buying champagne for everyone, trying to chat up birds . . .'

She just, like, glowers at me. She's still trying to work out how I even know.

'Trying to relive his youth,' I go. 'It's long gone, Toddy. *Long* focking gone!'

All *she* can come up with, in terms of a comeback, is, 'Fock you, Ross!' and I end up just laughing. See, victories over Erika are so rare that they have to be savoured.

'Black hair and red eyebrows,' I go. 'Yeah, a *rul* catch, Erika – a *rul* catch.'

It's at that exact moment that the old man suddenly appears through the plastic ribbon curtain at the back of the shop. 'Hello there, Ross,' he tries to go. 'I thought I heard your dulcet tones.'

He's wearing – the state of him – a blue and white striped apron with a focking ridiculous little white hat.

'What has you in the Merrion Shopping Centre?' he has the actual balls to go. 'Come to visit the city's newest purveyors of coagulated milk protein, who've put Sheridans of South Anne Street, Dublin 2 – let me tell you – on the proverbial back foot?'

I just laugh in his face.

'Everyone knows this place is an obvious front,' I go. 'You're laundering the moo you stashed in Andorra.'

That softens his cough. I watch his face just drop – believe me, he has *no* desire to go back to Stoney Lonesome.

'And that hat's so gay, by the way, it could marry a focking dude in Sweden.'

He mutters and stutters for a few seconds; then sort of, like, regathers himself and asks what I think of the government pushing ahead with the public sector pension levy and hang what the unions think! Of course he might as well be speaking, I don't know, Swahilish to me.

'Wait a minute!' he tries to go. 'Is that a frown I see on your face there, Ross?'

I'm there, 'No, I'm actually trying to work out what the fock you're talking about.'

'Well, thank the Lord for that,' he goes. 'Thought you might have become infected with all this talk of *doom* – to say nothing of *gloom*!'

I'm there, 'I can't see how it's going to affect me personally – so why would I give a fock?'

'Well, good for you,' he just goes. 'The very attitude that made this country great for eleven and a little bit years – and will again, you mark me. You're a chip off the old block,' and then he turns to Erika, obviously *having* to include her. 'The *two* of you – a pair of, quote-unquote, go-getters. Economic downturn, how are you!'

He rubs his hands together then, delighted with himself for whatever reason.

I'm there, 'I don't know why you're mentioning her in that. What's she done, except end up getting mentioned in, like, a divorce case?'

She looks at me like she wants to rip my dick out by the root.

'Oh, you heard?' he just goes, not even embarrassed about it. 'Lies and innuendo!'

I'm there, 'Is that what you think?'

'Of course – you know why it's suddenly come up, don't you?'

'Go on, why?'

'Well, it's obvious, isn't it? That restaurant business of his – word on the grapevine is that it's in trouble. Lot of restaurants in the same boat. Overstretched, you see. Tried to grow the business too quickly, all based on borrowings. Obviously, trade is down and the banks are getting nervous. *She* – the wife – well, she realizes she's no longer married to a man of means. Wants out. And she'll do anything to *get* out, even if it means traducing the name and reputation of your sister here . . .'

'Half-sister.'

'Who just happened to be there for her husband when he needed a friend . . .'

I laugh. Then I look at Erika and she just gives me a big, shit-eating grin. She can do no wrong in his eyes.

'And now this woman wants to drag her name through the papers – except it's not going to happen, because Mr Hennessy Coghlan-O'Hara is on the case, as ever! Talking about a High Court injunction and all sorts – stop these bloody newspapers dragging her name down into the gutter. We're meeting him for lunch. I'd ask you to join us, Ross, but it's a bit . . .'

He pulls a face, which I take to mean awkward. '*Sub judice*,' he goes. 'Pardon the Latin . . .'

I'm trying to think of something unbelievably hurtful to say back to him, roysh, but he just keeps blabbing on.

'So how's young Sorcha?' he goes 'How's *she* weathering the – inverted commas – storm?'

'Not great,' I end up having to go, 'not that it's any of your focking business. She'll turn it around, I'm sure . . .'

At the same time, roysh, I'm wondering is this just, like, wishful thinking?

I'm there, 'I mean, we all know how determined she is. Do you remember her debating at school? Even the argument she made that time for rerouting the Liffey to put Crumlin and Drimnagh on the Northside – she had practically the entire Conrad Hotel on its feet.'

'You see, *that's* the spirit that'll see us through this thing! As old Denis Fehily used to say, what is a diamond but a piece of coal that did well under pressure! If I know Sorcha like I think I do, she'll have that shop turned around quicker than she can say –'

'BCBGMAXAZRIA,' I go.

He's there, 'Exactly. It's like I said to JP's *old dad* only the other day . . .'

I'm there, 'You met JP's old man?'

'Yes! In Shanahan's, don't you know! Oh, he's making a real go of that new business of his – Last Resort Asset Reclaim or some such. I said to him, "You know what? I have to admire the way you and that son of yours have bounced back." He said he was sick to the teeth of hearing about this so-called financial crisis. I said, "Precisely! Do you think Messers McManus and Desmond are talking about a financial *crisis*? No, no, no. If I know those two chaps, they'll be staring down the ninth fairway of the old Green Monkey – for my money the most difficult par five *in* the game – ruminating on this financial *opportunity*."

'You tell Sorcha that you heard it from your old dad – we have as much to fear from this recession as a field has from the fire that burns away the residue of last year's harvest and prepares the ground for the next growing season. Recessions rejuvenate, Ross. They take old, tired ground and they make it rich and fertile again.'

Erika takes off her white coat. Even though I'm pissed off with her, I have to say that I like what she's wearing underneath. The old man takes off his as well, then pulls on his camel-hair. As I'm walking out the door, I hear *him* go, cheerful as you like, 'Manchego is a sheep's-milk cheese from Spain, in case you're caught on the hop again, Erika. Whereas the Mimolette is a bit like an aged Edam, except sweeter and ever so slightly fruity.'

What is it about people who 'do the whole travelling thing' that makes them think the rest of us are interested in every boring detail of their trip?

My inbox is literally full of their shit.

Claire – as in Claire from Bray – is the latest of Sorcha's friends to go to South-East Asia and send constant e-mails to everyone she's ever met in her life, giving us her thoughts on the place, like she was the one who focking discovered it.

I open one or two, just at random.

'Where do I even begin?' she goes. 'It's useless even to try to convey in words the beauty of this part of the world!' Except she then goes on to try, in paragraph after focking paragraph, mail after mail.

I read a few more and it's all the usual blah.

'You honestly haven't lived until you've observed the dawn chorus at Chiang Dao . . . Sitting there by the side of the road, just eating noodles! . . . Did the whole full-moon party thing – although Ko Pha-Ngan is SO commercialized. Avoid at all costs! . . . We went rubber-tubing down the river in Vang Vieng! Aaaggghhh! . . . No tourists there, just locals . . . Hoping to hook up again with some Aussie friends we met in Luang Prabang . . . Could live on almost literally nothing here . . . We walked across the bridge over the River Kwai – amazing to think, the ACTUAL bridge! – even though I've never seen the film. Does anyone know what it's even about? . . . Did Hanoi. Did Bangkok. Did Ho Chi Minh City . . . Before I set eyes on Halong Bay, I knew literally nothing about karst formations . . . Ran out of cash – ended up sleeping on the beach! . . . Trekking in the far north – you have to avoid Chiang Mai if you want a more authentic experience . . . Did Phonm Penh, did Phuket, did Vientiane . . . The temples are SO peaceful – we stayed in one all day, just soaking it in . . . The beach at Ko Phi Phi Leh is the one from the actual movie *The Beach*. We've ticked SO many things off the list at this stage . . . Watching the sun set from Sunset Beach is oh my God one of THE most jawdropping sights I think I've ever seen . . . The rumour is you can shoot a cow with a bazooka . . .'

And blah blah focking blah.

It's as I'm, like, deleting them all from my inbox that Sorcha decides to finally return my call from this morning. See, something suddenly occurred to me last night. The last two times I called into the shop, Honor's been there – in other words, she hasn't been in, like, Pre-Montessori? And I can, like, hear her in the background again now.

Little Roedean is costing me, like, twenty-five Ks a year.

Sorcha reacts to just a simple question by pretty much tearing me a new one. 'If you must know, Ross, I took her out because a little boy in her class has gone down with swine flu.'

'Swine flu? Do you know what that so-called school charges per term?'

'Swine flu doesn't just affect poor people, Ross.'

'Well, that's news to me.'

'Anywaaay,' she goes, like the subject is closed for discussion, 'I've taken her out for a couple of weeks, just as a precaution. That other little boy's in hospital. And speaking of hospitals – what are you doing the weekend after next?'

'Er, I don't know – why?'

'Chloe's having her hip replaced.'

'Again?'

'Don't give me that, Ross – it's the *other* hip this time?'

This, famously, is the result of her wearing nothing but designer heels that cost the price of a small family cor every day for, like, twelve or thirteen years. Some chiropractor apparently told her she'd the gait of a ninety-year-old woman.

'We're all rallying around,' she goes. 'Make sure to tell Fionn and JP.'

I'm like, 'Rallying around? Where?'

'The Beacon Private.'

'The Beacon Private?' I laugh. 'Even though she's almost as big a bitch as Erika?'

'She might be a total bitch, Ross, but she also *happens* to be Honor's number two godmother.'

And Erika's her number one. I'll say it again. It'll be a focking miracle if she grows up without issues.

'One upside,' the old dear goes, 'of this *thing* that's obviously happening is that it's so much easier to get tradesmen. Angela rang for an electrician last week – do you know, he came that very afternoon.'

We're sitting – just the two of us, if you can believe that – in the Lord Mayor's Lounge of the Shelbourne Hotel.

'And Delma,' she goes, 'she's just had her new individually designed, hand-crafted kitchen installed. She said there was none of the usual nonsense you get from these types. Came in, did the job and left. They didn't even mind when she told them they'd have to eat their luncheon-meat sandwiches – or whatever they had with them – in their van. Although she did have to dock them fifty euros when she found their bread wrappers in her perennials. Oh, they've threatened her with the small claims court but they'll get nowhere.'

She's had, like, a facial peel this morning and it's made shit of her skin. 'They could stick your head in the sea and use you as focking shark-bait,' I make sure to tell her. I grab a warm buttermilk scone, cut it in half, then dump a shitload of blueberry compote on to it. 'Being honest,' I go, 'I don't even know what the fock I'm doing here.'

'*I* invited you,' she goes. 'I thought it would be nice to spend some time together – like any mother and son.'

'Well,' I go, 'it's good to see you're finally getting around to it. I'm still only twenty-nine, of course.'

And before anyone storts feeling sorry for her, I should point out that the only reason she wants me – and even Delma and Angela – is because she's got fock-all else to do.

The big news is that, after three bestselling so-called books, she's finally run dry, in more ways than one. Writer's block, *she's* calling it, though the actual truth is that she's been found out. She's supposedly taking a time-out – to try to 'reconnect with her craft' – but of course she's going off her cake with fock-all to do all day.

See, all the great battles in her life have been fought. The last was the campaign to stop the Luas coming to Foxrock – they're routing it instead through Leopardstown and Carrick-mines. And now that the country's supposedly focked again, there's no actual money out there to do the kind of things she made her name organizing mass protests against.

To stay sane – her word, not mine – she's agreed to host a new food programme, *FO'CK Cooking*, on RTÉ in the after-noons, before *Seoige*.

'Next Monday, I thought I'd do my ballotine of Anjou pigeon,' she goes. 'It's *like* Heston's, but with my own twist, of course – Jabugo ham, shaved fennel and a bavarois of vanilla mayonnaise . . .'

I'm practically salivating here. The shit she can do with a Le Creuset and a pound of mince, in fairness to her.

I reach for the clotted cream.

She's there, 'It's a truly wonderful thing to be doing some-thing you love and to be appreciated for it. And it's like I told Mary Kennedy in the canteen yesterday – good food is the perfect antidote to all this negativity we're hearing at the moment.'

'I take it you're talking about the whole current economic blahdy blah?'

She sort of, like, clicks her tongue in disgust. 'Brian Dobson has started standing up to read the news,' she goes. 'What kind of message is that to be sending out? Oh, I'll say it to him when I see him.'

I'm thinking, how even *old* is Mary Kennedy? I would so love to have sex with Mary Kennedy.

She asks me if I've heard from the old man and I end up having to laugh. 'Him? Yeah, no, I called in to the shop yesterday. Other than that, I haven't seen him since the Grand Slam. He made a complete tit of himself in Cordiff, can I just say. He was shouting at Jack Kyle, ten rows back, "Sixty-one years of hurt, Doctor! Over at last!"'

She even laughs, to be fair.

I'm there, '*And* he was wearing one of those leprechaun hats that you get in Caddle's Irish Gifts – with the big focking buckle on the front?'

'I expect he was excited,' she goes. 'He waited a long time to see it. He's been predicting it every year for as long as I've known him.'

'Well, aport from that, the answer is no, I haven't seen him – not really.'

'I'm not making excuses for him,' she tries to go, 'but he *has* been busy.'

'What, with his new daughter and her mother? And his cheese shop? And that ridiculous plan of his to turn Mountjoy into, like, a six-star hotel?'

She smiles, I think the word is, like, thinly? 'Well, the hotel has been a kind of catharsis for him,' she goes. 'None of us can even imagine, Ross, the horrors he must have endured in that prison. The drugs. The violence. The table tennis. To say nothing of the carbohydrates, morning, noon and night. He doesn't like to talk about it, but still waters run deep. I think turning the place into a hotel is his way of painting over that period in his life . . . And yes, he's also in love.'

I just, like, roll my eyes.

'We *should* all go out for dinner,' she even goes, like it's the most natural thing in the world to say. 'Perhaps to L'Ecrivain. You and I, your father and Helen, your sister . . .'

She shoves a whole Shelbourne Fancy into her mouth, practically sideways. It makes me think of a clip I saw on the internet once of a focking python eating a kangaroo. 'Do you mind me saying,' I go, 'it totally weirds me out the way you're, like, cool with it?'

'Cool with what?'

I'm there, 'Er, him suddenly living with Erika's old dear on Ailesbury Road for storters? And you all being friends. I just think that's focked up, that's all.'

She stares up at the Louis whatever-the-fock chandelier, suddenly lost in thought. 'Well, I'm a romantic novelist,' she eventually goes. That's seriously pushing it, but I end up letting it go. 'I know what a wonderful miracle it is to find, as it were, your *other*.'

That stops me dead in my tracks, roysh, because I know she's thinking about Trevion. See, if I hadn't threatened to expose him as a US Ormy deserter, she'd probably still be with him in the States, basically married. Instead – like Oisinn – no one knows where the fock he is.

I feel the sudden need to say something. See, I've never been big on uncomfortable silences. 'If I could turn back the clock,' I go. 'Blahdy blahdy blah.'

'There's no need to apologize,' she goes. 'We agreed to draw a line, remember?'

I shrug. *I* didn't.

She decides to change the subject.

'I met Oisinn's mother,' she goes. 'In Marian Gale. The poor woman – oh, she's aged two years, Ross.'

I nod. It's nice that she *gives* a fock – they *were* Senior Cup Mums together.

I'm there, 'I know. I met her myself coming out of David

Lloyd Rivervew. She was cancelling his membership – which is never a good sign.'

'How could he do it to her, Ross? Just disappear like that. No note! Not even a phone call!'

'He had a lot of problems,' I go, 'debts and blah blah blah. It all just got on top of him. But don't you worry, I'm going to find him. I've been making phone calls, suddenly asking a lot of questions – like focking Columbo. You know me when I put my mind to something.'

She smiles, but she doesn't really say anything, except, 'Shall we get more tea and coffee?' and her neck pops up like a focking periscope, looking for a waitress.

I'm like, 'Just going back to the whole, I don't know, recession thing – you seem to be one of the few people I know who isn't actually worried.'

'I just feel it should simply be ignored until it goes away,' she goes.

I actually laugh – probably relief as much as anything.

I'm there, 'Sorcha's one person who'll be happy to hear that. Her shop looks like it's about to go tits-up in a ditch. No one's buying anything.'

She puts on, like, a sympathetic face?

'Yes, I called to see her this morning,' she goes. 'I told her, you hang on in there, girl! People still want quality, despite all these seventy percent off sales we're reading about. Oh, just vulgar!'

'I think Pia Bang closing her interiors shop was a major shock to her, though. They've been, like, friends since for ever.'

'Well, it's like Harry Connick, Jr says, Ross – this too shall pass.'

'That's actually a good quote to remember, in fairness to you.'

God, she's so focking ugly when she smiles.

'You know,' she goes, 'during the 1916 Rising, there were forty British soldiers garrisoned here, in this very hotel! The so-called Volunteers riddled this room with bullets, Ross. Riddled it! And do you know what the people did? They simply lifted their teacups and moved to the drawing room.'

I didn't know she knew so much about history. I suppose there's a lot of shit I don't know about her – and, being honest, don't want to know.

The waitress comes over.

'Ross will have, what, another coffee?' the old dear goes.

I tell her yeah, as long as she's paying. She just smiles. 'Yes,' she goes, 'and I'll have my Oolong.'

Keelyn says she has *never* been spoken to in the way Sorcha spoke to her. 'Even when I switched courses,' she goes, 'from Biochemistry and Molecular Biology to just Environmental Biology – and my dad was, like, *so* mad – he never shouted at me like your wife did.'

'Soon to be ex-wife,' I remind her. 'And even though I'd never in a million years defend the way she acted, she *does* have a point – as in, shops just can't go around giving people money off shit, just for the crack of it. See, the more you make shit affordable, the less people actually want it.'

I heard the old dear telling Delma on the phone that that's what happened to Waterford Crystal. It's basic economics, when you think about it.

Still, Keelyn says, she was surprised when I rang her out of the blue like that – as in, like, *pleasantly* surprised? – and I take that as my cue to slip my hand under the covers, and run it up and down her bare thigh.

And of course she loves it – loves it like chocolate cake.

'Well,' I go, 'as I said to you on the phone, I thought Sorcha was way out of line the way she spoke to you and I wanted to make it up to you. Plus, I won't lie, I did cop the way you were looking at me in the shop that day.'

She's there, 'Looking at you?'

'Er, yeah – and that's not meant to *sound* big-headed?'

Of course she tries to play it the big-time innocent. 'I wasn't looking at you in any particular way.'

I just give her knee a little tweak. 'You were, Keelyn – believe me. You might not have even realized it . . .'

She sort of, like, swats my hand away, says Oh! My God! three or four times, then tells me that I *so* shouldn't flatter myself. 'I actually think you've *disimproved*?' she tries to go. 'And that's not me being a bitch. I even said it to Gretchen Kennedy.'

'I'm happy to say, not everyone would agree with you. Who the fock is Gretchen Kennedy?'

'She's, like, my best friend? She was in UCD at the same time as us.'

'Don't remember her.'

'You were with her, like, three times – as in *with* with?'

'Doesn't exactly narrow the field, Keelyn.'

'Well, anyway, I said it to her, that day I saw you in the shop, either you were never as good-looking as everyone thought you were, or your looks are actually fading.'

I can tell you, she wasn't saying that at, like, eleven o'clock last night, when I was pleasuring her cross-eyed and she was screaming her hosannas loud enough to wake up half The focking Grange. There's another letter of complaint on the way from the property management company – that's as sure as she dropped a jeans size with the workout I put her through.

'Again,' I go, 'I'd just add that not everyone would agree with you.'

She's there, 'Hey, don't be so defensive. I'm just saying, *I* think you used to be really, *really* good-looking? But then again you're, what, thirty now?'

'Twenty-nine.'

'Twenty-nine, whatever.'

She suddenly reaches for my chest and takes my Leinster Schools Senior Cup medal in her hand. 'And how long are you going to go on wearing this thing?'

'What do you mean, how long?'

'Ross, this was, what, ten years ago? It's, like, get *over* it already?'

If she wants me to repeat the dose I gave her last night, she's going about it the wrong way. 'If you must know,' I go, snatching it out of her hand, 'I'm never taking it off.'

'Never?'

'That was the deal we made back in 1999, me and *all* the goys. We said we'd wear them forever . . .'

She laughs. That gap in her Jasmines again. She could eat a focking coconut through a tennis racket. 'Oh my God,' she goes, 'that is *so* sad.'

I'm there, 'Sad or not, I could write you out a list of players who never got their hands on one of these babies and never will. And I'm not just talking about Drico, the obvious – even though it *does* eat him up inside every time he sees me, Grand Slam or no Grand Slam. But Jamie Heaslip is another example.'

'Ross,' she goes, suddenly whipping back the sheets and swinging her legs out of the bed, 'the point I'm trying to make is, what does it matter now? Nobody cares any more.'

She storts walking around the room then, picking up clothes where they landed last night and throwing them on her.

'Where are you going?' I go. 'Do you not want to stay for . . .'

She sits on the side of the bed and pulls on her Uggs. 'I don't *eat* breakfast?' she goes.

I was actually going to say another treatment. I've got a horn on me like a focking railway sleeper.

'Anyway,' she goes, suddenly standing in the doorway,

'thanks for last night. I feel a lot better about the whole Sorcha thing now.'

'Obviously don't mention this,' I go, 'if you happen to run into her.'

What can I say? None of us will ever really *know* women, will we?

2. 'A Million-Euro Mortgage Doesn't Make You a Millionaire'

Amie with an ie thinks that Manolo Blahnik should be indicted for – oh my God – *war* crimes? And Jimmy Choo as well. 'Those shoes of theirs,' she goes, 'they're, like, the *real* weapons of mass destruction?'

The birds know she doesn't mean it. She's upset. They're *all* upset. Hospital waiting rooms aren't exactly top of anyone's fun list and, having worn pretty much nothing but designer heels themselves since they were seventeen years old, they wouldn't be human if they weren't worried about their own sherbets.

'It's an actual fact,' Sophie goes, 'that most shoes are designed by, like, gay men?'

You could suddenly cut the atmosphere with a knife. Sorcha's like, 'What's that got to do with anything?' because some of her best friends in first year in college were gay.

'Er, it stands to *reason*,' Sophie goes, 'that they hate women, doesn't it? It's, like, why else would they make something so beautiful so deadly.'

Fionn looks up from his newspaper and pushes his glasses up on his nose. It's obvious he's going to say something about the state of the country. What he ends up saying is that in ten years' time, all of those destination spa hotels they put up in, like, Wicklow and Kildare will be *our* Iranian palaces – as in, they'll just be, like, museums, to remind people of the shame of our decadent past.

I roll my eyes, thinking, yeah, that might pass as conversation in the school staffroom, Dude, but not here.

Except JP ends up actually encouraging him. He says, yeah, what Chloe's going through in there is the perfect metaphor for our age, isn't it? As in, we all walked tall for a time, but nature always claims its forfeit.

Of course there ends up being a whole conversation then about how bad shit is out there and how it's affecting us each personally. Amie with an ie says the Berkeley Court is doing rooms for, like, twenty euros a night now, which is, like, cheaper than a taxi home for her. Even *The Dubliner* is saying that staying out is the new going home.

Sorcha just stares at me. I could be wrong but I'm pretty sure there's, like, a tear in the corner of her eye. 'We had our wedding in the Berkeley Court,' she goes, a definite edge in her voice, like it's somehow *my* fault? She shakes her head and looks away. 'Oh my God, it's just, like, everything. Did I tell you guys about the Denby?'

Everyone nods.

Sophie says let's not depress ourselves. Chloe wouldn't want us sitting around all miserable. I disagree. Like I said, she *is* a bitch. I remember how horrible she was when Sorcha finished fifth in the UCD Fashion Show Young Designer of the Year competition. In dorker moments, I've heard Sorcha say that arthritis in her hips is the least she deserves.

But Sophie's right about us being all, I suppose, down about shit? She's there, 'Let's just have, like, an everyday conversation, like normal people.'

No one says anything for ages.

Then Amie with an ie says she's just storted the second season of *Californication* and she's loving it. Fionn says he's nine episodes into the first season of *Prison Break* and – please! – no one tell him what happens, although JP says that if he likes *Prison Break*, he'll love *Dexter*, which he can lend him, because he's just finished, like, the second season? Sophie says she's eight episodes into the third season of *Six Feet Under* and five episodes into the first season of *Lipstick Jungle*, while Sorcha is seven episodes into the first season of *Mad Men* and also seven episodes into the second season of *Damages*.

I'm just sitting there thinking how one of my great regrets in life is not having had sex with Chloe more often. She has a face like a two-day-old helium balloon, but she rides like an electric bull.

'Oh my God,' Sorcha suddenly goes, '*what* is keeping that surgeon? It's, like, how difficult could it be?'

Amie with an ie puts her orm around her shoulder and tells her everything's going to be okay. The important thing is that we'll be the first people she sees when the anaesthetic wears off.

'Whose hip is she even getting?' I just happen to go – not an unreasonable question, I would have thought. They all just suddenly crack their holes laughing. And I'm like, 'What?'

JP's there, 'Ross, she's not getting it from a donor. You don't leave someone your hips when you die.'

'Don't you?'

'No,' he goes, laughing, again not able to stop himself. 'She's getting a prosthetic one.'

I'm like, 'Oh,' my mind suddenly working at, like, a hundred miles an hour, or possibly more. 'Because I was actually thinking when they took her in, imagine if you were given a hip from some random skobe from, I don't know, Coolock or Sallynoggin or *any* of those. You get out of hospital, blah blah blah, it's all coola bualadh, until Saturday afternoon, when you wake up and suddenly find yourself in, I don't know, the off-licence or the Ilac Centre. As in, the thing's got focking GPS, built-in . . .'

Literally everyone laughs, roysh, and I'm thinking, see, this is what I'm famous for, in other words, putting a smile on people's actual faces.

Of course I'm straight on my feet, roysh, and I'm suddenly doing this hilarious shit, as in, walking without actually bending my knees, like the dude out of that Wallace and Gromit – *The Wrong* focking *Trousers* – up and down the waiting room, going, 'Where are you taking me now? Oh, no – Paddy Power in, I don't know, focking Firhouse, to put the labour money on a horse . . .'

The head nurse – a *total* focking goose-flesher, by the way – comes out of the nurse's station and tells me I'm going to have to either keep the noise down or leave, except I can't, roysh, because I'm on, like, a roll now? At the top of my voice, I'm giving it, 'Where are we going now? Oh no – the 75 bus to Tallaght, to see Shamrock focking Rovers play against, I don't know, whoever else there is! *Nooo!*'

Fionn and JP are, like, holding their sides laughing, while Sorcha, Sophie and Amie with an ie are crying pretty much tears. 'Oh my God,' Sophie just about manages to go, 'you are *so* funny.'

I'm there, 'It'd actually be a good movie, wouldn't it?'

The nurse – she really *is* a disgrace, looks-wise – reminds me that this is a hospital, full of people who are either sick or having important cosmetic procedures and any more disruption from me and she'll be forced to phone for security.

But the important thing is, roysh, everyone's laughing. One of the things I've always really loved about myself is that in times of – I think the word is, like, adversary? – I've always been able to inspire people and boost their spirits.

But then, roysh, without any warning at all, the big double doors swing open and Chloe is suddenly pushed through them on, like, a trolley, still out of the game.

The birds have suddenly forgotten about my words of, I suppose, inspiration. They're running alongside Chloe, talking to her, even though she can't actually *hear* them? They do say that kind of shit helps with, like, coma victims and blah blah blah. Amie with an ie tells her that they'll all go for a medi-pedi when she gets better, in maybe Revive, or The Beauty Suite, we're talking, like, the full Indian rose scrub?

The next thing, roysh, the trolley takes a right turn into what turns out to be the recovery room and we're all suddenly left outside again, looking through a big round window at Chloe, spitting zeds, the heavy bandaging visible under, like, her hospital gown.

Sorcha bursts into tears. It's all very Izzie focking Stevens. She says what if Chloe can never wear amazing shoes again? I put my orm around her and tell her that won't happen. Don't even think it.

Sophie just, like, stares through the window and says if she can't, she's going to ask her for her Viktor & Rolf aubergine closed-toes. As in, like, the *patent* ones?

It's Erika who answers the door. It's, like, ages since I've even been in her gaff, although the old man seems to have got his Deep Heat under the table, given the way he's shouting his focking mouth off in there.

At first, roysh, she's not going to even let me in. She goes, 'Hennessy's here,' like she expects me to go, oh, pity that, I'll talk to the old man some other time.

Instead, I just go, 'So focking what?' and she obviously can't think of an answer to that, because she sort of, like, rolls her eyes, then steps to one side.

I'm there, '*What* is your issue? I'm not going to steal him away from you, if that's what you're worried about. I'm only here because my cor insurance is due.'

'You're here to bleed money out of him. God, he must be so proud of you, Ross.'

There's, like, no way I'm taking that from her. 'Remember,' I go, 'you haven't *known* him that long? This is all still new to you. Give it time – *you'll* learn.'

She gives me this look, like a girl who's just dropped a wet fart in her wedding dress, then she leads me down the hall to his new study, which, I can't help but notice, is almost identical to his old study – as in, the one in Foxrock? – right down to the oak-effect panelling and the photograph of him with Dermot Desmond and David Duval in the lobby of the Sandy Lane Hotel in Barbados.

I don't *know* why it pisses me off? It just *does*?

'Here he comes,' is his first reaction when he sees me, 'the greatest unfulfilled talent in the history of Irish rugby,' trying to suck up to me. He's smoking a Cohiba the size of a focking chilli dog – as is Hennessy. 'Did you see the Harlequins match?'

I'm there, 'Course I saw the focking Horlequins match.'

'Whither the ladyboys tag now, eh, Ross?'

Hennessy tries to get in on the act then. 'They certainly proved they can win ugly.'

'They most certainly did,' the old man tries to go. 'I was just saying to your godfather here, Ross, I know it's the – inverted commas – old enemy of Munster next, but I'm rather coming to the view that this might be Leinster's year . . .'

I'm there, '*I* said that ages ago.'

'Did you?'

'Yeah – *ages*! In focking Idle Wilde in Dalkey. It was even *after* we lost to Castres. I was having a bit of brekky with Fionn and JP, like we do the morning after every big game. I'd the eggs focking Benedict, if you don't believe me. Then I said I've a feeling we're going to win the European Cup this year. That was *my* actual analysis – ask them.'

'Not necessary,' he goes, still trying to butter me up. 'I believe you. Your reading of the game was always second to none.'

I look over my shoulder. Erika's standing in the doorway of the study. There's, like, a definite tension between them? 'We, er, might reconvene,' the old man goes to her, 'in, shall we say, twenty minutes?'

I suddenly cop it. They were obviously talking about the whole Toddy Rathfriland thing when I walked in on them.

'I doubt it'll be twenty minutes,' *she* goes. 'He's only here for the money for his car insurance,' then she swans off down the hall to the kitchen with her focking nose in the air.

'*What* is her issue?' I go. 'Why does she always have to be so unpleasant?'

Hennessy makes his excuses then. He says he's going to ask her to make another pot of that French vanilla coffee of hers, then he focks off and leaves us to it.

'This is very cosy,' I go, nodding at the walls. I'm talking about the photo of him sitting on Hennessy's shoulders, the night he was elected to Dún Laoghaire-Rathdown County Council, then the autographed picture of Tiger Woods I gave him – his pride and joy, even though I actually forged the signature myself when I woke up one Christmas morning with no present for the focker.

See, all this shit used to be in his study in Foxrock.

'Anyway,' I go, seeing no point in wasting time here, 'Erika's right, my insurance *is* due. And the bad news for you is that it's going to be, like, four and a half grand . . .'

He's suddenly giving it, 'Whoa, Ross, not so fast. Let's you and I have a little catch-up – well, we've hardly seen each other since Cardiff . . .'

'Maybe that's because, unlike Erika, I'm not into playing happy families.'

He ignores that one and goes, 'The big news is that plans for the Mountjoy Hotel and Conference Centre are at an advanced stage and the signals that Hennessy and I have been getting from the Office of Public Works, re our submission, have been of a very positive nature . . .'

'Whoopee-focking-doo.'

'The good news doesn't end there either. No, I've asked your mother if she'd be interested in running A Hungry Feeling, the lobby café. You know she's taken a sabbatical from her writing – got this new cookery show of hers on RTÉ. Well, imagine, when we're opening our doors, if we could say, 'Menu in the lobby lounge devised by Fionnuala O'Carroll-Kelly, the star of RTÉ's *FO'CK Cooking*.' Oh, it'd be a coup, Ross, and no mistake.'

He balances his cigor on the edge of the desk and says he had an ortist draw up an impression of what the café's going to look like, just to try to persuade her, then he storts rooting through drawers, obviously looking for it.

I'm about to tell him not to bother his hole, I've zero interest anyway, when all of a sudden – for whatever reason – this piece of paper on his desk catches my eye. I've no idea how, roysh, but it's like I instantly know that this is what he was discussing with Erika and Hennessy when I walked through the door. It's, like, screaming out for me to read it, so I sort of, like, turn it towards me, then stort giving it the old left to right.

The first thing that leaps off the page is the signature at the bottom, we're talking Regina Rathfriland, who I immediately take to be Toddy Rathfriland's wife.

It turns out to be her, I suppose you'd have to call it, *testimony*?

'It must be here somewhere,' the old man's going, turning the place over behind me. 'I had my hand on it this morning.'

'Just try and find it,' I go, just to buy myself some time. 'Maybe I can help you talk the old dear into it . . .'

I stort reading.

It's like, *Toddy always kept late hours. That's the nature of the restaurant business. I can't say exactly when I suspected that he was having an affair. He'd withdrawn from me a long, long time before that. I think it was something that slowly dawned on me. Maybe it was the sudden improvement in his mood. He definitely started to take more of an interest in his appearance. His hair's dyed, everyone knows that, but he was suddenly having it recoloured every two weeks, instead of every, say, six. And much blacker than he used to. Definitely a shade or two. I thought it put years on him, not took them off . . .*

Blah blah blah.

Ah, here we go. *One morning he was on the phone. I came home from gospel choir practice — I admit, I'd started to sneak around, hoping to catch him in the act — and I heard him say Sugar Tits. Yes, Sugar Tits. But like it was a pet name or something. Then I started to question myself, as you do. I thought maybe I'd misheard him — trying to give him the benefit of the doubt, you see. But then he said it again, clear as a bell this time. I love you too, Sugar Tits . . .*

I actually laugh out loud. So much for the old man's *lies and innuendo.*

I didn't confront him about it. Oh, it was partly shock and partly being scared. I didn't want to bring it to a head immediately. It would mean our marriage was over — which it was in that moment, don't get me wrong — but I needed time to come to terms with it.

But about a month later, I decided I was ready. I told Toddy I was going to London for a few days to visit my sister Naoise, which I wasn't at all. I stayed in the Grand in Malahide, which is only a mile from the house. I suppose I was setting a trap. I knew he'd bring her — whoever she was — to the house, because that's Toddy. He'd want to show her everything he owned, because that's how just pathetically insecure he is . . .

49

The old man's still opening and closing drawers, going, 'Perhaps Helen took it . . .'

I'm there, 'Just keep focking looking, you dope.'

I thought he might at least wait a night or two. But no, it was that very night. I left the hotel at about eight o'clock, intending just to drive past the house. There was a black Ford Explorer parked in the driveway . . .

Yeah, Erika drives a black Ford Explorer.

I parked out on the road, used my remote control to open the gates, then let myself into the house, as quietly as I could. I tiptoed upstairs, even though it wasn't necessary. I could have driven ten horses up there and they wouldn't have heard for the noise they were making in that room.

I had to see it, even though I knew it was going to be painful. So I pushed the door . . .

Toddy was on top of her, naked, except for – and this is difficult for me – the pink Gant tie that I bought him as a present when he opened The Garden of Eatin in Howth.

She had no clothes on either and he had smeared her body with this, well, this cardamom pear sorbet that I had in the freezer. It's funny the things that go through your mind at a moment like that – I remember thinking, Toddy's never been a sorbet eater.

She was the one who noticed me first. Like I said, he was on top, with his back to me. She was lying on her back, looking at the door. Anyway, she saw me standing there and it didn't seem to bother her one bit. In fact the opposite was the case. She looked me straight in the eye and, honest to God, she actually smiled at me, obviously getting some kind of sick pleasure out of me catching them in the act. She didn't tell him either. She just tightened the tie around his neck, two or three twists and said, 'Keep going, Toddy – don't stop now!'

'Perhaps I'll just check with Hennessy,' the old man goes. 'See if *he* can't tell me what I've done with the bloody thing . . .'

He slips out of the room. I'm thinking, so much for his sweet, innocent daughter.

I grab the page and bring it over to the fax machine. It's the one we had in Foxrock, roysh, so I know straight away how to use it. I put the page in place and press the copy button. It goes through, like, an inch at a time, spitting the photocopy out the other end, again, bit by bit. I'm constantly looking over my shoulder, expecting him to blunder back into the room at any second.

It takes about a minute, roysh, but it eventually goes through. I put the original back on his desk, then fold up the copy and stick it in the sky rocket of my chinos.

Then I spot his cigor, balanced on the side of the desk, still smoking away. I pick it up, then hold the lit end to the nice cream-coloured corpet, burning a dirty big hole in it. Then I lay the cigor down beside it.

It's at that exact moment that he comes back, going, 'Found it, Ross! Panic over! Seems Helen was perusing the thing over breakfast this morning. Can you smell burning, by the way?'

I'm there, 'No.'

He hands me the so-called ortist's impression. I barely even glance at the focking thing. 'Amazing,' I go, handing it straight back to him. 'The tosser deserves a gold stor for that.'

He's there, 'And you can imagine how packed it'll be – what, with your mother's prawn and harissa couscous, to say nothing of her venison sausages with mash and leek gravy? Are you sure you can't smell something, Ross?'

I'm like, 'How the fock would I know? Maybe you dropped your focking cigor on the floor – have you considered that?'

His eyes immediately go to the edge of the desk, where he left it, then to the floor below. 'Oh, no,' he goes, the big drama routine, reaching down and picking it up. 'Look what I've done to the Axminster!'

I'm there, 'Anyway, klutz – like I said, I need four and a half grand. Transfer it to my account, will you?'

'Yes, of course,' he goes, barely able to tear his eyes away from the damage.

I decide to hit the bricks, though I only manage to get as far as the door before he's in my ear again.

'Oh,' he shouts after me, 'your mother's booked L'Ecrivain for next Friday. For the five of us. A kind of extended family dinner. You and I might work on her together. A Hungry Feeling, what? Bit of persuasion? The old O'Carroll-Kelly pincer movement?'

I'm just like, 'Whatever.'

Or maybe I don't say anything.

Complimentary green tea beberos. Yeah, that's exactly *my* reaction. 'Er, what?'

'Don't give me that,' Sorcha goes. 'It's a premium matcha tea, Ross. In fact, it's practically a superfood?'

I'm there, 'Is it?' except, of course, she's got a face on her now, because she knows I'm Scooby Dubious.

'I don't remember even asking for your opinion,' she goes. 'If you must know, it's, like, a 900-year tradition in Japan. It's grown under the shade of handmade bamboo-reed canopies and it's got, like, antioxidants, B-complex and, oh my God, *loads* of other stuff in it.'

I'm there, 'Babes, I'm not dissing the actual tea. I'm just not sure that giving it out for free is the way to get bodies into your shop. What you seem to be forgetting is that people – especially Irish people – love ripping the piss when it comes to, like, free shit. They're going to go, "Hey, don't have to spend four or five snots on a macchiato on the way to work any more – job's a good 'un!"'

She just, like, stares into her Flirtini – flattened by the old Straight Talk Express.

I'm there, 'Look, Babes, one of the things that even you'd

have to admit about me is that I've never been afraid to tell it. What I'm saying is, I don't think it's going to help you sell any extra clobber. In fact, all you're actually going to do long term is piss off Storbucks. And you know how I feel about that.'

'You sound just like Erika.'

'Erika?'

'She said the same thing.'

I pull a face.

'I think Erika would be better off concentrating on her own problems. I've found out one or two things, let's just say.'

'Things?'

'Yeah, no, she basically broke up that dude's marriage and my old man knows the full focking story.'

'You're making it sound sleazy, Ross, which I happen to know it wasn't.'

'I'm just making the point, Babes. All *his* focking talk – not wanting to see his daughter's name being dragged through the gutter – when he knows all along what she did. And now *I* know what she did.'

'You couldn't know.'

'Oh, I know. And it *was* sleazy, by the way – even though I'm a fine one to talk. Actually, I'm thinking of putting the whole thing up on my Facebook page.'

'What whole thing?'

'Hey, you'll see. Just keep your eyes on my status updates, especially one that says, *Ross has become a fan of "Toddy Was Never a Sorbet Eater!"*'

Saba is rammers, especially for a Monday night in a country that's *supposedly* focked? I ask her if she fancies another Knick-erdropper Glory, although obviously I don't call it that. She says no. 'I don't even know what I'm doing here,' she goes, sort of, like, making to stand up. This is before our *storters* have even arrived? 'I should be with my daughter.'

I reach over and sort of, like, touch her orm. 'Honor's fine,' I go, which she *obviously* is, because Sorcha's old pair have her for the night.

She's there, 'Maybe I should just ring and check on her.'

'Or maybe,' I go, 'you should just chillax. How long is it since you had a night out?'

She doesn't answer, just sits back in her seat again. I catch the waiter's eye and tell him I'll have the same again drinks-wise.

Did I mention that she looks incredible?

'Anyway,' I go, 'let's just forget about the whole current economic thing. It's, like, so depressing. Let's just change the subject.'

'Okay,' she goes, spreading her napkin across her lap. 'I heard you slept with Keelyn.'

It's like, whoa, she pulled that out of nowhere. I'm there, '*Excuse* me?'

'Don't even try to deny it, Ross. She came into the shop today and told me that you slept with her.'

She snaps her chopsticks aport.

I'm there, 'Is *that* what she's claiming?'

'Come on, Ross,' she goes, 'the only reason she slept with you was *so* she could come into the shop and tell me. For someone who prides himself on being a male slut, you don't understand women, do you?'

'Hey, I never claimed to – if some of the most intelligent men in, you'd have to say, history couldn't understand them, what chance have I got?'

My drink arrives – another Sidecor.

I'm there, 'Do you mind me saying, you don't seem as pissed off as I thought you'd be?'

She shrugs. 'Why *would* I be? We're both free agents,' then we end up just sitting there for the next few minutes, neither of us saying shit.

It doesn't take long for the conversation to return to the whole current eonomic business.

'I'm only doing what your dad suggested,' she eventually goes. 'I'm talking about his letter in last Saturday's *Irish Times*? He said there's still money out there *during* an actual recession, Ross. You just have to find out what it is that people want – preferably something original – and give it to them . . .'

I reach across the table and give her hand a bit of a rub. 'Okay, I'm sorry,' I go.

'All I'm saying, Ross, is I'm really trying.'

'I know you're trying. Like I said, I'm really sorry and shit?'

This, you might be surprised to hear, isn't me suddenly trying to get in there while she's vulnerable. No, this is one of *those* situations – like when you ask your new girlfriend to hide in the bathroom while your ex gets the rest of her shit together. It's called being a gentleman.

'You know Guess is gone from South Anne Street?' she suddenly goes.

I let go of her hand and nod sort of, like, sadly. I tell her I heard. I just didn't know whether to say anything.

'It's like, if that can just be *gone* one morning,' she goes, 'it's, like, oh my God, what chance is there for anyone else? Calum Best opened it, Ross.'

'I know, Babes. I know.'

I can't bring myself to tell her that Nine West went tango uniform in the rhubarb this morning as well. I know I should, but she seems so already down?

She's suddenly, like, staring over my shoulder at all the black and white photos on the wall of all these – I have to say the word – *Asian* people, driving tuk-tuks and doing basically whatever else. She says that some days she feels like just taking off and doing something really mad.

I remind her that she's been talking for ages about trekking the Annapurnas to raise money for river blindness. Maybe it's time to give that a whirl. She just shakes her head. 'I'm talking, like, *totally* mad,' she goes. 'Like just dropping out of the whole – I don't know – rat race. Maybe backpacking around Thailand, Vietnam and Laos . . .'

She shrugs, then takes a sip of her drink. 'Claire came home last weekend,' she goes, 'and – oh! my God! – the experiences she had!'

I'm there, 'Experiences? As in?'

She's like, 'As in, loads, Ross. I can't give you specifics. Have you not been reading her mails?'

'The odd one. They're shit.'

'Well, *loads* is all I'm saying. She even got some Asian writing tattooed on her wrist.'

'Claire is from Bray,' I remind her. 'She can carry that kind of shit off.'

'I'm not *saying* I want a tattoo, Ross. I'm just saying that sometimes I want to just, like, flip out and do something wild. Like, just as an example, another day, she got talking to this guy who was just reading a copy of *The Sorrow of War* outside an internet café in Hanoi. It turned out he was from, like, Greystones. Can you believe the coincidence of that?'

Er, considering that half of focking Ireland's over there at any given time, yeah.

'It *is* pretty amazing,' I go.

She's like, 'It's more than amazing – it's, like, fate, Ross. Because now they're back here and they're actually madly in love. They called in to the shop on Saturday – Garret's *his* name – and she looked amazing, Ross, even though she was only wearing this, like, printed tea dress from Urban Outfitters?'

'But *you* couldn't just take off like that anyway,' I suddenly go. 'We've got an actual daughter together, remember?'

She immediately looks guilty for even thinking it and I feel guilty for reminding her.

Our main courses arrive. I go to pick up my fork and she asks me if she can say something that might sound a little bit, I don't know, cheesy?

I'm there, 'Cheesy? Shoot, Babes – let me be the judge of that.'

'Okay,' she goes, 'I was thinking about what you were saying that day in the shop – about us maybe putting the divorce on hold?'

I actually stop, a prawn from my Pad Thai frozen in mid-air somewhere between my plate and my Von Trapp.

I'm there, 'Excuse me?'

She goes, 'I'm saying I don't want to get divorced, Ross. Not at the moment. Everything's just – oh my God – *so* already depressing? I'm asking can we just let things sit for a while?'

I'm wondering has the Keelyn thing reminded her that she still has feelings for me. I don't want to take advantage of the situation, but I still end up having to go, 'Are you saying I could get back in there – if I wanted?' and don't ask me why, roysh, but I end up nodding at her chest.

She goes, 'No, Ross, you can't *get back in here*, as you put it. We're over. We were over a long time ago. And you being with Keelyn was – oh my God – *so* a reminder of *why*? The thing is, I don't *want* to be married to you – but it's just that I don't want to be divorced from you even more. Can you understand that?'

And there's me, not a focking didgeridoo what's she's banging on about.

I'm like, 'Yeah, of course – a hundred percent.'

One F rings me while I'm in the scratcher watching *Loose Women*, which isn't anything like the programme it promises to be, by the way. He says he's looking for a favour. It turns out some colleague of his in the *Plumber's Shithouse Companion* – or whatever rag it is he writes for – is looking for my old dear's number.

I go, 'Dude, my old dear's number is, like, a state secret. You have no idea how seriously she takes that whole privacy thing. What do they want it for anyway?'

'Ah, they're ringing around various RTÉ celebrities,' he goes, 'and trying to embarrass them into taking a cut in their wages.'

I'm there, 'Now that is what I call journalism.'

'Thanks.'

'Okay, take this down . . .'

'Bet you never thought you'd be sitting in the front of a flat-bed truck,' JP's old man goes to me.

He's right – although my defence is that at least *I'm* only along for the ride.

'Lot of people out there doing a lot of shit they never thought they'd be doing,' he goes. 'You see the news last night?'

I shake my head. Not unless it was the one that Glenda Gilson was reading. Jake Gyllenhaal and Reese Wither-spoon's reps have denied rumours that the couple are set to split.

'People queuing,' he goes, 'for fucking burger jobs. And I'm talking about good people – solicitors, architects, accountants, quantity surveyors. I'm telling you, this country is royally fucked,' except he says it like it's an actual *good* thing?

JP's sitting on the other side of me, behind the wheel. 'What my dad means is that *we're* only going to get busier,' he goes. 'I mean, this truck is only the start of it, Ross. We're already talking about hiring.'

I get the distinct feeling that I'm about to be offered a job. I quickly change the subject. I ask them what we're even repossessing here and JP says a hot tub.

We all hop out of the truck. It's pissing so hord you'd nearly feel the urge to stort rounding up two of every animal.

'It was bought on hire purchase,' JP goes. 'The guy stopped making repayments about six months ago.'

His old man grabs a toolbox from the back of the van.

'No sledgehammer?' I go.

He actually laughs. He says no, they always get the hot tubs without a fight. 'You take someone's E-Class, his A6, his X5, his Continental GT, you could be driving away with that bastard sprawled across the bonnet, sobbing his fucking heart out. But the hot tubs, they generally come quietly . . .'

'People are embarrassed by them,' JP goes. 'Remind them of how stupid they were.'

I suppose we were all guilty of stupidity. I paid ninety squids for a Nigella Lawson saltpig for Sorcha one Christmas. I'd say even the word 'saltpig' is going to, like, disappear from the language.

The front door of the house opens and out walks this dude, probably about my age, two o'clock in the afternoon, still in his dressing-gown, although a lot of my critics would say that *I'm* one to focking criticize.

'It's back here,' he goes, leading us around the back of the gaff, not seeming to give a shit. Seems to just want it gone, just like JP's old man said.

It's at, like, the bottom of the gorden. There's, like, two or three steps up to this little decking area, then in the corner of it there's this, like, humungous bath, as big as the one I saw Hugh Hefner sitting in on *Cribs*, except this is at the back of a gaff in Luttrellstown.

JP says we might need a bigger truck, but his old man says

no, you'd be surprised how small these things are when they're, like, broken down.

The dude they're, like, repossessing it from just shakes his head. He's like, 'What *was* I thinking?'

The rain's hammering off the tarpaulin cover like a donkey pissing on a flat rock.

'Ah, I saw people do crazier shit,' JP's old man goes. Then he shrugs. 'They were the times.'

The dude just nods.

'I don't know who we thought we were,' he goes. He looks back up at the house. 'A million-euro mortgage doesn't make you a millionaire – that's the lesson, isn't it?'

Of course he's saying it to the man who might have even sold him the gaff.

'Ah, maybe we'll all deal with it better the next time round,' JP's old man goes. 'Hey, have you got the assembly instructions for this thing? Makes it easier for us.'

The goy just nods, then turns around and trudges back to the gaff.

The second he's gone – I swear to fock – JP's old man storts taking off his clothes. First he whips off his Barbour Stockman, then he takes his shirt and his pink cable-knit Ralph off over his head together.

This is in the pelting rain, remember.

'Er, what are you doing?' I end up *having* to go.

'Well,' he goes, tipping up the steps, then ripping back the tarpaulin, 'if I'm guessing right . . .' He sticks his hand into it. 'Still hot,' he goes, delighted with himself. 'See, they never *can* resist it – one last guilty dip.'

He steps out of his Kurt Geigers, then in one movement whips down his yellow cords and his boxer shorts, while me and JP stand there watching his grey flabby orse disappear over the side like a focking elephant seal finding the ocean.

60

JP just shrugs, then storts whipping off his own threads and, the next thing anyone knows, *he's* in there as well.

So – suddenly feeling like a spare tit just standing there – I end up having to just follow them in.

The water, it has to be said, *is* amazing – as in, roasting hot?

JP's old man fannies about with the controls and gets the jets going and all of a sudden, roysh, you could nearly forget you were sitting in the total raw in some random stranger's gorden in the middle of, I don't know, wherever the fock Luttrellstown is.

'So what about it?' JP's old man suddenly goes. I have to nearly squint to see him through the fog of eucalyptus steam. He's lying back with his head resting on a leather pillow and his eyes closed. 'You want to join us? The team that helped build the Celtic Tiger – re-formed and taking it back!'

I'm there, 'I don't know, Mr Conroy . . .'

'Do you want to know what I like about you, Ross?'

'I've no conscience. You told me that when I was selling gaffs for you.'

'Well, I wasn't blowing smoke up your hole either. I meant every word of it. Now I'm going to tell you something I *haven't* told you before. Do you remember that bird Alice, used to do the accounts for me, with the big milkers?'

'Is she one of the ones who took the sexual harassment case against you?'

He suddenly opens his eyes.

'Why are you bringing that up? I'm telling you a nice story here.'

'Sorry.'

'Okay. Well, *before* all that, Alice was a medium. And I'm not talking about her fucking bra size here. She had powers, Ross. Genuine powers. Could contact the dead and all sorts of shit.

Anyway, the very first day you walked through my door, your first day at work, I caught her looking at you . . .'

'She *did* have a thing for me.'

'No, I mean looking at you funny. See, I thought the same as you. I thought, oh, here's another poor mare about to get her heart kicked around in the dirt. But then you were on the phone. Ah, you were trying to bleed an extra thirty grand from some pair of newlyweds – for some fucking ant chamber on the Lucan Road. Yeah, they were the days. And Alice was just looking at you, like I said, funny.

'So the next thing, she jumps up from her desk and she runs out of the place. Out the fucking door. So I ran after her. She was standing outside Hemingways, trying to light a fag, except her hands were shaking too much. Cut a long story short, I says to her, "What's wrong?" And *she* says, "That guy in there – the new guy? – he has no aura."'

'No aura?'

'That's what she said. No aura. Means you're empty. Fucking dead inside. Here, take it as a compliment. JP and me, we could certainly use someone like you. In these times – you know what I'm saying?'

I don't know *what* to say. I'm a bit, I don't know, taken aback? I'm there, 'Er, I think I might, er, pass on it.'

'The money's great,' it's JP who goes.

'Yeah, no, I know things are *supposably* bad out there? But I honestly hadn't figured on getting a job . . .'

'Well,' JP's old man goes, 'if you change your mind . . .'

The owner of the gaff suddenly arrives out again, with the instruction manual in his hand. 'Don't mind, do you?' JP's old man goes, sort of, like, indicating the water with a flick of his head. The poor focker doesn't know what to say, looking at these three randomers, stark Vegas naked in his gorden.

'Er, no,' he ends up going, setting the instructions down on top of the patio log burner. 'I'll, er, leave you to it.'

JP's old man is suddenly squinting back at the house.

'That your wife,' he goes, 'looking out the upstairs window?'

The dude has a look over his shoulder.

He's like, 'Yeah,' and then, for whatever reason, he adds, 'She *was* in recruitment.'

JP's old man nods, I suppose you'd have to say, thoughtfully? He says she sure is a pretty lady.

The old man says he's already looking forward to dessert. The cheese board rolled past a minute ago and he says he'd bet ten euros to my twenty that he smelled Roomano.

I shrug, as if to say, what makes you think *I* give a fock?

He goes, 'Dutch, don't you know, despite the Italian-sounding name. Bears a certain resemblance to the Parmigiano Reggiano, except with caramel and butterscotch notes.'

'*Chaaarles*,' the old dear suddenly goes, sort of, like, pleadingly – the same voice she used to use when she wanted a piece of Lladró or a new baby seal for her back. 'What was your cholesterol the last time you had it checked?'

'Oh, something or other,' he goes, then he sticks his head back in his menu.

Erika chips in then. 'Fionnuala, it's like talking to the wall,' she goes. 'Mum and I have been trying to get him to slow down . . .'

Helen shakes her head. 'Yes, if it's not the shop, it's the hotel. If it's not the hotel, it's some other idea he's had. Four o'clock this morning, there he was, bolt upright in the bed, night light on, scribbling away with that Mont Blanc pen of his.'

I check the old dear's face for a reaction – *she* bought him that pen, as a thank you present, when the council gave up trying to stick a halting site on Westminster Road – although she genuinely doesn't seem to *give* two shits?

'Oh, it's just this recession,' *he* goes, suddenly looking up again. '*It isn't so much that hard times are coming; the change observed is mostly soft times going!* Marx said that. Karl or Groucho, I can never remember, though I can check it for you.'

I'm just, like, staring at Helen, wondering what the fock she even sees in him. I've always thought she looked like Diane Lane.

'The point I'm making,' he goes, 'is that there's never been a better time for business. Interest rates are low. Oil is cheap. No pressure on wages. There's nothing like it, eh, Ross, for getting the old haemoglobin pumping?'

I'm there, 'Don't focking include me in that,' but he just keeps blabbing on. It's impossible to hurt the focker.

'I saw Paddy Kelly the other day . . . cycling! Paddy bloody Kelly – him with all his Rolls-Royces – and there he was, sitting on – quite literally, Fionnuala – one of these famous push-bikes. Well, I knew things hadn't been going quite so well for him. I shouted out to him. "That's the spirit, Paddy!" Or something of that colour. Although Erika thinks I might have clipped him with my mirror taking the turn on to Ailesbury Road.'

'You *did* clip him,' Erika goes, but at the same time she's, like, laughing?

The old man laughs then. It's, like, way too cosy and it pisses me off that *he's* still in obvious denial about the person his daughter actually *is*?

The old dear throws her tuppenies in then.

'Charles, I know you're excited, but you and Helen should be *enjoying* these years together.' Then she smiles across the table at the woman who's basically scoring her husband. 'God knows, you waited long enough.'

I think she really *is* over him.

Helen's there, 'Thanks, Fionnuala,' and I'm honestly about two seconds away from hurling.

The waiter suddenly appears – he's, like, French by the sounds of him – and asks us if we've any questions about the menu. The old dear actually laughs.

'You're obviously new,' she goes. 'I'm Fionnuala O'Carroll-Kelly. I'm a regular in L'Ecrivain,' except she totally overdoes the pronunciation, so it sounds like Llleccckkk-ruvon.

The dude just nods, then goes, 'Well, zis week, we haff ze special menoo – fife corsees for seeksty-fife yoro . . .'

The old dear suddenly stands up. The legs of her chair screech along the wooden floor, causing pretty much every conversation in the place to stop. 'How dare you!' she goes. 'Do we *look* like the kind of people who want the sixty-five euro menu?'

The poor focker hasn't a bog. He's like, '*Madame?*'

'Have another waiter sent to our table,' she goes, 'this instant! And it'll be *à la carte*, like it always was and always will be,' and she sits down again, then turns to the couple at the next table and goes, 'Early birds! Grill menus! This used to be the happiest place in the world to live! A survey found that out – hard as it is to believe it now!'

There's suddenly this, like, awkward silence in the restaurant.

I'm just there, 'Get a focking grip on yourself, you cocktail-crazed good-time girl . . .'

Erika suddenly pins me with this look and – this is unbelievable – goes, 'Ross, don't speak to your mother like that.'

This is Erika, remember.

The rest of them are all delighted, of course. The general vibe is that Ross has met his match at last. Let him stick that in his flan crust and bake it.

A new waiter appears. Helen says she can't decide between the scallops and the Challans duck, then the old dear says she could have one as a storter and the other as, like, a main course?

'Do you know what *I'd* love?' I suddenly go, staring straight at Erika. 'Sorbet!'

She just freezes. You can see her, roysh, in that split second, trying to work out where I'm getting my actual information from.

'Sorbet?' the old man goes, obviously not making the connection. He's as slow as bananas digesting, see.

'Yeah,' I go, 'I don't know what's making me think of it. I've just got this sudden craving for the stuff.'

He's like, 'Well, it's just the thing to freshen the palate, Ross. It's very popular in some places.'

And I'm there, 'Some places more than others, eh, Erika?'

The old dear obviously hasn't a clue and neither has he, although I can tell that Helen has suddenly copped it. Erika storts taking a sudden interest in her menu again, totally humiliated.

I laugh. I'm thinking, that's you back in your box.

We all order. I end up asking for the scallops followed by the duck as well. The waiter focks off and that's when the old dear's phone suddenly rings. She looks at it, sitting there on the table – the ringtone's some focking Snorah Jones song.

'Number blocked,' she goes, picking it up. 'It might be RTÉ. They're having awful problems getting their hands on Dwarf Cape gooseberries for my show on Monday.'

'A regrettable sign of the times,' the old man goes. 'Better answer it, then.'

Which she does.

'You're *who* from what newspaper?' she's suddenly going, at the top of her voice.

The old man and Helen exchange, I suppose, concerned

looks. After, like, five or ten seconds of silence, the old dear goes, 'A *paycut*? Why in heaven's name would I volunteer to take a paycut?'

Obviously, roysh, we can only hear, like, *her* side of the conversation? 'Well, good for Pat Kenny!' she goes. 'But that's *his* concern.'

The old man tells her to just hang up.

'*Share the pain?*' she practically screams down the phone. '*National interest?* How did you even get this number?'

You can imagine me at this stage. I'm practically on the floor laughing, to the point that I suddenly need the Josh Ritter – eight inches of dirty spine that wants crimping.

Anyway, to cut a long short, I hit the jacks and do whatever needs doing. Five minutes later, I'm stepping out of Trap Two, a good three pounds lighter, when who's standing right in front of me – this is *in* the gents, remember – only Erika, with a face on her as mad as a focking meat-axe.

It's automatic, roysh – I've always been a slave to the one-liner – I end up just going, 'Hey, Sugar Tits – how the hell are you?' and what happens after that, I can't exactly say, because it happens in, like, a blizzard of movement.

One minute, I'm heading for the sink to wash the old Christian Andersens, the next my head is being cracked off the tile wall and I'm struggling to breathe with this feeling of sudden tightness in my throat.

It's only when my head and my vision clear, roysh, that I realize I'm lying flat on the toilet floor and Erika is standing over me, with the heel of one of her black Christian Louboutin courts pressing down on my windpipe.

'Where is it?' she goes, her face so red that I'm convinced she'd be capable of *actually* killing me here.

I'm barely able to get the words out. I'm like, '*Where's . . . what?*'

She presses down horder, with pretty much her entire body weight, and I swear to fock, I think my Adam's apple is about to burst.

'*It's in my . . . sky rocket*,' I end up having to go.

She's there, 'Give it to me,' the tone in her voice telling me not to even think about focking with her.

I reach for my chinos and whip it out. She takes it and then, with her foot still gripping my throat, pops it into her XOXO clutch.

'*I'm . . . sorry*,' I go. '*I was tired of the whole . . . I suppose happy families thing . . .*'

'You ever pull a stunt like that again,' she goes, sort of, like, grinding her foot now, to the point where I'm actually retching, 'and I'll kill you.'

Then she takes her foot off my throat, checks her make-up in the mirror and focks off back to the table. I end up just lying on the floor for a good five minutes – even with other customers coming in and out. They all just step over me. One or two ask me if I'm okay, but I just lie there trying to get my breathing back to normal.

Eventually, roysh, I get up, fix myself, then go back out to the restaurant. They've all, like, finished their storters and my scallops are sitting there, basically cold.

'Hope you don't mind,' the old man goes, 'I helped myself to one of your thingamys.'

I'm just there, 'Er, no . . . it's cool.'

I can't even look at Erika – focking scared, I admit – though I know *she's* looking at *me*, grinning like a focking undertaker.

'What's that there?' the old man suddenly *has* to go then, sort of, like, indicating the right side of my neck with his butter knife.

I put my hand to it. There's something there, all right. It's, like, an indentation, maybe half an inch deep.

'It looks about the size of a Louboutin heel,' Erika goes, with real badness in her voice.

Real focking badness.

I wake up in some random bed in some random gaff in Rathgor of all places, alone and just lying there while my eyes adjust to the light.

I search my head for a name.

Estelle?

No.

Stella?

Could be.

I *do* remember her going out the door, though – it must be, like, hours ago now – saying she had to go to work, telling me to let myself out.

Hang on. No, Stella was what I was drinking. That was it. Cocoon closed down last night. Another victim of the blahdy blah. You'd almost feel sorry for Eddie Irvine if he didn't own half of focking Monte Corlo.

I remember being all full of concern, asking him, 'What's going to happen to all the hairdressers, Irv?' and he said he didn't know. Then he got this, like, distant look in his eyes and said I was always popular with that crowd, that I went through Toni and Guy like a dose of contact dermatitis.

Which was nice of him.

But whoever I went home with last night, I've no memory of what she even *looked* like?

I roll out of the bed and throw the old threads on, then tip out to the sort of, like, living room. There's, like, a photograph on the sideboard of what I presume is *her*, sitting in a water taxi, with the Sydney focking Opera House in the background. Another one who's done *the whole travelling thing*. I pick it up and give her the quick once-over.

She's not great, but then she's not exactly a daywalker either, just average. Parsley. Vanilla. Cheese and focking onion.

I really need to raise my game.

My phone rings in my pocket. I'm thinking, it's either her, making sure I've gotten the fock out of her gaff, or it's JP or Fionn, checking have I still got the old Lemony Snickets for the Leinster v Munster match next weekend.

We still owe those fockers at least one, by the way.

It ends up being none of the above. It's, like, Sorcha. And from the, I suppose, commotion I can hear in the background, it's immediately obvious that something's wrong.

I'm there, 'Is everything okay with Honor?'

'Er, yeah,' she goes. 'It's just that it's, like, absolutely packed in here today? The Gords have even been in, threatening to charge me with, like, public order offences,' and something – maybe something in her voice – tells me that she doesn't mean that in, like, a good way.

'It doesn't look like I'm going to get out for lunch,' she suddenly goes. 'Would you be an absolute angel, if you're in town, and get me a slice of quiche from Fallon & Byrne? Mossfield organic cheese and bacon lardons, if they still do it.'

I'm about to ask her what bacon lardons are when, all of a sudden, I hear this woman's voice on the other end of the line go, 'This is lukewarm!' then Sorcha go, 'Oh! My God! I am *so* sorry!' and then the same woman again go, 'Maybe if you got off the focking phone, you might be able to get my order right.'

Sorcha immediately hangs up.

By the sound of things, she's in obvious trouble, so I decide to hit town. This, after all, is my – still – wife. I walk out on to the street, grab an Andy McNab and get the dude to drop me at, like, Stephen's Green. I literally peg it down Grafton Street, hang that left turn just after Bewley's and don't stop running until I reach the actual Powerscourt Townhouse Centre.

When I get there, I literally can't *believe* the sight that awaits me?

There's a focking line of people out the door – not the door of the shop, I should add, we're talking the door of the actual shopping centre? – we're talking five or maybe six hundred people, men *and* birds, young and old, standing on the pavement, two- and three-deep, all the way up South William Street, way past the rear of the actual Westbury.

Of course, I'm thinking, no, it couldn't be, but then I stop and ask some random bird – think Emily Deschanel but as, like, an emo? – what everyone's queuing for and she sort of, like, shrugs, then goes, '*Something* for free.'

Green tea beberos. What did I tell her? Irish people would sell your focking orse for ports.

The mood of the crowd, it has to be said, is pretty hostile, as I follow the line inside the shopping centre and up the steps. People are making a big show of checking their watches and quoting their focking wait time to each other. 'An hour,' some dude with floppy hair and a scorf goes to no one in particular. 'That's my entire focking lunchbreak!'

Then, as I get closer, I hear this bird say that she's been waiting even longer than she waited yesterday and that it's just not good enough.

I make my way through the throng of people to the actual shop and I look through the window to see Sorcha, dressed up like a barista, standing behind the counter, her old dear's Burco bubbling away behind her and three Aeroccinos on the permanent go.

Of course she's working like a cat burying shit on a wooden floor, making sure everyone gets their . . . whatever the fock these things even are. And at the same time she's going, 'I've

just got exclusive new lines in by Percy, Literature, Nicole Miller and Sue Wong. And Radcliffe jeans, which I think are even more slimming than Sevens, if you can believe that.'

Then other times she's going, 'All those items on that rack are ecologically sound!'

But of course no one's paying the slightest attention to that. They're collecting their drinks, then turning around and walking straight out of the shop. And that's if she's lucky. Some of them have the actual towns to complain.

'They're not nearly as nice as I thought they'd be,' I hear this one old dear go, though she's still focking drinking it, I notice.

Sorcha tries to tell her that she's going to be doing green tea espressos from tomorrow, but all to no avail. The woman actually laughs in her face and goes, 'Well, I, for one, won't be coming back.'

The next person in line, this big fat bird, is just like, 'Are you going to serve me or are you just going to stand there with your mouth open?'

I know we're, like, technically not a couple any more, but I can't even begin to tell you what it does to me, seeing Sorcha treated like that, a girl, remember, who recently changed her Facebook status from 'Single' to 'It's Complicated' for me.

She suddenly looks up from her, I don't know, frothers and her various other bits and pieces.

'Ross!' she goes, and I swear to God, roysh, the look of, I suppose, desperation in her eyes breaks my actual hort.

'It looks like you could do with some help,' I end up just going, no stranger, a lot of people would say, to playing the hero.

She smiles at me.

'Go on,' I go, 'hand me that other apron,' which she immediately does.

She thinks, of course, that I'm going to put the focking thing on. Instead, roysh, I get the apron and I twist it into something resembling a bullwhip. Then – without saying another word – I just stort lashing people across the focking shins with it – *foo-tish!* – going, 'Out! What the fock do you think this is, a soup kitchen? Out! Out!'

It's honestly like that scene in, I suppose, the Bible, where Jesus went basically apeshit in the temple. There's all of a sudden panic. People are turning and running, screaming, for the door.

Foo-tish! Foo-tish!

I'm cracking the fockers across the backs of their legs and at the same time I'm giving it, 'Out! Out, you focking para-sites!'

There's suddenly, like, a bottleneck of people at the door, all trying to squeeze through the same space to avoid the wrath of the old Rossmeister.

That's when I spot the big fat bird who said that shit to Sorcha about standing there with, like, her mouth open? She makes, like, a dive for a gap that doesn't actually exist and she gets sort of, like, jammed there in the crush of bodies.

It's like looking at Gavin Quinnell's orse sticking out of a ruck.

'Looks like you want it *to go*,' I give it, then I shape up, roysh, to make it a good one.

Foo-foo, foo-foo, foo-foo, foo-TISH!

Right across the old Derry Air. She roars like a focking bull taking an orseful of buckshot.

'You want more whip on that?' I go.

These lines are just coming to me, by the way. I suppose you pick them up over the years going in and out of Buckys.

Foo-foo, foo-foo, foo-foo, foo-TISH!

That finally releases the blockage. The people at the front

sort of, like, fall through the doors, then the ones behind them clamber over their bodies to get out.

I shut the door and put the catch on, then turn around to Sorcha, expecting her to suddenly throw her orms around me, as grateful as she was the first night I ever slept with her.

Her reaction, though, takes me by total surprise. 'How *could* you?' she goes.

I'm there, 'Er, *excuse* me?'

'They were customers, Ross!'

'They were freeloaders!'

'*Someone* might have bought something! I heard one girl admire those hibiscus jacquard-print minidresses by Milly.'

'Well, I heard another bird say it was a disgrace that you weren't doing pastries. A *disgrace*, Sorcha!'

She tries to look away.

'There's a recession happening out there,' I go, 'and you can't pretend otherwise. Babes, you can't make eye contact with people these days without them asking you to validate their focking porking.'

She knows that deep down I'm right.

'Well,' she goes, in her usual sulky voice, 'you scared Honor.'

I'm like, 'Honor?' suddenly looking around me.

There she is, roysh, sitting on the pink PVC sofa opposite the changing rooms, chatting happily to herself and flicking through the copy of Ross Kemp's *Gangs* that Ronan bought her for Christmas.

I go over and scoop her up into my orms. 'Daddy!' she goes, which is always nice to hear.

Whoa! I'm suddenly thinking to myself. How many weeks has she been out of Pre-Montessori now? I'm like, 'That swine flu scare can't still be going on . . .'

Sorcha just turns away from me. 'Don't give me that,' she goes.

Which is a strange reaction.

I grab her by the shoulder and, like, spin her round. I'm like, 'Sorcha! Whoa! What the fock is going on?'

It's Honor who ends up answering. 'Mommy is sad,' she goes.

I just stare at Sorcha. I'm like, 'That much is obvious, Honor. But I'd prefer to hear it straight from the horse's mouth.'

Sorcha takes, like, a deep breath.

'She was expelled,' she goes – out with it, just like that. It rocks me back on my pretty much heels, I can tell you.

I'm there, 'Expelled?'

Sorcha shakes her head. 'Expelled, sent home, whatever you want to call it . . .'

That's when it all finally comes out.

'Because I didn't pay her fees.'

'But *I* pay her fees,' I go. 'Hennessy set up that direct debit to your account . . .'

But then it suddenly hits me. 'You've been using the money to keep this focking place going.'

The tears suddenly arrive. The only surprise is that they're hers and not mine.

'The bills were piling up on me,' she goes. 'I've been struggling to make the repayments on the loan I took out to refit this place. Then there's, like, rent, rates, suppliers. Something had to give . . .'

'Oh, and that something just happened to be our daughter's education?'

She ends up losing it with me then. 'The one thing I always wanted, Ross, ever since Honor was born, was to have something that I could one day pass on to her . . .'

I'm thinking, you will – a six-figure overdraft.

'So don't put that on me,' she goes. 'Don't put that on me, even if it *is* true.'

77

I feel automatically bad then, seeing how upset she is and everything? 'When was it that she was expelled?' I go.

She's there, 'A week before Christmas. I asked for more time to pay, but . . . It was – oh! my God! – horrible, Ross! They pulled her out in front of her entire Mathematical Reasoning class. Made her pack all of her things into a black plastic bag. Plastic, Ross!'

'That's out of order.'

'I'll tell you what else is out of order. She wasn't even allowed to sit her Royal Academy of Dance ballet examination.'

'Jesus.'

'So much for Pre-Montessori providing a comprehensive educational approach from birth to adulthood based on the observation of children's needs.'

I shake my head, I think the word is *ruefully*?

'Well, I *did* tell you to stop ordering in new shit,' I go. 'I'm not one for saying I told you so, which is lucky for you, in this case. But what I still don't get is, why can't you just tap your old man for the moo? He must be good for it – family law solicitor, blah blah blah.'

'Because,' she goes, 'I'm too proud to ask my parents for money – can you understand that?'

'Being honest, no.'

'You heard my dad talk about me at his sixtieth birthday party, Ross. He described me as one of the great success stories of the Celtic Tiger. I can't let him know the mess I've got myself into – it'd break his, oh my God, heart.'

'Don't cry, Mommy,' Honor suddenly goes, and it's amazing, roysh, how the innocence of a child can put everything into sudden perspective.

Sorcha sort of, like, laughs, wipes her tears away with her open palm, then takes Honor out of my orms.

'You know what the worst thing is,' she whispers to me,

'every morning when she wakes up, she puts her little boater on her head, thinking she's going to school . . .'

I suddenly feel like *I'm* about to cry? And that's even before she delivers the even worse news.

She takes, like, a deep breath. 'They're threatening to repossess the house.'

I'm there, 'Who?'

'See,' she goes, 'I *knew* this is how you'd react.'

'I only said who?'

'Who the fock do you think, Ross? The bank!'

'But why?'

'Because of all the money I owe them.'

'Jesus, we've just come through the Celtic Tiger – everyone owes them money.'

'Well, I've . . . missed a lot of repayments.'

'I focking suspected that. How many are we talking?'

She looks away again. 'All of them.'

'All of them? Fock's sake, Sorcha. I thought that last dude you went out with was supposed to be some kind of hotshot auditor?'

'Don't try to lay this on Cillian,' she goes, pretty much spitting fish out her hole. 'No one could have predicted this recession, Ross – not when I took out that loan.'

'So now they're threatening to take the roof from over your heads . . .'

'Yes.'

'Have you talked to them?'

She shakes her head. 'I've been avoiding their calls.'

I'm there, 'Jesus Christ, Sorcha. It's time you took your head out of the basic sand. You're in serious trouble here. You need to, like, face up to that fact?'

Her face suddenly softens. She doesn't say anything for ages, just keeps combing Honor's hair with the tips of her fingers, until Honor eventually gets annoyed by it and sort of, like, slaps her hand away.

'Well, maybe, I'll make an appointment to see them,' she, in the end, goes. 'First thing Monday morning. They do say that, don't they? Whatever you do, don't ignore the problem. Go and talk to them and make, I don't know, *some* kind of repayment plan.'

I'm there, 'It suddenly sounds like you're talking sense.'

She smiles at me, then gives me the cow eyes, which I never can resist. 'Ross,' she goes, 'will you come with me?'

'The auction rooms – I'm told – are *full* of repossessed X5s,' Garbhan says, then I pull a face, as if to say, fock, *where* is it all going to end? Blathin's old man seems to agree with me.

'Parents with professions – *real* professions – are asking schools for time to pay their children's fees,' he goes. 'I heard an economist on the radio this morning – I can't remember which one – saying this could be the end of the Irish middle class as we know it.'

And this coming from an obstetrician. Maybe my old pair are wrong afer all.

Tina's hanging off the edge of the conversation, probably delighted to hear that people are finally suffering on this side of the river.

I subtly check her out. Clothes-wise, she's a disaster area – we're talking Ground focking Zero. She's still wearing, like, her white hospital uniform – I don't know if I mentioned that she's working as, like, a trainee nurse in Beaumont now? – having just come off a fourteen-hour shift, with just a fleece thrown over it, then Uggs, which aren't even real ones, and big hoopy earrings that wouldn't look out of place with a Chinese gymnast handstanding on them while planning an aerial focking dismount.

It's her son's girlfriend's first day as a teenager – she could have made the effort. 'It's focking Clonskeagh,' I go to her out of the side of my mouth.

She either doesn't hear or pretends not to.

'I'm not sure if it'll be the end of the middle class in Ireland,' this Garbhan dude goes. 'The IMF would step in long before it ever came to that . . .'

I just nod – all I *can* do in the circs. But then Tina's suddenly about to open her trap. I'm thinking, don't embarrass yourself any more than you already have.

'I wootunt see dat as bean a good ting,' she tries to go. 'De foorst ting deed do if dee kem in would be to cut poobalic seervices. In utter words, it's the poo-er bein made to pay again for de greed of de rich.'

I turn to Blathin's old man. 'She doesn't mean any offence, Dr Roberts. Possibly just thinking out loud . . .'

'No, she's quite right,' *he* goes. 'It was greed and speculation that got us into this mess. Nothing else. And there is evidence there – I've seen the data – of a sudden spike in diseases such as tuberculosis and cholera in countries that received aid from the IMF.'

I just nod.

I'm there, 'I suppose that's one way of looking at it.'

'Well,' he goes, 'what other way is there?'

The three of them are suddenly stood staring at me, waiting for an answer.

If I learned anything from being in school, it's how to bluff my way out of these situations. I sort of, like, laugh to myself – like it's a private joke? 'You do *not* want to get me going on the whole world affairs thing!' I go. 'We'd be here until focking midnight!' then I turn around and go off to work the room.

First, though, I need a drink – especially after all that heavy talk – so I hit the kitchen, where the booze is all laid out on the table. There's no sign of the Celtic Tiger being over in this gaff, by the way – they've pushed the boat out in a major way.

I grab a glass, then dip it into the punchbowl.

I'm just looking around, thinking how porties have certainly changed since *I* was their age. Blathin's old pair hired, like, a sushi chef to cater the event – that's what kids are eating these days – and a team of beauticians to give Bla and her friends makeovers.

'Excuse me,' I hear this woman's voice go, reaching for the gin. I look up and I end up nearly shitting my pants. It's Granuaile Kneafsey, a bird I used to, well, *know*, back in my Club 92 days.

I'd love to be able to say it ended well.

I'm like, 'How the hell are you?' thinking, the past is the past – we're at a kid's birthday porty, which is no place for a scene. 'I presume you got the morning-after pill that time, did you?'

Except I say it a bit loud and one or two heads turn our way, including – shit! – Blathin's old dear. She's not exactly a fan of mine as it is.

Do you ever get the feeling that it's going to be one of those days?

Granuaile looks at me, pretty appalled, it has to be said, then just shakes her head. She pours herself probably a larger whack of gin than she originally intended. I take a sip of my punch, which is weak as piss.

'So,' I go, trying to come in from a different angle, 'are any of these kids yours?'

'No,' she goes, like she's just barely managing to keep her rag with me, 'I'm Blathin's teacher.'

It's a small world – well, especially if you've been around it as many times as I have.

'This punch needs something,' I go, acting a bit Jack the Lad, if I'm being honest. 'Oisinn – I'm not sure if you remember him; big dude – he used to make one back in the day. I'm trying to remember what was in it . . .'

There was definitely gin, now that I think about it. I'm like, 'Are you finished with that?' and I take the bottle out of her hand and lorry a shitload of it into the bowl.

There was also brandy, unless I'm very much mistaken, except there's none on the table, so I grab the Southy and use that instead. Then vodka. Oisinn loves a focking voddy. I tip maybe half a bottle of that in, then throw some JD in on top and give the whole thing a bit of a stir with the ladle.

'This is going to be actual rocket fuel,' I go. 'Don't be surprised if I end up swinging from the focking chandelier!'

Granuaile looks me up and down and says I haven't changed, which isn't intended as a compliment. I just shrug.

'Never will,' I go, then I fill my glass and go off looking for Ro.

He's in the living room, surrounded – I'm proud to say – by girls, in other words Blathin and all her friends, who are, like, hanging on his every word. Birds from this side of the town love a whiff of danger. The boy's only ploughing ground that his old man worked for many happy years.

He's, like, reeling off all the injuries that his friend Gull managed to get compensation for before he was finally jailed for fraud.

I'm just standing in the doorway, so unbelievably proud of him. There's, like, serious competition for his attention as well and I notice Blathin use her wheelchair to block off this one girl who tries to get too close. You can see that this bird – Kandra – totally loves herself.

I leave Ro to it and move on.

I go back into the dining room, where I spot this little huddle of young mums – a personal favourite of mine – and I roll in there like a focking bowling ball.

'Sushi,' I go, for openers, shaking my head. 'When I had my thirteenth, it was, like, miniature goat's cheese quiches and pancetta-wrapped chipolatas. How times change, huh?'

You can see them all looking at me, at the same time thinking, who's this obvious player?

'Well, *my* daughter loves it,' this one woman, the spits of – being honest – Agyness Deyn, goes. 'I bring her to Dundrum and I go off shopping and leave her and her friends at the sushi bar . . .'

I'm like, 'Raw fish, though. Jesus!'

She laughs. 'I know. My ex-husband gives out to me – he says, "She's a twelve-year-old girl, Doireann, not a penguin!"'

I laugh then. I never miss a trick, though. 'Did you say *ex*-husband?'

You focking bet she did, because she's giving me the not-so-subtle message. You can see the other ones looking at her like she's some kind of fallen woman.

I turn my body slightly, to separate her from the herd. 'Do you mind me paying you a compliment?' I go. 'I love birds with short hair.'

She laughs. She's like, 'Oh . . . thank you.'

I'm there, 'Well, I've said it – it's out there now. I hope you don't think I'm cracking on to you, but the hair, the cheekbones, even, I have to say it, the big lips – you've got it all going on . . .'

She laughs, except it's, like, a nervous laugh? Then she takes a sip of her champagne, obviously thinking, pull yourself together – he's, like, ten years younger than you.

I'm there, 'Like I said, that's not me coming on to you . . .'

It's important to keep saying that, get them thinking, er, why not? See, they actually *like* you having to work for it?

We chat for the next, maybe, hour.

I keep giving her more little compliments – one of my tricks of the trade – then I tell her that I'm in pretty much the same boat as her relationship-wise, as in, divorce going through the system, blah blah blah. And you can picture me, I'm sure, with a sincere focking face on me.

The upshot of all this is that we sort of, like, agree in principle to go for a coffee some time, as friends, nothing in it, of course. She keys my number into her phone, going, 'It's just a coffee!' and I'm thinking, yeah, you keep telling yourself that, girl.

You can see the other women looking at her, thinking, *what is she doing?*

I'm a master of my craft – ain't no bout-a-doubt it.

I'm actually telling her that they do a pretty amazing flat white upstairs in Donnybrook Fair when all of a sudden a scream from the kitchen pretty much pierces our eardrums.

Doireann's hand goes to her mouth. 'That's Kandra!' she goes. I immediately put two and two together and realize that *she* must be Kandra's old dear. She goes pegging it out of the room, roysh, and I follow her – out of curiosity as much as anything.

It's when I'm in the hallway that I hear another girl scream, 'You slut! You focking slut!' over and over again. I'm thinking, that's not a phrase you'd associate with Mount Anville – certainly not the junior school anyway.

When I reach the kitchen, I end up having to do a double-take, because I literally can't believe what I'm actually *seeing?* Blathin – we're talking sweet, innocent Bla – has gone totally apeshit. She's got a hold of Kandra's hair, roysh, and she's shaking the girl's head like she's trying to pull it out.

'You're all focking over him!' she's at the same time going. 'He's *my* boyfriend, you slut! You focking slut!'

And – get this – Ronan's stood in between them, trying to loosen Blathin's grip but the girl's either too strong, roysh, or

in too much of a rage. Even with Doireann's help, he can't get her to let go.

I'm looking over at Tina, as if to say, it's all ahead of him – take it from someone who knows.

That's when I hear this sudden splash on the tiles beside me and I look down to see that another one of Blathin's friends has spewed her sashimi all over the floor, splashing my Dubes, I might add, in the process.

Blathin's old man comes running over to help Ronan and Doireann and he's the first one to cop it, I suppose being a doctor and everything. 'Jesus Christ,' he goes, after he's managed to prise the two of them apart, 'they're drunk!'

Has it ever happened to you, roysh, that you instinctively *know* that something's your fault, it's just that you haven't found out *how* yet?

'Drunk!' he's going. 'How on earth did they . . .'

I see his nose suddenly twitching, like he's smelt something, then I watch him follow the trail all the way to the punchbowl. The fumes from it would be enough to put you on your back. 'Someone's spiked the Mini Mosa!' he goes and there's, like, a collective intake of breath. 'Someone put alcohol in it.'

The girl who yacked on my shoes suddenly falls – I'm not exaggerating – face forward on the focking floor.

I'm thinking, shit! This is bad! This is very, very bad!

'Someone spiked the what?' I go – you can picture me, playing the big-time innocent.

The woman beside me goes, 'The fruit punch, for the kiddies,' and I pull a face, roysh, as if to say, what kind of a focking animal . . .

'It was you!' someone suddenly shouts.

I'm there, 'Sorry?' getting ready to deny it.

Except it's focking Granuaile – who saw me do it. She's waited a long time for this moment. Forward she steps. She

88

looks at Blathin's old dear. 'It was him,' she goes, nodding in my general postcode. 'I watched him. He put everything in there. Vodka, Southern Comfort . . .'

The looks I'm suddenly getting.

Shit! There's, like, a boy and a girl – couldn't be more than eleven – wearing the faces off each other outside the back door. Luckily, no one seems to notice – they're all too busy giving me daggers.

'Okay,' I go, holding my hands up, 'in my defence, I *would* add that I didn't know that it was for the kids. I just wanted to liven things up a bit in here. Jesus, I've been at focking autopsies with a better atmos.'

There's a lot of oh-my-Gods from the other mummies and daddies. I spot Ro, backing into a corner of the kitchen, trying to be invisible.

I'm thinking, okay, Ross, shut the fock up now – except, roysh, my mouth keeps going? 'It's actually not even my cocktail. It's a mate of mine called Oisinn invented it. He calls it Liquid Cocaine . . .'

Ross, stop focking talking!

Blathin's old dear, who, like I said, has never been a fan of my whole act, fixes me with this look of absolute hatred. 'Get out of my house,' she just goes.

There's, like, total silence in the kitchen, to the point where I can hear another girl in the next room tossing her cookies.

'Get used to it,' I just go, trying to get them to see the funny side. 'A couple of years' time, they're all going to be going to Wesley.'

'Get out!'

I don't need to be told a third time.

3. It's the Stupid, Economy

I shake my head.

'Luke Fitzgerald!' I go, except I say it in, like, an admiring way? 'The names I've called him over the years. But right now, I don't care where he went to school. That try. There's no one happier for him in this so-called stadium.'

JP's quiet. See, he *always* gets nervous when Leinster play? He says there's still, like, half an hour left. And it's, what, 18–6? Which is far from over.

I tell him not to sweat it – it's in the bag. Even Fionn agrees with me. Munster are basically bottling it in pretty much the same way that *we* did three years ago?

'Wherever he is in the world,' I go, 'I just hope that Oisinn's watching this.'

I'm looking around me at all the supporters in red jerseys. Even though they objected – some of them with threats of violence – to our IRISH BY BIRTH, MUNSTER BY THE GRACE OF A DEFECTIVE GENE banner, I'm beginning to feel, believe it or not, *sorry* for them?

This news takes Fionn by surprise.

'You always said they despised our civilization,' he goes, 'and wanted to destroy our way of life . . .'

'I did say that, I know.'

'When we're singing "Ireland's Call", you always change the line to, "The *three* proud provinces of Ireland . . ."'

'That's also true. Maybe it's just because Drico and the boys are down there putting out the gorbage this time, but I'm storting to feel nothing but genuine pity for Munster. I mean take a look at some of their fans. There's a dude two rows back, red hair growing in four directions at once, mouth like a box of broken Doulton . . .'

Fionn *and* JP both look over their shoulders.

'I mean, recession or not, we're still unbelievably privileged compared to these people,' I go. 'Think about it – where we're from, there's always something for us to do, be it Toys for Big Boys, the internet, blah blah blah . . . Electricity at the flick of the switch. But these people have literally nothing . . .'

'Except Rog, Big O and the rest of them,' JP goes.

'Exactly.'

Fionn's there, 'And they're not exactly doing them proud down there today.'

JP's still looking around him. 'Goys,' he goes, 'you'll never guess who's sitting, like, six rows back there . . .'

Me and Fionn instantly turn around, going, 'Who?'

The two of us are getting on pretty well these days, even though *he's* so far in the closet he's practically finding his Christmas presents.

'What did they call him?' JP goes. 'Was it Mocky?'

Mocky – I never knew his *actual* name? – captained the Newbridge College team that we made shit of in the Leinster Schools Senior Cup final ten years ago. 'It *is* him,' Fionn goes. 'And that's that dude, Muiris Bán, beside him, their prop. And their number eight – what was he called? Something Óg . . .'

I laugh.

'Fock, the years haven't been kind to them,' I go, because they've all, like, packed on the pounds. Mocky still has a lash-back, I notice. 'Hey, let's have a bit of fun here . . .'

'Ross, don't,' Fionn tries to go, because he knows I'm about to stort ripping the serious piss. I never can resist it with those fockers.

I stand up.

'Mocky,' I go, singling *him* out, I suppose, because he made the Irish schools team and Fionn and JP here didn't. I make the world-famous L sign with my thumb and forefinger. 'Focking loser!' I go.

He looks at me, roysh, with his face all scrunched up and confused – pretty much the same face Sorcha's granny pulls when she's trying to use the TV remote.

'Put it on my soul,' he eventually goes, 'but 'tis *him*!' and suddenly the three Newbridge goys are all staring at me in, like, total shock. 'God save the hearer! We were only after being talking about you!'

I raise one eyebrow, smooth as eggs. I'm like, 'All good, I presume.'

Mocky looks at the other two, like he can't actually *believe* the nerve of me? 'He's a right one, isn't he? As mild a man as ever on stirrabout smiled!' and then they all laugh, whatever the fock it even means – focking Kildare – then he looks back at me. 'God bless the mark! I swear by all the brindled Bibles of the Pope, 'twas *not* good. In fect, we were recalling the day of the Schools Cup final, collecting our runners-up mittles. We were talking about thet good-for-nothing slattern thet was stood at the bottom of the stips – cocked up to the height of his vanity – saying, "You're shit!" to each and ivery one of us . . .'

'I stand by that analysis,' I make sure to go.

That's when Muiris Bán totally loses it with me. He's like, 'The devil fire your ribs, you stump of a fool!' which – as you can imagine – draws quite a bit of attention from the Leinster contingent. 'You'll be better off with a bit of sense!'

He looks like he's about to get out of his seat to come down to me until Mocky makes him see reason. 'Hold you whisht,' he goes, grabbing him by the orm, 'for there's no cure for misfortune than to kill it with patience.'

The other dude – Something Óg – throws his thoughts into

the mix then. 'In the presence of my maker, he thinks 'tis out of his own poll the sun does rise!'

'I'll grant you,' Mocky goes, 'he's a brave man on his own floor! And the very divil for causing thrubble! But I swear you, by the black curse thet Finn put on the *bairneachs*, thet even a noble horse can't run for ever!'

The three of them seem to find this hilarious. The shit that must pass for comedy in that port of the world.

'Yeah, whatever,' I go. 'We handed you your orses ten years ago,' and then I flick my thumb in the direction of the pitch. 'Just like we're handing you your orses out there today.'

They look at each other then, totally confused. Actually, they're permanently confused – that's what happens when your old pair are brother and sister. '*We're* from Linnstar as well,' Mocky tries to go.

I laugh. It just *sounds* so ridiculous? I'm there, 'Dude, Kildare's *hordly* in Leinster . . .'

He's there, 'My love for ever, is it no sense you have? Have you ever looked at a mep?'

There *is* a map that's supposed to exist. I'm like, 'I'm proud to say no.'

'It actually *is* in Leinster,' Fionn *has* to go then, forgetting whose side he's supposed to be on, the occasion bringing out the focking schoolteacher in him. 'Why do you think they were playing in the Leinster Schools Senior Cup, Ross?'

I'd honestly never thought about it from that angle.

'Well,' I go, still staring Mocky out of it, 'my point is, you might technically *live* in Leinster? But do you honestly believe that the likes of Dorce and Fitzy and Johnny Sexton down there are representing you and the way you choose to live your lives?' I laugh, then shake my head, mainly for effect. 'As far as rugby is concerned, Leinster storts at Terroirs and ends at Foxrock Church.'

Mocky turns to the other two and they exchange what would have to be described in hindsight as *knowing* smiles? 'Look at you,' he goes to me, 'at the height of your glory. Well, you may cut the sign of the cross on yourself that it stays fine for you. *Sha*, there was niver a tide flowed west but didn't flow east again!'

I don't get the chance to hit him with an amazing comeback line, because it's at that exact moment that a roar goes suddenly up and I turn back to the pitch, roysh, expecting to see that Munster have got a try back.

Except they *haven't*?

Drico's suddenly in, like, acres of space, with the ball tucked under his orm and Rog baiting after him like a focking shoplifter leaving, I don't know, Todds.

'He intercepted him!' JP's going. 'He read his focking mind.'

I'm there, 'He's got the legs! He's got the focking legs!'

Drico touches the ball down under the posts and we go absolutely mental. Everything else is forgotten, including the borney with the mullers. It's like, game over. We certainly won't be hearing 'The Fields' sung again this side of Christmas.

It's only, like, half an hour later, roysh, as we're leaving Croke Pork, that Mocky pops into my head again, in other words something he said that obviously stuck in my mind.

I'm there, 'Goys, what did he mean when he said, there was niver a tide flowed west but didn't flow east again?'

JP just shakes his head, I suppose just wanting to enjoy the moment. He's there, 'I presume it's something that just got lost in translation.'

'Is that Ronan?' I go, because he seems to be disguising his voice.

He's like, 'Who wants to know?'

I'm there, '*Who wants to know?* Ro, it's me – your old man.'

'Ah, Rosser,' he goes. 'Sorry, I'm out and about – on one of me skites.'

Him and his skites. Still, he seems surprisingly okay with me.

'Look,' I go, 'I just wanted to, er, you know, apologize for what happened at Blathin's porty, even though it wasn't technically my fault? How is she?'

'Ah, she's foyin now . . .'

'That's good news. I heard she had to have her stomach pumped.'

'She did, yeah.'

'Jesus,' I go, 'I've *been* that soldier once or twice myself. It's no picnic.'

Weirdly, he laughs. 'You were probably older than torteen, but.'

I laugh then. 'Just a bit, yeah. Still, it might actually put her off ever drinking again, which long term might be a good thing . . .'

'Heh, heh – true, Rosser . . . True, man.'

Something's not right.

'Ro,' I go, 'is everything okay?'

'Er, yeah . . .'

'It's just you don't seem, I don't know . . . I thought you'd be pissed *off* with me? It can't have been easy for you – the whole porty ending up in A&E . . .'

'It's awreet,' he goes.

'Are you sure everything's okay?'

'Er, yeah. I have to go, Rosser.'

Claire and whatever-the-fock-he's-called got engaged – that's Sorcha's big news from last weekend. He took her for a walk on Saturday afternoon, don't laugh, roysh, but along Bray Seafront, where he got down on one knee and, with the sound of the waves crashing behind him, popped the question.

'So when's the baby due?' I go.

She just glares at me. She's there, 'That's not the only reason people from Bray get married, Ross,' but I can tell deep down that she *wants* to laugh?

Then something suddenly occurs to me, as it would, I'm sure, to anyone. 'Saturday afternoon?' I go. 'Er, *why* wasn't he watching Leinster make shit of Munster? They're in the European Cup final, Sorcha.'

She's like, 'That's the amazing thing about him. He has – oh my God – *zero* interest in rugby, Ross. Or any sport.'

I actually laugh out loud in her face. 'He's beginning to sound like a *real* catch,' I go.

And there the conversation has to end, roysh, because all of a sudden we're shown into this little room and, the next thing we know, we're sitting across a desk from a bird called Aibhril, who turns out to be Sorcha's branch manager.

She's focking disgraceful-looking, by the way. I don't know what the bank were even thinking. Big Taylors, no chin, hair the shade of the nation.

In front of her, on the desk, she's got a file as thick as foundation English and she's going through it, roysh, page by page, sort of, like, nodding to herself – this is without even *acknowledging* our presence?

We're sitting there like a couple of spare ones, before she eventually closes the file over, looks up and goes, 'You borrowed, I see from your file, two hundred thousand euros . . .'

'Yes,' Sorcha goes.

'To refurbish a . . . *fashion boutique*?' and she says fashion boutique like she might as well be saying head shop.

'It wasn't so much a refurbishment as, like, a total refit?' Sorcha goes, not picking up on it. 'I wanted to restyle it along the lines of Kitson in LA, which is where – oh my God – *all* the major celebs go to shop. That's why there's always, like, paparazzi outside?'

You can tell, roysh, that this cuts no ice whatsoever with the bank bird. This is the same crew, bear in mind, who six months ago were throwing moo at actors and focking surfers.

'This two hundred thousand euros . . .' she goes, obviously loving the power, 'paid for what exactly?'

Sorcha manages to keep the head. It's the debating background again standing to her. 'Oh my God, everything!' she goes. 'The new interior, the sound system, the pink PVC sofas, the giant plasma screen televisions playing catwalk footage from all the major fashion shows. Plus, I opened out into the unit next door – that's, like, the vintage section? As in, Sorcha & Circa . . .'

The bird – if you could call her that – is scribbling all this shit down.

I throw one in then. 'Here, what about all those framed prints of, like, whales and lions and giraffes,' I go, backing her up, 'with those big words underneath them – Synchronicity and Grace and, I don't know, Pride . . .'

'Well,' Sorcha goes, defensively, even though I'm *on* her side, 'that's because if customers are inspired, they *will* buy – a girl who actually did retail in college *told* me that?'

'What else?' the bank bird goes, like all that she's just heard isn't even enough. She's *all* business, this bird. I suppose when you look like that you've got to play to your strengths. 'Two hundred thousand euros is a lot of money. The refit couldn't have cost more than, what, seventy? What was the rest of the money for?'

'Sorry, excuse me,' Sorcha goes, screwing up her face, 'can I just say, there were none of these questions when I asked to borrow the money in the first place?'

The bank bird has the actual balls to laugh. It's obviously some private joke. 'I understand that,' she goes, still smiling, 'but, as you may have heard, credit conditions have changed somewhat in the past six months.'

In other words, as Cinderella said to Snow White, everyone loves you while your goose is shitting golden eggs.

I'm looking at Sorcha suddenly, wondering what *her* comeback's going to be. 'You're asking what *else* did it pay for?' she goes, a definite snippiness coming into her voice now. 'Okay, in a word, research . . .'

'Research?'

'Yes, *research*,' Sorcha goes, then looks at me for back-up. I have to say, though, I'm pretty focking curious myself. She's there, 'I spent nearly a year living in LA, basically studying retail . . .'

You can tell immediately that the bank bird's struggling with this. '*Studying* retail?' she goes.

She means obviously shopping.

'Er, *yes*?' Sorcha gives it. 'If it wasn't for the time I spent in the States, I wouldn't currently be the only shop in Ireland doing Jay Godfrey sheaths. I wouldn't have been literally the first to get in the new Jimmy Choo Idol platform sandal. *And* the Dior by John Galliano bag . . .'

She's losing her. You can see it. You've got to know your audience. I doubt if this bird has ever worn anything decent. I'm not being a bastard, roysh, but what would be the point?

Luckily for Sorcha, though, the phone on the desk suddenly rings and then – for whatever reason – the bank bird has to suddenly excuse herself and step out of the office for a minute. The second she's gone, Sorcha turns dog on me.

'What the hell are you doing?' she goes.

I'm genuinely there, 'What? I haven't done a basic thing.'

'Exactly,' she goes. 'You're just sitting there with your focking mouth open.'

'Excuse me, I was the one who brought up the whole framed animal prints thing.'

She sort of, like, rolls her eyes, like she's *totally* lost patience with me? 'Where's this famous *way* with women that you're supposed to have?'

I'm suddenly thrown. 'Sorcha, what are you saying?'

She sighs, then looks over her shoulder, like she's looking for someone else to share my focking stupidity with. 'Flirt,' she goes.

I'm there, 'Flirt?'

'Yes, flirt – tell her she looks like someone.'

I pull a face. 'She does. Rupert focking Grint. But I don't think *that's* going to melt her Magnum, Babes.'

That's when she all of a sudden does the weirdest thing. She reaches for my shirt, roysh – this is my pink Apple Crumble that I'm wearing – and before I manage to ask what the fock she thinks she's playing at, she undoes the second button, exposing an extra one or two inches of skin. I'm, like, way too in shock to even say shit. She looks at my chest, roysh, like she's studying, I don't know, some focking picture or other in the National Gallery, then she obviously thinks, ah, what the hell, and opens the third button down as well.

I'm suddenly there freezing my tits off – literally – but before I get a chance to do the buttons back up the bank bird arrives back, all apologies, and of course her eyes are immediately out on stalks, staring at my Rory Best.

She could hang her focking cape on these pecs and she knows it. She tries to be professional, though, and gets straight back to business. 'Okay, can I just outline one or two of *our* concerns,' she goes, 'and I'm speaking for the bank now. You haven't made any repayments on this loan . . .'

'Well,' Sorcha tries to go, 'retail has been affected right across the board. I mean, look at the Royal Hibernian Way – it's practically a no-go area.'

'*And,*' the woman just goes, 'you've ignored repeated letters from us, detailing our concerns regarding these arrears,' and while she's fluting through the file, looking for actual copies, Sorcha storts giving me the eyes and mouthing the words, 'Fock's sake, Ross! Do something!'

Now, I've chormed some of Ireland's most beautiful women horizontal – ask around – but this is suddenly a lot of pressure to be heaping on me.

Sorcha keeps giving me the death rays, so suddenly I sort of, like, clear my throat, as if I'm about to make a statement, and the bank bird suddenly stops what she's doing and looks up at me.

'Must, er, must get pretty boring,' I end up going, 'looking at facts and figures all day. Do you mind me asking, do you ever let your hair down?' and at the same time, roysh, I'm touching my schools cup medal and – this is going to *sound* sleazy? – I'm giving her what Oisinn used to call my Strangers Have the Best Candy smile. 'Where do you tend to do your socializing?'

She's too in shock to even answer. She just looks at me, her big ugly mouth slung open like something out of Wrights of Howth's window, with no actual words coming out. You can see her suddenly telling herself to get her shit together and focus. This is supposed to be a place of business.

She's looking at me, going, 'Em . . . Em . . . Em . . . Oh, the letters . . .' and then she turns to Sorcha. 'You haven't acknowledged any of our correspondence – and that's going back over several months . . .'

'Well,' Sorcha goes, 'I'm not making excuses, but I've been mostly concentrating on my summer range? I think this year's going to be all about vintage-inspired styles with quirky modern twists, like angular heels, square toes and sultry colours,' and at the same time, roysh, she's kicking me under the desk, presumably telling me to give the girl more of the magic.

'Be that as it may,' she goes, 'you've also failed to make any recent repayments on a pre-existing loan . . .'

She shuffles through the file.

'. . . of fifty thousand euros. Which you took out in September 2006, I see from your application, to restyle the shop along the lines of the Betsey Johnson shop in Covent Garden, London . . .'

'Do you know who you're an actual ringer for?' I hear myself suddenly go. 'Jessica Stroup – and that's not me being sarcastic.'

She just, like, stares at me, loving it deep down, of course. Then she looks back at Sorcha.

'Look,' she goes, suddenly *sounding* reasonable? 'You can't go on just pretending this problem doesn't exist. Remember, we're here to help you. We're not *just* a lending institution. We're also here to offer you financial advice, to help you meet, head-on, the challenges of the new economic paradigm, going forward.'

Sorcha looks at me. I'm thinking, don't bother, I didn't catch a focking word of it either.

'So,' Sorcha, 'what exactly would your advice be?'

The bird looks at her, roysh, and goes, 'Close the shop down, sell the stock and start paying us our money back.'

Of course that doesn't go down at all well. Sorcha's like, '*Excuse* me?'

'Your shop,' the bird goes, 'is no longer a viable commercial proposition.'

Sorcha stands straight up. I'm thinking, oh fock!

'Firstly,' she goes, 'it's not a shop – it's *actually* a store? And secondly, would you mind cancelling my subscription?'

The bird is like, 'Subscription?' not unreasonably in my humble op. I look back at Sorcha. I'm thinking, no, she's not going to say it, is she? But she is. She clicks her fingers, going suddenly all Tyra Banks on the girl, and goes, 'Yeah – because I'm *tired* of your issues!'

Then she turns around and focks off, leaving me sitting there with the ginger minger. It's pretty embarrassing, it has to be said, me having gone out on a limb like I did. I stand up.

'Just to let you know,' I go, 'that stuff I said was all horseshit, just to try to get you to . . .'

'Goodbye!' she just goes, suddenly going back to her work.

Hell hath no fury – and blahdy blahdy blah blah.

Sorcha's waiting outside – as mad as I've ever seen her. 'Can you *believe* what that woman said to me?' she goes.

Of course, I don't make the kind of noises she's looking for, because – despite having a face like a busted orsehole – I think the woman had a point.

'And did you *see* the way she was looking at you?' she goes. 'Er, you're my *husband*?'

Something – possibly instinct – tells me that there's a whole world of trouble ahead of us.

'Babes,' I go, 'don't take this the wrong way – that *cancel my subscription* shit? That's okay to say to, like, Sophie or Amie with an ie or any of them. You can't, I'm presuming, go around saying it to, like, the bank?'

She looks at me like she could snap my neck in two. '*Where do you tend to do your socializing?*' she goes. And she says it in this, like, mentally deficient voice – which hurts, it has to be said. '*Do you know who you're an actual ringer for?*'

I tell her to keep her focking Spanx on.

'It was actually a lot of pressure,' I go. 'It was like trying to come up with my usual cracking lines with a focking drumroll sounding in my ear.'

She looks me up and down and tells me I'm – oh my God – *useless*!

Hilarious.

There's, like, a photograph of the old dear on the front page of the *Mail*, coming out of, I don't know where, but laden down with shopping bags.

The headline's like, 'Recession? What FO'CK-ing Recession?' and then underneath, it's like, 'Author and TV chef drops €200 in astonishing TWO-HOUR shopping binge!'

I'm standing in the petrol station on the Rock Road reading this shit.

It's like, *Bestselling-author-turned-celebrity chef Fionnuala O'Carroll-Kelly sought to forget about her own financial crisis yesterday – with a little retail therapy. The stunningly attractive host of* FO'CK Cooking *is the only RTÉ high-earner still refusing to accept a cut in her reputed €500,000-a-year salary to help ease the station's crippling financial position.*

But the multimillionaire author of such international bestsellers as Criminal Assets *and* Karma Suits Ya *yesterday braved the storm of controversy caused by her stand by taking to Grafton Street for a shopping spree that was straight from the movie* Pretty Woman . . .

It's only then I realize that they've, like, superimposed her face on to Julia Roberts's body. I thought she was looking a bit *too* well for her.

In little more than two hours, it says, *the estranged wife of disgraced former councillor Charles O'Carroll-Kelly spent an astonishing €200. The splurge included €27.50 on a Miniamo wire cupcake tree from Stock Design on South King Street, €12.50 on a copy of Jane Austen's* Lady Susan *in Dubray Books on Grafton Street and €12 on a silver-plated candle snuffer from Avoca Handweavers on Suffolk Street.*

And she wasn't finished there. She also visited Carluccio's on Dawson Street, where she picked up a bottle of aceto balsamico di Modena for €26.25 and a large packet of Conchiglioni Puglia pasta for €3.95 . . .

It's too focking funny for words. A year ago, you were off your meds if you weren't buying three investment aportments on the Black Sea. Now you can't be seen buying shit. I'd feel sorry for her, roysh, except it's too actually hilarious.

O'Carroll-Kelly is the last of the taxpayer-funded station's Big Fish still holding out against pressure to accept a pay revision commensurate with the new economic realities. After filming her show yesterday, however, she hit Grafton Street, clearly intent on shopping her blues away. She rounded off the day with a visit to Brown Thomas, where she paid €22 for two Villeroy and Boch espresso cups, €40 for a Revol crème brûlée-scented candle, €60 for a jar of La Prairie concealer and €36 for a jar of Diptyque apricot hand balm.

Fellow shoppers stood by open-mouthed as she swept through the exclusive department store like a tornado. 'You'd swear there was no recession going on at all,' said one shocked on-looker. 'She was literally shopping without a single thought for anyone else's financial circumstances. It was obscene. I had my eight-year-old daughter with me and I had to put my hands over her eyes.'

An RTÉ insider said, 'As a role model, she would certainly seem to be setting the wrong example by spending money so openly at what is a difficult time for a great many people.'

Something's eating Ronan. I can just tell. We're in Dr Quirkey's Good Time Emporium and he hasn't kicked the coin cascade once. I also happen to be beating him at Hummer Racing Extreme Edition, which never happens. It's like he's not even *trying?*

He's also smoking a lot more than usual.

I'd like to be able to say that he'll tell me when he's good and ready, except I can't be even *sure* of that? The kid is only, like, three IQ points away from being considered officially gifted. It's the strangest focking thing to be twenty-nine years old and to have a twelve-year-old son who's already smorter than you'll ever be.

Ronan's screen says Game Over. Me, I'm through to the fourth level for the first time ever, though I don't bother playing it. I catch his sad little reflection in the glass and I leave the wheel and turn to him.

'Did you, er, see that cocaine seizure in Drogheda?' I end up going. 'Eighteen millions' worth. Whose prints would you say are on that?'

He doesn't answer. His little head is down.

I'm there, 'We'll get the *Sunday World* this weekend. Williams will have put a name on it. He always focking does. Matter of fact, I'll pick up a first edition in Spar on Saturday night, then drive it over to your old dear's.'

He looks up at me. 'But you go out on a Saturday night,' he goes.

I'm there, 'Well, maybe this Saturday, I'll give it a miss. Get you the paper instead. You've got to stay ahead of the curve, don't you, especially if you want to be a criminal mastermind yourself one day?'

He says he supposes so.

I'm there, 'Look, Ro, is it still the porty? Again, I'm sorry I gave your girlfriend alcohol poisoning . . .'

'It's not that,' he goes.

'Okay. Look, there's not a lot that I can teach you as a father, Ro. You're, like, very, very nearly a boy genius, whereas me, well, there's little or nothing going on inside my head – that day in Clonskeagh just proved the point. Possibly the only thing I *do* have over you is life experience. I think what I'm trying to say is that if there's ever anything, Ro, that you want to talk to me about, you *can*?'

He just nods. It doesn't look like he's going to say anything until suddenly, unexpectedly, he goes, 'It's Bla . . .'

I knew it.

I'm there, 'Are her old pair breaking your balls because of me?'

But he just goes, 'How do you . . .' and then he suddenly stops. 'How do you know if you're not in love any mower?'

That totally floors me. I'm there, 'You're saying you think you might have fallen out of love with her?'

He doesn't answer, just shrugs his little shoulders.

I take a breath. 'Well, there's no hord and fast rule, Ro. But what I would say to you is this. Sometimes when we think we're confused about our feelings, we're not really confused at all. We just don't want to face up to them, especially if it means hurting someone. But deep down, my guess is, you know how you feel.'

He just stares into the distance over my shoulder. 'I was watching this programme,' he eventually goes, 'thudder week – was one of them David Atten Buddahs . . .'

I'm there, 'They *can* be good,' wondering where the fock this is going.

'Was all about the migration . . .'

'The what?'

'Thee were wildebeests, Rosser – there's a million of these shams, maybe mower, and thee move in this massive heerd, looking for food and warther. And thee get bleaten slaughtered, so thee do – lions and leopards and cheetahs picking them off, then even crocodiles when thee do be crossing the rivers . . .'

'Jesus.'

'So I was just watching it, thinking, I'd have luffen to have seen that . . .'

'What do you mean, you'd have *luffen* to have seen it. You're, like, twelve – who's to say you one day won't?'

I stop. I suddenly know where this is going. It's me who ends up saying the unsayable. 'You think you won't be able to go to – I don't know, is it Africa? – because Blathin's in a wheelchair . . .'

He doesn't answer.

'Ro,' I go, 'people in wheelchairs go on safari all the time

– that's my guess anyway. Do you want me to check it out online? I could even go into Trailfinders – ask the hord questions. No better man.'

He shakes his head, like I'm missing the obvious point. 'It's not just that, but. It's not just Africa. There's gonna to be loads of things we're never gonna be able to do thegedder – do you get me?'

'I think so.'

'Ine afraid . . . afraid she's gonna . . . hold me back . . .'

'That's your answer, then, Ro. If you really loved her, you wouldn't think of it as *being* held back.'

'So what kind of a fooken pox does that make me?'

'It doesn't make you a focking pox at all.'

'What, wanting to break up with a boord because she caddent walk?'

'That's what I'm trying to get you to see, Ro – you want to break up with her because you don't love her. And because you're twelve and because you've got so much living to do and you shouldn't even *be* in a serious relationship anyway, even with someone from Clonskeagh. I've always thought that, even though I love Bla. But when you think about it, Ro, her being in a wheelchair is the reason you're *not* breaking up with her . . .'

He knows, deep down, that I'm talking sense, but he's eaten up with guilt just thinking the things that he's thinking. Where did he get his sense of shame from? It certainly wasn't from my side of the family.

'Ro,' I go, 'you're going to have to finish it with her and not even think about the fact that she's in a wheelchair . . .'

'It's heerd.'

'Of course it's hord, telling a bird you've no interest any more. But it's one of those things you just have to face.'

That night with Breege suddenly pops into my head. I'm one to focking talk. I'd rather fall six storeys to my death . . .

Still, if the worst thing anyone can say about me as a father is that I'm a hypocrite, then I won't have done too badly. I hand him a euro.

'Another shot of Hummer Racing?'

He just nods.

I watch him feed the coin into the slot, roysh, then grip the wheel.

'Ready?' I go, then the race storts.

I slam my foot on the pedal and he's in my mirror straight away, a hundred, two hundred, three hundred yords behind me, clipping trees and sliding into ditches, his poor little head full of thoughts that only grown-ups should ever have to deal with.

The last person I expected it to be on the phone, after what happened that night in L'Ecrivain, is Erika. I even say it to her. 'This is a surprise.'

'Look, can we call a truce?' she just goes.

I'm there, 'Er, cool,' genuinely taken aback.

'We can't go on fighting the way we always have.'

I'm like, 'Er, I suppose I agree,' port of me waiting for the punchline. See, it's hord to get used to her being anything other than a total and utter bitch.

'Fighting for Charles's attention like two teenage girls!'

I laugh. I'm there, 'I suppose I'm prepared to admit that I was, like, *jealous* of you? I mean, don't get me wrong, I still think he's a dick – you'll find that out given time – but he used to have, I don't know, time for me. Now it's suddenly all you and obviously your old dear . . .'

'I think I can understand that.'

'Well, that's a stort.'

'Look,' she goes then, 'I did something stupid . . .'

I get the instant impression she's talking about Toddy Rath-friland. 'Are you talking about Toddy Rathfriland?'

108

'Yes. Ross. It was a stupid thing to do, getting involved with someone like him, and I got myself into a lot of trouble. Whatever you think about him, Charles was there for you growing up, Ross. He wasn't there for me. That's why he's so keen to fight my battles for me now.'

'Did Hennessy get that injunction to stop it being in the papers?'

'Yes, but do you understand what I'm trying to say?'

'I suppose.'

'What you did that day, Ross, taking that *woman's* deposition . . .'

She lets it hang there for twenty seconds until I realize that what she's looking for is an apology. 'Okay, that was out of order,' I go. 'And, I'm admitting, *bang* out of order.'

There's another, like, ten seconds of silence on the other end, before I hear her go, 'Okay, then let's forget about it. We need to talk about Sorcha.'

'Sorcha?'

'I hear the bank didn't go well.'

That's one thing you'd have to say about Erika. She's a focking wagon at the best of times – but she can also be a good friend. 'Er, that's one way of putting it,' I go. 'Sorcha just won't listen to reason.'

'Ross, they're going to repossess her house.'

'*Hello?* I was *there*, remember?'

'She needs to close the shop.'

'That much is obvious.'

'Okay. I'm going to work on her.'

'And how do you propose to do that?'

'I've been helping her do a stock-take the last couple of days. Anyway, in passing, I offered to show the books to Charles – just for an independent third-party view? And she agreed.'

'Sorcha loves my – sorry, *our* – old man. Hopefully he'll look at the accounts and tell her the place is focked seven ways till Sunday.'

'Now, what *you* need to do, Ross, is come up with some money, enough to keep the banks happy and stop them foreclosing on the house.'

'Er, I'm pretty sure I can manage that.'

'Tell me you're not thinking of asking Charles for it.'

'Okay, give me another few minutes, then . . .'

She ends up losing it with me a little bit. 'Can you not do anything yourself, Ross? You really need to man-up here.'

'Excuse me?'

'This is your wife we're talking about. You were a pretty lousy husband to her. Could you at least *try* to be a better ex?'

It's, like, an hour later, while I'm watching *The Afternoon Show*, that the weirdest focking thing happens. I'd be tempted to put it down to coincidence if I didn't already believe it was Father Fehily, I don't know, smiling down on me from above.

The doorbell goes and I check the little screen, except I don't instantly recognize the bird who's standing outside, even though she seems to know me.

'Hi, Roth,' she goes, 'ith Ailith.'

I've always had a thing for birds with lisps, focked as that might sound. I'm there, 'Okay, come on up,' and I buzz her in.

She airkisses me on both cheeks. It's how are you and blah blah blah and I still have no focking idea who she is, remember, until she finally gets down to business. 'That thing we thalked about the lath day,' she goes. 'Are you thill intrethted?'

She's no Blake Lively up close, in fairness.

I'm there, 'The last day, yeah,' trying to bluff her. 'What a day that ended up being . . .'

She sees straight through it. 'You have no ithea who I am, thoo you?'

I'm there, 'Not a focking clue, no – being honest.'

'Then why thid you leth me in?'

'Good question – because you might have been a looker . . .'

'A looker? Roth, we meth that night . . . in Cocoon?'

Ailish! *That* was her name! I recognize her now, from her photo in front of the Sydney Opera House. Don't remember any speech impediment, though.

'No offence,' I go, 'but I was really, really pissed that night . . .'

She's like, 'Not *thoo* pithed – I'm happy to thay!' She smiles, then she sort of, like, shivers with excitement at the memory. 'I had thuch an amathing nithe.'

Jesus, she's as soppy as a sponge. I tell her to sit down – sort of, like, indicate the couch.

She's there, 'I'm prethuming, then, you thon't remember the converthathion we hath,' and she doesn't give me a chance to answer. 'Have you ever hearth of an aparthment development called Rotha Parkth?'

I laugh. 'You mean Rosa Parks?' I go. 'Well, yeah, as it happens. I've a very good friend who works in repossessions – he's never out of the focking place.'

'Okay, well, I work for Ethie Torsney . . .'

'Eddie Torsney?'

'Yeth – he's the builther.'

'I know him. He's been all over the news. Okay – I'm still trying to work out how this is any of my beeswax.'

'Well, you thaid that night that you might be intrethted in moving . . .'

'Moving?'

'To Rotha Parkth?'

I laugh. 'Look – being honest? – I probably only said that to get into your, you know . . .'

Her face drops. 'Oh,' she goes. 'You theemed prithy genuine.'

'Well, that's just a skill I've learned – like a mind trick?'

She's literally crushed. But I suppose I'm, like, curious now. 'Do you mind me asking, how did the subject even come up?'

She's there, 'Well, when you thold me you lifthed in The Grange, I thaid to you that Ethie was looking for an aparthment in there.'

'I wouldn't blame him. What is it that sign on the dualler *still* says? *Few Addresses Generate This Kind of Dream*? End of.'

'There *are* vacanth aparthments in there, but Ethie wants a penth houth.'

'Wouldn't blame him either. Look at this place . . .'

'And I thaid to you that he'd be prepared thoo offer you a penth houth suite in Rotha Parkth, brand new, fully furnithed – it wath originally the thow aparthment – ith about thwice the thize of thith place.'

'Like I said, it was probably only to get you – not being crude – but lengthways.'

'Pluth,' she all of a sudden goes, 'one hunthreth thousanth euroth . . .'

There's, like, silence from me all of a sudden. She senses my sudden interest. Oh, she's good – wetter than a focking logride, but good.

'One hunthreth thousanth euroth, Roth. There are very few people can thurn their nothes up at that kind of money – in the currenth economic climath.'

She's not wrong either. I'd have the poppy to stop Sorcha and Honor being made homeless. I'd even have enough to put Honor back in Little Roedean. Plus, Erika's possibly right.

It might well be time for me to man-up. A hundred Ks is a hundred Ks. Now is not the time to be selfish.

'But Rosa Parks is an absolute shithole,' I go, 'with all due respect. I mean, there's only, like, twenty percent of the aportments even occupied. JP told me there's one entire building with only, like, five people living in it.'

She's like, 'Noth for much longer.'

I'm obviously there, 'What do you mean?'

'Well, thrictly between uth, Ethie's thone a theal with UCD, to leth out almoth all of the remaining vacanth as thtudent dormitoreeth. From Theptember, Rotha Parkth ith going to become bathically an exthtenthion of the UCD camputh.'

It's like she *knows* what buttons to press with me? 'Fock,' I end up going. 'Orts students walking around morning, noon and night, wearing half-nothing, porties, blah, blah, blah . . . Be just like the old days . . .'

'Tho whath thoo you think?'

What I think is, it's like a focking lookalike competition in China – in other words, everyone's a focking winner.

'Maybe I need to sleep on it again,' I go, even though I know – and she knows – what my answer's possibly going to be.

We smile at exactly the same time. She gets the words out before I do. 'Perhapth we thould thleep on ith thegether.'

I honestly couldn't have put it better myself.

The New Westies. That's who Paul Williams is putting that eighteen million yoyos worth of coke down to. It's a new one on Ro. He practically rips the paper out of my hands, then his little head is suddenly going from side to side, taking in every word, his face lit up like he's reading his first bench warrant.

He's giving me the edited highlights, of course. *No regeerd for human life . . . Even more rootless than the originiddle Westies . . .*

I know I'm only feeding his obsession with that whole

world, but it's good to see him back to something like his old self, even if it's just for a short while.

Tina asks me what I'm doing here on a Saturday night. Well, what she actually says is, 'Why ardent you out tonight?' making it sound – like everything else that comes out of her mouth – like an accusation, at the same time pulling her ski pants out of her orse.

Don't ask me *how* I ever went there.

'Er, I'm spending some time with our son?' I go, except I say it, like, sarcastically? '*If* that's okay with you.'

She doesn't care one way or the other. She's on her way out herself. It's obviously single mums' night in the Broken Arms in Finglas.

'Me fadder was gonna pop in and look arthur him,' she goes. Living next door to your old pair is another one of those things that's, like, so working class. 'He'll be delighrit, he can go for he's few beers arthur all.'

She says goodnight to Ro, then she can't resist one last dig at me about Blathin's porty. 'If you're gonna be givin him spidits,' she goes, 'give him vodka and oddinge juice – it's much bether for their little stomachs, Ross . . .'

She cracks her hole laughing, then disappears out the door, leaving a focking vapour cloud of *Coleen X* in her wake.

Me and Ro end up sitting there for practically the entire night, watching boxsets of *The Wire* on the big plasma TV that I helped JP repossess.

And you know the script, it's all, '*Grab a hound, yo,*' and '*You can't go round droppin Five-Oh – now they takin doors . . .*'

'Jesus, Ro,' I go, at some point in the evening, 'I honestly can't understand a focking word of this.'

He laughs. 'Grab a hound means get a Greyhound bus,' he goes. 'Droppin Five-Oh is shootin coppers. Takin doors – well, if you came up arowint here, you'd know what takin doors means . . . Do you want me to stick the subtitles on, Rosser?'

I'm there, 'Er, I don't think so! That sounds too much like work to me.'

It's maybe, I don't know, half an hour later that I bring up the whole Blathin thing. He seems all right now, but I've never seen him as sad as he was the other day. I'm there, 'Have you done the dirty deed yet? As in Bla, blah blah blah?'

He doesn't say anything and I take his silence to mean no. 'I did the doort on her,' he eventually goes. I feel my eyes go suddenly wide. He's there, 'With Kandra . . .'

I just shake my head. It turns out he's more like me than I ever gave him credit for. 'That's who you were with that day when I rang you – when you said you were on one of your famous skites . . . You sounded like you were up to something all right.'

'I feel shit abourrit, Rosser.'

All of a sudden Keelyn pops into my head. Keelyn and a thousand others. 'Ro,' I go, 'I'm telling you this as someone who has a lot of experience with the old Deadlier of the Species. You've got to tell her – and soon. Because if you don't, I can guarantee you this, Kandra will.'

'Seriously,' this Garret dude goes, 'once you've *been* to Thailand, you can never go back to eating Thai food in Ireland ever again.'

'Well, you *can*?' Claire goes. 'But it's *so* not the same.'

Sorcha and Erika are sitting there just nodding, like they're listening to the tales of two, I don't know, intrepid explorers. Who *gives* a fock? The point is, Sorcha and me have already spent time in that neck of the woods – in other words, Indonesia? – while Erika wouldn't be orsed going any focking place where the electrical system couldn't take her BaByliss Pro 2000 and her ghd.

Listening to them dissing *our* Thai food makes me feel, in a weird way, patriotic.

'How is it different?' I end up going. Erika's loving watching me put them under pressure, having always hated Claire's guts. 'I'm only asking,' I go, 'as a fan of Saba, Diep, all those – how is it not the same?'

Claire rolls her eyes – this is someone from Bray, remember, rolling *her* eyes at *me*? 'If you'd ever eaten food,' she goes, 'from a stall in Thailand, Ross, you'd know.'

'I ate food from a stall once in Bali. Ended up with the Hershey squirts and a hole like the Japanese flag.'

Sorcha shoots me a sudden filthy – the exact same look she gave me on our pre-marriage course, when I squeezed one out, then asked the priest in front of four other couples whether it was maybe something he'd eaten.

Erika gives me a secret smile, though.

He's a dick with ears, by the way. I hate these people who come back from supposedly travelling and insist on dressing like they're still away. He's wearing, like, board shorts, Birkenstocks and a short-sleeved shirt – er, it's *pissing* today? – and up and down his orms he's got all these different coloured bits of wool and string tied – friendship bracelets he was given by people he met once, maybe twice, and who'll be following the boring twists and turns of his life on Facebook until the day they die.

I *could* add that he's sitting with, like, one foot up on his own seat and his orms folded across his knee – so chilled out from all the travelling and all the experiences that he's forgotten how to sit in a focking chair properly.

He's no fan of mine either – I can tell that from the tude he's giving me. I suppose if they *are* getting married, she's probably given him her full service history. Which is why he can't even look me in the eye – see, my name's all *over* that logbook.

Our grub finally arrives. Whatever about Thai food, Sorcha says, one thing that is *always* amazing is the wings in Elephant and Castle.

Everyone agrees.

'So,' she goes then, 'how are the wedding plans coming along? Have you set a date?'

'It's going to be in late August,' Claire goes.

Sorcha's like, 'Oh my God, that's only, like, three months away.'

Claire smiles, then looks at *him*. 'We've decided it's not going to be, like, a big wedding?' she goes.

Then *he's* like, 'We just think weddings are *such* a rip-off. Like two grand for flowers, three grand for a dress. Er, thanks, but *no* thanks?'

Sorcha's nodding in agreement – this the girl who spent a hundred and fifty Ks on *our* wedding, a day that ended up in tears and threats of annulment before a drop of the forty-euro bisque had passed anyone's lips.

'That's the thing about doing the whole travelling thing,' Claire goes. 'You meet people from all walks of life – the States, England, Australia. And you realize that the whole, I don't know, commercial thing, it's just . . . oh my God!'

'It's all for show,' *he* goes.

She's there, 'That's what I mean. It's like, we don't *need* to hire the ballroom in the Shelbourne Hotel to make this commitment to each other? Especially with the credit crunch. *Or* pay, I don't know, two grand to hire a fleet of cars for, what, a couple of hours?'

Jesus Christ, it's a wonder they ever let these two across the focking Dargle.

'In Thailand,' *he* goes, 'they don't go in for these big, three-hundred-euro-a-plate weddings. God, we're obsessed in this country. *Their* weddings are, like, pretty much spiritual.'

'We're actually going to include some aspects of the traditional Thai wedding in *our* day,' *she* goes. 'We're going to get a monk to bless my mum and dad's house before we leave for the church . . .'

I'm there, 'That'll be a first for Ballywaltrim.'

She decides to ignore it. 'Then, for the reception, we're going to go back to the house to do the whole *Rod Nam Sang* thing, where, after the meal, Garret and I will sit on the floor – in, like, the *wai* position? – with a chain of flowers connecting our hands, with our families and friends all sitting round. Then my dad – who's big-time Catholic, so he needed obviously a *bit* of persuading – is going to soak our hands in water poured from a conch shell and wish us luck. Then everyone else will do the same . . .'

It's funny to see the different reactions to this. Sorcha's got this, like, fake smile just frozen on her face – like one of those people you see in the papers, receiving those giant novelty cheques and grinning so hord they look like they're about to shit a carjack sideways.

Erika looks like she's about to throw up – she even pushes away the rest of her Chandler Bings.

'And does your mum definitely have the room in the house?' Sorcha goes.

Claire's like, 'Yeah, because the *sun room* will be finished by then?'

'And,' *he* goes, 'it's going to be a pretty small gathering, really just close family and friends.'

'That's the reason I wanted to talk to you,' Claire goes and the next thing I'm expecting her to tell us is that we're not going to make the cut. Instead, roysh, she goes, 'Sorcha and Erika, would you be my bridesmaids?'

My jaw just drops. To say it's a big turn-up would be like saying Dolph Lundgren is a big Swede. I mean, there's no real surprise with Sorcha. They've been friends since they were, like, fifteen, when they both worked in Gorta on Lower Liffey Street as part of, like, transition year?

But Claire's always hated Erika and Erika's always hated Claire. I suppose it shows you how hord-up she is for mates.

Anyway, this turns out to be *the* main topic of conversation after Claire and Garret leave – apparently, porking, like, everything else, is a total rip-off in this town. They also want to hit HMV, to see if they can get *Bridge on the River Kwai* on DVD.

'Jesus Christ,' I end up having to go, 'you used to call her *The Charwoman's Daughter*, Erika – do you remember that?'

It was when she found out Claire's old dear used to clean Pres Bray three evenings a week. It used to drive Erika mad that she was always trying to fit in with, I suppose, *our* kind.

'I was awful to her,' *she* even goes. 'Why would she ask *me* to be her bridesmaid?'

Sorcha shrugs. 'She *did* get very into Buddhism while she was away.'

Erika considers this for a few seconds, then goes, 'I'm going to be a bridesmaid at a credit crunch wedding. I wonder should I mention that I'm allergic to crimplene . . .' and we all laugh, even Sorcha.

It's great watching Erika be a bitch to other people.

Ten minutes later, the three of us are walking up Grafton Street – *I'm* porked in the Royal Surgeons – and I decide it's time to hit them with *my* amazing news.

Sorcha actually says thanks for paying for everyone and I tell her it's cool. I didn't see *him* sticking his hand in his pocket, by the way. I wonder is that, like, a Thai custom as well, stinging every other focker for the Harry Hill.

'Money's not an issue for some of us,' I go. 'Which, by the way, is something I wanted to talk to you about . . .'

She's like, 'What do you mean?'

'What I mean is that you and Honor can stop worrying about the current economic blahdy blah.'

Sorcha *and* Erika both just stop – this is outside Laura Ashley – with looks of genuine surprise on their faces. 'What are you talking about?' Sorcha goes.

'What I'm talking about is, I've managed to get the old Cora Venus together to get the bank off your back – and to put Honor back in Little Roedean.'

'Ross,' she automatically goes, 'I couldn't take money from your mum and dad.'

I laugh. 'Er, it's not *from* them? For once in my life, Babes, this one is down to me.'

I look at Erika. She's more in shock at this than she was to be asked to be Claire's bridesmaid.

Sorcha's there, 'You haven't done anything stupid, have you, Ross?'

I'm there, 'Like gotten a job? Er, no – what I can tell you, though, is that it's all legal and above board.'

'Are you saying . . .'

'I'm saying our daughter's going to be back playing the glockenspiel again quicker than she can say, I don't know, *konnichiwa*. And you don't have to worry about being focked out on to Newtownpork Avenue either – at least for a few months.'

And the way she looks at me – the way they *both* look at me? – makes me prouder of myself than I've possibly ever been.

'You haven't told me what you think yet.'

My voice echoes through the empty aportment. See, I wanted, like, an independent opinion from someone who knows his property. JP just shrugs. 'Big and spacious,' is all he goes and that – unbelievably – is the nicest thing he can think to say.

I'm there, 'Dude, it's an unbelievable pad. Imagine the focking porties I'm going to be able to throw. And what about the jacuzzi? Alpa-focking-cino.'

He's there, 'You couldn't exactly describe it as trading up, though.'

He steps through the French doors, out on to the balcony. 'I mean, instead of looking down on the N11,' he goes, 'you're looking down on, what, the M50? You're still just watching traffic go by.'

Er, this coming from a Formula One fan?

'Plus,' he goes, 'no one lives here. Look at this place. It's been abandoned. The builder's never going to sell the rest of these aportments, so it's never going to be finished. A lot of these blocks are going to end up bulldozed.'

Of course that's where he's wrong.

I'm there, 'I told you what Ailish said. He's actually going to finish the whole thing this summer – it's about to become port of the UCD campus.'

JP stares out over the mounds of muck and bricks and abandoned diggers. 'We're in Ticknock, Ross. You couldn't see UCD from here with the Hubble focking Telescope.'

I just let it wash over me. 'Yeah, you come back and say that to me when this place is Tequila Central!'

He just shrugs. 'Okay,' he goes, 'as long as *you* know what you're doing . . .'

I tell him I do.

The next thing, Ailish steps out and joins us on the balcony. 'Tho,' she goes, clapping her hands together, like she's talking to a four-year-old, 'thoo you know anything about the *original* Rotha Parkth?'

Which is pretty insulting to my intelligence, it has to be said. I'm there, 'Yeah, I know how to work the internet,' possibly a bit *too* defensively? But I want to let her know that I'm not

121

the type to just rush into something like this without fully researching it first.

She's there, 'Wathn't thee an amathing woman?' obviously having Googled her herself. 'You know, when thee refuthed thoo give up her theat on that buth all thoth yearth ago in America, thee became a hero for noth juth black people, buth for women thoo! And for anyone who wanth a bether worlth! Ith like, "Go Rotha – you thell 'em, girl!"'

I'm there, 'I suppose fair focks to her would be my own basic attitude as well.'

JP's just staring at me, judging me. I told him that me and her did it on the floor of my kitchen, though I didn't mention that she was a focking sap.

'Ith tho, tho thad,' she goes, 'that Rotha never lifthed long enough to thee thith plathe. Thadly, thee patht away in Octhober '05 – the very week thath An Bord Pleanala granthed final planning permithion, with one hundreth and thixthy-theven condithionth attached . . .'

I'm there, 'Bummer.'

She nods. 'Of courth the tragedy ith we're not thure if thee even knew about thith plathe. Ethie and I were hoping to bring her thoo Ticknock thoo perform the official opening theremony – which made her death doubly thad . . .'

I'm just staring at her, thinking, okay, have you stopped babbling yet? 'Tho,' she goes, 'whath thoo you think, Roth?'

I'm just there, 'Is the hundred Ks still port of it?'

'Abtholutely.'

'Then you've got yourself a deal.'

Her face lights up. I don't even look at JP, though I can tell he's giving me, I suppose, disapproving looks, so I leave him out there on the balcony, and step into the kitchen with Ailish to do the business – I'm talking about the business, this time, as opposed to the bidiness.

She produces the paperwork and spreads it out on the island in the kitchen. You could focking honeymoon on the thing, it's that big.

I actually love signing my autograph. Most of the time that I *did* spend in class during my final two years at school, I spent just practising it. I do it, like everything I do, with a bit of a flourish, then Ailish reaches inside the jacket of her trouser suit and goes, 'I think *thith* belongth to you.'

She puts the Ant and Dec down on the old Numerär birch worktop in front of me. I pick it up and end up just standing there, staring at it for, like, thirty seconds. 'Look at all those noughts,' I can't help but go. 'One, two, three, four, five, six, seven . . .'

The word 'Fuck!' suddenly slips from Ailish's lips and, for whatever reason, she suddenly snatches it from my hand. She looks at it for, like, a second or two, then hands it back to me, the panic suddenly over. 'Roth,' she goes 'thoo of those noughth are *afther* the dethimal pointh?'

I'm there, 'They all count, Baby. They all count.'

Fionn's early. We're meeting in, like, Kielys and he's already sat at the bor, reading – this'd be *very* Fionn – a *book* of all things?

'How the hell are you?' I go, then I give the borman a nod. Two pints of the old Milk of Amnesia. I'm there, 'What are you reading?' deciding not to even bother about the whys.

He's straight away on the big-time defensive, thinking I'm going to rip the piss out of him, of course. 'It's, er, a book . . .'

'Continue.'

'A book about physics. I'm reading about the possibility of profound symmetry transformations in the hot soup of quarks, antiquarks and gluons.'

I'm left just looking at him in total awe. 'Is it possible to weigh someone's brain?' I go.

He laughs. 'What?'

'Exactly what I said – is it possible to weigh an actual brain?'

'It is possible, of course.'

'Well, I'd love to know what your focking brains weighs, Fionn. If ever you find out . . .'

'I'll be sure to tell you.'

'Do. Something unbelievable, I bet. Jesus.'

He laughs again, then pushes his glasses up on his nose. The thing is, roysh, I've always given the dude a hord time – Goggleboy, Captain Nerdstorm, Filburt Shellbache – but if anyone else ever did, he knows deep down that I'd be the first one decking them. That's how far back we go.

We stort shooting the shit. I tell him about Ro and Bla – how your first hort is always the hordest to break. I tell him about Sorcha's shop being in a jocker and her performance the other day in the old Hilary Swank, then about me moving to Rosa Parks.

'Are you sure that's wise?' he goes. 'I've passed that place once or twice – it's still a building site, isn't it?'

I'm there, 'Not for much longer, Fionn. Not for much longer.'

I ask him how school's going, as in the old teaching?

He's there, 'Fine. I've probably taken a bit too much extra-curricular work, with the Maths Olympiad and the Young Science Innovators.'

I don't think I've ever met a man more in need of a ride.

'How's McGahy?' I go. 'Still a dick?'

He laughs. 'Tom's, er, much the same as a principal as he was as a teacher.'

In other words, yes.

I'm there, 'I can't imagine what it'd be like having him as a boss. I hope you don't take shit from him.'

The dude just laughs.

I'm halfway through my second pint when he suddenly goes all deep on my ass. First he mentions, roysh, that we're going to be, like, thirty next year? Then he goes, 'Do you ever look back on the years, Ross, and think, what have I done with my life?'

The thought has never focking occurred to me – that's being honest. I'm there, 'Fionn, *you*'ve done loads – you've degrees coming out your ears.'

'Yeah, I know. And I'm very happy teaching. I know we're all supposed to be up in arms about this pension levy, but, to be honest with you, I'd nearly do what I do for free.'

'Hey, whatever bloats your goat.'

He laughs. 'No, I just mean, do you ever look back and . . . Ah, I don't know *what* I mean.'

The thing is, roysh, *I* suddenly do? It's the first time it's ever occurred to me but I think Fionn might actually be lonely. I know for a fact that he hasn't been with a bird since, well, Aoife died and that must be, like, three years ago now.

'Fionn,' I go, 'do you not think it's time – you know, time you maybe met someone else?'

It feels a bit Jodie Morsh saying it to him but he can't spend the rest of his life sitting in listening to Elbow and playing focking Jenga by himself. He must have balls like camel humps.

'That's what my mother says. You know, *I've grieved long enough, Aoife wouldn't want me to spend the rest of my life on my own . . .*'

'Well, she wouldn't. I think it's time you maybe put yourself back on the morket.'

'I know you're right. But it still feels, I don't know, weird – just the idea of it. Like I'm cheating?'

See, *I've* never had any issue with cheating – he's talking to the wrong *buachaill* here. I order two more pints of the old Prep H.

He's like, 'It's difficult anyway – you know, meeting someone?'

and I'm there, 'Dude, a surprising number of birds are actually *into* glasses – they do exist, is all I'm saying.'

'I'm not talking about my glasses, Ross. I'm just saying, as you get older, it obviously gets harder. There's less out there – statistically, I mean.'

I'm there, 'Statistically?' I even laugh. 'Jesus Christ, Fionn, what have statistics got to do with anything? Every bird you meet doesn't have to be the bird you're going to marry. Choose 'em, use 'em and lose 'em – it's what *I've* always done. And do you see me all depressed about turning thirty?'

He smiles at me. We've had our differences over the years but he's still a major fan. 'You know,' he goes, 'sometimes I wish I'd been a bit more like you.'

I laugh. 'There's room for only one Ross O'Carroll-Kelly on this planet that we call, I suppose, Earth?'

'Well, maybe I wish I'd let myself go more often.'

I remember we're heading for Edinburgh this weekend for, like, the Heineken Cup final? I make, like, a mental note to get him *the* most shiftfaced he's ever been.

The old man asks me for my thoughts on all this – quote-unquote – share the pain rhetoric that's coming from the government.

I just stare him out of it. He's got, like, cappuccino froth on his nose, but I don't tell him. It makes it easier for me to hate him, if that doesn't sound too weird?

'*From each according to his means,*' he goes, just shaking his head. 'I never thought I'd live long enough to hear those words pour from the mouth of an Irish cabinet minister. Thirty years ago, you'd have been shot in the street for that kind of talk.'

I look across at Erika, as if to say, are you beginning to see it now?

'Thee've trun anutter twenty-five cents on a packet of smokes,' Ronan goes. The poor kid's putting a brave face on things. 'Hitting the weak again. Here, you've something on your nose there, Grandda . . .'

This is us, by the way, in the restaurant in the middle of the Powerscourt Townhouse Centre, waiting for Sorcha to show her boat. The old man's had a look at the books and we're all waiting for his honest opinion. You know mine. I've already shelled out the guts of fifty Ks to get Honor back into Pre-Montessori and stop the old Hilary Swank putting the two of them out on the road. I don't want that shop bleeding me for the rest.

Sorcha even said it herself. Working in town these days is like doing the dayshift in a battlefield hospital – you go in every morning and find out who went in the night. Jack & Jones. Harriet's House. Sasha. Golden Discs. It was touch and go for Karen Millen for a while. And Oasis.

Now – without wanting to come across as a bastard – it looks like *her* turn has finally arrived.

She comes in and sits down. Her and Erika give it a bit of blahdy blah. Claire – oh, yeah, this *is* hilarious – she's just chosen their bridesmaids dresses. She got them from – get this – Yo Thai in Donnybrook, as in the restaurant above Kielys. They had, like, a closing-down sale last weekend, flogging off everything from the plates and cutlery to the waitresses' uniforms – which, incidentally, is what the girls are going to be wearing on the day.

Sorcha puts, like, a positive spin on it by describing them as silk-effect kaftans.

Erika goes, 'Silk *what* kaftans?' not unreasonably in my HO.

'Effect,' Sorcha goes. 'Well, it's *actually* acetate, which is usually, like, a lining fabric?'

I laugh. Erika laughs. Even Sorcha can't help smile. 'Come on,' she goes, 'they're trying to save money.'

I'm there, 'Speaking of which . . .' deciding it's time to get down to business. Sorcha suddenly looks at the old man – I know it's not a word – but *expectantly*?

'Well,' he just goes, giving himself plenty of fanfare, 'I've looked at the accounts – just as you asked – and one thing strikes me very clearly. You're not making enough money in retail sales to meet your shop's outgoings.'

I end up just shaking my head. 'Thank you, Stephen focking Hawking. Are you saying you needed to take the books *away* to work that one out?'

But Sorcha nods like she's just learned something new. 'What *isn't* in there, Charles, can I just say, are the two sales I made this week. A Christian Lacroix pleated dress and a Gerard Darel crochet bag . . .'

Then *he's* suddenly nodding, roysh, like this is new information. I end up totally losing it then. And we're *talking* totally. Because, at the end of the day, *I'm* the one who's going to end up paying for this.

'*Gerard Darel?*' I go. 'Sorry, we're supposedly here to decide whether we're going to keep flogging this dead horse – or are we going to decide to, like, shut it down?'

Erika nods. 'Sorcha, you said it yourself,' she goes, 'people aren't spending money. They're scared. And if the major high street names are in trouble, what chance have independent operators like you got?'

I'm there, 'Sounds like we're coming to a decision here . . .'

Ronan pipes up then. 'Why doatent you burden it?'

Sorcha, Erika and the old man all look at me.

'He means *burn* it?' I go. 'My twelve-year-old son is suggesting we commit orson, presumably for the insurance.'

The old man – if you can believe this – goes, 'Let's hear the little chap out, Ross. There's no such thing as a bad idea – that's one lesson I've learned from forty-something years in business.'

'Ine just sayin',' Ro goes, 'you know Nudger?'

The old man's like, 'Yes! I shared a landing with his brother. How is he?'

'He's moostard, Grandda. Moostard. In anyhow, this happens to be a sideline of he's. Calls heself a conflagration specialist. He has a cussint, woorks in the fire brigade – knows how to make it look like an electrical fault . . .'

The old man's actually there nodding away. 'What are we looking at in terms of overheads?' he even goes.

That's when I really flip. 'Overheads? What the fock *is* this – *Dragon's Den*? You're not burning anything, Ro.'

Sorcha goes, 'I don't think I could bring myself to do it anyway, Ronan. What, destroy all those beautiful creations? The Giuseppe Zanotti gold gladiators? The tulle strapless Lanvin – as in, the exact same one that Katherine Heigl wore with gold Loubs when she went brunette that time. Oh my God, I literally couldn't stand there and watch them go up in flames.'

'Plus,' Erika goes, 'you're not even *on* electricity any more. You had the shop converted to wind power . . .'

I'm there, 'Exactly! Which no one seems to be factoring into the equation.'

A waitress stops by to take Sorcha's order. And to tell Ronan that he can't smoke in here – she gives *me* a filthy then? I'm there, 'Believe me – I've *no* control over him.'

Sorcha asks for a soy milk latte. Then she turns to the old man and says she thinks that maybe me and Erika are right – maybe she should just close it down. Erika's there, 'You'd be cutting your losses, Sorcha.'

I'm like, 'And what *have* you lost, when you think about it? I mean, your old man only set up the shop for you to give you something to do when you finished college. I mean, what the fock else were you going to do with an Orts degree?'

She knows we're talking sense. In fact she's on the point of actually agreeing with us. She's nodding her head and she's about to say okay – her mouth is even forming the little *o*, when the old man has to go and open his trap.

'That sounds very much like defeatist talk,' he suddenly goes, waving his cappuccino spoon at me. 'Are we all just going to give in now? Surrender and become Communists, like our friends in Kildare Street?'

'Charles!' Erika goes, meaning shut the fock up.

Sorcha's there, 'No, no, Erika, let's hear your dad out.'

He goes, 'I'm simply saying, Sorcha, that this isn't the attitude that brought about what looked for a few years there like being an economic miracle!'

His words seem to, like, stir something in her.

'You know what, Charles? You're right. Nespresso have just brought out *five* new flavours. Except they're not calling them flavours – they're calling them personalities. It's like, at least *someone's* trying to keep this Celtic Tiger going.'

The old man's like, 'There you are, see. That's the spirit. As Winston Churchill said, success is the ability to go from one failure to the other with no loss of enthusiasm.'

Winston Churchill! I'm trying to boot him under the table, to tell him to shut the fock up, except the damage has already been done.

'I've always tried to ask myself,' Sorcha goes, 'whenever I've had a difficult decision to make, in life as well as fashion – what would Stella do?'

That's how there ended up *being* fourteen wind turbines on the roof of this shopping centre.

'I don't think Stella would just give in,' she goes. 'She didn't give in when people in the fashion world were being – oh my God – *so* bitchy about her.'

'There'll always be critics,' the old man goes. 'I can tell you, for my part, I've said some terribly harsh things about Declan Kidney, which I now regret. Go back and read the letters pages . . .'

Sorcha's face is suddenly full of – I'm pretty sure the word is, like, resolve? In other words, her mind is made up. She's there, 'I'm going to keep the shop open . . .'

Erika tries one more time. 'Sorcha, I think you should think about this more carefully.'

She's like, 'No, Erika. I was thinking anyway, shops like mine are *so* needed right now. I don't know if any of you have noticed but 1980s fashion is suddenly back – and, oh my God, it wasn't even good the first time around. Shoulder pads, tight jeans, plimsolls, Members Only jackets. And, oh my God, garish colours. Somebody's going to have to offer an alternative.'

She all of a sudden stands up. I know her well enough to know that this conversation is over. She goes, 'Thanks, everyone – now, if you'll excuse me, I've got a business to run.'

If you could call spending the afternoon on Facebook and TMZ running a business.

I turn to the old man, except I don't get a chance to say a word. He just goes, 'Looking forward to Auld Reekie, Ross?'

I'm like, 'What?' giving him a serious filthy.

He's there, 'You and your chaps, you're heading over for the Heineken Cup final tomorrow, aren't you? Edinburgh! The Athens of the North! *Nisi Dominus Frustra!*'

I look at Erika as if to say, you see what *I've* had to put up with for the last nearly thirty years?

I look over and watch Sorcha disappear back into her shop. There *is* no talking to her. There's going to be a price to pay for this and somehow I already know that I'm the one who's going to be paying it.

4. Lions and Tigers and Bare Bottoms, Oh My!

'We dinnae see many of yeer kind aroond here,' the cop goes and by *our kind* he presumably means streakers. 'Cannae take the cold, most ae them.'

He's pacing the back of the paddy wagon, talking to us – if I'm being honest – like an actual schoolteacher.

'Ahm just wondering what tae charge ye with – public indecency or looid behaviour.'

'Could we at least have . . . a blanket?' Fionn tries to go. I notice that the earpiece on one side of his glasses is missing. He's never been good on the sauce. 'I mean, aren't we entitled to one under the . . . what, Geneva Convention?'

'Ahm no sure,' the dude goes. 'Ah'll see is there a copy ae it lying aroond the station. See does it say anything aboot doss bastards coming over here trying tae make an arse ootae the Edinburgh fucken police.'

I laugh. I can *afford* to? While they're sat there freezing their National Concerts off, I'm still dressed as Leo the Lion, sweating like a teenage disco.

I'm as pissed as one as well.

The costume is a long story, which, by the way, I'll tell in my own time . . .

The cop gives me the serious death rays. 'Are ye no ashamed or yeerselves? Are ye no embarrassed? What aboot yeer families?'

I tell him he clearly doesn't know my old pair. Being dragged buck-naked into a police van in front of seventy thousand people wouldn't even be a topic of dinner conversation in our house.

I look at Fionn. 'But *you*,' I go, unable to keep a straight face, 'I'm surprised at *you*,' except he knows what I actually mean is proud. 'Is this what you meant by letting yourself go?'

He's grinning like a shot fox. He's totally off his tits – drinking like a rock star, all night and all day. I hope for the sake of his career that the TV cameras didn't catching him running *starkas bollockas narkas* across the field – although, in fairness, what RTÉ usually do is go, in a really snooty voice, 'Some attention-seekers on the pitch – let's not indulge them by giving them what they want.'

'Are you not worried about getting the bullet?' I go. 'Because that's what'll happen if McGahy gets wind of this.'

He's too mullered to even care. He's been throwing it down his Jeff Beck for, like, fifteen or sixteen hours straight, although, in fairness to him, I was the one egging him on.

JP's sat on the bench beside me, his eyes closed and his mouth open, trashed.

'Dude!' I go, shaking him, trying to wake him, but all he does, roysh, is try to snuggle into me, to warm himself off my fur.

There's suddenly all this, like, banging on the side of the van. Outside, we can hear the chants of 'Legends! Legends! Legends!'

The cop says we certainly seem to have our admirers. Then he finally throws Fionn and JP a blanket. JP's just lands on his head and he goes on sleeping.

My mind keeps drifting back to the match. 'Johnny Sexton,' I suddenly go, just shaking my head. 'He played for Ireland A when I was coaching Andorra. You could see it then. He just has it, the focker . . .'

I drunk-texted him this morning, giving him the same advice I used to give to Rog before every match. 'Eat nerves, shit results!' and he was straight back with, 'Thanks, Legend,' probably realizing that there's still shit he can learn from me.

We were sitting in McDonald's on Princes Street at that stage, the three of us racing the gherkins from our Big Macs down the inside of the window, JP winning because he had the presence of mind to wipe his free of the special sauce, which – you'll know if you've ever played the game – can slow your runner up.

I think we were all still hammered from Renords the night before. No sleep was the rule we all agreed on. Fionn, who, like I said, famously can't take his drink, switched to gin and tonics sometime around midnight. Seeing this as an attempt to, like, wuss out, I made sure every one was a double.

Then we were, like, drinking at the airport, drinking on the flight, drinking in the taxi to the match . . . It was midday and I was so wankered drunk I could have sworn I heard the poor focker ask whether we were going to do a streak across the pitch if Leinster won.

I might have went, 'What?'

'I'm serious,' he went. 'We fuggen said it, didn't we? Years ago. It was fff . . . Oisinn's idea. We said if Leinster ever won the Heineken Cup . . .'

I put my orm around him and laughed. 'Dude, that was back in the days when we couldn't get out of our focking pool.'

He just pushed his glasses up on his nose. He was like, 'We still said it.'

I laughed it off, thinking that was the end of it.

This bird came out from behind the counter then – her orse like two F50 pistons in those tight little slacks they make them wear – and storted spraying, then wiping down, the shit we'd made of the window. She didn't say a word to us, just cleaned up our mess, which made us all feel instantly guilty and I was on the point of telling her that she looked like Selita Ebanks when I heard someone shout that Leinster were a man down and they needed a volunteer.

I staggered to my feet. It was, like, an *instinct* thing more than anything? In my totally focked state, I really did think that Sexton had bottled it and that Michael Cheika had sent a minion to Mackey Ds to find a replacement kicker.

See, I blame the Dutch for brewing it.

I had my hand in the air, roysh, before I even turned to see the old dude in the Leinster blazer, holding a lion's head in one hand, then what looked like a giant actual Babygro in the other.

I'm going to be honest, roysh, I actually got a bit of a fright seeing Leo with the stuffing ripped out of him like that, to the point where JP even felt the need to go, 'It was never a *real* lion, Ross? It was just a costume.'

It was eventually explained to us, roysh, that the dude who in normal circumstances would be wearing it today had been turned away by Ryanair because he arrived at Dublin Airport with only his driving licence and no actual *passport*? The costume was brought over with the training kit and the balls and blahdy blahdy blah. And now they were in the serious shit, he said, because they'd no one to wear it.

'You've just found yourself a saviour,' I suddenly heard myself go. 'Go tell Michael Cheika to just focus on the match . . .'

The thing weighed a focking tonne. And if I storted knocking the beer back a little faster than usual in the hours before kick-off, I would add, in my defence, that it was only out of fear of dehydration.

The downside of all that drinking, of course, is that there are one or two blind spots in my memory of what *actually* happened? I do remember grabbing an Andy McNab to Murrayfield and it ended up having to be one of those wheelchair-accessible jobs, because you couldn't have squeezed me into anything else in that suit.

I remember Fionn and JP cracking their holes laughing at me – more mullered than I was – then taking pictures with their camera phones and saying how they really wished Oisinn was here to see it.

Of course the laughter stopped when we arrived at the ground, then three or four Leinster blazers grabbed me and ushered me down to actual pitchside, in front of the stand where Fionn and JP were sitting back in Row focking Z. I could hear them behind me shouting, 'You're focking crazy!'

The view I had of the match was as good as sitting on the old Dame Judy. I did have work to do, though. In my horren-dified condition, I tried to, like, remember as best I could some of the moves I'd seen the lion do at, like, Donnybrook and the RDS, and the crowd, I thought, responded positively, even *if* I fell a couple of times, owing to the fockload of drink I'd taken on board.

Of course it's easy to work the crowd when you're winning. Leinster went 9–3 up, Drico and Sexton with the kind of drop goals that we usually call Saddams – the execution wasn't the cleanest but who the fock cares?

I was giving it loads of fist-pumping, roysh, and running along, a few times in front of the actual Leinster bench, with my orms in the air. Like I said, it was easy like a Sunday morning.

Of course then the match suddenly turned. Stan Wright was sinbinned, Ben Woods ended up getting over for a try, then two Julien Dupuy penalties had me – and a lot more Leinster fans, I'd imagine – feeling suddenly, disgustingly, sober.

The fight had actually gone out of me. Leicester had scored, like, ten unanswered points and I dare say I wasn't the only one thinking, that's us focked.

Of course Leo the Lion would *never* think like that and I got, like, a shorp reminder of that when another one of Leinster's blazers tapped me on the shoulder, when I was sitting down, taking a breather, and went, 'Dance, you idiot! Dance!'

That was all I needed to hear.

I storted suddenly giving it loads again, gesturing to the crowd, even pointing to Leicester's tiger mascot and jokingly making, like, a throat-slitting gesture, which succeeded, it has to be said, in raising the noise levels from the Leinster contingent.

I wouldn't like to claim the credit for what happened next. That's for other people to say. But with the roars of the crowd in his ears, Rocky Elsom went rampaging downfield and Jamie Heaslip ended up scoring a try.

I missed Johnny's conversion, because I celebrated, roysh, by running thirty yords, then sliding on my stomach, which the Leinster fans loved but which I didn't attempt a second time because I ended up spewing my ring inside the actual suit, which explains the hum in the paddy wagon now.

Just after Johnny kicked what turned out to be the winning points, I wandered over to the stand to try to pick out the goys, mainly to get their reaction. Even from that distance, we're talking twenty rows of seats back, with my eyes going in all directions at once, I could see that Fionn – Mr Spontaneity for once – had taken his Leinster jersey off and was rubbing what turned out to be Vicks VapoRub all over his upper body.

It turns out it helps your body retain heat and makes it difficult for cops and stewards to get a good grip on you.

I was thinking, okay, someone stop him before this turns ugly. But when I squinted my eyes, roysh, I could see that JP was doing exactly the same thing.

But then the final whistle went and, well, I had more work to do. While the players celebrated on the field, I was stood in front of the Leinster fans, again striking various poses.

That's when, all of a sudden, the noise level went up a notch and two of the whitest human beings I've ever seen flew past me in a blinding flash, followed by the whiff of menthol.

They were suddenly pegging it across the pitch, both of them, stark Vegas naked – everything hung out for everyone to see.

It was pretty focking hilarious watching the Feds and the ground staff trying to grab them. They just kept slipping away and you could see even some of the Leinster players laughing as they waited to collect the cup.

I had no original intention of joining them until I saw the Leicester tiger, the sneaky focker, trip Fionn up, then I decided, in my very drunken state, that it would be a good idea for me to go over and deck him.

The next thing anyone knew, there was literally fur flying. As everyone I think accepts, there is nothing funnier in the world than two men in giant animal costumes hitting each other. Fionn and JP might have literally slipped back into the crowd had they not copped me thumping the stuffing out of the Leicester tiger and pretty much collapsed with laughter. It was that moment of hesitation that proved fatal. They were on us in an instant.

'A couple ae weeks in Saughton,' the cop suddenly goes, 'that'll poot manners on you boys.'

Saughton sounds like it could be *their* Mountjoy? A shithole, no doubt.

That's when Fionn ends up making his plea for, I don't know, leniency. 'Ossifer,' he goes, shivering under his blanket, 'is there any chance you might just . . . let us go?'

'Let ye go?' He even laughs. 'Why would ah dae that?'

'I don't know – because we're in the middle of a recession . . .'

'What's that got tae dae wiyit?'

Fionn shrugs.

'I don't know. It's just . . . We come from a country they used to call the . . . Singy Pore of . . . of Europe,' he goes. I don't think I've *ever* seen him so off his tits. 'Hard as that is to believe now, you fff . . . It's all redundancies and fucking, I don't know, repossessions and people losing their . . . their retirement savings. Shit, it's a depressing time, isn't it? But then . . . then we go and win the European Cup . . .'

I'm literally wiping away tears with the palm of my hand because what he's saying is actually true.

'Taking off our clothes,' he goes, 'it just . . . seemed like the right thing to do . . . The only thing . . .'

They've storted rocking the van now, the Leinster supporters – and still the chant continues: 'Legends! Legends! Legends!'

'So who are they ooy there?' the cop goes. 'The fucking dispossessed?'

Fionn obviously likes this because he sort of, like, smiles and goes, 'Yeah.'

It's then, roysh, totally unexpectedly, that the cop's face suddenly softens. He sort of, like, smiles himself. 'Ma father,' he goes, really drawing out his words, 'he never had a bean. Know what he told me before he died?'

We're all there, 'Er, no . . .'

'He said that when Celtic won the European Cup, it mightae been the only day he was truly happy in his whole puff.'

He walks to the back of the paddy wagon.

He's like, 'Wrap they blankets aroond yeer waists, boys,' and he suddenly opens the door. There's, like, a roar from the Leinster fans surrounding the van.

'Go oan,' the dude goes, 'oot tae fock – before I change ma maind.'

Birds who call each other 'Chicken' are always out and out bitches – has anyone else ever noticed that? 'Mrs' is another one. Sophie and Amie with an ie are giving Chloe plenty of both.

It's like, 'Are you okay, Mrs?' every time she moves a focking muscle. Or it's, 'Can I get you anything, Chicken?'

Of course, the second she hobbles out on to the balcony for a cigarette, they're flaying the focking skin off her back. 'Er, hello?' Sophie goes. '*How* long is she going to need those crutches?'

Amie with an ie laughs. 'I know, it's like – er, it's *only* a new hip?'

The three of them called around, like, an hour ago, with a chocolate fondue set as a supposed flat-warming present, even though it's an obvious regift. The real reason they're here is to have, like, a nosey at the new gaff.

'Do you have any, like, neighbours?' Sophie goes.

I'm there, 'Not yet. I think there's, like, eight aportments in this block of sixty that are occupied. In fact I'm the only one living above the third floor. Except that's *all* about to change. Watch this space!'

Chloe hobbles back in from the balcony. 'It's actually a really nice aportment,' she goes, like I *give* a fock what any of them think. 'It *could* do with some books, though.'

She must cop my reaction, roysh, because she goes, 'No one's saying you *have* to read them, Ross. I'm just saying they make, like, amazing furniture. I've got something like twenty in mine. My sister's in, like, interior *design*, don't forget?'

She hobbles back over to the sofa and, like, manoeuvres herself back into a sitting position. Amie with an ie goes, 'Are you okay, Mrs?'

Chloe just nods.

Sophie says her own aportment in Sandyford Industrial Estate – as in the one she's renting out to that Estonian couple – has gone from being worth €468,000 to being worth, oh my God, €410,000. *And* the couple are thinking of going back to Haapsalu. 'Haapsalu!' she goes. '*Hello?* Who's even heard of it? That's how bad things in this country have obviously gone.'

Amie with an ie says if she thinks *that's* bad, her mum and dad's house in Booterstown *was* worth €860,0000 *before* the whole Celtic Tiger? Then it went up to, like, €1.3 million. Now it's worth, like, €860,000, and there's general agreement among them that this is an *actual* disgrace.

My head is beginning to focking throb.

'Oh my God,' Sophie goes, '*on* that actual point – Ross, *what* is your mum doing?'

I'm like, 'What?'

'Er, the *spending*?'

I don't know why I end up defending the woman. 'It's *her* focking money,' I go, 'which means it's *her* business what she spends it on.'

'Well,' she goes, 'I actually agree with – I can't remember which paper, but the one that said she was being unpatriotic.'

It's at that exact point, roysh, that I hear voices in the hallway outside – and not the kind you'd expect to hear in a development as prestigious as Rosa Parks. They're the voices of, I think the politically correct phrase to use is *disadvantaged* people?

'Ssshhh!' I go.

The girls shut the fock up. I tip over to the door and have a look through the spyhole.

There's two – as Ro would call them – *shams* outside in the hallway, maybe mid twenties, you know the kind, we're talking cheap sweatshirts and we're talking runners that cost the price of a week's holiday somewhere.

It's immediately obvious, roysh, that they're trying to break into the vacant aportment next door, probably for the copper piping. I'm there, 'Sophie, throw me the phone . . .'

The Feds take their time answering.

I'm like, 'Yeah, I've got skobies trying to break into the vacant aportment next door to me – can you send a fleet?'

The dude's like, 'Veecant?' – focking *CSI Belturbet*. 'Sure, what's the heerm in thet?'

I can't believe my actual ears. 'Sorry?'

'Is it the builder owns it?'

'Er, yeah?'

'Sure them builders is the worst criminals of the lot, what they're after doing to this counthree. It's them what should be behind bars – them and the banks . . .'

Then the line just goes dead. And I end up having to take the law into my own hands.

'Be careful!' Chloe goes, as I grab, like, an empty JD bottle from the recycling bin, then reef open the front door. Of course the two schnacks don't even flinch.

I go, 'Just to let you know, I've actually already *called* the Feds?'

They look at each other, totally scoobied. 'Ah,' one of them goes, 'he tinks we're tryin to break in, so he does.'

The other focker laughs. I'm thinking what's so funny? 'We liff hee-er,' he goes.

Now, you can imagine me – my hort pretty much stops in my chest.

He's there, 'Ine only lookin for me key, so I am.'

I'm still thinking, hoping, that I maybe misheard them? 'Look,' I go, 'take the copper, the lead, whatever you've come for . . .'

'Are ye not listenin to me, are you not? We liff hee-er.'

It's Chloe who ends up asking the question that's frozen on my lips. 'Ask them how people like them can afford to live somewhere like this,' she shouts out into the hall.

'Because,' the one who's looking for his key goes, '*we're* not payin for it. It's the fooken soshiddle.'

I'm there, 'The what?' in my innocence.

'The soshiddle welfeer,' he goes. 'There's fooken hudrits of vacant apeertmints in these blocks . . .'

I'm there, so focking gullible: 'But it was supposed to become, like, student accommodation?'

He actually laughs at me. 'Sure the soshiddle's the only crowd writing out big rent cheques these days . . .'

I suddenly feel like a focking Guilbaud's lobster who's just copped my old man grinning into the tank at him. How could an obvious sap like Ailish stitch me up like this? Of course it's obvious. It's called the current economic climate.

I watch the two of them continue searching for their keys. Then they eventually find them. One of them sticks out his hand and goes, 'I'm Tetty,' though what he obviously means is Terry.

I shake it, in a sudden daze.

'And this is Laddy,' he goes, in other words Larry, 'the brutter . . .'

And to think the old dear said this recession wasn't going to affect me. Now it's suddenly living next door.

The two boys are loving my, I suppose, discomfort, of course. 'Nice meetin ye,' Larry makes sure to go, 'neighbour!'

'*What* is wrong with you?'

Sorcha practically roars the words at me. I'm sitting in the middle of the shop, feeding Honor an ethical, probiotic yoghurt, looking around me at all these cordboard boxes full of – get this – *more* new stock?

'You *know* what's wrong with me,' I go. 'I moved out of my gaff – I've ended up living next door to poor people – just to get the bank off your back and this one back in Pre-Montessori. And you're still ploughing money into this . . .'

I even kick a box of Yigal Azrouël dresses, looking for the right word.

'Ross!' she goes again. 'You're putting that yoghurt all over Honor's face.'

She pretty much snatches her out of my orms, which is when I suddenly snap out of it. She's right – poor Honor looks like a bucket of paint with eyes.

'My point still stands,' I go. 'You can't even sell the shit you have . . .'

'I'll thank you not to use language like that in front of your daughter. And do you *think* I'd just go and order in all this stock without having a plan?'

The next thing I know, roysh, she's looking over my shoulder, going, 'Hey, Erika!' and she's dumping Honor back in my orms.

I'm thinking, this kid is heading for a child shrink as sure as her mother's heading for the focking bankruptcy court.

Erika looks incredible and I'm only mentioning that as a statement of fact. I look back at Sorcha, then ask her what's going on. She says it's called torgeted morkeshing and I'd know that if I *cared* about retail and the problems it's facing at the moment?

That evening certificate course she did in the Smurfit Business School has obviously gone to her head.

'Erika,' she goes, 'I'll be an hour at the very most. Honor, Mommy will be back soon,' and then she reaches down behind the counter and whips out – I don't believe it – a focking megaphone. I try to ask her, 'What the fock?' but she's out the door before I can even get the words out.

'I told her she should just hire Claire to stand outside Bewley's with a sign,' Erika goes. 'Claire would do it too, with this wedding coming up. How else is she going to pay for twenty-two Massamam curries?'

I'm suddenly getting the picture here. 'Are you telling me she's heading for Grafton Street with that thing – to, what, drum up business?' Erika doesn't answer, although her silence says yes. 'Why didn't you talk her out of it? I thought you were on my side in this thing?'

'She's my friend,' she goes, like that's ever been an excuse for anything. 'I might not *agree* with her standing on Grafton Street advertising her shop through a loud-hailer. I might think that the most sensible thing to do is to just shut it down. But I'm going to be here, Ross, every afternoon for as long as she needs me . . .'

'Well, personally, I think she's gone mad . . .'

'Mommy's not mad,' Honor – totally out of the blue – goes. 'It's just the recession, Daddy!'

My mouth just drops open. Erika's does too, in fairness. Then I end up semi-losing it – I can't put it any stronger than that. 'See?' I go. 'A little girl of not even four years of age shouldn't even *know* a word like that. This is because of what she's been exposed to in this shop.'

I pick her up in my orms and storm off after Sorcha. It doesn't take me long to find her. I actually hear her before I see her – her voice going, 'Eighties style *is* making a comeback due to the fashion industry's 25-year-recycling rule – but what I want to tell you here today is that it doesn't have to be that way . . .'

She's standing outside Boodles – the flower-sellers there don't look like happy rabbits about being forced to listen to her either. 'There *are* other retro trends you can follow that don't necessarily mean cheap. The whole ethnic tribal thing is *so* in right now – animal prints are getting a total overhaul and belted trenches and safari jackets are going to be huge this year, even stretching into the autumn . . .'

She's using all the public-speaking skills she picked up in school – focusing on a particular point in the distance, which seems to be the *Never Mind the Recession – Look at Our Prices* shopfront opposite her, then every so often glimpsing at these little prompt cords that she's holding.

It's pretty obvious, though, that people are only stopping to, like, laugh at her, which is difficult for me to just stand there and watch.

Obviously, I say fock-all, though, because I don't want people to think that I know her.

'Another look that's going to be – oh my God – huge this year is Disney Chic. Those of you who read *Elle* and *Marie Claire* will know that the catwalks this spring have been flooded with crazy-shaped shoes, big bangles and full swishy skirts – and all these trends and more can be found in the exclusive Sorcha & Circa in the Powerscourt Townhouse Centre . . .'

I'm on the point of walking straight up to her to tell her she's making a basic tit of me, as well as herself, when – possibly out of frustration at not being listened to – she suddenly storts picking out individuals walking past and basically critiquing what they're wearing, except it's not so much critiquing as ripping the piss.

It actually storts off, roysh, hormless enough. She's there, 'You there, the girl in the leather Members Only jacket with the sleeves rolled up and the Ray-Bans on your head – stacked bangles, which are available in Sorcha & Circa, are a simple way to work a globetrotting trend into that look.'

Which is a reasonable enough thing to say. But then, roysh, it storts to get really personal.

'That girl over there,' she ends up going to this totally innocent fat bird who just happens to waddle by, 'I know the whole *Flashdance* thing is suddenly back but that sweatshirt and those leggings do absolutely nothing for a girl of your size. If you want to downplay those curves, why not follow Milan's obsession this spring with delicate layers, wispy fabrics and cascading ruffles, adding ballet pumps to give everything a more ethereal edge. Also, masculine, tailored jackets offer a softer, slouchy twist to the fuller female frame – and all are available from Sorcha & Circa . . .'

The bird actually stops, her mouth just flapping there in the wind. The next thing, roysh, Sorcha's trained her eye on some other poor unsuspecting cow, this one coming out of the Corphone Warehouse.

'Those colours,' she goes. 'Yes, I'm talking about you, in the shocking-pink tank, with the tangy lime T underneath? All they do is draw the colour from your face and highlight – no offence – your bad complexion . . .'

You can see the bird – she's rough as guts, roysh, and big-time WC – actually considering going over and decking her. I'm even getting ready to step in.

'Tone-on-tone neutrals and creams,' Sorcha keeps giving it, 'add sophistication to any look and can detract from badly pocked skin like yours.'

The bird turns around to no one in particular and says she's going to boorst her, the snoppy fooken bitch, and I feel like telling her that people like her shouldn't even *be* on Grafton Street. It's the mobile phone shops that keep bringing them in.

Before she can do anything, though, Sorcha has moved on to someone else.

'Jeans tucked into ankle boots shorten and thicken the lower leg and, as you can all see, add two pounds to the rear . . .'

I decide, roysh, that I can't take any more of this and I turn to leave. As I do, Honor goes, 'Daddy, what's Mommy doing?'

I just shake my head and tell her she's *trying to earn a living* – and the way things are going, we might all be doing it before we're very much older.

'Yeth?'

'Dont give me *yeth*,' I practically roar down the phone. 'Why haven't you been returning my calls?'

She's there, 'I'm thorry, Roth, I've been tho, tho bithy . . .'

'Busy avoiding me, more like.'

'The thing ith, I should have thold you thith before – I'm sort of, like, *theeing* thith other guy – I thought you under-thtood, we were never going to be a therious thing . . .'

I'm like, 'Whoa, let me give this to you straight. I've no focking interest in you. It was a use and abuse situation. End of. My problem is you stitching me up . . .'

'Thtitching you up?'

'Er, in a *major* way? I've got skangers living next door to me all of a sudden – it was supposed to be all students . . .'

'Yeth, unfortunately the thtudent thing fell through. Plan B was the thothial welfare . . .'

I'm there, 'Horseshit – that UCD thing was obviously never a runner . . .'

'Roth,' she tries to go, 'Ethie's had to thake an enormouth hith – heath loothing a loth of money and the bankth are threatening thoo . . .'

'Don't give me that. Eddie knew what he was doing. He knew he had to get out of there before he turned the place into practically Ballymun. When you met me you told him you'd found him a sucker. Even though you probably said *thucker* . . .'

'Thath very hurthful.'

'Well, I'm beginning to wonder is that even a *real* speech impediment you have . . .'

148

'Whath?'

'I'm just saying, obviously nothing's as it focking seems with you. Maybe it's just put on, to make yourself sound more stupid – lull people into a sense of blahdy blah.'

'How thare you!'

'Hey, I *worked* as an estate agent back in the good old days. I know all the tricks . . .'

'Well,' she goes, 'if you thid work ath an ethtate agenth, you'll know that it wath all legal and above boarth . . .'

'Have you even thought about what Rosa Parks would think of all this if she was alive today?'

'Fuck Rotha Parkth!'

I'm left in just total shock. 'That's, I don't know, blasphemy.'

She's there, 'Live with ith, Roth – ith called the rethethion!'

I wake up in the early afternoon underneath a bird called Abhlach, a DBS Diploma in Internet Morkeshing student who I met in Dakota and who agreed to come home with me without telling me that it was Dare You week.

Oh, I was, like, stripped and ready for action, raiding the old johnny cache and hunkering down for a long night ahead, when I noticed her sitting on the edge of the bed with her orms and legs folded and a face on her like a kicked-in can of Chum – tell-tale signs for an experienced campaigner like me.

I was there, 'Are you saying it's your . . .'

She looked at me, shocked, I think, at how comfortable I was talking about, like, *women's* issues?

She was like, 'Yeah, I just got it today.'

I just shook my head. 'I can't believe you're perioding me.'

'Sorry,' she went. 'I should have maybe mentioned it in the taxi.'

I'm thinking, no, you should have maybe mentioned it *before* I spent a focking Brody Jenner buying you a Cosmo.

I don't think there's a man alive who'd have blamed me if I'd put her out on the street. And I definitely would have if I'd still been living in The Grange. But Ticknock is miles from anywhere and it's obviously not safe around here with pretty much *Adam and Paul* living next door.

So I let her stay, which is, again, the gentleman in me coming out.

Anyway, where all this is going, is, the next day, we're talking two, maybe three o'clock in the afternoon, I wake up with *her* dead weight lying on top of me and someone beating out a morse code message on the focking doorbell.

Now, in normal circumstances, I'd just ignore it, but whoever's outside just keeps pressing it at, like, five-second intervals, which means I end up having to roll Abhlach off me, throw back the old Outlaw Petes and go and see who it is.

I'm one hungover grover, by the way.

I check the little CCTV screen and I get an immediate fright. It's Sorcha's old man and straight away I'm wondering what the fock I've done. But then I'm thinking it might not be anything major. Sorcha's got her thirtieth birthday coming up this summer – maybe he just wants to warn me to stay away, possibly even serve me with *papers* to that effect?

Either way, I decide not to answer it.

'Who is it?' Abhlach shouts.

'Edmund Lalor,' I go, 'a prick with ears. He's the father of the old Bag for Life. I'm going to crack on not to be in . . .'

Of course what I don't realize, because I'm not used to this intercom yet, is that I've got my finger on the focking speaker button.

Jesus, I'm so slow sometimes, they could put deckchairs on me and call me a focking cruise ship.

He puts his face right up to the camera lens and goes, 'Let me in, you little tidemark,' which is a thing he's always called me.

I'm there, 'Er, cool – just, er, push the door there, Mr Lalor. It's, like, the ninth floor.'

Maybe sixty seconds later, I hear the elevator go, then in he walks, no greeting, no pleasantries, nothing. I bring him into the kitchen. '*She's* just a friend in there,' I go, flicking my thumb in the direction of the bedroom, 'just in case you're wondering . . .'

But he doesn't *give* a fock. He gets straight down to business. 'Why is my daughter standing on Grafton Street like some carnival barker?'

I actually laugh.

'Whoa, that's straight out of left field,' I go. 'I thought this was going to be about her thirtieth. Where's she having it, by the way – has she decided yet?'

'A colleague of mine from the Law Library rang me at lunchtime. He said he saw my daughter standing outside Bewley's, using a megaphone to try to drum up custom for that shop of hers. I said, no way – couldn't have been her. My Sorcha would never stoop so low. I said I'd have to see it with my own eyes. So I went to Grafton Street myself . . .'

'And *did* it turn out to be her?' I go. I don't *know* why, maybe just playing for time.

'Sorcha's grandmother has coffee in Bewley's every Friday morning. What would she think if she saw her like that?'

'Well,' I go, 'she'd certainly be wondering is that all a UCD education is worth these days . . .'

He takes a step closer to me – he's in no mood for *my* bullshit – and he sticks his finger practically in my face. 'You better tell me what the *fuck* is going on?'

'Okay,' I end up having go, 'her shop's in trouble.'

'Trouble?' he goes, looking genuinely bewildered.

I'm there, 'Yeah. Er, *financial* trouble?'

'That can't be true. No, she told me herself that she was

meeting the challenges of the new economic paradigm head-on.'

I nearly laugh – that's obviously more Smurfit School horse-shit.

I'm there, 'Dude, take it from me – the girl couldn't sell Johnny Hayes a dummy pass.'

He's seriously pissed off, of course, that *I* know all of this shit and *he* doesn't? 'I'm sure she would have told me if it was as bad as you say.'

I laugh.

I'm like, 'Dude, she ended up nearly losing the house,' bad and all as I feel for telling him.

'The house?'

'Yeah, she couldn't make her loan payments and the banks were going to turf her out on to Newtownpork Avenue – until *I* stepped in, of course, as the last-minute hero.'

'Why didn't she tell me any of this? We've never had secrets?'

'Look,' I go, mainly to try to make him feel better, 'you know Sorcha – she's, like, really proud and blah blah blah. She didn't want her precious daddy to find out what kind of shit she was actually in.'

You can see his little mind working overtime, trying to think of a way of blaming me for it. 'You *let* her get into this kind of trouble.'

'Whoa, horsy! I'm the one who's been telling her to shut the shop down.'

'Well, obviously not firmly enough. If you had . . .' but then he suddenly loses his train of thought, distracted by some-thing. 'What's that . . . *awful* noise?'

'It's *Christy Moore Live at the Point.* I've got poor people living next door . . .'

He doesn't know how to respond to this information.

'It's "Nancy Spain",' I go, 'thirty times a focking day. And that's all because I traded down, to make sure your daughter and granddaughter didn't end up living in a focking bus shelter . . .'

Again, he can't bear the thought of me being the man of the moment. He smiles, but not in a good way, then pretends to be interested in a photo on the sideboard of me standing next to Declan Kidney, giving him the rabbit ears. He's obviously working up to telling me something.

'You know,' he goes, loving the sound of his own voice, 'when you broke Sorcha's heart, I made it my life's ambition to destroy you.'

'You've told me that before – loads of times.'

He just nods.

'Sorcha asked me to put the brake on the divorce proceedings for a little while – you know that as well, I expect. Not to give you false hope, of course – she's got you *well* out of her system . . .'

I wouldn't be so sure about that but I let him continue.

'I tried to talk her out of it, of course. Let's crush the little bastard into the dirt, I said. But her mother said no, give the girl time to reflect on what she's doing, if that's what she wants. But me, I can't wait to get back to it.'

'I bet you can't.'

'You see, I'm very, very good at what I do. And obviously I've a passion for this particular case. I could cripple you, Ross – financially speaking of course.'

'I'm not sure Sorcha would want that.'

'Of course she wouldn't. But I still could. I want you to appreciate the power I have over you.'

I'm there, 'What exactly are you saying?'

He laughs, I suppose, cruelly. 'I don't care whether Sorcha's shop remains open or closed for business,' he goes. 'What I'm telling you is this. I'm going to walk down Grafton Street tomorrow morning, and if I see my daughter there, demeaning herself again, I'm going to obliterate you in the divorce courts, regardless of what she and her mother say. If she's back on that street with that loud-hailer in her hand, I'll make sure it's you who ends up paying whatever debts she has . . . for ever!'

Then off he goes.

It's often occurred to me that there's nothing like the threat of poverty to suddenly concentrate the mind. I sit down at the table, mulling over my dilemma, until a plan eventually comes into my mind.

I tip back into Abhlach, who's watching *Murder, She Wrote*, outstaying her welcome by a good fourteen hours at this stage. I grab the remote and just mute it.

'Okay,' I go, 'I think we'd all agree that that was a pretty shitty stunt you pulled on me last night, with your period, blah blah blah,' and she looks at me, roysh, still trying to play the innocent. 'But you can make it up to me by doing me a favour.'

I pick up my chinos from where I dropped them last night, then I grab a whack of notes out of the pocket. She's going, 'What are you talking about?'

'Don't worry, you're probably going to enjoy it. Do you know a shop called Sorcha & Circa in the Powerscourt Townhouse Centre?'

She shakes her head.

'Well,' I go, peeling off five hundred snots, 'it exists. Only focking barely – but it does. I want you to go and spend this in there . . .'

She's obviously surprised.

'Why?'

'That's for me to know. You've just got to promise me you'll spend every focking cent of it in there. As in, don't be nipping around the corner to Rococo.'

'You're *giving* me five hundred euros? To spend on, like, clothes?'

I laugh.

'*And* no sex,' I go. 'Yeah, we might as well be focking married, huh?'

I pull back the sheets and gesture for her to get out of the bed. Then I grab my phone and stort scrolling down through my contacts, looking for exes who are still on talking terms with me.

'Remember that – oh my God – really flirty Saloni Alexia dress that I actually wanted for myself?' Sorcha goes. 'Well, I actually *sold* it this morning? With a pair of strappy Chanel ankle boots.'

I'm there, 'That's cool.'

'I'm sure I know her, by the way.'

'Who?'

'The girl who bought them. Maybe from Annabel's . . .'

Shit.

I quickly get her off the subject. 'Business-wise,' I go, 'you really seem to have turned a corner. Fair focks would have to be my basic attitude.'

She smiles – happy that I'm happy *for* her – and says she sold three Milly of London dresses yesterday alone *and* that pair of neutral-seam-detail jodhpurs that she's had, like, *for ever*?

'I just knew we'd ride this recession out,' she goes. 'See, the key to it, as we learned in college, is to keep money in circulation . . .'

I'm certainly doing that – down five focking Ks in just over a week.

As we're talking, Sorcha's putting Honor's little coat on her and I ask her where they're headed anyway at, like, four o'clock on a Sunday afternoon. At first, roysh, she's not going to tell me, but eventually I get it out of her that Claire has found – oh my God – *the* most amazing previously loved wedding dress online.

See, when *I* hear that, I end up needing a moment – that's how hord I laugh. 'You mean second-hand?' I go, then of course Sorcha's on the immediate defensive.

'No, I *mean* previously loved, Ross.'

This wedding just gets funnier and funnier.

'I've already told you – they don't have much money.'

'As if that's an excuse! Who even sells their wedding dress?'

The reason I ask is that, look, *our* marriage wasn't one of those happy ever after jobbies, yet Sorcha still pulls on the old Vera Wang when she's having one of her blue days, even if it is just to eat her own body weight in Dairy Milk and watch movies with Patrick Dempsey and Anne Hathaway in them.

'Okay, don't laugh,' she goes, 'but it's this, like, website she found? It's for people who *had* wedding plans but, for one reason or another, they didn't go ahead.'

I actually *do* laugh.

'Are we talking people who were, like, jilted at the altar? Because I thought that shit only happened in *EastEnders*.'

She shakes her head, like I'm the *only* one who watches too much TV?

'We're talking about people who had second thoughts,' she goes. 'Anyway, Claire's going to be here any minute, Ross, so if you wouldn't mind . . .'

She sort of, like, indicates the front door, telling me to hit the bricks. I'm there, 'Er, not a chance,' and then I scoop Honor up in my orms. 'I wouldn't miss this for the world.'

'Ross,' she goes, 'it's in a place called Kilcroney,' which I know is supposed to scare me off. But nothing could. I get the feeling that this is one experience *not* to be missed?

I look at Honor and I go, 'Would you like your daddy to

come along with you?' and Honor sort of, like, squeals, then claps her hands and goes, 'Daddy,' and I'm like, 'Yeah, that's right, kiddo – road trip!'

There's a sudden ring at the door and it's Claire.

'Ross wants to come,' Sorcha tells her. *She* ends up being weirdly cool with it, though. She's like, 'Let him if he wants to,' even though she knows I'm there just to rip the actual.

So we pile into Claire's Renault Clio, then we're off.

Kilcroney ends up being in Wicklow, which I should have guessed. Poor Honor's little face as she watches the worst of it zip by – she'll never stray further than the Loughlinstown roundabout again. Which is no bad thing. Teach them young. Of course straight away I stort getting the subtle digs in.

'Has *he* got his suit yet?' I go. 'If you want, I could go through the death notices in the paper – find someone who won't be needing theirs any more.'

Sorcha's like, 'Ignore him, Claire,' and Claire says she learned that lesson a long time ago.

He rings when we're halfway down there. She answers by going, 'Garret, I've got you on speakerphone,' just in case he's about to say something weird. *I've got the handcuffs and the rubber nappy on – come straight home.* That kind of shit.

He asks her if she's tried the dress on yet and she says no, we're only, like, driving down there now.

Then she goes, 'I probably should tell you – Ross is here as well.'

He's like, 'Ross?' and then there's all of a sudden silence on the other end of the phone. It's obvious he's bulling at the idea that I'm going to see the dress before *he* does?

So I go, 'Hey, Garret,' all happy, like a man with a tit in either pocket. 'I've had an amazing idea about your suit. Can you get an *Evening Herald* if you're out?'

He doesn't rise to the bait. He just goes, 'Claire, we'll talk about this later,' and she's like, 'Gar, he only came for the drive,' but he's there, 'I said later,' and he just hangs up.

'It might just be pre-wedding nerves,' Sorcha tries to go, ready to defend him, but Claire's like, 'No, he just gets – oh my God – *so* possessive.'

I suddenly cop why she was so happy to have me along for the ride. She's using *me* to fock with his head. Women. You could stay awake all night and you still wouldn't be up early enough for them.

It takes forever to find the gaff. The satnav stops talking to us somewhere around Kilmacanogue, presumably writing us off for dead. But we eventually find the place – a surprisingly all right gaff, it has to be said.

Julie is the bird's name. It's all, 'So you're the bride – congratulations!' and blahdy blahdy blah.

She brings us into the kitchen and we all make horseshit conversation about the drive down and the recapitalization of the banks and how bad things are out there at the moment. She's not actually that bad. She's maybe twenty-four, twenty-five. She *could* look like Emily Browning if she did something with herself.

All I want to know, of course, is why she's flogging the Eton Mess.

'I only bought it three months ago,' she goes.

Sorcha's like, 'We saw the photos online. Oh my God, it's *so* beautiful. It *is* a Rosetta Nicolini, is it?'

'It is, yeah.'

Sorcha and Claire smile at each other.

'Daddy, what's that smell?' Honor goes.

'Ssshhh!' I go. 'It's Wicklow, Honor. It'll be over soon.'

'It's next Saturday we were supposed to get married,' Julie goes. This is, like, totally out of the blue.

Claire puts on this, like, sympathetic face – totally fake. 'I'm *so* sorry,' she goes, then she sort of, like, grips Julie's upper orm.

You can tell what she's thinking is, hurry up and get the focking thing.

She disappears into the bedroom to get it. I'm there, 'I wonder what happened,' and Sorcha tells me to behave myself, knowing my previous.

Sixty seconds later, she's back. Claire and Sorcha practically buckle at the knees when they see it. There's a lot of hands over mouths and a lot of oh my Gods, then Claire says she *has* to try it on – oh my God, *right* now!

She doesn't disappear into another room to do it either. She strips down to her Biggie Smalls right there in front of me, then even goes, 'Oh my God, Ross, don't ever tell Garret you saw me in just my bra and knickers.'

It's like, er, yeah – like *she's* not going to let it slip?

'Do you mind me asking,' Julie goes, 'what colour are your bridesmaids' dresses?'

Claire turns to Sorcha, the last word in fashion. 'Would you say egg yolk?'

Sorcha nods.

'Egg yolk!' Julie goes, a little big shocked – she tries her best to hide it but you can hear it in her voice, like when someone tells you they've named their kid Blaine or some shit.

Claire's there, 'Yeah, egg yolk, with, like, white pagodas on them?'

'Pagodas?'

I get in then. 'Did you ever eat in the restaurant that used to be above Kielys?'

Sorcha interrupts before she has a chance to answer and tries explain that the actual theme of the wedding is Thai. From the way Julie looks at her, she might as well have said it was fancy focking dress.

Claire puts the thing on over her head, then Sorcha storts pulling it this way and that, basically adjusting it.

'Do you mind *me* asking,' *I* suddenly go, 'because it's focking killing me at this stage – why was the wedding called off?'

'Ross!' Sorcha goes, like she's giving out to an actual child. But the thing is, roysh, Julie seems happy enough to talk about it.

She's there, 'Breffni was cheating on me,' she goes. 'With my best friend. I'm just happy I found out before I made the biggest mistake of my life.'

Then she opens this sort of, like, long cupboard with the ironing board in it and there's, like, a full-length mirror on the inside of the door. Claire checks herself out in it, striking various poses, and she seems to like whatever the fock it is she sees.

'Oh, yes!' she's going. 'Oh, yes! *Wait* till Erika sees me in this!'

'So what shoes are you going to wear with it?' Julie goes. 'I had these beautiful white Louboutins that my sister bought me in New York . . .'

Claire's there, 'Okay, this is going to *sound* bad? But I fell – oh my God – in *love* with this one pair? They just *happen* to be from Barratts but they *are* really nice . . .'

Julie's there, 'Oh . . .'

'They *are* amazing shoes,' Sorcha goes, trying to back her up. This is the same Sorcha, remember, who'd sooner cut her own toes off with a blunt scissors and wear focking horse shoes than put anything from Barratts on her actual foot.

I turn around to Julie and I'm like, 'So what's the Jack – how did you find out, about him and your so-called bezzy mate?'

'I saw them out together – in Bray one night.'

'Bray!' I instantly go. 'That's where Claire's from! Lovely port of the world, I'm told.'

I'm too busy ripping the piss to notice how upset Julie is suddenly becoming. 'It was all planned . . .' she goes, her eyes filling up.

Sorcha tells me to stop, I'm making her sad. I tell her I disagree – she seems to *want* to get it off her chest?

'I sometimes think, if I could only talk to him. It might have been just pre-wedding jitters . . .'

You can see Claire suddenly thinking, fock, is she going to change her mind about selling this thing?

'Er, after the way he obviously humiliated you,' she goes, 'you'd be mad, Julie, to even want him back.'

Julie dabs at her tears with the back of her hand and tries to change the subject.

She's there, 'So who's doing your make-up? Are you going to Brown Sugar or one of those?'

Claire looks at Sorcha – *guiltily*, if that's a word? She's like, 'No, it's not one of the well-known ones? Well, what I'm actually doing is – there's this new, like, beauty college that's just opened up on the Main Street in Greystones. They're always looking for models . . .'

'*What?*' Julie goes, genuinely disgusted.

From my long and often sorry experience of birds, I'd say she's less than ten seconds away from flipping the tits here.

'When you think about it,' Claire tries to go, 'these are the make-up artists of the future. They're the ones who are going to be working in all the well-known places once they qualify.'

'Oh my God, take the dress off,' Julie suddenly goes. She's not focking about either, just from the way she says it.

Claire's there, 'What?'

'I said take it off!'

'No, I've decided I want it.'

'What, so you can go mud-wrestling in it? Take it off!'

I tell Claire not to orgue. I've heard what they do to GAA referees in these ports. Except that's exactly what she *does* do? 'I will *not* take it off. I'm paying you what you wanted for it – four hundred euros – and that's it . . .'

The next thing any of us knows, roysh, Julie has made a sudden lunge for Claire. She grabs two massive fistfuls of the dress and she's twisting it in her hands, at the same time going, 'Take it off! Take it fucking off!'

I'm standing there thinking, see, this is what ends up happening when you try to do shit on the cheap.

'It was for *my* big day!' Julie's going. '*My* big day!'

'Ross!' Sorcha goes. 'Get her off her!' which I decide I probably should do, especially when Honor storts getting distressed about what she's seeing – two natives basically going at it. I hand the kid to Sorcha, then I grab Julie's fingers and try to unlock them from the – it's a gay word – but *fabric*?

The problem is, she's unbelievably strong, roysh, and the angrier she gets, the tighter her grip becomes. At the same time, Claire and Sorcha are both screaming at me to do something. They're going, 'Do something, Ross! Do something!'

So I end up grabbing Julie from behind, by the two shoulders, putting one foot on Claire's chest, then sort of, like, pulling Julie backwards with every bit of strength in my body.

The next thing any of us hears is this humungous rip.

Claire goes flying in one direction and hits the focking wall. I go the other way and land sprawled on the kitchen floor, with Julie on top of me, still holding two pieces of the focking dress.

Sorcha helps Claire up. I hear her go, 'My mum will fix it – she's an amazing seamstress,' then the two of them – get this – just leg it out of the house, leaving me there, still wrestling on the floor with Julie.

She's strong, it has to be said, with a bite like a focking donkey, though I manage eventually to get the better of her, thanks to my superior fitness, then stumble, battered and bloodied, out into the gorden. Claire, still in the dress, has the engine of the Clio idling and the front-passenger door open.

I dive in, head first, then manage somehow to get the door closed and Claire doesn't drop below a hundred Ks an hour until we return to civilization.

'Why me?' Malindi goes.

God, she's thick as pig shit. Which is saying something coming from me. How she made it in PR is a focking mystery. 'Because it's got to be birds that Sorcha doesn't know,' I go. 'Otherwise she'll get suspicious.'

This is us in the Brown Thomas café, by the way.

She takes the money off the table like she's just woken up out of a twenty-year coma and has just clapped eyes on the euro for the first time. 'I haven't seen you for, like, two years . . .'

'Like I said, I wasn't ready to go down that whole relationship road.'

'Presumably because you were married – which you failed to mention by the way in the three months we were seeing each other.'

'Look, I get *why* you're pissed off?'

'Then you ring me, totally out of the blue, ask me to meet you for coffee and you offer me five hundred euros to spend in your wife's shop . . .'

I'm on the point of actually giving in. I go to take the money out of her hand but she whips it away quickly. 'I'm not saying I *won't* do it,' she goes. 'In fact, yeah, I'll accept this as compensation for the way you treated me.'

I laugh and I tell her fair enough. She drains the rest of her cappuccino, then focks off without saying another word.

I'm left just sitting there. I'm actually just texting Fionn – he's totally ashamed of his antics in Edinburgh, by the way – when all of a sudden I hear this sort of, like, squeaking noise, like a wheel that needs oiling, then I look up to see Blathin approaching, her old dear pushing her in the chair.

I'm there, 'Hey, how the hell are you?' trying to, I suppose, gloss over what happened the last time we saw each other. 'Do you want to join me for a coffee?'

Blathin's old dear pushes her right up to me – you could say she pushes her into position – then, without any warning, Bla hits me the most unbelievable slap across the face. Even the sound of it is, you'd have to say, perfect, and you can see people looking up from their bruschettas and their organic fish cakes, in admiration as much as curiosity.

It's pretty clear there's been a development between her and Ro. She goes, 'I know where he gets it from,' which is almost certainly unfair on him.

I look up at Amanda, as if to say, hey, this shit happens every day – they're only kids, for fock's sake.

That's when the second slap – *her*, this time – reddens the other side of my face. 'And *I've* been waiting to give you that,' she goes, 'since the day of the party.'

Amanda's sort of, like, reversing Blathin out of there when my phone comes alive on the table. I immediately recognize the ring as Ro's – Omar Little whistling 'The Farmer in the Dell' – and Bla must recognize it too, roysh, because she just goes, 'Tell him to have a nice focking life!' at the top of her voice, as her old dear pushes her back though Gifts and Household, towards the elevator.

I answer. Of course everyone in the place is glued to the focking drama now. 'Rosser?' he goes, in a sort of, like, *hushed* tone?

I'm there, 'Hey, Ro.'

'She's arthur findin out, Rosser.'

'Okay.'

'Yeah, you were reet. Kandra opened her mouth.'

'I thought she would.'

'She's goin bleaten mental, Rosser. Ine stayin out of her way.'

'You're learning, Ro. You're definitely learning.'

Woof!

   Woof, woof!

   Woof, woof, woof!

   For fock's sake!

   Woof!

   Woof, woof!

Christy Moore, I've gotten strangely used to. Damien Demspey – I can learn to live with him. Even Christy Dignam, singing 'Wish You Were Here' on permanent repeat from one end of the night to the other – in a funny way, I think I'd miss it if it ever stopped.

But that focking borking coming from next door's balcony. It's, like, they shouldn't even *have* a dog in there?

It's eleven o'clock in the morning and I'm wide awake and I end up jumping out of the bed – I admit it – in a bit of a rage. Before I even know what I'm doing, I'm suddenly out in the hallway, hammering on Terry and Larry's door, thinking it's about time I told them a thing or two.

It's Terry who answers – he's, like, the older of the two? 'Ah, howiya,' is his opening line, then he sort, of, like, totally wrongfoots me, roysh, by inviting me in.

Their gaff, I straight away notice, is a lot nicer than mine – Eddie focking Torsney – and every room is like one of those ready-made demonstration rooms you see in Ikea. 'So,' Terry goes, leaning against the exact same Lagan worktop that Sorcha has, 'how's effery little ting?'

I'm there, 'Not great. There's something I wanted to . . .'

'Keepin the head abuff wather, says you.'

'What?'

'Keepin the head abuff wather . . .'

'Er, yeah . . .'

'Like the rest of us, wha?'

'Yeah, I suppose.'

'So this is, wha, a soshiddle call?'

I'm like, 'Er, no, as I was about to say, there's a couple of things I wanted to talk to you about. Look, I know we didn't get off to the best of storts . . .'

'Wha, you threatenin to call the loar on us?'

'Yeah, I admit it – a lot of that was down to me, jumping to certain conclusions, because of the way you dress, the way you talk, blah blah blah. The other thing was, I actually got conned out of my previous place, which is how I ended up getting dumped next to . . . well, next to you.'

It's hord to tell from his expression exactly what he's thinking. He's just like, 'Continue . . .'

This guy must be, like, five or six years younger than me. And here I am having to explain myself to him.

I'm there, 'I think we'd all agree that it's not an ideal situation . . .'

'How do you mee-in?'

'In that we're, like, very different people.'

'Diffordent?'

'Er – *obviously*? But, for better or worse, we *have* ended up living beside each other, and if we're going to get along we're both going to have to put in the effort.'

He gets suddenly serious. He turns the handle on the Alsvik single-lever mixer-tap, which *was*, like, dripping? 'Is there somethin in pertickiller?' he goes. 'Somethin dats bodderin ya?'

'Well, okay, being honest, it's the dog.'

'Rooney?'

'If that's what he's called, yeah. You must be able to hear the borking yourselves . . . .'

'Laddy!' he suddenly shouts, without taking his eyes off me – he's obviously calling Larry. 'Come in hee-er a minute, will ya?'

His facial expression hasn't changed, roysh, but there's, like, a definite shift in the mood all of a sudden.

Larry walks into the kitchen. He immediately storts looking me up and down, sizing me up.

Terry keeps just staring at me. He's there, 'Tell Laddy what you're joost arthur sayin to me.'

I laugh, roysh, to try to, like, *defuse* the situation? 'Look, it's not a biggie,' I go. 'It's just your dog . . .'

'Rooney?' Larry goes.

'Yeah, *if* that's his name. It's just his borking's driving me a little bit mental.'

The two of them look at each other and it's like they've got this secret means of, I don't know, communication. 'He'd be veddy hoort to hear dat,' Terry goes, 'wootent he, Laddy?'

Larry nods. 'Veddy hoort – fact, Tetty, I tink we should let dis fella hee-er tell him to he's bleaten face.'

I'm there, 'Goys, like I said, this only needs to be as big a deal as we make it.'

Larry's not listening, though. He wanders over to the sliding door leading out on to the balcony, then pulls back the net curtain.

I end up having to do a focking double-take. Out there, beyond that sheet of glass, is *the* most terrifying animal I've ever seen. It's a Rottweiler, roysh, except it happens to be built like a focking tiger and it's, like, pacing back and forth, we're talking, I don't know, half a tonne of rippling muscles and pure pent-up focking anger.

As soon as he spots me through the window, he suddenly stops pacing. His eyes go wide and you can see him sort of, like, adjusting his back legs, presumably getting ready to make

a lunge. Even through the double glazing, I can hear him breathing – he growls in the same way that other dogs exhale.

I tell them I'd better be getting back – meant no offence, blah blah blah – when all of a sudden, without any warning, Larry just flicks the catch and slides the door open.

All I hear is, like, a roar, then I'm suddenly like that dude in *Jurassic Pork*, who was sitting on the shitter when the Tyrannosaurus Rex came through the door. Larry dives one way, Terry dives the other and this – literally – monster comes tearing towards me.

It's honestly like being hit by a focking Subaru Forester. All the air disappears from my lungs and I go down like a dynamited building, with this savage beast tearing at me, while I'm kicking and thrashing, going, 'Not the face! Not the face!'

Gggrrr! Gggrrr! Gggrrr!

I make two or three attempts to get back on my feet, but he's too strong for me, pinning me down with his big muscly legs, and in the end I just curl up into a ball, resigned to being basically eaten.

Gggrrr! Gggrrr! Gggrrr!

It's then, roysh, that I hear the laughter – Larry and Terry, breaking their actual holes. I do, like, a quick inventory, if that's the word, to see what bits I'm missing. The answer, I realize, is nothing. It's suddenly obvious that I haven't been bitten and that the only thing I can *actually* feel is Rooney's dead weight on top of me and his warm, sickly sweet breath on my neck.

I manage to just about move my neck to have a look and that's when I realize that he's not savaging me at all.

He's focking humping me.

Gggrrr! Gggrrr! Gggrrr! Gggrrr! Gggrrr! Gggrrr!

Terry and Larry are pretty much on the floor laughing.

I'm going, 'Get him off me! Get him off me!' looking at the animal hanging on to my focking leg for dear life, with his eyes rolled back and his tongue flapping around like a focked roller blind in a Force 10 gale.

Gggrrr! Gggrrr! Gggrrr!

The two boys take their time before they help me as well. It eventually takes all their combined strength to drag him off me, then they pull him – still panting like a focking phone pest – back out on to the balcony, where he regathers his breath and, for all I know, lights up a cigarette.

Terry helps me to my feet, while Larry goes, 'I tink Rooney has a ting for you,' which seems to be the funniest line either of them has ever heard.

This shiver goes up my spine. I head for the door, too scared to even check whether he's left a deposit on my chinos.

'Hee-er,' Terry goes, 'I'll make shewer he's a gentleman and rings ya.'

5. A Closed Shop

Danuta Jankauskas is the new Ross O'Carroll-Kelly. Or that's the word that JP and his old man have been putting around the Merrion Inn.

See, when I heard they'd hired this six-foot, nineteen-year-old Russian stunner to help them with the old repossession business, my instant reaction – like everyone else's – was that the poor girl was going to have her orse handled more times than a prize cow at auction.

Because Mr Conroy is a filthbag – always has been.

But then, roysh, when the stories storted to filter back to me about how amazing she was at the ort of actually repossessing shit, I thought, no, no, no – this is, like, a ruse? They're using her as bait to try to get me to take that job offer, knowing how much I love a challenge.

I suppose what I'm admitting is that I was curious. If she really *was* all she was being cracked up to be, well, I had to, like, see it for myself?

When I first clapped eyes on her, sitting in the front of the flatbed truck, I'll be honest, roysh, I actually laughed. There was no way I could take her seriously. She wasn't six foot, she was taller – six-two, six-three – and a ringer – and I *mean* a ringer – for Maria Kirilenko.

I opened the passenger door and sort of, like, indicated for her to scooch up, but she just looked at me, roysh, coldly. Wasn't *even* coldly– this was, like, contempt, like I was a fly she could reduce to mush if only she could be orsed.

So I ended up having to get in the driver's side and I sat in the middle. JP was driving this particular day because his old man was in court – I presumed fighting one of the many sexual harassment cases that were all that remained of his once famous estate agency business.

Now, no one could honestly say I *didn't* make the effort with Danuta? I asked her where exactly in Russia she was from but she said Novosibirsk like she could have been telling me to go fock myself. I even cracked on that I'd heard of it – nice to be nice – but she just rolled her eyes, then under her breath went, 'Stoopit boy,' and storted fiddling about with her actual iPhone.

I turned to JP – we were halfway to Shankill, at this stage – and looked at him as if to say, *what* is her issue? He just shook his head, as if to say, fair focks to you for making a major effort, Ross – you're actually great like that – but do not even *think* about going there.

To change the subject, he said he met Sorcha coming out of Crunch Fitness last night. 'She was in much better form,' he went. 'She seems to think this recession was just a blip.'

I was there, 'Er, really?'

'She said that if the evidence of *her* shop was anything to go by, we've definitely turned a corner as a nation . . .'

'That's, er, good to hear.'

'And *she* did that course, didn't she?'

'Focking Smurfit School, yeah.'

'Well, she says consumer confidence has returned with a vengeance. People are back spending.'

I certainly was. It was only, like, the first week in June and I was already down nearly eighteen grand. The Cora Venus from the Rosa Parks move was disappearing fast. The one upside, of course, was that Sorcha hadn't been making a holy tit of herself on Grafton Street. Still, I knew I was going to have to switch from clothes and shoes to bags and accessories if I was going to keep the illusion of, I suppose, prosperity going for any longer.

While this conversation was going on, Danuta was basically mute, except for the odd time when she looked up from her iPhone to, I don't know, pronounce comment under her breath on the driving skills of other drivers on the road. 'Indicate, you fugging beetch,' she'd go, or 'You harr in ze fast lane why – because you harr turning right in fife miles time?'

To break the tension as much as anything else, I asked JP what he was even repossessing today. He said a bouncy castle and I was suddenly sat there wondering what would a bouncy castle cost and is *that* how bad things have actually gone?

The next thing I knew, we were pulling up outside a red-brick gaff in the middle of some random housing estate in – like I said – Skankill. JP killed the engine.

'It's a *big* bouncy castle,' he went, obviously reading my mind. 'Three grands' worth.'

I thought, even so . . .

We all hopped out of the truck. I had a sly look at Danuta, who, with her hand, was smoothing out the creases of her skinny jeans while looking – being honest – incredible.

JP had barely set foot in the front gorden when this woman – if anything, you'd say she was an older version of Jordana Brewster – came pegging it out of the gaff, going, 'No, please! Not today!'

It has to be said, it took me kind of unawares.

JP, roysh, did his best to blank her and it's *me* she ended up telling that it was Lila and Giovanna's joint birthday porty and could we not show some humanity by coming back some other day.

I went, 'It's actually nothing to do with me. I'm along for the ride,' and then – speaking of rides – I turned around to see what Danuta was up to. She was still standing next to the truck – get this – checking out her focking manicure.

I laughed – *had* to.

I went, 'Your old man was right, JP. She's a real go-getter,' then I followed him around the back of the gaff, while Jordana Brewster chased after us, calling me in particular a selection of names, none of which was especially original.

JP wasn't shitting me when he described it as a *big* bouncy castle. It was literally the biggest one I'd ever seen – we're talking two storeys high – and definitely modelled on Princess Fiona's one in, like, the first *Shrek* movie? See, I watched all that shit with Honor, which is how I know.

There must have been, like, fifty or sixty kids – we're talking half the actual neighbourhood – playing on the thing, jumping up and down, hanging out of the windows and blahdy blahdy blah.

Kids being basically kids.

There were, like, ten, maybe eleven other parents there too and they were suddenly looking at me and the J-Dog as if to say, who the fock are these two suddenly arriving?

I was just, like, hanging back, wondering how he was going to clear all of the kids out before he deflated the thing. By this stage, roysh, the Jordana Brewster one had copped that JP *was* in actual chorge and she storted to concentrate her anger on him. She was, like, stood in front of him, asking him why he couldn't let the children, no, the kiddies, have one day – one last day – of fun in the thing, had he *ever* been young himself and did he have *any* Christian compassion in him whatsoever?

Personally, I thought the questions were storting to hit home. The seminary, or whatever you call it, left its mork on him.

I was leaning against the side of the old Hampton Orangery, watching JP struggle with his conscience in the face of this serious guilt-tripping. That's when I heard the clop, clop, clop of Danuta's high-heeled boots on the gravel pathway and I turned to see her coming around the side of the gaff, her walk as cool and confident as that of a basic catwalk model.

Everybody turned to see her and, once they saw her, they couldn't take their eyes off her, because she was – like I said – a sight worth seeing. Everyone – we're talking men *and* women – just stood in total awe as this magnificent creature strode, all sultry but full of – you'd have to say – purpose, towards the air-pump that was keeping the castle inflated and then, without even batting one of her three-inch eyelashes, kicked the switch to the off position.

The sound of the motor stopped and the walls of the castle immediately storted to fall.

The gorden was suddenly filled with the sounds of children screaming. Except the adults, roysh, were too in shock to move. And I'm included in that.

It took, like, fifteen seconds for the entire structure to collapse. Two or three kids managed to, like, jump clear in time, but the rest of them were trapped in this, I don't know, latex landslide.

It was only then that the parents got over the initial shock phase and storted to react. It was like watching the Red Cross going in after one of those, I suppose, tragedies that Sorcha's always contributing money to, sifting through the folds, pulling out crying children missing their shoes.

I was suddenly thinking about Honor – as in, what if *she* was trapped in there? – and for a moment I was actually considering helping with the rescue effort.

But that was when I sensed the mood of the gathering suddenly turning from one of shock and panic to one of – you'd have to say – anger. 'You focking animals!' one of the parents suddenly shouted at Danuta.

I looked over at JP, who was watching all of this with a worrying lack of concern.

'Dude!' I went – except I had to say it a second time before he even heard me. 'Dude!' and then I gave him the eyes, as if to say, we better make like shepherds and get the flock out of here.

He shook his head at me and that's when Danuta opened up on one of the parents.

'Who harr you to call us aneemals?' she went. 'You cannot pay, you fugging giff beck. Git your fugging cheeldoren out of there – we wheel be beck een one hour to collect,' and then, with a flick of her hair, she walked – all hips and shoulders – back to the truck.

Me and JP followed a few paces behind. *He* put his orm around my shoulder and said it had finally happened – we're talking the thunderbolt.

He said he was in love.

Rebel TV chef Fionnuala O'Carroll-Kelly was at it again yesterday – shopping up a storm while the rest of the country faced up to the gravest crisis to hit Ireland since the Potato Famine . . .

This story is, like, splashed across the front page of *The PAYE Daily Monkey* or whatever it's called.

The former multimillion-selling author and host of RTÉ's FO'CK Cooking *is continuing to hold firm in the face of pressure from station bosses to accept a revised pay deal. And while hundreds of thousands of Irish people face up to life on the dole – and even on the streets – the sixty-year-old presenter . . .*

Sixty? I'm thinking, Jesus Christ, are they going to add five years to her age every week until she finally caves?

. . . sent a clear message to the rest of the country yesterday – FO'CK the lot of you!

That's good, you'd have to say.

Our photographer captured the millionaire socialite in the midst of yet another of her famous shopping binges yesterday afternoon, this time in Dundrum Town Centre, where in little more than an hour she spent a STAGGERING €38 on a miniature ornamental bird cage in House of Fraser, an ASTONISHING €22 on a bottle of Re-charge Black Pepper Bodywash in Molton Brown and a MIND-BLOWING €54 on a copy of Andrew Pern's Black Pudding and Foie Gras *in Hughes & Hughes.*

Asked how he felt about the idea of O'Carroll-Kelly lording it up on what is essentially public money, unemployed father-of-six Damien Fennessy, who lost his job when Dell closed in Limerick, said he was 'sickened'.

Fighting back tears, he said, 'Share the pain is the message we keep hearing from our politicians – well, she's certainly not feeling any. Black pepper body wash? If I brought that into the house, my kids would probably eat it.'

Fionnuala had no words of comfort for Damien and tens of thousands more like him yesterday. Asked by our photographer for a comment, she simply said, 'I'm having a wonderful day, thank you.'

I'm still actually laughing at this when my mobile suddenly rings and, by sheer coincidence, there's some bird on the line saying she's from, like, RTÉ and shit? I presume at first that she's ringing to tell me the old dear's had a sudden meltdown and been corted off to the booby house. Except it turns out to be not that at all.

This bird's from, like, *Nationwide*, that programme that's always on after the news, with that whole Country People Do the Darnedest Things vibe?

She tells me they're doing an item on the way in which the downturn in the economy has narrowed the social divisions within Irish life, even in terms of simple propinquity. Of course you can picture me. I caught so little of what she said that I couldn't tell you whether she'd even finished her sentence, so I give it a good ten seconds before I decide that it's safe to answer.

'Er, is there actually another way you could put that?'

She has the cheek to laugh. 'Yes,' she goes, 'we're doing a feature on how the recession has – if you like – taken the various socio-economic classes, which became polarized during the years of the boom, and thrown them back together again.'

It's a good job I'm already lying down. I'm there, 'Er, give it one last shot.'

'Okay, for instance, I don't know if you saw it but in Galway yesterday there were engineers, solicitors, quantity surveyors, queuing up alongside non-skilled workers for Subway sandwich franchises.'

The only reason I'm entertaining this, by the way, is because she has, like, a cute voice and I'm guessing she looks a little bit like Leighton Meester.

'In addition to that,' she goes, 'a lot of people who bought apartments when the property market was at its most buoyant are suddenly discovering themselves living alongside people who've been housed by the Department of Social Welfare in the exact same properties . . .'

I suddenly get it. 'Someone's clearly been talking,' I tell her.

She doesn't seem at all embarrassed. She said she overheard my old dear telling Miriam O'Callaghan that I was living next door to people who challenged the notion of human beings as evolution's final word. I actually didn't think she cared that much.

'What we'd like to do,' she goes, 'is maybe talk to you *and* your neighbours about some of the tensions that are perhaps involved.'

I'm there, 'Have you asked them?'

'We have, yeah.'

'And they're up for it?'

'Yeah, they're happy to be interviewed.'

'Okay, then I probably *should* say something. Warn the public to be vigilant – or *they'll* end up living next door to skanks. This is all going to depend obviously on whether it's Mary Kennedy doing the interviews, or, I don't know . . . the dude.'

She says it's almost certainly going to be Mary. Then I tell her I think I could *definitely* add something to this whole debate. Come on over.

The second she's off the phone, I'm out of that bed like I've pissed it. I give the place an unbelievable going-over, Flash Wiping every surface, throwing all the clutter into the hot press, even making three or four attempts to flush the toilet.

To cut a long story short, two hours later, roysh, there's a knock on the door and I practically tear the thing off its hinges I open it that fast. And there I am – at long last, is the way I feel – face to face with Mary Kennedy.

'Hey,' I go, smooth and nice, yet at the same a *little* bit flirty?

'Hello,' she goes, sticking out her hand. I laugh and tell her I *think* we can do better than that? I kiss her on either cheek, then I think, ah, what the hell, and I repeat the dose.

Of course Terry and Larry hear the commotion in the hallway and come out of their gaff at that exact moment. 'Jaysus,' Terry, naturally, *has* to go, 'what counthree are *you* living in – Ferrants?' trying to make a show of me in front of her.

I'm there, 'Er, this is how *civilized* people greet each other? We don't all shout, "Hee-er, Wanker!" like you did to me in the corpork this morning.'

Mary laughs. 'Please,' she goes, 'save it until we start filming!'

Terry's like, 'Ah, we widdle, don't you woody. We've plenty to bleaten say, so we have.'

'He toordened eer dog gay?' Larry goes.

I'm there, 'I did *not* turn their dog gay.'

Terry backs him up, of course. 'Ya did, yeah – pooer Rooney. Do you not member him tryin to royid ya?'

'Of course I remember him trying to ride me . . . But *I* had nothing to do with turning him gay. He was obviously gay before.'

'I'd luffen to see ya say dat to he's face,' Larry goes.

Mary laughs, then says she's going to interview me first, then pop next door to talk to them in, say, twenty minutes? The two boys are like, 'Feerd enuff, Meerdy,' then she breezes past me into the gaff, the sweet smell of – I'm pretty sure – *Fifth Avenue* by Elizabeth Orden following her like the contrails of an F15.

Oh, there's also some director dude, two cameramen, then one or two, I don't know, technicians or whatever they're called, who set up everything while Mary and me shoot the shit. She asks me if I think my old dear will ever write again and I tell her, with a bit of luck, no. Then they sit us down, mike us up, and *she* storts hitting me with the hord questions.

'You and your neighbours, you're from, I think it's fair to say, very different backgrounds . . .' she goes.

I laugh.

'You can say that again,' I go, trying to give not only Mary, but also the viewers at home, a little flavour of what I'm like.

She's there, 'You're from quite a privileged background.'

'And proud of it.'

'Money. Status. Private, rugby-playing secondary school.'

'All of that.'

'I suppose what I'm asking,' Mary goes, keeping her eye on the bigger picture, like the pro that she is, 'is how have you all been rubbing along, if you like, now that you're neighbours here in the stunning, stunning Rosa Parks?'

'That's a very good question, Mary. Well, you saw us out in the hallway there. Sometimes it's like World War . . . I don't know – whatever one we're up to. Look, I'm not going to

181

make any secret of it. I gave up a perfectly good aportment in the old Spirit of Gracious Living to move here. I got stitched up in a major way. And as you can imagine, I wasn't exactly a happy camper when I found out I was sharing the penthouse floor with – no offence – the lowest of the low . . .'

Mary seems a bit taken aback by that. 'Well, on the contrary,' she goes, 'I think a great number of people would take offence at that description.'

I'm losing her, so I decide to reel it in a bit.

'Yeah, no, to go back to your question about the main differences between us, I'd say the hours we keep is a major one. See, I tend to do a lot of my sleeping during the day, when they're up and about and making a lot of noise, doing whatever it is they do in there. Then at night, when I'm playing Xbox or listening to music or – as *has* been known to happen occasionally, Mary – entertaining female company . . .'

I give the camera a little wink.

'. . . *they're* hammering on the walls, telling *me* to keep the noise down.'

I continue in this vein for, like, twenty minutes or so, giving it to her and the viewers as it basically is. And it's *all* good stuff – take it from someone who watches a lot of TV.

Anyway, it's *as* they're packing up their shit that one of the technician dudes turns around to me and happens to mention that I'm a brave man. I just nod. I can take a compliment.

I'm there, 'Like I said, I didn't *choose* to live beside them? But you can't just roll over either. Otherwise, the next thing you know, they're sticking a pigeon loft on your balcony.'

I say my goodbyes to Mary, then she disappears in next door. 'Good luck,' I shout after her.

'No, no,' the technician dude goes to me, 'what I mean is the way you speak to them. You know who they are, don't you?'

I'm there, 'Er, no . . .' genuinely not having a clue.

'Well,' he goes, 'I could be wrong . . .'

I don't like the sound of this.

'I mean, I thought I recognized them out in the hallway there.'

I'm like, 'Who are they?' the concern pretty obvious in my voice.

'Well,' he goes, 'I *think* they call them the New Westies.'

I'm there, 'Er, please tell me you're shitting me.'

'No,' he goes, 'you know the crowd I'm talking about.'

Know them? They've been all over the news for the past two weeks. I'm there, '*Blah blah blah was believed to have been murdered as part of the ongoing feud between the New Westies and Skobie Gang B . . .*'

'Exactly,' he goes. 'But, like I said, I could be wrong.'

'Holdall' is one of those words you only ever hear used in relation to criminal activity. I'm wondering – as I watch, through the spyhole, the comings and goings of the two next door – whether anyone in history has ever had an honest reason to own one.

Of course, my old man made pretty much the same point when he ran in the local elections on, like, a law and order platform, arguing that the way to stamp out working-class crime was not better gun control but better holdall control, and that those who deal in these 'instruments of misery' should be required – *by law* – to keep a register of anyone who buys one.

It's actually the old man who flashes into my mind as I take in this fish-eye view of Terry and Larry making their seventh trip up from the underground corpork in the space of an hour, each time carrying one of these, again, holdalls in either hand, stuffed to practically bursting point with, well, I can only guess what, but I'm pretty sure it's not shopping.

I suddenly hear Omar whistling. I pull my eye away from the spyhole. It's Ro returning my call from last night. The poor kid's still got the major guilts, I can instantly tell. Of course, he's young. He'll get over it when *he* gets his first straight red from a bird.

'She sent me the cheerm bracelet back,' he instantly goes. 'The one from Tiffany's.'

See, that's changed from my time. The Mounties *always* held on to the shit you gave them. Same as Alex and Holy Child Killiney. It was the Loretos – Dalkey, Foxrock, the Green – who'd usually fock stuff back at you.

'Why don't you, er, give it to Kandra?' I go, trying to put myself in his shoes.

He's there, 'Ine not seein Kandra. I told you, Rosser, I was only wit her that once.'

'Well, hang on to it for the moment,' I go. 'There's going to be loads more girls, Ro – believe me.'

Through the door I hear the lift ping. I look out through the spyhole again. The two boys are going back down to the corpork to fill up their holdalls again. I tell Ronan I have a question for him.

'Have you ever heard of two – I suppose – goys, called – are you ready? –*Terry and Larry Tuhill*?'

He laughs for maybe the first time in months. 'Tetty and Laddy Tuhill?'

'Yeah, now think carefully, Ro.'

'I doatent have to think. *They're* the New Westies, Rosser . . .'

'Are you absolutely sure?'

'It was in that *Sunday Wurdled* you brought me. They're into all sorts of shit, them boys. Thrugs, guns . . .'

'Shit!'

'From what I hear, Tetty's the Avon Beerksdale of the operation and Laddy's apposed to be the Stringer Bell . . .'

'Fock! I think I may have, er, made a few derogatory remarks about them on RTÉ's *Nationwide* . . .'

'What the fook did you do that for?'

'It's a long story. It's supposed to be going out on Friday . . .'

'Rosser, them boys don't dance.'

'Er, I *know* that, Ro? I'm the one living next door to them . . .'

There's, like, silence on the other end, but I can almost hear him smiling down the phone. 'You're wha?'

'Why do you think I'm shitting babyfood here? I thought they were just a couple of hormless skanks!'

He cracks his hole laughing. I'm glad to to hear he's suddenly over Bla. 'Here,' he goes, 'I might call into them – welcome them to the neighbourhood and that.'

I end up losing it and letting a roar out of me. 'You stay away from that underworld scum!'

It's at that exact point, roysh, that there's a sudden knock on the door. Not *even* a knock, more like a hammering, like someone's hitting it with the heel of their hand.

I'm thinking, shit, they definitely heard what I just shouted. Ronan's hung up, by the way, and left me to it.

Thump! Thump! Thump! Thump! Thump! Thump! Thump!

The only thing to be done, I decide, is to get into bed, get under the covers and pretend not to be in. But the hammering just continues.

Thump! Thump! Thump! Thump! Thump! Thump! Thump!

I put my eye up to the spyhole and it's with a sense of massive relief I discover that it's not Terry and Larry at all, it's actually, like, Erika? I open the door and I'm suddenly there going, 'Come in, come in,' but as usual, the happy feeling of seeing her lasts all of five seconds.

'What the hell is going on?' is her opener.

I tell her I was just about to pack. I have to be out of the country before *Nationwide* hits the screens on Friday.

'I'm talking about Sorcha,' she goes. 'I'm talking about the shop,' and I automatically look away.

'Yeah,' I go, 'I, er, heard it's suddenly flying . . .'

I sit down and flick on the TV. Lisa Cannon's catching up with *X Factor* finalist Eoghan Quigg.

Erika could bore a hole in my forehead with the look she's still giving me. 'Bit unusual, isn't it?'

'Unusual? As in?'

'The economy's still in freefall. Retail sales are at a twenty-year low. The Grafton Street area is full of vacant units. A lot of shops are only surviving because they're having all-year-round, fifty-percent-off sales . . .'

'Your point being?'

'My *point* being that in the past month, Sorcha's turnover is the same as it was for the *twelve* months of last year.'

She's shorp, I'll give her that.

'Well,' I try to go, 'it might have been her taking the message to the streets that day. There might be something in that shit she was saying about people actually *wanting* quality at a time like this?'

There's no bullshitting this girl, though. She knows me too well. She just stares at me until I end up having to look at her. And once I do that, there's nowhere to hide. 'Okay,' I end up having to go, 'I've been giving money to birds to spend in the shop . . .'

She's delighted, of course. 'That's what I thought. These are all your . . . *tarts*, are they, who've been coming in?'

I actually resent that word. I'm like, 'Pretty much, yeah. How did you know?'

She smiles but not in, like, a good way? 'They were all of a type, Ross.'

Maybe I should have sent in one or two hogs, even just to keep it realistic.

'So now the only other question,' she goes, 'is why?'

I shrug. 'Sorcha's old man threatened me.'

'Threatened you? Physically?'

'No, although he's done that plenty of times in the past. No, he threatened to ruin me – as in, financially? I think one or two of his barrister mates saw her on Grafton Street with the focking megaphone. You can't blame them, they were probably thinking, er, *how* much did it cost Edmund to put her through Mount Anville again?'

'And he said he'd ruin you?'

'Yeah, in the divorce. Said unless I got her off the focking street, he was going to make sure *I* was the one who ended up paying her debts. Can I just point out, Erika, I was the one telling her to close the shop . . .'

In fairness to her, she agrees with me. She sits down, roysh, suddenly not so aggressive – more like an actual *sister*, in fact?

'I even had to trade down,' I go, 'just to get the old Hilary Swank off her back. That's how I ended up living in this focking . . . building site . . .'

'What *is* that barking?' she goes.

I shake my head. 'It's next door's dog. He's actually supposed to be in love with me. And that's not me being big-headed.'

She looks at me like it's the most focked-up thing she's ever heard.

I'm there, 'Erika, you're not going to tell her, are you?' and she just laughs.

'Of course I'm going to tell her.'

'What, just to be a bitch?'

'No, *not* to be a bitch . . . Ross, have you even thought about what's going to happen when you run out of money?'

'Well,' I go, 'I've enough to maybe see it through the summer. I figured the recession would probably be over by then. Do you know how long they usually last?'

She shakes her head.

'This one,' she goes, 'might even outlive us. And all you're doing is giving Sorcha false hope and putting off the inevitable. You know she stood up at the AGM of the City Centre Business Association last weekend and said the recession was nothing more than a media invention.'

'And how did that go down?'

'As well as you'd expect . . . You can't go on doing this, Ross. Besides, I've better things to do with my time than to go on serving bogus customers in some shop that's already failed.'

I'm there, 'She's going to go chicken jalfrezi. I mean, probably worse than the time I nailed her little sister.'

'Let *me* talk to her,' she goes. 'If she knows that your intentions were good . . .'

I end up just shrugging. There's at least two very large shitstorms blowing this way and deep down I just know that I'm about to get splattered.

'She swims. And I don't just mean as a hobby. When she was only, like, fifteen, she was a first reserve in the Russian team for the 2004 Olympics – I *think* in the 200-metres individual medley . . .'

This is JP, by the way, totally smitten with Danuta, only, what, two dates in?

We've had her Cuban fusion cooking. We've had her two Konik ponies called Raisa and Vladena. We've had her encyclopedic knowledge of Russian ballet.

'What about the age thing?' Fionn goes.

That did cross my mind as well. She's, like, ten years younger than him?

'It's not a thing,' JP goes. 'It's not like going out with a nineteen-year-old girl from, say, Dublin – Uggs and Facebook and robbing drinks at last orders. Danuta's different. You've met her, Ross, she's . . .'

She's horder than Dolphin's Born, is what she is. I don't say that, though. I just go, 'Stunning,' and keep up the fake smile.

'Exactly,' he goes, 'and it's also nice to go out with someone with a different, I don't know, worldview to your own. I mean, she's got me doing all sorts of crazy shit. She's got me, for instance, reading Nabokov . . .'

I roll my eyes – can't help it.

Fionn, though, says he loves Nabokov. He *would*, of course. Even when he's on his summer holidays, he can't help being a schoolteacher.

'I told you she was studying literature in Trinity, didn't I?'

'Yes,' I go. 'At least twice.'

'What I *don't* get,' Fionn goes, 'is how she ended up doing repossessions.'

I'm thinking, if you saw her in action, Fionn, you'd get it straight away.

'Well,' JP goes, 'that's *her* old man's line of work too – as in, back in Russia? I mean, she's been helping him from the time she was, I don't know, ten or something. So when she saw my old man's classified ad in *In Dublin*, she thought, hey, job's a good un . . .'

We're all tanning it, it has to be said, for a Thursday night in Café en Seine.

'Goys,' I go, 'maybe try to remember to keep your clothes on tonight, will you?' and they both laugh, in fairness to them.

JP's there, 'McGahy never found out, Fionn, no?' and Fionn goes, 'No. God knows *what* he'd have said.'

I'm like, 'Would have been another excuse for him to hate rugby, I can tell you that for free.'

'You know,' Fionn goes, 'I don't regret it – what we did. I know I'd drunk an awful lot, and, yeah, I was embarrassed initially, probably worried for my job as well. But it felt good to cut loose for once – like we used to when we were young.'

'Well, some of us never stopped,' I go. 'Just *as* a matter of interest, have you had any, let's just call it, trade since we had our little chat?'

JP's there, 'What's all this about?'

'I was telling Fionn it's time to get back in the game. He needs to be back out there – like you – getting down and sweaty again.'

Fionn's there, 'Ross! Jesus!' all embarrassed.

I'm there, 'Okay, left hammer, sitting at that high table over there – she's drinking, I think I'm right in saying, a Cosmo? She's been giving you the deep meaningfuls all night.'

He has a sly George Hook over his shoulder and turns back with a look of, like, total disgust on his boat. 'You pick out the only girl in here tonight who's wearing glasses?'

I'm there, 'Well, I'm just saying, you've got to have something in common – you always read that in these magazines, don't you, that that kind of shit's important?'

'We *are* allowed to breed outside our species, you know?'

'Whoa, beam me up, Snotty! I'm *actually* trying to help? As it happens, I don't even think she's *that* horrendous – nice shopfrontage on it.'

He's there, 'Well, I can look after myself, thanks all the same.'

I'm like, 'Fair enough. Oh, by the way, did I tell you, I might soon be joining Oisinn in hiding?'

The two goys look at me as if to say, whoa, don't say that Rossmeister, you're needed around here.

I'm there, 'Yeah, no, all of those people who said that I'd one day get my comeuppance – they might be about to finally have their moment. See, I've been paying people – exes of mine, basically – to spend money in Sorcha's shop . . .'

'Why?' they both go, at the exact same time.

'It's a long story. Anyway, she's about to find out about it. On top of that, well, I've said some pretty horsh things about the two yahoos next door on tomorrow night's *Nationwide*. And then of course it turns out that they're both major underworld figures . . .'

They're both just staring at me with their mouths wide open.

'So,' I go, 'if I'm suddenly found floating in the sea, chopped up in a milk churn, with my balls in my mouth, you'll know why. And that's just what Sorcha's going to do to me!'

Of course it turns out that the reason Fionn and JP are staring at me open-mouthed is that she happens to be standing right behind me. See, I was just *born* unlucky?

I spin around on the stool.

'Don't bother, Ross,' she goes. 'Erika told me everything,' and she looks at me like she knows she *could* actually kill me, then get off on the grounds of justification. 'You bastard,' she goes. 'All your little whores . . .'

'That's horsh.'

'. . . coming into my shop and – oh my God – laughing at me behind my actual back . . .'

Fionn tries to get in between us then. Of course, he represented Norway in the Model UN. 'Sorcha,' he goes, 'sit down. Let's talk about this thing . . .'

'Stay the *fock* out of my affairs,' she goes, then she turns to me. 'So how much of it was real?'

'What?'

'I want to know, Ross. How much money did you spend in my shop?'

I sort of, like, sigh. 'Thirty-something grand – we're talking ballpork?'

She's like, 'Thirty-something grand?' and at the same time you can see her doing the calculations in her head. Then her face suddenly drops. It's obvious, roysh, that it's her entire turnover for the past few weeks.

'Hey, I was the one trying to tell you to close the shop down,' I go.

She's there, 'You *focking* bastard!'

'To be fair, your old man threatened to bankrupt me in the divorce if he saw you on Grafton Street with that megaphone again . . .'

Her expression suddenly changes from one of anger to one of, like, sadness. She shakes her head and tells me that this is the worst thing I've done to her – this coming from the girl I gave oral thrush to the night before her graduation.

She goes, 'I'll never forgive you for this, Ross. Never . . .'

Five to seven on Friday evening and they're stood at my door with twenty-four bottles of Fink Bräu, grinning like two focking donkeys eating glass.

Of course I can't come up with an excuse quick enough. Before I can say a word, they just borge in. Larry goes, 'What were you doin, havin a wank?'

See, this is how they talk the whole time.

I'm there, 'Er, *no?*' except they're not even listening now. They've, like, settled themselves on the sofa and they've switched the TV over to RTÉ1.

'Eer big night, wha?' Terry goes to me. 'Here, me ma has all her neighbours arowint to see it in hers. Fooken mad proud, so she is . . .'

Oh, fock.

My hort's suddenly pumping like a pimped-up Vauxhall Nova. 'It's, er, not today,' I go, trying to bluff them. 'I'm pretty sure it's, like, next *Friday?*'

And of course no sooner have I said it than the credits roll and Mary Kennedy's going, 'On *Nationwide* tonight . . .' and there *we* are, coming up in a moment, squeezed in between an item about a new holistic healing centre for Tullamore and one about a group of nuns from Ballyduff who make Braille bibles for blind street kids in Belize.

'See, it'll be another ten minutes at least,' I go, 'let's see what else is on for the moment,' hoping to find some, maybe, *soccer* to distract them?

'Here, Tetty,' Larry goes, 'I hope he's not arthur sayin sometin derogatoddy abour us and he doesn't want us to see it.'

I laugh. 'Yeah, roysh,' I go, making a grab for the remote. 'As if . . .'

'Leaf that fooken telly as it is,' Terry goes, like a man who's used to getting his way.

Oh, fock!

It's, like, the nuns who are up first. All the work is done by hand and blahdy blahdy blah. I'm sitting there, roysh, trying to remember some of the shit I said. All I know is that very little of it could be described as good.

I stand up and wander over to the French doors, thinking, maybe I'll go over the balcony again. Climb down there and never come back. Just leave this place to the focking elements.

'Sit dowin!' Terry goes.

'I was just going to grab a lungful of air . . .'

'Sit fooken dowin!'

I do immediately what he says.

Larry's there, 'Dat's good woork dem nuns is doin – will we trun a few bob at dem?' and his brother goes, 'Yeah, why not?' and I'm thinking, underworld characters who give money to charity . . .

Jesus.

The report seems to go on for ever. But eventually, roysh, it ends and then *we're* suddenly up. The two boys cheer when they see Mary Kennedy standing in the hallway between our two doors. 'Yeeeaaahhh!' they both go, raising their bottles to the screen.

'Go on, Meeerdy!'

'Now,' Mary goes, 'the economic downturn that we are currently experiencing has been described by economists as the most socially democratic recession ever to hit Ireland, affecting people across a whole range of economic groups. One of the most interesting features of the downturn, according to a recent study by NUI Maynooth, has been a blurring of many of the social divisions that once existed in this country. Here, in the beautiful South Dublin suburb of Ticknock, I visited two sets of neighbours from vastly divergent social backgrounds and spoke to them about the tensions involved in living next door to each other in the new, post-Tiger Ireland . . .'

The next thing, roysh, on come the opening notes of Coldplay's 'In My Place' – which *is* a clever touch – along with a montage of slow-motion images of me playing *GTA 4* on the Xbox and doing sit-ups with my top off, then Terry and Larry smoking in their tracksuit bottoms and their wife-beater vests, then wrestling with Rooney out on the balcony.

Then it cuts to the two of them, sitting side by side, on the sofa. 'For me,' Terry goes, 'the heerdest ting – bein honest wit ya – has been de language baddier. Does be veddy heerd sometimes to wontherstand him and I'm shewer it does be heerd for him to wontherstand us. Like, he does say *goys* when what he means is *feddas*. He does use diffordent words. But then *we'd* often say *royid* – "Did you get the royid off her?" – whereas he does say *scooore* . . .'

'*Did you scooore her?*' Larry goes, then the two of them crack their holes laughing.

The next shot is me going, 'Hash. The focking smell of it, constantly. In the lift. In the hallway. Focking everywhere . . .'

I have a quick look at the two boys. They're sitting there watching with their mouths just open.

Meanwhile, I'm up on the screen going, 'Don't get me wrong here, I've got nothing against hash per se. I just think it's a gateway drug that can lead to more serious shit, like holidays in Benalmadena and going to see Pink Floyd tribute bands . . .'

Then I give the camera one of my sly little smiles.

Okay, I'm thinking, *they're* going to stort slagging *me* off any second now – to, like, balance the whole thing up?

'When we moofed in foorst,' Larry goes, 'we tought, he's a snoppy little so-and-so next doh-er. Like, he'd almost look dowin he's nose at you when you met him in de lift. Sure, he rang de loar on us, foorst day we moofed in, tought we were stroking de gaff. But den de both of us – Tetty *and* me – we decided dats probley just de way he was raised. I tink now, we'd both say, he's actually a veddy nice toype of a fedda . . .'

That's not what they focking think!

Shit. I'm up again. 'The first thing that entered my head when I saw them, roysh, was that they were the kind you always see on the news, coming out of court, one hand cuffed to a Gord, the other covering their faces with a tabloid newspaper . . .'

They're still just staring at the screen. 'Goys,' I try to go, 'just to say, this was *before* I found out who you actually were?'

Except they don't answer. And I go on hanging myself up there.

'Those kind of people, you know the sort, their only ambition in life is to own pubs and restaurants in focking Alicante . . . All their washing hanging over the balcony rail – er, hello? . . . I'd say, roysh, in all honesty, having them living next door to me has probably knocked about sixty, possibly seventy Ks off the value of my aportment. So *you* tell *me* whether that's, like, a good thing.'

They suddenly both stand up at exactly the same time. I'm literally shitting myself, expecting them to pull a couple of Glocks. I get ready to dive for cover behind the Blake occasional table, honestly expecting to die in a hail of bullets and birch-veneer splinters. Except their *actual* reaction takes me by total surprise.

'Eer fooken ma's watchin dis!' Terry goes, more *disappointed* than angry?

I'm there, 'I know – you mentioned. It's just, look, no offence, I thought we were *all* going to be slagging each other off. I thought you were going to be talking about Rooney trying to, you know, *ride* me that day . . .'

'What, you tink I'd say sometin like dat knowin me ma was gonna be watchin?'

They've obviously got a different relationship with their old dear than I have with mine. 'Well, yeah . . .'

He shakes his head. 'Dat Rooney ting was just a joke, Ross. But what you're arthur just sayin abour us . . . it was veddy hoortful . . .'

I suddenly can't even look at them. It's weird, roysh, because they're giving me the major guilts, even though I know deep down that these are the country's two biggest dealers in, like, illegal drugs and fireorms?

'I tought we were frents,' Larry goes.

I'm like, 'Friends?' because it's honestly news to me.

'Yeah, frents!'

He shakes his head then and picks up the tray of Fink Bräu. 'Mon, Tetty,' he goes. 'We'll thrink these next doh-er – bether company,' and off they go – to my considerable relief, it has to be said.

It's, like, five seconds after the report ends that Fionn rings. 'Do you need a bed for tonight?' in his opening line. He's obviously watched it. I end up just laughing, which obviously surprises him. I'm there, 'Would you believe me if I told you they watched it here *with* me?'

He's like, 'What?'

He probably thinks I'm, like, delirious with fear. 'They called in, with beers from Lidl . . .'

He sounds suddenly full of concern. 'Are they holding a gun to your head there, Ross? Cough if they are.'

'No, they're gone, Dude. See, that's, like, the weirdest thing? I honestly thought there was going to be, like, frogmen out searching for me tonight.'

'Are you telling me they're not even angry, Ross . . . after *that*?'

'No, they were just, again, disappointed . . .'

'Disappointed?'

'Yeah, exactly the same as Sorcha.'

'Well, thank God for that.'

'Big time – disappointment is something I can more than live with.'

Claire calls around with what's-his-face, while I'm watching a rerun of the Heineken Cup final on Sky Plus. Then she *proves* that she knows fock-all about rugby by going, 'Oh my God, Brian O'Driscoll's wearing blue! Does he not play for, like, Ireland any more?'

It's one of those questions that I wouldn't even dignify with an answer, so I end up just blanking her.

He ends up sitting – get this – *cross-legged* on the sofa, like he's doing yoga or some shit, and I'm thinking, I swear to fock, if he puts dirt on my cushions, I'll take one of those Birkenstocks and give him something to focking meditate on.

What's his even name again?

'Is this a *big* game?' Claire goes, the way birds do when they want you to mute the TV.

I'm like, 'Er, you *could* say that, Claire, yeah.'

Then *he* has the actual cheek to shake his head and go, 'I'm sorry, I just don't *get* sports,' with a big smirk on his face as well, like he finds everyone in the world just a bit focking ridiculous.

It's like, yeah, maybe if *I* went into Trailfinders and booked a Qantas around-the-world-in-three-stops trip, I'd end up being as cool as him.

Claire has the cheek to laugh at *me* then.

She's there, 'Oh my God, is *that* what I think it is, Ross?' and what she's talking about is my Leinster Schools Senior Cup medal. 'Are you telling me you wear that whenever you watch a rugby match?'

'No,' I go, 'I wear it all the focking time. I just take it out from under my shirt when I'm watching Leinster play.'

'Oh, dear!' *he* goes, the patronizing prick.

So I go, 'Yeah, Claire, like *you've* never seen your reflection in it, panting like a focking dog,' and that shuts the two of them up long enough for me to enjoy Johnny Sexton's drop goal. 'Is there a reason, by the way, that you two are even here?'

That's when *she* makes a big show of clearing her throat and goes, 'Okay, obviously it's only, like, two months until the big day and we want to square off as many things as we can now, just so we can, like, relax and enjoy it.'

'Cool,' I go, quick as a flash, 'I'll have the Cantonese spring rolls followed by the king prawns in black bean sauce . . .'

She gives me an absolute filthy. *He* just tries to ignore it, the focking Zen master over there.

'Or is it just going to be chicken balls with curry sauce for everyone?'

The whole Bray thing is something she's never going to be able to live down – neither should she.

'To make sure the day runs smoothly,' she goes, 'we're trying to identify areas of potential conflict early on and, like, tackle them?'

'Meaning?'

'Well, I heard about the little stunt you pulled with Sorcha's shop . . .'

'That's nothing to do with you.'

'And I know she told you she never wants to see you again . . .'

'Again, none of your focking business.'

'We just want to make sure that none of the ill-feeling between you spills over into our wedding day, the theme of which is *supposed* to be serenity and oneness?'

'Is that everything?'

'What?'

'Is that everything? Because I'd really like to go back to enjoying my Saturday afternoon . . .'

The two of them exchange looks. 'Well, no,' *she* goes, 'I also had a favour to ask . . .'

I sort of, like, snort at her. Bray people would live in your ear, then stick three foreign-language students in the other one.

'You know the e-mails that I sent to everyone,' she goes, 'about my travels around Asia?'

I don't even give her the satisfaction of an answer.

'Well, Garret thinks I should put them all together and publish, like, a book?'

I laugh. No option.

'And I was wondering, do you think your mum would give me any advice on how to go about getting it published?'

'Definitely,' I go. 'She's the one with the track record for writing boring shit that feels like actual work to read.'

I suddenly remember what it said on the radio this morning. O'Carroll-Kelly is now the last of RTÉ's high-earners holding out. Which means she'll be as pissy as a dipso's mattress. 'Definitely give her a ring,' I tell her. 'Here's her number . . .'

I can see her through the glass, sat slumped on the floor with her back to the wall, looking totally defeated, her fingers playing with something, which turns out to be a buckle that Honor pulled from a pair of Mary Jane five-strap peep toes. It's the only evidence left of what this place used to actually be.

I give the window another quick tap. 'Please, Sorcha!' I go. 'I didn't ever want to see this day.'

That for some reason gets her attention. She peels herself up off the floor and walks to the door. She looks horrific, by the way, like she hasn't slept in two nights.

It turns out she *hasn't* slept in two nights.

She unlocks the door and opens it, except only an inch or two, not enough to let me actually in. 'I used to wish you had something wrong with your brain,' is her opening line, 'as in, like, a tumour?'

Of course that rocks me back on my heels. 'I know you're upset, Babes, but that's possibly a *bit* over the top?'

'Whenever you did something awful,' she goes, 'like when you slept with my little sister, or the time you swore you saw Stella McCortney in the lane beside Iskanders eating a shish kebab, I used to always say to my mum, maybe he's got something pushing down on his brain and – oh my God – *making* him act the way he does?'

In fairness to her, she *has* always tried to see the good in me.

'Mum *and* Dad would be just like, "Cut him out of your life, Sorcha, like a leg gone bad with gangrene." But I'd be there, "No, you see this kind of thing on TV all the time! *Chicago Hope, ER* . . . " actually defending you, Ross! Thinking that if I could just get you to go for an MRI, it might suddenly explain everything.'

I shake my head.

'It's nice of you to think that way,' I go, 'but it'd probably just be a waste of hospital resources. I act the way I do, I can tell you for a fact, because that's just the way I am. I'm a dick. Love me or hate me . . .'

She looks me up and down and I feel her attitude towards me suddenly soften. 'Ross, I know you did what you did because my dad threatened you . . .'

She suddenly opens the door wide enough to let me in. It's, like, *so* random seeing the shop like this? It's weird the way our voices echo off the walls, with everything but the corpet stripped out of it. I tell her I thought she might have had, like, a closing-down sale but she says she couldn't have faced it.

'Sell those new Rupert Sandersons, for instance, for, like, fifty percent off? I was the first shop in Ireland to get them after BTs, Ross – I literally couldn't do it . . .'

She sits back down on the floor and I plonk myself down beside her. She asks me if I saw the photograph of Sean Fitzpatrick in the paper this morning. 'With a suntan,' she goes, before I get a chance to even answer, 'as if nothing even happened . . .'

That poor focker's getting blamed for everything. Him and my old dear. It's like the old man always says – people love a lynching.

'God, if I could get my hands on him . . .' I go, agreeing with her – you'd *have* to with the form she's in?

We're both quiet then.

'Holly Willoughby said this was one of her favourite places to shop when she was in Dublin,' she suddenly goes, looking sad and distant.

I tell her I know. I remember.

'And Michelle Heaton.'

I tell her I know that too.

She produces a bottle of champagne. It's, like, good shit as well. She says Pia Bang dropped it in to her last night, when she was clearing the stock out. You'd have to say fair focks.

She's there, 'I *asked* her – what am I supposedly celebrating, Pia? It felt weird because I still think I've, oh my God, failed? She said I should be celebrating the fact that I ran one of the best clothes shops this city has ever seen . . .'

I ask her if she wants me to open that bottle, then she, like, hands it to me. I peel away the foil, twist off the metal cap and pop the cork. It's a sound that I haven't heard in too focking long.

It's only then that I realize we've no glasses. I take a sip straight from the neck. Fizz ends up coming out of my nose. I hand the bottle to Sorcha and she does the same.

'You don't need Pia Bang to tell you how good this place actually was,' I go. 'How many times did the *Irish Times Magazine* put it in the "What's Hot" section?'

'Once. But *Image* had it in too, and so did, like, *Irish Tatler*?'

'I rest my case.'

She hands me the bottle and I take another mouthful.

My eyes do a quick sweep of the place, which only two days ago was wall to wall with Madison Marcus and Lauren Moffatt and Jodi Arnold and Helmut Lang. It was KLS. It was BCBG and CC Skye. It was Mulberry, Blueberry, Strawberry and Blackberry. Orange, Banana and Shabby Apple. Mike & Chris, Paul & Joe, Sass & Bide. Westwood Red and Graeme Black. It was Citizens of Humanity. Daughters of the Revolution. Spoiled Little Mamas.

And how easily it all tripped off her tongue.

You can prevent heavy prints dictating your shape by adding a waist-

cinching belt . . . And don't discount hot pinks and reds. They're going to be providing a bold contrast to pastel shades everywhere this year . . .

How long will it be before everyone's forgotten what that shit even means? Before they've forgotten that Sorcha's was the first shop in Ireland to do jeans by Gold Sign, Earnest Sewn and Kitson Own. Miu Mius, Jimmy Choos and Jason Wus. 291 Venice, 3.1 Phillip Lim and 7s For All Mankind. Balmain, Bertin, Cardin. Susana Monaco. Shoshanna and on it goes – Moschino, Malandrino, Valentino. Yamamoto, Take-moto, Kishimoto. Jellycat. Baby Phat. No Added Sugar. Rich and Skinny . . .

It's no wonder her actual hort is broken.

I hand her the bottle. She's throwing it into her as well. I ask her what's going to happen to the unit and she says it'll probably end up being another Carroll's Irish Gifts. She's upset. I tell her not to think like that. That won't be allowed to happen. The Powerscourt Townhouse Centre is still the Powerscourt Townhouse Centre, even if the world around it *is* going to shit.

She shakes her head, like she's no longer certain of even that. She says she doesn't want to come across as, like, a snob or anything? But no one ever went into liquidation by over-estimating the public's desire for Guinness fridge magnets, jester hats in county colours and songs about dead IRA men.

And there's real bitterness in her voice when she says it and the worst thing is that, deep down, I know it's probably true.

'This country,' she goes, 'is totally focked, Ross. And I mean – oh my God – totally!'

It's definitely the angriest I've seen her since a few months back, when those – again, racist – Muslim dudes were up in court for plotting to blow up airplanes. I just happened to call into the gaff and found her in the living room, staring madly at their photographs on Sky News, saying *they* were the reason she wasn't allowed to bring her Sisley Confort Extrême Day

Cream in her hand luggage when she was coming back from the States last year.

That's how badly things *can* affect her?

So I try to keep things jollying along. I take another swig from the bottle and tell her I remember the weekend the shop actually opened. She smiles then. 'We had champagne then as well,' she goes. 'And we drank it this exact same way . . .'

No glasses then either – that's right.

'I remember when the stock was delivered,' she goes. 'Oh my God, there must have been, like, fifty or sixty boxes? It was, like, Friday lunchtime and I was supposed to be opening the following day. So you and my mum came in . . .'

'And we helped you.'

'The three of us worked right through the night . . .'

'I remember us getting a Chinese.'

'Nine o'clock in the morning we finished setting it up. Then we opened the champagne – do you remember that?'

'Yeah, the people were already queuing up outside. We didn't open the doors until we'd finished the bottle.'

She smiles.

She's there, 'See, you could actually *do* things like that in those days? People had money. They had to spend it some-where. You knew they'd come back.'

'We worked something ridiculous,' I go, 'like thirty-six hours straight.'

She's there, 'We must have been, like, high on adrenalin or something?'

I nod.

I'm there, 'That was the Celtic Tiger, of course. We all did a lot of crazy shit.'

I offer her the bottle but she waves it away.

'Oh my God,' she goes, suddenly remembering something, 'Claire said your mum was really rude to her.'

'Rude to her?'

'Yeah, see, she wants to publish her travelogue as, like, a book? And she rang your mum for some advice.'

'I *told* her not to.'

'Did you?'

'Yeah, she's getting hammered on the whole *pay* thing? She's the last one holding out. I told her the old dear was spitting feathers, might need to leave her a week or two. They can't be told – people from Bray.'

We both go suddenly quiet again. I think the champagne is going to *both* our heads? I ask her what she's going to do now, expecting her to say something like, I don't know, become an ambassador for the Rainforest Alliance, which has always been an ambition of hers, liaising with the likes of Storbucks and Nespresso on their sustainability programmes. But she doesn't mention it. In a weird way, I think even *that* dream has died?

'I'm going to take some time out,' she goes, 'to make sure I connect with my grief. I'm not having a thirtieth birthday porty, by the way.'

'What?'

'I've cancelled it.'

'Whoa! I wouldn't say Il Segreto were happy with you,' because she had the upstairs room booked.

'Well,' she goes, 'I just figured – oh my God, what's there to even celebrate?'

I tell her that sounds heavy but she doesn't answer. We sit there for another five minutes. I finish the champagne. We're probably both quite pissed.

She goes, 'Ross, what kind of a world have we brought our daughter into?'

I tell her I don't know. I've been trying not to let this whole current economic thing get me down but every day I recognize this town less and less.

I'm there, 'I had a dream the other night that me and Honor were sitting on this mountain, looking out across nothing but fields. And I said to her, "I remember when this was *all* apartments."'

Then I turn my head to find Sorcha sleeping soundly on my shoulder.

6. Crème de la total Mare

The old dear – finally – caved on the whole paycut thing. I hear it on the lunchtime news as I'm waking up with a hangover that knows my name and a slightly chunky bird from Glenageary who, happily, doesn't.

She's like a fuller version of Leah Remini, this bird, and she rides like she actually invented it. Now, though, we're going to have to say goodbye, because I've got shit to do.

See, it's not every day I get to look my old dear in the face and laugh.

I give the girl a glass of water and a few porting words of wisdom – 'neither of us should be ashamed of what happened last night, far from it, in fact, casual sex and blahdy blahdy blah blah' – then drop her to the Luas Station in Sandyford. I think she ends up dazed at the slickness of the manoeuvre as I leave her there, in the pissings of rain, still clutching the tenner I pressed into her hand. I don't *know* why I do that? Oisinn always said it was a bit, I suppose, sleazy.

Anyway, ten minutes later, I'm pulling into RTÉ. I throw the beast into Ryle Nugent's porking space – fock him – then tip over to TV reception.

The bird behind the desk – the one who's a ringer for Shanna Moakler – knows me only too well and she immediately picks up the Wolfe when she sees me coming and dials the old dear's extension.

Literally five seconds later, while she's still waiting for an answer, the old dear comes bursting through the double doors, with her make-up all over the shop and her BlackBerry slapped to her ear, giving out yords to someone in this, like, loud, screechy voice.

I honestly haven't seen her this upset since Jackie Lavin stuck her XC90 in her porking space at Foxrock Golf Club while she was still lady captain.

It turns out, roysh, that this has got fock-all to do with the paycut she's agreed to. Listening to her side of the conversation, it soon becomes obvious that RTÉ have asked her to stort cooking dishes on her show that better reflect what they're calling the new economic realities.

'You think you can just change the name of my programme from *FO'CK Cooking* to *FO'CK on a Budget* without any consultation whatsoever?' she's giving it at the top of her voice. 'A piece of advice for you – do *not* be anywhere near me the next time I've got my Stellar Sabatier in my hand,' and then she just, like, hangs up.

I actually laugh, then ask her what's the Johnny McRory. She's, like, too upset to nearly speak. She just hands me this big, I suppose, whack of paper, we're talking all A4 sheets, which she tells me, when she finally gets her shit together, is a list of all the ingredients she's no longer allowed to use on the show.

I leaf through it and read some of the things. We're talking bulghar wheat. We're talking colocasia. We're talking black cohosh. We're talking *even* Mascarpone?

'Six months ago,' she goes, not unreasonably in my humble op, 'everyone in Ireland was eating those things. It's back to the bloody caves we're headed.'

Bee balm. Pandanus. Even lemon verbena.

'Do you know what they're suggesting I cook with tomorrow? Swede, Ross!'

There's real anger in her eyes. I've seen the same crazy look in police mugshots of Catherine Nevin.

'What's swede?' I obviously go.

'It's like a rutabaga,' she goes, 'except for poor people. And they're asking *me* to go on national television and encourage people to . . .'

Her voice trails off. It's like she's suddenly had an idea.

'Maybe if I chopped it up,' she suddenly goes, 'I could do one of my famous lanttulaatikkos . . . Ross, just tell me, is daikon on the proscribed list?'

I give it the old left to right. Luckily it's in, like, alphabetical order? I'm there, 'Er, yeah, it is.'

'You're joking!' she goes. 'Well, what about canola oil?'

I laugh. I'm there, 'Yeah, that too.'

'Okay,' she goes, still trying to hold it together. 'Maybe I could do my faux proletarian hotpot, with pumpkin, sausage and root vegetables. I'm presuming they've not gone completely insane and banned me from using savoury kielbasa . . .'

I flick through the pages and then I'm like, 'Er, would you believe it if I told you . . .'

'Oh for heaven's sake,' she just goes – this, remember, in the middle of TV reception. 'You can get kielbasa in Aldi. A friend of Delma's went once – she saw it with her own eyes . . .'

I'm in a jocker laughing at this stage. 'Sorry to disappoint you – it's on the banned list.'

'Okay,' she goes, still trying to control her breathing, 'don't panic, Fionnuala. Just think . . . Okay, no one – and I mean no one – who has tasted my rutabaga and apple casserole has anything other than loved it. If I put enough cinnamon in, no one need ever know it's – ugh, I can barely bring myself to say the word – *swede*!'

'Well,' I go, running my finger down the *c*'s, 'you're all right with cinnamon.'

'Sense!' she goes. 'At last! What about all-purpose flour?'

I'm there, 'Good to go – that's not on the list.'

'What about light-brown sugar?'

'Again,' I go, 'well within the rules.'

She's like, 'What about seakale and haricots verts?'

She cops my expression, roysh, and she immediately knows and that's when she suddenly can't hold it together any longer. She lets, like, a scream out of her, and Rachel Allen, who's arriving for work, does a full three-sixty in the swing door and goes back out into the corpork again.

'Famine food,' the old dear's suddenly screaming at her through, like, an inch of plate glass. 'That's what they're asking me to cook, Rachel! Focking famine food!'

Then she storms through the double doors again, demanding a meeting with – don't ask me – but Cathal Goan. I give Rachel a little wink to tell her it's safe to come in now, while hoping to fock that someone had the cop to hide that Stellar Sabatier.

I'm totally gay, I'm telling Fionn, for these new Black Forest lattes that they're doing in Buckys. They *taste* like a cake but they're an actual *drink*? Close your eyes and you could forget that there's even a recession on.

We're in the one in Blackrock, by the way.

I take another sip, then ask Fionn why he wanted to meet up. 'Here, is it about JP's new bird?' I go. 'Because what you're not hearing from him is that she's mental and colder than a witch's tit.'

'No,' he goes, 'it's about, er – actually, let's just wait till Erika arrives.'

I'm there, 'Erika?'

'Ah, here she comes.'

I turn around. She's walking past the sign for the blade grinder recall and she looks – I make no apologies for saying it – really, really, really, really well. 'Have you said anything?' she goes to Fionn before she even sits down.

Fionn's like, 'Not yet.'

Then she just fixes me with a look and goes, 'Ross, you need to talk to Sorcha.'

There's a real, I don't know, intervention vibe to it – like back at school? I'm there, 'Sorcha? What are you shitting on about?'

'She's been under a huge amount of mental strain,' Erika goes, 'with the shop . . .'

'The shop's been closed, what, nearly two weeks now?'

Fionn chips in then. 'We know, Ross. But the struggle she went through, trying to keep it afloat, it must have put enormous pressure on her.'

'Well, thank fock it's over is what I say.'

Fionn and Erika exchange a look, like they can't believe how actually stupid I am? 'Fionn's mum saw her yesterday,' Erika goes, just blurting it out, 'in Fallon & Byrne – in the food court . . .'

'And?'

Fionn takes, like, a deep breath. 'Ross, she saw Sorcha put some items into her bag . . . And then leave the shop without paying for them.'

'What?' I'm in, like, total shock. 'What kind of items are we even talking?'

'My mum thought okra, lingots blancs . . .'

'You're *actually* taking the piss here.'

'And some purple salad potatoes.'

'Jesus Christ!'

I'm in actual shock. I can't believe this is, like, *Sorcha* we're talking about? As in, *the* most honest person I know. The girl who was head of the Justice, Peace and Integrity of Creation group at school, who was even a Minister for the Eucharist in Killiney Church until Mass storted clashing with *90210* on a Sunday morning.

I literally can't take it in. I'm there, 'How much even *is* okra?' still in shock, I suppose.

Erika looks at Fionn, then back at me. 'Ross, why is *that* important?'

I'm there, 'I don't know. I suppose it isn't. What I mean is, you know, maybe she just forgot to pay for it . . .'

Erika shakes her head. 'When Fionn rang me and told me, it tallied with one or two things I saw over the past few weeks.'

'Weeks? Are you saying this has been going on for weeks?'

'She's been under a huge amount of strain, Ross. And, yes, there *was* one day in D4 Stores . . .'

'Stealing from Gayle Killilea and Seán Dunne?' I go. 'Jesus, how low can anyone stoop . . .'

'Ross,' she goes, 'you really *need* to watch her. We all do.'

I sit back in my ormchair and look up at the ceiling, as if to say, what more can this recession possibly throw at me?

If Terry and Larry had left me alone since the whole *Nationwide* mix-up, it was only because they'd been away on their summer holidays. And I only knew that because their old dear had been dropping by twice a day to feed Rooney – fock knows what but my guess, knowing what her boys do for a living, would be human body ports.

I saw her just the once, half nine in the morning, getting into the lift in front of me, with this blonde bird – a focking spare rib in a Juicy tracksuit, who I immediately took to be Terry and Larry's older sister. I hung back, of course, remembering that she'd had the neighbours in to watch the interview and half suspecting that my comments about her sons knocking a lot of Ks off the value of my aportment might not have gone down well with her.

My gut instinct proved to be right, because that night, when they arrived to give the dog his dinner, I could hear the mother in the hallway going, 'He's in dare, de doorty pox. Ife a good moyunt to knock . . .'

Then the daughter, who turned out to be called Tanya – they so often are – went, 'Why doatunt ye? Say it to he's face, Ma – snoppy fooken bastoord.'

Happily, roysh, they didn't knock. Instead, they sought to even up the score by throwing Rooney's shit over the glass partition separating our two balconies – Tanya constantly in her mother's ear, telling her that what they should be doing is force-feeding it to me.

Because courteous living . . . is a civil right.

It was – if you can believe this – an actual relief to have Terry and Larry back. I saw them through the spyhole arriving home at, like, nine o'clock in the morning, suntanned and freshly tattooed, with their Duty Free bottles clinking away at their sides.

I felt this unbelievable urge to go out and hug them, though I wisely managed to resist it.

They were, like, quiet for the rest of the day, obviously sleeping off the effects of the overnight flight from Tallamolinos or wherever the fock they were. That afternoon, roysh, I hit Dundrum, just to get a few things – not important. It was while I was on my way back, still on the actual M50, that I saw the banner – WELCOME HOME TERRY AND LARRY – hanging between two balconies on the floor below mine. That's when I realized that the Deportment of Social Welfare had moved more of them in and that Rosa Parks was fast becoming a kind of Wheatfield without the hope of eventual release.

Still, I decided to mind my own beeswax as best I could.

That night, I – let's just say – *entertained* a young lady called

Erin Boylan – or Erin Go Braless, as we used to call her, for reasons I won't explain out of, like, *respect* for the girl?

She was on her back, with her legs in the air, blaspheming at the ceiling while I did *my* thing, managing to maintain my stroke despite the noise from the obvious porty that was in full swing next door.

'Is that Leo Sayer?' Erin went at some point in our, I'm going to call it love-making, referring of course to the music. 'It *is* – that's "More than I Can Say". Oh my God, my mum *loves* Leo Sayer. *How* random!'

After this brief, I don't know, interlude, we went back to doing the bould thing, except we were interrupted from our exertions again a short time later by the sound of someone banging on the aportment door.

I was up on my elbows, going, 'Ignore it,' except the longer we did, the more – I don't know – *persistent* the banging grew?

Eventually, roysh, I had to hop off her, throw on the old Cantos and the Leinster training jersey and answer it.

It turned out to be some fat dude, who introduced himself to me as Daso from number 475, which I took to mean 475 Rosa Parks.

'Mon,' he went, 'de boys want a woord,' and from the confident way he turned, it was obvious he hadn't even considered the possibility of me refusing the invitation.

I followed him out into the hallway, then in next door, where – I was right – a porty was in full flow.

And it *was* Leo Sayer, by the way. I saw his *Greatest Hits* on the coffee table. Someone had obviously been using the case from the CD to chop up lines of coke.

'You Make Me Feel Like Dancing' just happened to come on as I walked into the living room, where ten, maybe fifteen teenage skobes were suddenly staring at me in what would have to be described as a seriously hostile way.

It reminded me of the time Sorcha persuaded me to take her to Iffey Valley Shopping Centre. I was as much in fear of my life that day as I was now.

Someone mentioned *Nationwide*, then someone else called me a wankoar, as my eyes searched the room for a friendly face. Even Rooney's would have been a welcome alternative to this.

'Mon out here, Ross,' someone – it turned out to be Terry – shouted from the kitchen. It felt weirdly good to see him, sitting at the table. *And* Larry, who was pouring shots of what *he* pronounced as Sudderden Comfort for five or six other heads who were just standing around.

Terry refused my offer of a high-five, though I was keen to give him the benefit of the doubt, presuming he'd never come across one before.

'Sithowin dare,' he went, signalling the chair opposite him. I pulled it out, docked my orse on it.

'How was the hollier?' I went, still shitting the old trackie daks, but finding some focked-up consolation in the idea that, even *if* I die here, at least the last face I'm going to see will be a familiar one.

He didn't answer.

'We goth off on de wrong footh,' he just went.

I was like, 'Agreed,' because it sounded like they wanted to put the whole Mary Kennedy experience behind them. He looked at the others, then nodded at my jersey – the horp on it. He was like, 'Ross hee-er's a rubby man.'

Of course, from the looks I ended up getting, he might as well have said I focked chickens.

It was all, 'Rubby? *Rubby?* I doatunt agree with dat.'

One of them – the, honestly, hordest-looking man I've ever seen in my life – went, 'Couple of feddas I knew insoyit – dee were from Limerick – dey were mad into der rubby.'

'That's the beauty of the game,' I ended up going, ever keen to spread the gospel, 'especially in Limerick – you've got both ends of society who follow it.'

'Boat ends?' it was Larry who went.

'Yeah. I don't know if you know this but "The Fields of Athenry" is actually *about* a criminal from that side of the country. That's why they love it down there.'

They all nodded like they found it suddenly interesting. That's the key to teaching, Fionn always said – you've got to find something to engage them.

'See me?' Terry went. 'I caddent make head nor fooken tayul of dat gayum . . .'

I laughed. It was, like, I *had* to? I was there, 'It *is* a pretty complicated game, in fairness to you.'

Terry went, 'But how's it woork? Explain it to us.'

Which, like a focking idiot, I attempted to do. 'Okay,' I went, 'have you got something I could use to represent each of the positions?'

From nowhere, roysh, Larry produced a fistful of what turned out to be pill bottles – full, of course. There were exactly seven of them. Of course I didn't even think about what was in them because I was suddenly in my element.

A lot of people are of the view that I was, like, *born* to coach?

I used the bottles to set up the backline – scrum-half, out-half, inside-centre, outside-centre, right-wing, left-wing, fullback – and then I explained to them a little bit about how the entire thing should, in theory, function. I also managed to slip in the fact that the backs are basically the glamour boys of the game and made sure to mention that I was one myself back in my playing days.

There they were, roysh, all nodding and it almost felt like I was back in Andorra again, passing on the gospel to people who've never been privileged enough to hear it before.

'Now,' I went, really warming to it, 'the forwards are generally much bigger . . .'

'Hee-er,' it was Larry who went, then he produced a cordboard box from under the sink, which he turned over on to the table.

My hort nearly stopped – actually, I'm pretty sure it did stop for two or three seconds.

Because what came tumbling out of that box, into the middle of the exact same Sandra Kragnert-designed Fusion table that Sorcha got from Ikea, were eight semi-automatic pistols. I recognized them immediately from a Public Enemy video that's on my YouTube favourites.

I was like, 'Errr . . .'

'Deer not loated,' Larry went. 'Keep goin . . .'

I was literally shitting myself, roysh, but I had no option but to keep going with the, I suppose, *lesson*? I took the eight guns and I laid them out in lines of three, two and three – front row, second row, back row – then, with my hands *actually* trembling, I tried to talk them through how the scrum and lineout worked.

'Of course,' I went, my voice shaking, 'the other job the forwards do is softening up the opposition, so the pretty boys like myself, Pivot and Johnny Sex can do *our* thing . . .'

Terry was just staring at me, across this highly illegal team formation, loving the sudden fear that he could sense in me. 'Eer ma was veddy upseth,' he went. 'De tings ya said . . .'

His poor mother. My balcony looked like a focking dirty protest in a dogs' home. I was like, 'Yeah, so I believe . . .'

He just nodded. 'We doatunt want any mower of you toordenin your nose up arrus in de lift, bangin on de wall, tellin us we're not in Fuerteventura now, stickin notes unther the doh-er, givin our abourrus hangin eer washin on de balcony . . .'

'Dude,' I went, 'that was all *before* I found out who you actually were?'

He nodded at the stash in front of us. 'Well,' he went, 'now you know. An anutter ting, Mr High and fooken Moythee, your fingerprints is now all over dem guns and thrugs . . .'

It's her.

Definitely, roysh, because that's the Betsey Johnson pleated coat I bought her for, like, her *birthday* last year?

I'm standing, like, a good twenty yords behind her, watching her push the trolley up the Soups and Sauces aisle. She suddenly stops and reaches for something. One thing she's *always* loved about Superquinn is their own-brand mulligatawny soup.

Honor is sitting in the little seat in the front of the trolley. Even from this distance, she cops me. 'Daddy!' she suddenly goes. 'Mummy, I can see Daddy!' and I have to quickly step behind a board advertising their Euro Saver Switch and Save Scheme.

I'm thinking, twenty-twenty vision – just like her old man.

'No,' I hear Sorcha go, 'Daddy's not here today, Dorling.'

Except I am. Unfortunately for her, I'm very much here.

I peek out, just as Sorcha's disappearing around the end of the aisle and into Pastas and Cooking Oils. I tip after her, hide behind a pallet piled high with kitchen roll, then have a quick peek out.

She's stopped again.

Except this time, roysh, I watch her take a jor from the shelf and look over both shoulders. Then – and it sends me cold, roysh, even though I *know* it's coming? – she slips the jor inside her coat.

See, I'd wanted Fionn and Erika to be wrong. My next-door neighbours are gangland criminals and now my still-wife is a common shoplifter. Talk about the good times being well and truly over.

I walk straight up behind her. I put my hand on her shoulder and she ends up nearly bombing her knickers. She whips around as if she's just been stung. 'Ross!' she goes. 'You frightened me!'

I'm in no mood for pleasantries, though. I'm like, 'Er, are you going to pay for those *carciofini di Cupello in oli extra vergine di oliva*?'

Of course she tries to act the innocent. She's there, 'What?' except I'm not going to let it go.

'Er, what port of *carciofini di Cupello in oli extra vergine di oliva* do you not understand, Sorcha?'

She looks away. She's busted and she knows it. I hold my hand out and she suddenly looks at me, madder than madness itself. She reaches into her coat – it *is* the one I bought her? – and plonks the jor into my hand.

I put it back on the shelf.

'*And* the wild lavender honey with walnuts,' I go, 'that I'm *pretty* sure I saw you take earlier?'

She's there, 'So, what, you're following me around now?'

She reaches into the other side of her coat and hands me that as well. She's actually *furious*? I decide I still need to give her some tough love, though. 'Do you want to end up sharing a cell with the focking Scissor Sisters?'

That draws a few looks, I can tell you. It's not the kind of thing you'd expect to hear shouted in Superquinn a year ago. Lidl maybe, but not Superquinn.

Sorcha just turns away from me. She's like, 'What do *you* care?' and she goes to push her trolley away.

'Oh, *I* care,' I go, chasing after her. 'If I didn't care, then why would I have gone on the internet last night and Googled loads of shit about basically shoplifting?'

I whip out a couple of sheets of paper – just shit I printed out. She rounds the corner into Cereals and Flour but I'm, like, determined to say my piece. 'It says in this particular orticle that an estimated forty percent of shoplifting cases aren't *acquisitive* crimes . . . And I even looked *that* up – this dude who supposedly doesn't care – and it means doing it for, like, gain?'

She keeps walking but I keep following her. 'Sorcha, you've been under unbelievable stress . . .'

'I'm fine!'

'I think you're far from it. I think you should maybe see someone – a doctor, for example?'

'I *said* I'm fine.'

Except I don't give a fock what she *said*. I'm going to give her a few home truths whether she likes it or not.

I'm there, '*Psychologists believe that up to twenty-two percent of all shoplifting is compulsive in nature and most likely a function of stress and/or depression.* And/or, Sorcha! And/or!'

She stops, picks a jor of wheat germ off the shelf and drops it into the trolley, still blanking me.

'Hey,' I go, 'this is not some random horseshit I picked up just anywhere – this was on the internet, Sorcha.'

But she just pushes her trolley on, not wanting to know a thing about the research I've done.

Two things are immediately clear to me. The first is that she's almost certainly going to keep doing this shit, regardless of what *I* say? The second is that it's not going to end well.

The thing about these high-definition plasma TVs is, you buy them because, in the shop, you've seen some amazing scene off National Geographic – a killer whale horsing a sealion or some dude heliskiing down the side of a focking glacier. But of course *you* get the thing home and you end up just watching *Coronation Street* on it, staring into the abyss of Blanche's nostrils while you're trying to eat your dinner.

Or, worse, the old dear's nostrils. I'm looking at her up there on the screen, thinking, if you swung on those focking nose-hairs, you'd expect to hear the Christchurch bells.

I'm in the sack, roysh, watching the latest episode of her show since it was renamed *FO'CK on a Budget* and it's possibly the funniest thing I've ever seen. She's showing the camera, like, an ordinary corn on the cob?

'Now,' she's going, 'when *I* want to eat sweetcorn – like most people – it simply *has* to be Fallon & Byrne, with their wonderful, wonderful vegetable range, all fresh, all organic and all locally produced. However, if you've been made redundant –*or* you've been shamed by the media into accepting an arbitary cut in your standard of living – a cheaper alternative *is* now available . . .'

The next thing, roysh, she puts down the corn on the cob and picks up what looks very much to me like a *tin* of sweetcorn, except from the way she's holding it, it might as well be white dog shit.

'Now, this is what's known as *processed* food – and, if certain people in this very building are to be believed, it's going to be *all in* for the next few years. Now, if you're anything like me, you'll be staring at this rather odd-looking, ribbed-aluminium can, thinking, "But how do I get the *food* – and I use that word advisedly – out of there?" Well, don't panic – you do it using one of these . . .'

I don't *actually* believe it. She's about to show the nation how to use a focking tin opener.

'As recently as the 1980s,' she goes, and you can tell she's struggling to even say the words, 'you would have found one of these items in most household kitchen drawers, although they became obsolete with the advent of farmers markets and the drive towards fresh, agrichemical-free produce with fewer food miles . . .'

The camera pans in for a close-up.

'This particular – if you like – *tin opener* is a classic, no-fuss butterfly model. It features a set of jaws – right here – which hold the can in place, while this little serrated rotating wheel here – are we getting it there on camera two? – punctures the can.

'Then – this is the difficult bit, though George Lee told me in the canteen an hour ago that we're all going to get plenty of practice at this – you twist this butterfly-shaped wingnut here and the serrated rotating wheel, as you can see, literally cuts through the metal . . .'

Her voice is breaking with emotion. I'm there laughing but at the same time shaking my head – much as I hate her guts – unable to believe that RTÉ – or anyone – could put another human being through something like this.

That's when my phone all of a sudden rings. I answer without checking who it is.

Big mistake.

'The best laid plans of mice and men!' he goes.

That's, like, his opening line?

'I'm focking busy,' I just go.

He's like, 'Oh, I'll bet. The apple doesn't fall far from the tree . . .'

I'm there, 'Actually, if you must know, I'm in bed watching your, I know you've forgotten, but wife, showing this once proud nation how to use a focking tin opener . . .'

I can tell he's in shock, roysh, but he tries not to let it show. 'Well,' he just goes, 'I'm having my own travails with this current economic business. My plan for the Mountjoy Hotel and Casino has had to be shelved, Ross . . .'

I'm there, 'Focking delighted!'

'Much as I hate to burden you with *my* woes. It seems the parlous state of the nation's finances has forced the government to put their plans for a new prison on hold . . .'

I'm there, 'They should just stick a big focking wall around Rosa Parks – save themselves a fortune.'

He goes, 'Means old Joshua Jebb's folly is going to stay the way it is for the forseeable . . .' He sighs then. 'All that planning,' he has the actual balls to go. 'All that work. I'm beginning to think maybe I erred, Ross, when I said this recession was going to pass us by. I'm feeling rather down today . . .'

'Well,' I just go, 'you're also depressing me. Ring your precious daughter – *she'll* listen, I'm sure.'

I hang up, just as the old dear is scraping sweetcorn out of a pot on to a plate. She eats a forkful of it and pretends to even like it, even though she has a face on her like an old-age pensioner licking anti-freeze off a hot stove. She's got, like, tears in her eyes, going, 'Tomorrow, we'll be looking at textured vegetable protein and other cheaper alternatives to meat . . .'

In a weird, focked-up way, she has me almost feeling *sorry* for her? Except, roysh, just as I'm struggling to come to terms with the sensation, I hear all this sudden talking outside in the hallway. I mute Cruella and have a listen.

From what I can make out, Terry and Larry are, like, thanking someone for calling in.

It's all *sowint* as a *powint* and we'll see you *arowint*.

Then I hear *his* voice and I realize that who they're talking to is – shit! – Ronan.

I suddenly don't give a fock how many guns they're, I don't know, *packing*? I reef open the front door and go, 'Er, Ro, can you come in here – as in now?'

'Ah, howiya, Rosser?' he just goes. You'd never know the Blathin business even happened.

Terry and Larry, of course, break into immediate smiles, seeing my stress, like they've suddenly found my Achilles' heel.

When I manage to prise Ro away from them, all he can go is, 'Thee say never meet your heerdoes – they're fooken wrong, Rosser . . .'

I decide at first *not* to give him the whole heavy father routine? See, I know enough kids to know that they'll usually do the exact opposite of what you tell them. Plus, if I told him the aportment was full of guns and drugs, you'd need to focking Taser him to get him out of there.

No, instead I try to, like, change the subject. Today happens to be the first day of his summer holidays. 'Six lovely weeks stretching out ahead of you,' I try to go, handing him a can of Cidona. '*And* you're young, free and single. Finglas had better lock up its daughters . . .'

Or at least the ones who aren't already locked up.

'Nah,' he just goes, picking up one of my dumbbells and performing a couple of stretches with it, 'not havin athin to do with boords for now . . .'

I laugh.

'Let me tell you something, Ro – the number of times I've said that over the years. No, unfortunately, they're as addictive as those cigarettes you smoke.'

At the mention of the word, he whips one out, then pats the pockets of his school trousers looking for his lighter.

'Tetty and Laddy,' he goes, 'they don't have boords . . .'

'Are you surprised? The focking state of them . . .'

'No, thee reckon thee only holt you back. If you're maddied to a life of crime, Laddy said, you caddent be maddied to anyone else – dudn't woork.'

'I'm not sure I'd agree with his analysis there, Ro. What about your big hero?'

'The Genoddle?'

'Yeah, *he* was very happily married. *And* he was doing her sister, wasn't he?'

He lights his cigarette.

'Yeah,' he goes, 'but Tetty and Laddy say boords are a distraction. And thee send you fooken mad if you ever have to do toyim . . .'

I end up losing it with him then, which is what I definitely *didn't* want to do?

I'm there, '*If you ever have to do time?* Jesus Christ, Ro, you're twelve . . .'

He seems all of a sudden hurt. 'Laddy had he's foorst J-Lo at torteen.'

'His first what?'

'Juvenile let-off.'

'Er, can I just remind you, Ro – a few months ago you were going out with a bird whose old man was an actual doctor . . .'

'So?'

'*So* . . . they were good people. Clon-focking-skeagh, if I have to remind you! And now *this* is the focking road you suddenly want to go down?'

Even *he's* a bit taken aback, because I've hordly ever had to shout at him before. 'I was only fooken talkin to dum,' he tries to go, actually shouting *back*?

I point at him – I actually point the finger – and go, 'I don't want you calling in there again. It's bad enough that I have to live next door to them. That's the recession. It's nobody's fault but it's an unfortunate fact of life. But I'm saying this to you, Ro, as your actual father – stay away from Terry and Larry.'

And the look he ends up giving me is the exact same look I got from Sorcha. It's a look of actual defiance.

So I'm sitting in Mickey D's at the bottom of Grafton Street with Honor, enjoying a spot of lunch and the company of my daughter while her old dear's in Dundrum, enjoying a day of retail therapy with, like, Erika and Claire.

Instead of a wedding cake – 'oh my God – *rip-off*?' – Claire's decided to have, like, a massive tiramisu and they've gone to, like, Brambles to – here's a word I forgot even existed – *price* them. This supposed wedding just gets funnier and funnier.

She's been texting me pretty much every day, by the way, still banging on about this book she thinks she's writing, going, oh my God, I know your mum's under *so* much pressure – I saw her on the show yesterday showing people how to defrost processed vegetables – but do you think she'd even look at, like, my chapter plan?

Anyway, there I am, roysh, feeding Honor her chicken nuggets, when all of a sudden I'm aware of someone standing over me. I look up and – speak of the devil – it's, like, Garret.

I automatically laugh. There's just something about this dude. Maybe I also instinctively know what's coming.

'Ah,' I just go, 'look who it isn't!' which is one of my famous lines.

He's there, 'Can I have a word?'

I laugh. 'It's about Claire, is it?' He doesn't answer. I'm there, 'Go on.'

The dick won't even look at me. 'The day you went to Kilcroney,' he goes, 'for the wedding dress, she said she caught you staring at her while she was in just her bra and knickers.'

I laugh.

'You might find it funny,' he goes, 'but you made her feel uncomfortable.'

'That's what *she* said?'

'Yeah, it is. And I believe her.'

'That's that, then.'

He sort of, like, laughs then – again trying to patronize me. 'I actually pity you,' he even tries to go.

I'm there, 'Pity me? Er, why?'

'Look,' he goes, 'I know you still have feelings for her.'

Now it's *my* turn to laugh? 'Dude, I've never had feelings for her. Yeah, I've been in there a fair few times – in there like swimwear. Which she made *sure* to mention to you, I bet.'

'Well, what *you're* going to have to accept is that that's in the past now.'

'Oh, believe me, it's well in the past.'

'So what about all these text messages, then, back and forth?'

'Dude, what are you shitting about?'

'I'm saying they have to fucking stop!'

'Whoa,' I go, 'where's that famous calm and serenity you supposedly learned in Thailand?'

Gone obviously because he points at me in, like, an angry way. 'Claire's told you she's getting married, how many times now? And you just won't accept it.'

'Dude, you're being played.'

'What?'

'You're being played. Like *Gran* focking *Turismo 4*.'

I can't believe that they're allowing someone this naive about women and their ways to even *get* married.

He shakes his head. He's like, 'You're still in love with her. *She* even says it . . .'

'Oh, well, if *she* says it . . .' The poor focker's whipped like Häagen-Dazs. 'Look, *she's* the one who's been texting *me*? Dude, grab yourself a chai tea, pull up a pew and let me explain to you a little bit about birds and the way they operate . . .'

I figure I owe it to mankind to pass on the lessons I've learned in the course of my life as a player.

'I can see it for myself,' he just goes, 'the way you look at her. She's marrying *me*. And you need to get over that fact . . .'

The conversation doesn't *get* the chance to go any further

downhill from there. Because it's at that exact moment that *she* rings him – as in, Claire?

He straight away has to hold the phone away from his ear. I can hear the screaming myself, even from here. It's not just *her* either. I recognize Erika's scream as well – the exact same noise she made when I spilled a glass of Pinot Noir on her Derek Lam georgette tunic dress in Thornton's last Christmas Eve.

'Calm down!' Dick Head is trying to go. 'Talk to me, Claire! What's wrong?'

'It's Sorcha!' *I* can even hear her go. 'She's going to kill us!'

I sit forward, suddenly interested. Even Honor goes, 'Mommy!' somehow sensing that something's wrong.

I'm there, 'Okay, *what* the fock?'

Garret pulls the phone away from his ear again. 'They're all in the car. Sorcha's driving and she's had some kind of, I don't know, freak attack,' he goes. He lowers his voice. 'She keeps ranting about the *Crème de la Mer* fish – do you know what that means?'

'The *Crème de la Mer* fish?'

'Think, Ross – because Claire said she's driving through Donnybrook at, like, a hundred and twenty Ks, breaking every red light . . .'

Garret continues to listen while I stort, like, racking my brains? 'The *Crème de la Mer* fish . . .'

'Shoplifting?' *he* suddenly goes.

I'm there, 'What?'

'Sorcha was . . . *arrested*,' he again whispers, not that Honor would even understand. 'She walked out of Molton Brown with a bottle of Active Cassia Bodywash . . .'

Then he corrects himself. 'Bodywash and Scrub . . .'

Claire is relaying all of this information in, like, a high-pitched, panicked voice. 'They took her to Dundrum and charged her, Ross,' he goes.

'I focking told her that was going to eventually happen.'

'Claire says when they got back to the car afterwards, she started just freaking out . . . the *Crème de la Mer* fish! I can hear her saying it now. Think, Ross! Think!'

'I'm focking trying, yoga boy!'

I hear more screams.

'Ross,' Garret goes, 'they've just gone over Leeson Street Bridge and all four wheels left the road!' and I'm instantly thinking of that scene in, like, *Ferris Bueller* where those two dudes take Cameron's cor for, like, a joyride. And that's when the answer suddenly pops into my head . . .

See, I made Sorcha watch that movie the night before she sat her finals, when she was *also* freaking out like this? She'd been up for, like, two days and nights, basically cramming. And any time I rang her, she kept banging on about the fish. It turned out a week or so earlier, she'd bought something from the *Crème de la Mer* counter in BTs – it might have even *been* a body scrub – but then she storted to get the sudden guilts about how much she'd spent. But she kept banging on about the tank at the front of the store, kept saying that humans aren't entitled to keep any creature in, like, captivity like that, although *I* have to say, those fish have always seemed happy enough to me.

I put her madness that night down to a combination of sleep deprivation and shopper's remorse. So I called out to her gaff on the Vico with a bottle of Châteauneuf and *that* movie on DVD. And what happened? She chilled out and ended up getting an actual first.

'Garret,' I go, 'gimme that focking phone,' which he immediately does, even though you can tell he hates the idea of me being the man of the moment. 'Claire,' I go, 'I'm going to need you and Erika calm . . .'

She goes, 'Ross, she's just taken the turn on to Stephen's Green on two wheels . . .'

Two wheels? I honestly *didn't* think that Opel Astra TwinTop had it in it.

I'm there, 'Okay, can you put me on speakerphone there,' which she immediately does.

'Sorcha,' I go, 'I suspect we haven't got much time here. I know you've been under a lot of stress but you have to realize – like I told you the night before your finals – that's *all* it is? Just try to relax . . .'

'Keep talking,' *he* goes, like I need instructions from him.

I'm there, 'Do you remember what happened to Ferris Bueller's mate when *he* calmed down that time? They only ended up having the best day of their actual lives. I mean, they ended up, I don't know, going up to the top of a really tall building, then to an ort gallery, then to . . . em, yeah, a really nice restaurant where you have to wear a jacket . . .'

Shit!

I mouth the words to Garret: 'What else? What else?'

He's like, 'What?'

I'm there, 'What else did they do? I mean, the movie made it seem like an unbelievable day – but Jesus Christ, if you add up all the things, it was actually shit . . .'

The next thing I hear is Claire screaming again. *And* Erika.

'They went to a ballgame,' some randomer at the next table goes, 'although they didn't stay long.'

I tell him thanks.

'Did you hear that, Sorcha? They also went to a ballgame and they didn't stay long!'

Claire suddenly shouts, 'Ross, she's turned down Grafton Street!'

I'm like, 'You can't drive down Grafton Street – it's . . .'

Garret's off the seat and out of McDonald's before I've even thought of the word *pedestrianized*. I hang up, lift Honor up and follow him out on to the street, with a sense that something pretty bad is about to happen.

At first, roysh, we see nothing. All we can hear are people's screams coming from the Laura Ashley end of things? Then a few seconds later, we can see people scattering everywhere, like in *Cloverfield* or one of those.

Then we suddenly see the Astra, tearing towards us, with the top down. Erika's in the front-passenger seat and Claire's in the back, both with their hands over their eyes. People everywhere are, like, diving for cover, into the doorways of Weir's, the O2 Store, Morks and Spencer.

I can suddenly make out Sorcha's face behind the wheel, madder than a Kilkenny farmer, and that's when I realize that she's going to do what I think she's going to do . . .

I throw Honor into Garret's orms, then I run to the main entrance of BTs and try to, like, clear it. I'm going, 'Move! Quick! We need to evacuate this basic area!'

There's one or two how-dare-yous, which you'd expect from BTs . . .

It's too late.

The next thing I hear is the sudden squeal of tyres, as Sorcha pulls hord on the wheel.

Then the cor suddenly comes crashing through the front doors in an absolute explosion of glass.

The entire make-up deportment screams, which is some noise, I can tell you. I manage to pull this Jamie Ray Newman lookalike out from behind the counter just in time, then I hit the deck, as Sorcha's front bumper smashes into the fish tank with a force that causes it to just burst.

It's, like, *buddoooossshhh!*

The airbags instantly inflate and a tonne of water spills out into the cor – as do the fish, not looking happy at all, it has to be said, about being suddenly free.

I'm picking myself up off the floor, watching Sorcha, Erika and Claire wrestling with the airbags, when another scene from *Ferris Bueller* comes to me.

'Shit!' I end up going. 'I should have mentioned him singing on that parade float.'

Erika's pissed like I've very rarely seen her pissed. 'No, Ross,' she goes, managing to free herself, 'you should have mentioned that she has a daughter to live for.'

7. *Sei parte ormai di me*

He's unbelievable. And I don't even mean that in a good way? All he can talk about is what he's going to do with all this suddenly free time on his hands since the Office of Public Works put the kibosh on his hotel and casino plan.

'Perhaps you can relax,' Helen goes, snatching a lump of Cœur de Neufchâtel out of his hand before he gets to take a second bite of it. 'Let's take that trip to France we've been talking about.'

He's there, 'A holiday?' horrified by the idea. 'I'll take a holiday when this recession takes one. Yes, Helen, I've had a setback and no mistake. But this current economic climate that everyone's so excited about, it's not going to defeat me. No, I'm going to master it – like our friend Santiago and his famous marlin.'

I'm just, like, staring at him across the counter. 'Er,' I go, 'the Feds have just added reckless endangerment using a motor vehicle to the already shoplifting and criminal damage chorges against my wife – and all you can do is bullshit on about nothing?'

He smiles – actually *smiles* at me? 'Don't you worry your head,' he tries to go. 'I've always said it about you, Ross – you're too much of a deep thinker. Hennessy's going to sort everything out . . .'

'And what if she ends up in prison? What am I going to tell our daughter?'

'It won't come to that, Ross. She's from a good background.'

'What the fock's that got to do with the price of radicchio?'

He laughs, like *I'm* the naive one?

'Everything, of course. *And* she's pleading guilty. It'll be dealt with summarily. She'll be in and out of there tomorrow in the blink of an eye. Probation Act, how are you!'

Helen asks me how Sorcha is – like I keep saying, the woman is, like, *way* too good for him. I tell her I haven't a bog. I haven't actually spoken to her since it happened. She's staying with her old pair in Killiney and she's not, like, answering her phone.

'Erika said Brown Thomas have agreed to cover the cost of the damages themselves,' she goes, 'and to write a letter to the court, asking for leniency . . .'

I'm there, 'Least they could do – the amount of bread she's dropped in that place over the years. And the fish, in the end, were fine. Mao on Chatham Street have agreed to, I don't know, foster them until BTs get the new tank in. I'm just hoping the judge will be swayed by that. It's her birthday tomorrow as well, you know – her actual thirtieth.'

'Well, whatever happens,' Helen goes, smiling at me, 'she's very lucky to have you, Ross,' and I have to say, roysh, it's amazing to suddenly get that recognition.

I decide to try Sorcha's phone again. I step outside the old cheesemonger's and dial the number. I'm walking past Nutley Newsagents when it's suddenly answered. Except it's not Sorcha who does the answering – it's her old man.

So I end up putting on this, like, German accent, roysh, trying to pass myself off as one of her mates from the summer she spent *au pairing* in Mannheim. 'Gute eefening,' I go. 'I vould like to shpeak vit Sorcha Lalor . . .'

He's there, 'Your photograph comes up on her screen when you ring, you little shithead . . .'

He does *not* sound a happy carrot-cruncher. If he was embarrassed by the idea of her trying to flog her threads on

Grafton Street, imagine how her crashing through the doors of Ireland's leading deportment store in the Astra he bought her is going down.

Er, *not* well?

'I just wanted to make sure she's okay,' I go.

He's there, 'Sorcha hasn't been okay since the day you blundered into her life. And she won't be until the day you're banished from it – which will hopefully be soon . . .'

'Can I speak to her?'

'Hennessy's prepping her for tomorrow. Then she's going to get an early night and hope to God that she's going to be sleeping in her own bed again tomorrow.'

'Okay, would you maybe just give her a message – good luck, I'm thinking about her, blah blah blah . . .'

'No,' he just goes.

I'm like, 'Well, would you even just tell her that I'll see her outside the court in the morning?'

He's there, 'No, no more messages. You just stay away from my daughter . . .'

In the background, roysh, I can hear Sorcha ask who he's talking to. 'It's no one,' he goes.

No one.

Then he just hangs up.

She looks amazing. Then she always *does*? Plus I'm sure Hennessy told her to undo those two extra buttons on her shirt. I guess judges are no different from the rest of us.

I hold her hand and ask her if she's okay. She says she's actually fine and that when this is all over she's going to go on a verbal fast retreat with her mum.

I give her hand a little squeeze and I go, 'Come on, Sorcha, how long have we known each other?' and that's when the tears suddenly come, standing there in the hallway of – believe it or not – the Bridewell District Court. It's obviously not how she envisaged spending her thirtieth.

She's like, 'What if I *do* end up sharing a cell with the Scissor Sisters?'

I tell her that's not going to happen. And it's *so* not. 'I only said that to you,' I go, 'that day in Superquinn to try to scare you straight. Even if the worst does come to the worst, they'd obviously keep people like you away from people like them . . .'

She's there, 'Do you think?' and I'm like, 'They'd have to! Think about it. Even if the world *is* turning to shit under our feet. And anyway, it's not going to come to that. Hennessy's pretty sure you're going to walk – especially because you're pleading guilty.'

She wipes away her tears with her open hand. 'If you're wrong,' she goes, '*you'll* bring up Honor, won't you?'

I shake my head and go, 'Let's not think like that,' but she puts her finger to my lips, roysh, and goes, 'Promise me, Ross! You're the best father that she could ever hope for . . .'

I look away.

I notice her old pair, her granny and her sister suddenly tipping up the steps of the court. The sister – whose name I can never remember – looks amazing, although now is obviously not the time to point that out to her. Too much history there. Instead, I go, 'Okay, I promise,' and then I tell her she'd better go and talk to her family.

As she's walking away I go, 'Happy birthday, by the way,' and she just stops for a second. She seemed to have forgotten it was today.

I grab a seat in what they call the public gallery. The court's not yet in session. It's amazing the shit you pick up watching *Judge Judy* practically every day of your adult life.

Hennessy cops me and he tips on over. 'Charlie tell you the hotel and casino plan fell through?'

I don't *actually* believe this?

I'm there, 'You want to talk about my old man's hairbrain focking schemes while my wife's about to go to possibly prison?'

'Hey, you little pissbag,' he goes, practically jabbing his finger in my face. 'You think I've nothing better to do with my time than clean up you and your sister's bullshit?'

That's an obvious reference to the whole, I don't know, Toddy Rathfriland thing?

I'm there, 'Er, I'd hordly call this *my* bullshit?'

'I'm doing this as a favour for Charlie,' he goes. 'And let me tell you something else. You wait till your loving wife and that old man of hers get you in the divorce court. You're going to wish she'd got life today . . .'

'I possibly will,' I go. 'Just make sure she doesn't.'

Hers ends up being the first case called and I can't tell you how much it upsets me to see her – this beautiful girl who played the flute in the Emmanuel Liturgical Music Project at school, remember – standing in a courtroom as the actual accused. Sister Zechariah would have puppies if she was alive today.

Sorcha's family and friends suddenly swarm into the – again – public gallery. Her old man gives me an unbelievable filthy and calls me a waste of skin. I tell him he's entitled to his opinion, then he ends up having to be held back by Sorcha's old dear and her granny, who prevent him from basically throttling me with his bare hands.

They eventually sit down.

'Hi, Ross,' the sister goes, like she's about to eat me with a focking spoon. I'm pretty sure it's Oonagh or Edina or some shit like that. Needless to say, I've got an instant one on me.

The girls also arrive. First Chloe, still on the crutches, followed by Sophie and Amie with an ie, who I hear mention that she's now finished all of *Californication* and is up to season three of *Weeds*.

Garret and Claire are next. *She* obviously has him totally para at this stage because he can't actually take his eyes off me.

Then in walks Erika, roysh, and sits down next to me and what's nice is that she's the only one so far to ask me how *I* am? I tell her I'm shitting mashed potatoes here and she just holds my hand.

Then it's suddenly game time.

This Gorda dude stands up first and gives an outline of what basically happened. The accused stole a bottle of body-wash *and* scrub – Garret was right – from Molton Brown in Dundrum Town Centre. After being chorged, she left the station and proceeded to drive in a reckless and dangerous manner in the direction of Dublin City Centre. Once there, she drove down Grafton Street at one of the busiest times of the day and crashed her cor through the main doors of the Brown Thomas deportment store, causing five thousand euros' worth of damage to two doors, a make-up display *and* a fish tank.

You can see the judge, roysh, looking at Sorcha over the top of his glasses, obviously thinking, *this* girl? Did all of *that*? Er . . .

He's clearly struggling with the idea – and it's not just because she's flashing her ta-tas at him.

'Am I hearing the correct case here?' he goes.

Hennessy spots his chance, roysh, and he's straight to his feet.

He's like, 'Yes, Your Honour – this is, as you've already no doubt gathered, a very unusual case, in which my client – a strikingly attractive young woman, as you can see – the mother of a young daughter, a professional woman with a business beset from all sides by the tumultuous currents of the current economic climate, under extreme duress, acted in a way that was most out of character for her . . .'

I turn to Erika and I go, 'He's good – there's no doubt about that.'

She says she knows. He's managed to persuade Regina Rathfriland, she says, to drop her name from the divorce proceedings, which is news to me.

'Can I also say,' Hennessy goes, 'that nobody was hurt in the incident . . .'

The judge is like, 'Fortunately!' and I'm suddenly sensing that this might not be the formality I *thought* it was going to be?

'Yes, Your Honor, it was very fortunate. My client accepts that. We are not contesting the facts of the case as they've been presented to the court today. I would, however, ask that, in determining a punishment, you take into account the untold pressure brought to bear on her in the months preceding the incident by her failing business. Your Honour might also consider this letter from Brown Thomas Group Limited, *to* the court, describing my client as a long-time friend of the department store . . .'

I turn to Erika. 'She's spent a focking fortune in there over the years – it's the least they could do.'

Sorcha's old man actually shushes me.

'I also have letters here, Your Honour, from an array of organizations – from the Burmese National League for Democracy to the Campaign to Save the Loggerhead Sea Turtle – thanking her for her support. In view of these ringing testimonials as to her caring nature, I would ask you to consider some alternative sanction to that of imprisonment, which would after all serve no purpose other than to deny a little girl her, I think you'd agree, very, very, very attractive mother. I would also submit that the signage indicating that

Grafton Street is a pedestrianized thoroughfare is clearly insufficient . . .'

'Enough,' the judge just goes. He doesn't seem like the kind of dude who'd let himself be shitted. 'Let me see those letters . . .'

Hennessy hands them to him and he goes through them, reading every single one, which takes about twenty focking minutes. Every so often, he'll look up and cop another look at Sorcha over the top of his glasses. I've never heard silence like it.

It actually beats Cordiff and Edinburgh combined for tension.

Eventually, roysh, he puts the letters down and actually addresses Sorcha. He's like, 'What do you know about the loggerhead sea turtle?'

Sorcha looks confused, like it's the last thing she expected to come up today. 'Just that they're – oh my God – among the most beautiful creatures in the sea,' she goes, 'and that we've hunted them to the point of, like, extinction? *And* that I actually swam with one when I spent a summer working in South Carolina . . .'

The judge just smiles. 'My wife swam with one too,' he goes and this, like, wave of relief just sweeps over me.

I turn to Erika. 'And to think I laughed in her face when she originally told me that story.'

'She's also a member of that campaign,' the judge goes, then he hands the letters back to Hennessy and clears his throat. 'I have no doubt whatsoever as to the good character of this woman who finds herself in front of me this morning. I have no doubt, too, that the pressure brought to bear on her by these unprecedented economic times was the sole determinant in these events that unfortunately occurred. However, in view of the danger that was presented to the public, I feel it incumbent on me to impose some form of sentence . . .'

Shit!

Sorcha looks around, not at her family, or at her friends, but at me. I give her a little smile as if to say, hey, we'll face it together, Babes – whatever *it* might actually be.

The judge takes his time to focking say it. 'That sentence is . . . that you perform four hundred hours of community service . . .'

'Yeeesss!!!' I hear myself suddenly go.

I punch the air.

'And that you keep up the good work in support of all these very worthwhile organizations . . .'

'Hennessy!' I shout. 'You little focking rooster!'

'And that the fellow there, wearing the baseball cap, be immediately removed from this court.'

My phone rings. I check caller ID and it's, like, Oisinn's old dear. I'd usually answer it straight away, roysh, to find out if he's obviously been in touch, except this time I consider *not* answering it? See, I know what day it is today.

But then, being a parent myself, I've got, like, *some* idea of what she must be going through.

So I do answer. I go, 'Hey, Mrs Wallace.'

I can tell she's been crying before she even opens her mouth. She's like, 'I'm sorry to be a nuisance . . .'

'You're anything *but* a nuisance,' I go, just so as *not* to hurt her feelings?

She's like, 'Do you know what day it is today?'

I'm there, 'Yeah, it's Oisinn's birthday,' because it was always two days after Sorcha's.

'His *thirtieth* birthday, Ross.'

'I know . . .'

He's, like, the first of the old SCT to get out of his twenties.

'Actually,' I go, 'me and the goys met up last night, had a

fair few scoops – don't you worry about that – and told our favourite Oisinn stories,' and then I immediately regret saying it because I realize I've made him sound dead.

And the thing that nobody – especially me – wants to admit is that he actually *could* be?

'I keep expecting him to walk through the door, like nothing ever happened. Where could he be, Ross?'

The answer, of course, is anywhere in the actual world.

Sorcha says she meant to ring me to say, well, you know . . .

I tell her, hey, it was a verbal fast retreat. I wouldn't have *expected* her to? I tell her I'm just happy she's okay – and, well, still at lorge.

She laughs. She looks incredible, even *in* just overalls.

She says she's been rereading *The Wasted Vigil* by Nadeem Aslam and it's given her – oh my God – a *totally* new perspective on life.

I tell her that sounds amazing.

She's quiet for a little while. Then she goes, 'I really thought I was going to jail, Ross.'

I laugh. I'm there, 'Er, that was *never* going to happen?'

She goes, 'But what was I like? I could have – oh my God – killed someone . . .'

'Hey,' I go, 'you're being too hord on yourself. You were focking bananas, don't forget.'

'I suppose.'

'No suppose about it. It's like I tried to tell you that day in Superquinn – the stress you've been under. It's the exact same shit as happened to Winona Ryder, remember?'

She nods. She knows that I'm talking sense. Then she, like, returns to her work, scraping the fly posters off the walls around the back of the George's Street Orcade. I tell her I still think they could have found something for her to do that

244

better suited her, I don't know, *talents*? I tell her to give me the scraper and I'll finish it for her – her focking orms must be hanging.

She says no, this is something *she* has to do herself? Otherwise she won't feel that she's been adequately punished. Someone told me once that they don't even have to supervise the detention in Mount Anville.

'Do you know what's funny?' she goes then. 'I feel like a geologist here, chipping my way through layers and layers of history. You can even see, like, the faultlines in our recent past. I took off a poster for a Turkish property expo and there, underneath, was an ad for Ireland's first one hundred and ten percent mortgage. Then I scraped that off and there was a poster for Il Divo at the Point . . .'

I laugh and shake my head.

'Il Divo,' I go. 'We really did lose the run of ourselves, didn't we? At least that's what everyone seems to be saying . . .'

She finishes another ten feet of wall, then asks me how *I* am, which is nice to hear. Of course I end up unloading all of my shit on her. Eight more aportments in my block have now fallen to social welfarites.

I'm there, 'I know we all *did* go a bit mental, but now things are going too much the *other* way? I'm just glad Rosa Parks isn't alive to see the focking tip they've made of the place.'

She smiles at me – you'd have to say *sympathetically*?

'Then, on top of everything else, Ronan's besotted with the two focking grunts next door . . .'

She suddenly stops scraping. She's like, 'Oh my God!'

And I'm there, 'You can say that again. He was supposed to call in to me yesterday. Thursday's always been our night in Dr Quirkey's – *you* know that. Didn't show. I was ringing him for, like, an hour. He eventually answered. Turned out he'd been in next door the whole time. I was like, "Er, are we not hitting O'Connell Street?" And he was like, "We're in the mittle of watchen sometin, Rosser – I'll catch you anutter toyum."'

'That must have been, like, *so* hurtful for you, Ross – as, like, a father?'

'It's not so much that. Look, I hated being around my *own* old man at that age? It's just, these two aren't anything like his other friends, dudes like Whacker, Nudger and Buckets of Blood. These two are *real* bad boys. We're actually talking guns and drugs. I actually saw them. They have these, like, wild porties where they listen to – believe it or not – Leo Sayer and focking snort the old devil's dandruff . . .'

'Ross, you have to keep Ronan away from them.'

'I know but it's, like, how? You tell a kid that something's off limits and they immediately want to go there.'

She smiles sort of, like, *inwardly*? I'm sure she's thinking about all the times her old man warned her off me. 'Maybe it's just him rebelling. I think he feels really bad about the way he treated Blathin. Maybe hanging about with these, well, hord characters is his way of pretending that it's not affecting him.'

'That's actually not a bad analysis. What did you say that book was called?'

She laughs.

'*The Wasted Vigil*.'

'Well,' I go, 'it's obviously done you *some* good? Either way, though, I'm going to have to have the chat with him about drugs . . .'

She kisses me on the cheek, tells me I'm an amazing father, then goes back to her scraping.

I mention that it was Oisinn's birthday last week.

She goes, 'Oh my God, the 31st of July! Has anyone even heard from him?'

'Not a word,' I go. 'His old dear rang me and she's . . . I

don't know, how could he do that to her? It's, like, I focking hate *my* old dear? But I'd still never put her through that – as in, not knowing? Jesus . . .'

'How are *you* getting on with, like, trying to find him?'

I shrug.

'Ah, I've kind of let it slide the last few months. I suppose I've had my own shit to deal with. I was mostly just ringing all his favourite hotels – which was, like, brain dead, given that the focker's skint . . .'

She says at least I'm trying and that's a great thing to hear for my confidence. Then she suddenly remembers something and stops scraping again.

'Oh my God,' she goes, 'I was supposed to pick up the photocopying from Reads.'

I'm like, 'What photocopying are we talking about here?'

'The Mass leaflets for, like, Claire and Garret's wedding?'

I crack my hole laughing. 'They're giving out photocopies?'

'They're on good-quality paper, Ross.'

I'm *still* laughing. 'This wedding just gets more and more focking hilarious.'

'Don't be nasty – they don't have a lot of money . . .'

'I'll tell you what,' I go, 'I'll go and pick them up *for* you.'

She's there, 'Are you sure you don't mind?'

I'm like, 'Hey, you've said some good stuff about me here today – it's the least I can do.'

'Ronan,' I go, 'nice of you to grace me with your presence.'

He doesn't even *feel* bad?

'As in, you didn't bother your orse calling in to see me last week. What were you doing in there anyway – or am I allowed to even ask?'

He just shrugs. 'We were watchin Paul Widdiams – *Doorty Money* – on tee-fee-tee.'

247

I'm all of a sudden hurt. Me and Sinead Desmond spent, like, four hours in the TV3 orchive putting that thing together for him. 'I actually thought you and me were going to watch it together.'

'Well, in anyhow,' he goes, 'Tetty and Laddy luffed it. There's no Criminal Assets Bureau ever gonna be findin deer assets, but.'

'You reckon?'

'Too smeert, thee are. Hidden all over the shop, so it is. Ah, the boys are the business, Rosser.'

I pull a face, like I, personally, could take or leave them. 'Look, do you mind me saying something to you?' I go.

He rolls his actual eyes.

I'm there, 'Just hear me out, Ro. I know, deep down, you possibly feel bad about the way you treated Bla – breaking it off with her just because she's in a wheelchair, doing the dirt with her mate, blah blah blah – but you don't have to pretend to be hord. It's all right to be sad about it . . .'

'Ine over it.'

'Well, I hope that's true. Another thing I wanted to say is, you know, dudes like Terry and Larry, they're young and they've got all this moo, all this power. A kid like you, born in that focking council Lego estate your mother brought you up in, I can see how your head could be turned by the likes of them. But don't forget, Ro, you *are* still a kid. What I'm saying is, you know, enjoy your childhood . . .'

I'm building up to mention the whole drugs thing, except his eyes are suddenly drawn to the muted television. The old dear's show is just storting. It has to be said, roysh, she's stuck it out a lot longer than I *thought* she would?

'*FO'CK on a Budget*?' Ronan goes. 'When did thee change the nayum?'

I'm like, 'A few weeks back. They told her to stort cooking

food that's more – I think the word is – *reflective* of the times in which we're living?'

He grabs the remote off the coffee table and highers up the sound.

'In these enviromentally conscious times,' the old dear's going, looking into the wrong focking camera as per usual, 'we are forever being urged to consider the amount of waste that each of us generates. And now, with unemployment, emigration and plummeting share prices once again features of life in Ireland, there has never been a better time for us to stop and think about the perfectly good food that we throw away – all of us – each and every day . . .'

The camera pans backwards, roysh, and there, plonked on top of the worktop beside her, is – get this – an *actual* dustbin.

I'm thinking, no – no focking way. I'm pretty sure Ronan is too.

'One of the arts that's being, if you like, rediscovered in these changed economic times is that of thrift. For a large number of people, cooking leftovers is once again a way of life. Today, I'm going to set aside the rights and wrongs of that, and show you how to make a delicious family casserole using ingredients that a great many of us would typically discard as waste . . .'

'Moy fooken Jaysus,' Ronan even goes – and *he* was raised on the Northside. I can't imagine how hord it must be for a kid of that age to have to watch his grandmother do shit like this on live TV.

She puts her hand into the bin, roysh, and she storts whipping out – I'm *being* serious here – fistfuls of basically vegetable peelings. You can tell from her boat that she's not happy – she looks like she's got an entire ball of Mozarella in her mouth.

'Now, this is something I've been guilty of in the past,' she goes, practically gagging. 'Peeling potatoes, carrots, courgettes, squash, then putting the skins straight into the bin – or, in my case, the electric garbage disposal. Anyone who lived through the Emergency, or the worst of the 1980s, will know that vegetable and fruit skins are simply loaded with vitamins, minerals, potassium and foliates . . .'

I watch her drop them into, like, a pot of water. 'I'm going to boil these up,' she goes, 'and these will form the base of our casserole . . .'

I tell him to turn it off. I mean, it's difficult for even *me* to watch? And anyway, we were midway through one of our famous father–son chats.

I'm there, 'Ro, I've been meaning to have a talk with you for ages now about drugs.'

'Alreet,' he goes, 'what do you wanna know, Ross?'

He's good value – I'll give him that. 'It's not what *I* want to know. It's what *you* need to know – what every kid needs to know.'

'Go on . . .'

'Er, I don't know – that they're bad, I suppose. It's not cool to actually take them . . .'

He sits there, roysh, just nodding at me, lapping up every word.

'If you're ever offered anything – I'm not just saying by those two yahoos either – remember, just say no.'

'Just say no?'

'Just . . . say . . . no.'

He's there, 'Er, reet.'

I didn't get the call-up for Garret's stag night. Not that I'm pissed off, even slightly. Er, go-korting, followed by pints in Break for the Border? Un-focking-believable. Then – and this is a total no-no as far as I'm concerned – they're *meeting up* with Claire's hen porty in Buck Whaleys, presumably to stop the lads from going to a lappy and making a decent night of it.

'Let me guess,' I said to Sorcha when she dropped Honor around to me at lunchtime, 'once you've been to a titty bor in Thailand, you could never go to one here . . .'

She laughed as well, in fairness to her. I was, like, happy to see her heading out – couldn't remember the last time I saw her get all done up for a night on the old tort fuel.

'Except I might not drink that much,' she went. 'I'm – oh my God – *so* wrecked after my community service this week and I want to take Honor into town tomorrow to get her a dress for the wedding. Don't want to be hungover . . .'

I was like, 'A dress?'

'Yeah, Claire asked me could she be a flower girl. Ross, I told you that.'

'I don't remember. Wait a minute – so who's actually *paying* for the dress?'

'Well, *I* am . . .'

I just break my balls laughing.

'Claire offered to,' she went, 'but she wanted to put a fifty-euro limit on it.'

I stopped laughing then and just shook my head sadly. That's the thing about people from Bray. It's one thing to be poor, but *they* make no effort to drag themselves *out* of the gutter?

'Are you *sure* you're okay taking Honor for the night?' she went.

I was like, 'Sorcha, I've been looking forward to this all week. I dare say Honor has as well. You just go and enjoy yourself.'

So it ends up, roysh, that I'm sitting in the gaff – this is, like, six o'clock on a Saturday evening, remember – looking after my daughter instead of getting ready for a night on the rip, that whole sensitive side to my personality that very few people get to see suddenly coming out again.

That's when JP suddenly rings and asks if I fancy a nosebag – he was on to Fionn and they're thinking of hitting Mao.

'No can do,' I go. 'I'm doing the whole Daddy Daycare routine while Sorcha's on the hen,' except *he's* there, 'Bring Honor with you – they *have* a children's menu,' and then I suddenly remember that Saturday night is porty night next door anyway. In an hour's time, the poor kid won't be able to hear Dora the Explorer over the sound of 'Thunder in My Hort', so I think, what the fock. I strap her into the baby seat, then hit Dún Laoghaire.

Fionn and JP are already there, with a cracking table and a bottle of Sapporo in front of them. 'Check out some of the looks I'm getting,' I go, trying to negotiate Honor into the little kiddies chair. 'Birds love goys who are good with kids . . .'

It's true. It's, like, eyes out on stalks everywhere. I give Honor a thick black morker that I happened to have in my pocket and also a menu and leave her scribbling away merrily, like a knacker on the Nightlink.

It turns out the goys have been talking about Oisinn. 'I had a call from his mum,' Fionn goes, 'on his birthday . . .'

I'm there, 'I did as well.'

'Did she seem drunk to you?'

'Drunk? No, it was the morning when she rang me.'

'It was the morning when she rang me as well. She sounded hammered, Ross.'

'Fock,' I go, 'I didn't cop that.'

'Well, JP and I were just discussing what we might do.'

'Or *not* do,' JP goes. 'I mean, you know how *I* feel – wherever he is, he's better off there than here.'

Fionn shakes his head. 'Well, let him stay where he is – as long as we can let Mrs Wallace know he's all right.'

The waitress comes over and takes our order. It's as I'm sitting there, staring at her Walter Mitties, that inspiration suddenly strikes me and it's another one of those occasions when it feels like Father Fehily is up there pulling the levers.

'Hang on a minute,' I go, 'isn't there supposed to be, like, a humanitarian fund to help Castlerock old boys who've fallen on basically hord times?'

JP nods. 'The Castlerock College Benevolent Fund for Rock Boys Who've Had, Like, a Bad Bounce of the Ball?'

I just laugh, then sit back and spread my orms wide. 'Why didn't we think of this before?'

'Think of what?' Fionn goes.

I'm there, 'Er, are you even *listening* to me? There's, like, a fund and it's there to help former players like Oisinn who, through no fault of their own, have got themselves into this kind of situation . . .'

JP throws his opinion in then. 'Oisinn is seventy-five million euros in debt, Ross.'

'Well, what kind of moo do you think is in this fund?'

'I'd be reasonably sure it's nothing like that. Ross, if they sold the school building and the grounds, they still couldn't bail Oisinn out of the trouble he's in.'

Fionn nods. 'And I doubt they would anyway – not with Tom in charge.'

McGahy, of course, is the one who pulled the school out of the Leinster Schools Senior Cup last year, claiming that – let me see if I can remember this – the presentation of adolescent athletes as God figures to their peers has succeeded only in turning our students into monsters. *If* you can believe that.

I'm there, 'I might go and see him, all the same.'

Fionn pulls a face, like he *doesn't* think it's a good idea?

'Hey,' I go, 'all he can do is say no. Best-case scenario, he comes up with enough of the folding green – even just thirty or forty mills – to get the banks off his back. Unless either of you has a better idea?'

They exchange looks that say, er, *I* haven't, just as our storters arrive. 'That's it decided, then,' I go. 'When does school stort back?'

'Not for another three weeks,' he goes. 'But Tom's like me, he always goes back the second week in August, just to prepare for the new term.'

There's *two* men, then, who need their Cheryl Cole.

'The second week in August? That's, like, next week.'

'Exactly.'

I shake my head then. 'I bet that focker thought he'd already seen the last of me . . .'

I look down at Honor's menu – she's made shit of it. 'Very good,' I go, because they *need* encouragement at that age, talent or no talent. I tell the two goys I know where she gets it from – as in, the ortistic streak? – because Sorcha finished seventh in the Texaco ort competition in school, with this amazing picture of a baby seal being basically clubbed to death, then out of his mouth, roysh, he had, like, a speech bubble and he was just going, 'Why?'

Neither of them says shit.

JP, I notice, is suddenly – I don't know – engrossed in his iPhone. 'Danuta's just getting off the Dart,' he goes.

I look at Fionn as if to say, what the fock is he talking about? JP picks up on it. 'Should have mentioned, she's coming in. Said she'd have dessert with us, then the two of us are going to walk the pier. It's going unbelievably well, by the way.'

'She's coming here?' I go, genuine fear in my voice. I'm about to tell him, roysh, that he's bang out of order, inviting a bird to crash our night like this, when I notice that he's suddenly staring at Honor with a look of what could only be described as total horror on his face.

'Oh! My! God!' he goes.

I turn around and look at her, roysh, and it ends up that she's got, like, a tiny smudge of black morker on her face, just above her top *lip*? I don't *get* his over-the-top reaction.

'Er, what's the issue?' I end up going.

He just throws up his hands. 'Ross,' he goes, 'it looks like a Hitler moustache,' and I end up laughing out loud then, because it actually *does*?

JP's *not* laughing, though. He looks as shocked as he did the time that me and Oisinn set fire to the bush outside the window of his dorm in Maynooth and he was convinced he was receiving messages from, I suppose, *Our Lord*?

I end up having to be all, 'Sorry, JP – what is your actual point here?'

'Danuta's grandfather died in the Second Battle of Kharkov, Ross. If she walks in and sees Honor sporting a Hitler moustache . . .'

I suspect she's not the type to see the funny side of it.

'Dude,' I go, 'chillax – I'll wash it off,' then I pour some water on to my napkin, roysh, and stort scrubbing Honor's upper lip. Then *I'm* the one suddenly not chillaxing because it won't actually come off.

Fionn's sort of, like, examining the morker. 'Ross,' he all of a sudden goes, 'it says here *semi-permanent*.'

I'm like, 'Oh, shit!'

'You're just going to have to turn it into a *full* moustache,' JP goes, like it's the most natural thing in the world to say.

I'm like, 'Whoa, are you asking me to draw on my daughter's face?'

'Ross, there's already a moustache there. I'm asking you to just, I don't know, thicken it out a bit . . .'

Fionn sort of, like, tuts, obviously *against* the idea? 'Ross, I really don't think . . .'

But then he's never seen Danuta in action, so his opinion doesn't really carry as much weight. 'Seriously,' JP goes, 'if you heard her talk about the Nazis and the way Oleg died – oh my God, she gets so angry . . .'

I just grab the morker and snap the top off.

He's there, 'Quick, Ross – she's going to be here any minute.'

I hold Honor's head steady, then I use the morker to – as JP suggested – fill it out a bit. I do two or three strokes either side. Then I sort of, like, pull back and look at her. It seems a bit, I don't know, uneven to me, so I add a bit more to the left. But then that side looks a bit, I don't know, *fuller*, so I do a bit more on the right.

Anyway, what happens is that Honor ends up with this huge moustache covering nearly half her face – and thick as a DBS first-year repeat.

Now before I stort hearing accusations of child abuse and whatever else, I should point out that Honor is actually laughing the whole time I'm doing it, thinking it's great crack.

Unfortunately, not everyone agrees with her analysis.

'*What* are you doing?' some focking do-gooder at the next table goes, just as I'm finishing up. She turns to her, I'm presuming, husband and goes, 'He's drawing a moustache on that little girl's face!' and suddenly all I can hear is, like, appalled voices shouting at me as the news, like, ripples through the restaurant.

'You're an animal,' another bird shouts.

I use one or two of the visualization techniques I learned back in my days as a kicker to block out the sudden hostility coming my way. In fact, roysh, I'm sitting there actually admiring the finished orticle when JP storts having another knicker fit.

'No, no, no!' he's suddenly going, with his head in his hands, giving it the full drama queen treatment.

I'm like, 'What now?'

He goes, 'Now she looks like Josef Stalin.'

Of course I ask the obvious question. 'Who the fock is Josef Stalin?'

Even Fionn looks at me, genuinely shocked. 'You've never heard of Josef Stalin?'

I'm like, 'What the fock *is* this – *Blackboard Jungle*?'

JP's looking over his shoulder in a total panic, expecting Danuta to arrive at any second. 'Ross,' he goes, 'I don't have time to explain to you who he was or any of the horrors that the Russian people suffered under him. But you need to do something about that moustache – and quickly . . .'

One of the qualities that made me the rugby player I was, of course, was my ability to think on my feet. 'Maybe I'll tack on a beard,' I go, 'and glasses.'

Except the husband dude at the next table suddenly gets involved again. 'If you draw a beard on that child's face,' he goes, 'I'm calling the Guards.'

Fionn's sitting there with his head in his actual hands.

I'm there, 'Er, it's not illegal, you know. Loads of kids get their faces painted.'

'Yeah, as lions and tigers,' Fionn goes. 'Not as Sébastien Chabal.'

But I snap the top off the morker again. That's when I hear the sound of chair legs scraping across the wooden floor. Another man has suddenly stood up and is staring at me in what could only be described as a threatening way. 'If you do it,' he goes, 'I will beat you senseless – and that's a fucking promise.'

I hesitate, roysh – and, it has to be said, fatally. I'm actually staring at the dude, wondering could I deck him if it *did* come to blows, when all of a sudden I become aware of a long shadow hanging over me – the shadow of JP's six-foot-something, psychotic Russian squeeze.

She's just, like, staring at Honor. It's the exact same look I saw on Sorcha's face when I made the mistake of showing her that dancing bear on YouTube.

'She, er, drew it herself,' is all I can think to say.

Of course she cops the morker still in my hand. 'You seenk zis is funny?' she goes. 'What Stalin deed to ze people of my country?'

The waitress arrives at that exact moment with our main courses.

I'm there, 'I'm going to level with you, Danuta, I'd never heard of this dude until about five minutes ago . . .'

She doesn't bat a focking eyelid – like that day in Shankill. She picks up my bowl of Five Spice Chicken and – honest to fock – just tips it upside down on to my lap.

'Aaarrrggghhh!!!'

I *actually* scream, as the soy sauce marinade soaks through my trousers and boxers and scalds my actual nut-sack. I'm, like, tearing at the crotch of my chinos, going, 'Aaarrrggghhh!!! Ffoooccckkk!!!'

Of course, Danuta is suddenly the hero of the hour. Everyone in the restaurant storts cheering and applauding her.

'Oh, yeah,' I'm going, between howls of agony, 'drawing a moustache on a kid with a semi-permanent morker is wrong, yet a dude getting his towns fricasseed is hilarious, is that it?'

That makes them only cheer louder.

A waiter tips over and tells me – *me!* – that he thinks I should leave, although deep down I realize that he's possibly talking sense. This audience is way beyond tired of my act.

So I pick Honor out of her high chair, and then, with twenty or thirty, I suppose, fellow diners abusing me – and with my knackers throbbing like they've been pressed in a focking waffle toaster – I make my way, very slowly, to the door.

Behind me, I hear JP say that he wonders whether there's

a fund for Rock boys who've had a bad bounce of *both* balls?

Which isn't funny. Which isn't even *nearly* funny?

'*I've been stung by a wasp*, the lady golfer screamed. *I've been stung by a wasp . . .*'

This is Hennessy, in case you didn't already guess, making a speech at the surprise porty my old man threw for him to celebrate his fortieth year in the legal profession.

'*Where did it sting you?* the golf pro asked. The lady golfer replied, *It was between the first and second holes.* Quick as a flash, the golf pro said, *Well, it sounds to me like your feet are too far apart on your down-swing . . .*'

The old man practically coughs up an organ, he laughs that hord.

'Enjoy your evening,' Hennessy just goes, then the entire room bursts into a spontaneous round of applause, by the end of which the old man is *still* laughing and shaking his head.

'Golf!' he just goes. 'Dear, oh dear!'

I'm there, 'You didn't even get that joke, did you?' and the thing is, roysh, he doesn't even *try* to deny it?

'Way over *my* head,' he goes. 'Though I suspect it's one of his world-famous *blue* ones – quote-unquote, and whatever you're having yourself.'

He looks around him and asks me what I think of the Arnold Palmer Room, like he *owns* the focking K Club? I tell him to cop on. I took Sorcha to see Rebecca Storm here and that was, like, years ago.

I call him a dickhead but of course it just washes over him. Because he suddenly spots Erika across the room, chatting to Helen and some friends of hers.

'Let's get your sister over here, shall we? I have a bit of news you might be interested in hearing,' and then he storts going, 'Erika! Erika!' at, like, the top of his voice.

Over she comes. She looks – I'm going to say it – amazing.

'Sorcha's looking for you,' is her opening line to me. 'She told me to tell you to ring her. Immediately, Ross.'

I'm there, 'Is it about Honor's moustache?'

She just shakes her head then, like she can't believe what an actual idiot I am, even after all these years.

The old man rubs his hands together then, like he's got something actually worthwhile to say to us. 'A lot of people wondered, when my plans for the Mountjoy Hotel and Casino had to be regrettably put in mothballs, what, if anything, old Charles O'Carroll-Kelly was going to do next. I think it's fair to say a good percentage expected the chap to just settle back into some form of semi-retirement, selling his slices of Montenebro and Lincolnshire Poacher – to all intents and purposes a spent force . . .'

I'm there, 'Is there any chance you might get to the point before I die of focking boredom?'

'Ross!' Erika goes, instantly taking *his* side. I never would have had *her* down as such a crawler.

'Well,' he just goes, 'the veil of secrecy can finally be lifted. It's time to tell you about my new business venture.'

I laugh. 'What are you wasting your focking time on now?'

He comes straight out with it. 'Shredding!'

'Shredding?'

Even Erika seems surprised.

'Oh, I know what you kids are thinking – hello, what's this? Has the *old dad* finally gone doolally? But think about it. The public is angry. They've suddenly got no money and they're looking for others to blame for their predicament. You've seen that with your mother, Ross, the way they've all turned on her . . .'

'Sorry,' I go, 'is this actually going anywhere?'

'The media have started asking some of their famous

questions,' he goes. 'Finally discovered the truth in what I said at my sentencing hearing – that this Celtic Tiger they were all so bloody fond of didn't come about without certain individuals, many of them friends of mine, being up to their necks in all sorts.

'Of course, when I said it, well, they thought it was just the rantings of a condemned man. But three years later, look – surprise, surprise – it turns out that old Charlie was right all along. It *was* all built on what they like to call corruption . . .'

'So where does the shredding come in?' it's Erika who goes.

He's there, 'Well, now, I'm rather firm in the belief that it's time for us, as a society, to get rid of the evidence.'

I actually laugh in his face. He's the same shady focker he's always been.

He's there, 'Your godfather over there was the unwitting inspiration behind the name, Ross.'

I look over at Hennessy. He's introducing some random Mary Steenburgen lookalike to JP's old man, who's airkissing her and at the same time trying to unclip her bra from the back. Another focker who'll never learn his lesson.

'There I was,' the old man goes, 'facing a difficult putt on the fifth at Elm Park, at the same time trying to come up with a name for the enterprise, something that captures the essence of this exciting new age in which we find ourselves living. Then I remembered the legal opinion that our learned friend over there gave me when the Criminal Assets Bureau arrived at the door with their so-called warrant and their bloody battering ram . . .'

'Shred focking everything?' I go.

He's there, 'Shred Focking Everything! I've even had it emblazoned across the side of the van.'

'Van?' Erika goes – she's as concerned as I am.

'Yes, I bought a van – Old Amnesia, I've christened her –

and I've already got a machine in the back of there capable of shredding three sacks of documents per minute!'

I'm like, 'You're so focking dodgy, you know that?'

'*If you can build a business up big enough, it's respectable,*' he goes. 'I can't remember who said that, but someone did.'

I don't know what he's waiting for – a standing ovation or some shit? I say fock-all, roysh, while Erika just sips her Sancerre. Then, after five or ten seconds of silence, we're talking totally out of the blue here, *he* goes, 'What do you say to being partners, Ross?'

I'm obviously there, 'Portners?'

He's like, 'Why not? The old team, back together again!'

'Honestly?' I go. 'I'd rather boil in my own focking spit.'

'Well, there's no rush, Ross. Take your time to decide.'

I can't go on avoiding Sorcha's calls. It's been, like, eight or nine times a day for the past week, so eventually I end up just *having* to answer?

'How the hell are you?' I go. It's like someone's suddenly slipped me a verbal suppository. 'I actually saw you the other day on South Anne Street, doing your community service and shit? Unfortunately, didn't have time to stop. What was it you were doing with that sort of, like, suction thing, by the way? I'm presuming it was, like, pulling chewing-gum off the street . . .'

She's in no mood for my pleasantries, though. She's there, 'What kind of way is that to return your daughter?'

I'm there, 'Errr, just to be clear here, are we talking about the moustache?'

'*I'm* talking about *you*, Ross, leaving her on the doorstep, ringing the bell and running.'

'Oh, that . . .'

'Yes, *that*!'

'Well, just to make it clear, I didn't *actually* run? I hid behind the front wall, just until you opened the door – had to make sure you were in, see.'

She's, like, seriously pissed off with me. 'Who drew that moustache on her face?' she goes.

I'm there, 'Would you believe me if I told you she actually did it herself?'

'No, Ross, because *she* said her daddy did it.'

'Okay, then, since *she* blabbed, I'm going to be honest and tell you it was actually a joint effort . . .'

'What kind of morker is it, Ross? It won't come off . . .'

'Er, all I know is, there was talk of it being semi-permanent.'

'Semi-permanent?'

She is *not* happy. 'Look, don't panic,' I go. 'See, I've been thinking a lot about that word. Do you remember that Italian bird you had working in the shop a couple of summers ago? Lazy as sin. *I* thought she looked like Petra Němcová . . .'

'Nadia?'

'Nadia, exactly. Well, *she* was semi-permanent, wasn't she? And you managed to get rid of her – eventually.'

My words come as pretty much *no* comfort to her?

'She's supposed to be a flower girl in, like, three days' time, Ross! And speaking of which, where are those Mass leaflets?'

My body goes instantly cold. I'm there, 'Mass leaflets?'

She pretty much *roars* it at me? 'Oh my God, the Mass leaflets you promised to collect from Reads!'

I'm just there, 'Hey, calm down – I collected them,' which I actually *did*?

'So where are they?' she goes.

That's what I can't for the focking life of me remember. I'm like, 'Er, they're here in front of me. I'm actually looking at them right now.'

'Okay, I'll call up and collect them from you in the morning.'

Shit.

'The morning's actually going to be tricky, Babes. I'm going to go see McGahy – see will the school throw us a few shekels to get Oisinn out of the shit.'

Fock. I suddenly remember. I went for one or two scoops in Ron Blacks after I collected them. I must have left the focking things there.

Sorcha sort of, like, sighs. 'On second thoughts,' she goes, 'I don't think I even want to see you at the moment. Just bring them to the church on the morning of the wedding – and don't even show your face if you've forgotten them, Ross.'

Then she just hangs up.

I sit back in my chair, thinking, okay, Rossmeister, how are you going to get out of this one with your good looks intact? I rack my brains for, like, twenty minutes, as the opening notes of 'One Man Band' come thumping through the wall. I grab a Ken from the fridge and think about it some more. Then it suddenly comes to me – so obvious I can't believe that it took as long as it did.

She answers on, like, the third ring. I'm like, 'Claire, what's the crack?'

She seems surprised that it's me. 'Ross,' she goes, 'did you collect the Mass leaflets from Reads?'

I laugh.

'Why is everyone suddenly panicking about the Mass leaflets? Yes, I focking collected them. I told Sorcha I'd bring them to the church.'

'Okay, would *you* mind actually giving them out on the day?'

'Yeah, whatever. Look, I need to ask you something. I've got this, let's just say, *friend* who's also getting married and he wants to do it on the major cheap like yourselves. He rang me there five seconds ago looking for some advice. Just answer me this, where did you get that Mass leaflet – as in, the original?'

'We actually got it off the internet. There's this, oh my God, amazing website, where they have, like, three hundred different wedding Masses that you can download . . .'

'Okay, so what's the actual address?'

'I'll send you the link . . .'

'Okay. And, again, just as a matter of interest, which Mass did you pick?'

'Well, *we* picked number 209, which is amazing, really, because that's the date we actually met – as in the 2nd of September?'

'Er, whatever – just send me that focking link, will you?'

'Okay, it's just going to you now. Oh and tell your friend not to forget to change all the names.'

'Names?'

'Yeah, they use just generic names – the Masses are all The Wedding of John and Mary, so they'll have to go through it and change all the Johns to whatever *his* name is and all the Marys to whatever *her* name is . . .'

It's a good job she told me that. I'm there, 'Cool. Anyway, look, I've got to go. Shit to do.'

I hang up, then click on the link. Twenty minutes later, I've managed to download Mass 209, I've changed all the Marys to Claires and all the Johns to Garrets and I've printed the thing out. First thing tomorrow morning, before I hit the school, I'll be stood outside Reads, waiting for the fockers to open.

And I'll have dodged a serious bullet.

She's a little breathtaker, I'll give her that. I'm talking about McGahy's new secretary here? A little focking breathtaker.

I'm giving her the famous Come to Papa eyes, but she's not paying me any attention, if you can believe that. She's listening to some tosspot on the radio saying that a period of austerity might help us all rediscover our soul as a nation, that we went from being a very poor country to a very rich one in such a short space of time that somewhere along the way we lost our moral compass.

I don't think she's even wearing a bra.

She suddenly catches me having a scope, so I end up going, 'There's, like, no getting away from it, is there?'

She's there, 'Sorry?'

If I had to describe her as looking like someone, I'd probably have to say Omarosa Manigault-Stallworth, except obviously white. 'Just the whole current economic bullshit. It's all anyone's even talking about these days, I don't know if you've noticed.'

'Well, it's people's livelihoods,' she goes, big serious boat on her. 'My mum and dad are really, really good friends with this couple – they look like they're going to lose their house.'

This sort of, like, catches me on the hop, so I just nod, like she might have a point after all.

Another reason I was pretty much worshipped as a rugby player was my ability to suddenly switch the direction of the play. Of course I end up proving that I've still got it.

'You think that's bad?' I go, rattling my brains for one or two of my own horror stories. 'Did you also know that Cooke's is gone?'

'Cooke's?'

'Er, as in Cooke's Café? It was actually one of the better ones, in fairness to it.'

'I've, em, never heard of it.'

Quick as a flash, I go, 'It's a pity it's gone, then – I'd have offered to take you there for, like, a meal and shit?'

It's the kind of line that could sound sleazy if it came from anybody else. She sort of, like, smiles, then goes back to whatever it is that secretaries do, obviously telling herself, basically, get a hold of yourself – at least *try* to keep it businesslike?

All the same, I'd bull her to exhaustion. See, McGahy cracks on to be all high and mighty but he's a dirty dog like the rest of us.

Some other tool on the radio is saying he remembers being in Dalkey at what would have been the height of the boom. He was having a coffee in Idle Wilde one Saturday morning, reading his *Irish Independent*, when one of these, you know, sports cars pulled up, too close to the path, and scraped its alloys right along the side of the kerb. The young man in the car – you know the type, pink T-shirt, shades on his head – he got out and, well, I don't know if it was embarrassment or not, but he didn't even look at the damage he'd done to his wheels.

I just roll my eyes.

'They try to blame everything on the Celtic Tiger, don't they?' She tries to look as if she's concentrating on something else. 'My own personal attitude is why can't they just leave it the fock alone?'

My phone suddenly beeps.

Sorcha says they're talking about me on *Lunchtime with Eamon Keane*. I text her back and tell her that it could have been anyone. It's Dalkey, for fock's sake.

The next thing, McGahy's office door opens and out walk – get this – four nuns. We're talking four *actual* nuns here? Of course, I can't resist it. I stort giving it, 'All the single ladies, all the single ladies . . .' obviously trying to put a smile on the secretary's face, whatever her name is.

You can tell she loves it, even though she's doing her best to *not* laugh?

Of course, *they're* not happy bunnies – as in the nuns – having the piss ripped out of them like that, and one of them even stops, stares hord at me, then tells me that she remembers me. She doesn't mean it in a good way either.

'It's okay, Sister Eunice,' this voice suddenly goes – McGahy, obviously. 'I'll handle this one.'

She carries on giving me filthies, then eventually backs down. I'm still cracking my hole laughing as I follow McGahy into his office. 'Sister Eunice,' I end up going, more to break the ice than anything. 'That's a name from my dark past. Do you know how many times she threatened to call the Feds on me?'

He doesn't answer. He just sits himself down on the other side of the desk. See, he's always had it in for me. Like I'm always saying – literally no interest in rugby.

'I take it you're back doing musicals with Loreto Foxrock,' I go, pulling up a chair opposite him. 'Bygones be bygones, blahdy blahdy blah. God, it's all ahead of Ronan. You know my son's storting here in a few weeks?'

'Yes, Ronan,' he goes. 'We're looking forward to having him. He's top of his class in the junior school.'

'Well, if I had my way, he'd be going somewhere else – somewhere that still plays rugby. But his mother thinks this place would be better for his education. It's, like, whatever sizzles your bacon.'

He has this look of, like, total boredom on his face. 'To what do I owe this pleasure?' he goes, which is such a focking teachery thing to say. So I end up getting straight to the point. I mention Oisinn's name and he continues to look at me – I swear to fock – blankly.

'Er, Oisinn Wallace?' I end up having to go. 'Hooker on the 1999 Leinster Schools Senior Cup team? Helped bring glory to this school?'

'Well, that's a matter of opinion,' he goes, the smug prick. 'And rugby is a game that's no longer played here at Castlerock College.'

I'm there, 'Dude, I know you've always had it in for the game. But we're talking about a goy here who mentioned the name of Castlerock in every interview he practically did over the years. We're talking *Elle*. We're talking *Vogue*. We're talking actual *Esquire* . . .'

'Ah,' he suddenly goes, his face brightening, 'this is the boy who invented all these . . . *fragrances*.'

'That's the dude. *Eau d'Affluence* and blahdy blah.'

'Yes, I read about him in – I think it was the *Independent* . . .' I don't think I'm imagining the delight in his actual voice. 'He's disappeared, hasn't he?'

'Pegged it is more the word. But yeah, no, he had serious debts.'

'Did he indeed?'

'Yeah, he'd have lost a fair few shekels in the whole property crash? He's supposed to have had a fair bit of bread in shares as well . . .'

'So he left his car at Dublin Airport and took off for God knows where.'

'Exactly. Anyway, there's two or three of us – his old team-mates, in other words? – and we're trying to, like, track him down.'

He's there, 'One or two banks and financial institutions as well, I'd wager,' grinning like the Grinny McDumbfock that he is. Then he sort of, like, shakes his head. 'Why are you telling me this anyway?'

'Well,' I go, 'he's a former student who's fallen on hord times . . .'

'He's not alone.'

'And it's a well-known fact, in rugby circles anyway, that the school has, like, a fund to help people like him.'

'Does it indeed?'

'Er, yeah? Namely the Castlerock College Benevolent Fund for Rock Boys Who've Had, Like, a Bad Bounce of the Ball?'

He just stares blankly at me.

'Well, does it even exist?' I go. 'Or was it always just talk?'

He's there, 'Oh, it exists. For genuine cases. Former students struck down by illness or incapacitated. It's certainly not for those who lost vast fortunes by engaging in greedy speculation . . .'

Greedy speculation? I actually feel like reaching across this desk there and decking him.

'. . . and who then chose to flee the jurisdiction,' he goes, 'rather than face up to their responsibilities.'

I just shake my head. I'm there, 'Who are you to say the fund isn't for those kind of people? I can tell you for a fact that Father Fehily would have wanted . . .'

'Father Fehily wanted a lot of things,' he just goes. 'Access to a warm-weather port for the German navy. The pushing back of the Oder-Neisse line . . .'

He's ripping the piss out of the dude's funeral homily now. I tell him he's out of order – and we're talking bang.

'Oh, don't worry,' I end up going, 'I know *why* you're being a dick here? It's because my old man withdrew his donation towards the new science block . . .'

He has the balls to laugh in my actual face.

He's there, 'I can assure you, we can – and will – build a new science block without the help of Charles O'Carroll-Kelly.'

'Well,' I go, 'you could have had a flood-lit, all-weather pitch as well. Seán Dunne's supposed to have ponied up for one for Clongowes, you know? But then *you* had to go and pull out of the Leinster Schools Senior Cup. No offence, but my old man takes his rugby seriously – so should everyone.'

He suddenly stands up and walks out from behind the desk. I'm thinking, where the fock is he going?

'Rugby,' he goes, disappearing behind me, 'brought nothing

but trouble and shame to this institute of learning. It's rather fortunate, as it happens, that you should have come to see me today – you've saved us the cost of a stamp.'

Inside, roysh, I'm thinking, what the fock is he banging on about now? He opens the door and I hear him go, 'Susan, can you give me one of those letters there – the one for Ross O'Carroll-Kelly?'

Susan. I was going to actually congratulate him on her, but he can forget about that now.

Suddenly, roysh, he's back in the room again and he's handing me an envelope, very official-looking, typed of course, with the words 'Castlerock College' across the top.

'What's this?' I go.

He's there, 'Oh, just some old business we're finally putting to bed. Do let me know if you ever catch up with your friend – there's one for him too.'

'I'll, er, look at it later,' I go. I don't know what the fock it is, roysh, but something tells me I shouldn't give him the pleasure of opening it here. 'So, just to recap,' I go, 'you're saying you can't do anything to help Oisinn?'

He's there, 'No, I'm saying I *won't* do anything to help him. And, as you can see, I'm quite busy here, preparing for the new term. So if that's everything . . .'

What a dick. I stand up. 'You're a disgrace to the name of this school,' I go.

He's just there, 'Goodbye.'

I walk out of there, making sure to really slam the door behind me. I morch past Susan's desk and ask her, at the top of my voice, how it feels to be working for an actual dipshit. She doesn't get a chance to answer because all of a sudden, roysh, who walks into the office only Fionn.

Poor fock. He did nothing with his summer, as far I can see, except read books. And now he's back at work – early, I might add. Still, if he's happy to be a sucker, there's fock-all *I* can say to him.

'Hey, Ross,' he goes, 'they've just been talking about you on the radio, you know.'

I'm there, 'There's no proof that it's me, Fionn – how many other goys do you reckon have done that?' and he shrugs, like I *could* actually have a point.

'How did you get on with Tom?' he goes.

I laugh like I was mad to think it'd go any other way. 'I don't know how you could work for someone who hates rugby as much as he does.'

He sort of, like, nods at the envelope in my hand. 'What's that?'

I'm like, 'I don't actually *know*?' and then I stort, like, ripping open the envelope.

It's funny, roysh, but before I even whip out the letter, I get this sudden feeling of, I suppose you'd have to call it, *dread*? Out of the corner of my eye, I notice Susan copping a sly look over, to get my reaction, and I immediately know that it's going to be bad news.

I read the opening lines and I'm suddenly sweating like a fat bird writing her first love letter. 'What's wrong?' Fionn goes, 'What does it say?'

I finish reading. Except I'm too in shock to even *talk*? I just hand him the letter.

It's like . . .

17 August 2009

Dear Member of the 1999 senior rugby squad,

It has been brought to the attention of the school author-ities that a member of the team that represented Castlerock

College in the 1999 Leinster Schools Senior Cup competition admitted, in the course of a recently published interview, that the drug methamphetamine had been administered to him prior to matches.

The Leinster Branch of the Irish Rugby Football Union has written to the school to point out that this substance is banned under the rules of the competition.

On 18 February 2009, Newbridge College, the beaten finalists in 1999, indicated by letter that they intended to take legal action to have Castlerock College retroactively disqualified from the competition on the basis of this admission, which was contained in the book *We Need to Talk About Ross.*

On 2 June 2009, meeting in emergency session, the Board of Governors of Castlerock College voted unanimously not to contest any such action. Subsequently, in conjunction with the Leinster Branch and the Board of Governors of Newbridge College, it was agreed, in the interests of fair play, that the result of the final, played on 17 March 1999, would be rescinded and the match awarded to Newbridge College.

Accordingly, we would ask you to return your winner's medal to the school at your earliest convenience.

Kind regards,
Tom McGahy
Principal

Fionn finishes reading the letter and hands it back to me. We're both so in shock, we end up having to lean against the actual wall? I feel instantly guilty. I'm the one who opened my big Von Trapp.

I go, 'This must be what Mocky meant when he said, there

was never a tide flowed – whatever the fock. Dude, please tell me they can't do this.'

He looks me dead in the eye. 'They can,' he goes. 'And it looks like they already have.'

8. From My Dead Cole Haans

'Oh! My God!' the birds are all going. 'She looks *so* amazing,' which she *doesn't* by the way?

And they know it.

Whatever bunch of beauty-school dropouts ended up doing Claire's make-up, she's obviously had some kind of reaction to it, which has left her boat all plump and shiny, while the dress has ended up looking a real mess after that day in Kilcroney, despite Sorcha's old dear's best efforts with the Singer.

In all honesty, she looks like a focking Pixar character wrapped in a net curtain.

Which, by the way, are the exact words I text to JP. Then I lean forward in the pew, just to get his reaction. Except he just mouths the word, 'What?' to me and I shake my head as if to say it doesn't matter.

His phone will be on silent, you mork my words – some shit about being in the house of God.

'Erika and Sorcha look great too,' Fionn, who's sitting between us, goes. Which *is* true and they're the only ones here who do. Claire's old pair, her two brothers, her Bray mates – they're all rough as guts, while *his* side aren't exactly easy on the eye either.

'I've been at some ugly weddings,' I go, out of the side of my mouth, 'but this is a real focking slaughterhouse, isn't it?'

Fionn's there, 'Hey, be nice,' except he *is* laughing?

'Brothers and sisters,' the priest goes, 'we are gathered here today to celebrate the union in marriage of Garret and Claire . . .'

Well, I'm thinking, at least I got the names right.

Oh yeah, I had to come clean about the Mass leaflets when Garret copped that they weren't on whatever focking paper it was they ordered. He actually pulled me, roysh, outside the church, while I was dishing them out, asking me what happened to the originals. I told him I was pretty sure I left them in Ron Blacks, which is why I printed out new ones – er, what's the major deal?

'Okay,' I go, turning to Fionn, 'this is where the laughter ends. Tell JP to sit forward in his seat there,' which he automatically does. 'Now, we've all had, like, a week to, I don't know, digest, dissect – whatever the actual word is – the news about our medals . . .'

'Ross,' JP goes, 'do you really think this is the time and place?'

I decide not to dignify that question with a response. 'We know this thing is happening,' I go, giving him a hord stare. 'What I want to know now is what are we going to do about it?'

JP pulls a face. He's there, 'What *can* we do?'

I shake my head. 'That doesn't sound like the JP who, for two years, was possibly one of the best three fullbacks for his age in the country – definitely top five . . .'

See, I'm suddenly full of, I don't know, resolve to fight this thing – that's what makes me a winner.

Fionn pushes his glasses up on his nose. 'Well, the question still stands, Ross. We've been retroactively disqualified.'

'So, what,' I go in, like, a *real* angry whisper, 'you're just going to hand your medal over to some focking farmhand?'

That rocks them both back in their pews.

'I'm really sorry, goys, but you're not listening to me. Which means I'm going to have to give it to you in a language you understand. You give that medal back to the school and this time next week it'll be hanging around the neck of Mocky or some other dangle-eyed chewbacon.'

They both look at each other. They know that, whatever way you slice it, that can't be right.

I'm there, 'I certainly didn't captain us to victory for that to one day happen.'

'*Ssshhh!*' some woman behind us goes and I half turn around and go, 'Hey, shush your focking self!'

JP's there, 'Do you really think there's a chance we could get to keep our medals?'

Of course, I'm suddenly loving the moment, suddenly playing it cooler than the other side of the pillow. 'What is it that dude always says? *From my cold, dead hands?*'

Fionn, for one, is definitely impressed. He's always seen me as a leader.

'Ross, are you saying you *have* a plan?'

I actually laugh – I *have* to. 'Oh, I've one or two little things bubbling away up there in the old head, don't you worry about that. We worked too hord for these medals to just give them up without a fight. I'm already going to talk to my old man – do you think he's going to stand by and just let this happen? Er, I don't *think* so? He's been dining out on my glory for ten years. Focker wouldn't have a social life if it wasn't for me. What I need *you* to do, Fionn, is get all the goys back together.'

'I don't know, Ross – most of them we haven't seen since the Debs.'

I'm there, 'Doesn't matter – you can get their contact details from the school. You haven't quit your job yet, have you?'

'What do you mean *yet?*'

'Well, I'm presuming you're going to.'

He doesn't answer.

I'm there, 'I focking *hope* you are. Anyway, you do the ringaround. All the goys will all have got their letters by now.

279

Obviously, they're going to be devastated. It'll be, *How can I go on?* and blahdy blahdy blah. Then you ring, going, "Er, what are you worried for? The Rossmeister General has a plan of focking action." Say some shit like, we've got one more game to play – and this time it's personal. Actually, don't use that, I'll keep that for when I see them . . .'

Then it's, like, eyes front again.

Something else occurs to me. 'By the way,' I go, 'don't tell Christian?'

Fionn's there, 'Why not?'

The thing is, roysh, I don't *know* why? I just don't want him finding out – maybe because, deep down, I know that it's all my fault.

'He's in the States,' I go. 'It'll be ages before he finds out – and by then, it'll be sorted. Just don't tell him.'

He's there, 'Okay, whatever you say.'

Honor looks amazing in that little dress that Sorcha bought her – even *with* the moustache? She's looking back, going, 'Daddy! Daddy!' and I'm waving away at her until she goes, 'My daddy drew on my face!' and people stort throwing me these horrified looks. Then Sorcha tells her she has to be quiet because Claire and Garret are about to exchange their vows.

Claire from Brayruit getting married. Who'd have honestly thunk it? I can be a bit, I don't know, sentimental at times, which is why I'm suddenly sat there thinking, Jesus, there's focking hope for everyone.

She's stood at the altar, giving it, 'I, Claire Theresa Sammon, take you, Garret John Hassett, to be my husband . . .'

That's when, out of the blue, I suddenly go, 'Fock! Nooo!'

Because I've realized, roysh, with a fright that almost stops my focking hort, that the text about Claire looking like a Pixar character in a net curtain – I sent it to *her* phone instead of JP's.

Literally everyone is turned around and suddenly staring at

me again. Sorcha's up there, mouthing the words 'Oh! My! God!' in my general direction, not a happy rabbit about it either.

He – in other words Garret? – looks like he wants to come down and finally deck me.

'Do you have something to say about this union?' the priest storts going. 'Apart from that vulgarism you just uttered.'

I'm there, 'Errr, no, you're cool.'

'Are you sure?'

'Yeah, you can, er, proceed.'

'That's most gracious of you.'

Anyway, they continue with their vows. Out of the corner of his mouth, Fionn goes, 'I take it you saw the Eucharistic Prayer,' and of course at that point I haven't a focking clue what he's even talking about.

I'm too busy thinking that I've *got* to stop her reading that focking text. But where's her Wolfe? She wouldn't have it with her, would she? No, of course she wouldn't. Could it be possibly back in the gaff? And if so, how am I going to get to it and delete that message before she sees it?

It's these kind of thoughts that occupy my, I suppose, *brain* for most of the next ten or fifteen minutes? Even when Garret is kissing the bride and the audience is clapping away, roysh, I'm sat there in an actual daze, trying to come up with a strategy to get my hands on that phone first.

JP's suddenly sat forward in his seat then. He's like, 'Has anyone looked at the Eucharistic Prayer?'

I turn to Fionn and I'm like, 'What is it about this focking prayer?'

'*We offer you our sacrifices of praise,*' the priest is going, '*for our own good and the good of those who are dear to us . . .*'

'When you changed the names on the version you downloaded,' Fionn goes, 'did you do it line by line?'

I'm there, 'I did in my Swiss. I just did a search and replace.'

'That'd explain it.'

'*We pray to you, our living and true God, for our well-being and redemption . . .*'

'Explain what?'

'Wait for it . . .'

'*In union with the whole Church, we honour Claire, the ever-virgin mother of Jesus Christ our Lord . . .*'

There's, like, a collective intake of breath. Claire and Garret are suddenly looking over their shoulders, directly at me, giving me serious daggers. Of course everyone else in the audience suddenly senses that, whatever happened, it's basically down to me, so they stort staring me out of it as well.

There's one thing that's certain. Even without them knowing about that text message, I've already managed to make myself *the* most hated person at this wedding. That much is obvious from the looks I get from the supposedly happy couple as they make their way down the aisle, orm in orm, followed by my wife and daughter, my sister and the focking cast of *Shameless*.

The most embarrassing bit is having to face the line-up. 'Well done, Ross,' JP goes, while we're waiting for our turn to say congratulations, 'you've made it another day to remember.'

I'm like, 'Dude, you honestly have no idea. I've just done that shit where you accidentally send a text to the person you're actually ripping the back out of.'

'Claire?' he goes. He's laughing, roysh, even though he knows it's not funny. He doesn't even ask me what it said. He just goes, 'Oh, shit!' presuming – knowing me – that it's *got* to be bad.

'Major congrats,' I suddenly go, sticking my hand out, 'you've got yourself a good girl there.'

Garret doesn't even shake it. He just goes, 'You couldn't even be happy for us, you're that eaten up with jealousy.'

What a prize prick.

'Well, if you're talking about me shouting out in the middle of the Mass,' I try to go, 'I actually thought the priest made a bit of a meal out of it? What is it, the first time he's ever heard the F word? *How* long has he lived in this town?'

I turn to Claire, then. I'm there, 'Congrats,' and I go to, like, hug her, except she pulls away, roysh, looks over my shoulder and tells JP that she's *so* sorry she couldn't invite Danuta, it's just the numbers and blah blah blah.

Sorcha and Erika are already standing outside in their Yo Thai waitress outfits, next to Chloe, Sophie, Amie with an ie and Fionn. I decide to, like, tip over and just brazen it out. 'I've said it before and I'll say it again,' I go, 'special occasions or not, Mass is focking boring, isn't it?'

Sorcha's holding Honor and just shaking her head, like she's basically given up on me.

'So what is it, Ross,' Sophie has to go, 'are you in love with Claire or something?'

'Please!' I go. 'I've been *in* there a load of times, don't forget – and I've *always* thought the girl was horrendous. A real focking mess.'

Of course her old dear happens to be standing right behind me at the time and I can immediately tell it's going to be one of those days when I literally can't do or say *anything* right?

Luckily, roysh, Erika changes the subject. 'Fionn,' she goes, 'you were talking about the Edvard Munch exhibition . . .'

Fionn pushes his glasses up on his nose.

He goes, 'Yeah, no, I was talking about *The Scream*, which is obviously his best-known work. I was just saying, he was on the record somewhere as saying that he got the inspiration to paint it after stepping out for a walk one evening and witnessing this brilliantly orange sunset, which art historians always believed was simply a reflection of his famous melancholy.

But I was reading this book recently – it said geologists have discovered that when Krakatoa erupted in 1883, it caused the sky over northern Europe to turn an unnaturally fiery colour, which is almost certainly what inspired him to paint his masterpiece nearly ten years later.'

There's lots of wows from the birds, humouring him basically. Then Sorcha says we'd better stort making our way up to the gaff. 'Where is it?' I go. 'Just beyond the second burnedout Nightlink on the left?' and then I hear Claire's old man asking one of her brothers, 'Who is he anyway?'

I end up giving Sorcha, Honor and Erika a lift. On the walk to the cor, Erika links me – there's a real, yeah, you're a total penis but you're still my brother vibe to it – and she goes, 'Isn't Fionn just *so* interesting?' and I laugh and go, 'Er, yeah, whatever blows your skirt up.'

We arrive at the gaff, roysh, and in we go. I sidle straight over to Claire, then whip out my phone and subtly go, 'God, I must turn this thing back on,' even though it *is* on?

Of course she ponies up the info I'm looking for. 'Yeah, I left mine up in my bedroom,' she goes. 'I didn't want any distractions today,' and then she remembers what happened in the church and goes, 'You *better* put that thing on silent during the *Rod Nam Sang* ceremony, Ross,' to which there's no *real* answer?

The meal, believe it or not, ends up being surprisingly all right, even if it *is* just the house special yellow curry from The King and Thai on the Quinsboro Road.

And it's actually really nice to be just, I don't know, sitting around like this, the old crew back together again – me talking about how there's no focking way in the world I'm giving up this medal, JP saying he's not either, and Amie with an ie saying she's tried to get into *Breaking Bad* but it's, oh my God, nowhere near as good as *Californication*.

At the same time, I'm watching Claire like a focking hawk, of course, to make sure she doesn't just nip upstairs to check her texts – to the point where Sophie actually turns around, roysh, being a total bitch, and goes, 'Oh my God, Ross, you can't take your eyes off her!'

About, like, an hour or so after the meal, roysh, Claire and *him* get up from the table and suddenly sit, I don't know, cross-legged in the middle of the kitchen floor. Some half-Thai, half-Irish dude called Johnny, who apparently runs a kick-boxing club in Fassaroe, is going to be the supposed monk for the ceremony.

They tell everyone to, like, crowd around, roysh, and I decide to use the sudden confusion to try to, like, slip upstairs. I'm thinking, happy focking days. Except Sorcha cops me, roysh, just as I'm disappearing around the door of the kitchen. She's like, 'Where are *you* going?'

Of course *I'm* suddenly the centre of attention again, with everyone just, like, staring at me.

'Er, to be brutally honest,' I go, 'this kind of shit really isn't my *bag*? I was going to use it as a chance to go for a hit and miss. My back teeth are actually floating.'

'Sit down!' Claire's old man just goes and you can tell from the way he says it that he's not expecting a debate.

So I end up having to sit through the whole focking show then – the chain of flowers, the conch shell, the full bag of chips – sober as fock and slowly losing the will to live.

When it's finally over, we each have to give a personal message of goodwill to the happy couple. I get totally caught on the hop and mine ends up being, 'Er, I think it's actually pretty cool, blah blah blah,' and I hear JP behind me go, 'Thank you, the Dalai Lama,' which one or two others seem to think is hilarious.

I don't actually rise to the bait. There's loads of shit I

could throw back at him but all I can think about is that phone.

Over the next couple of hours, I make two or three further attempts to get upstairs, but I keep getting constantly cornered, firstly by Chloe, who mentions that Kelly Rutherford has named her son Hermès, which she thinks is *so* an amazing name for a baby, then by one of Claire's brothers, who tells me that if this wasn't such a happy day for his family, he would beat me to a bloody pulp, then dump my sorry carcass into the Dargle.

I'm thinking, dude, you don't even know the worst of it yet.

Another hour passes with me still trying to get out of the room and upstairs. But then Sorcha dumps Honor into my orms to take a photo of the bride and groom cutting the tiramisu.

Then it's suddenly the first dance, which ends up being 'World of Our Own', in the middle of the sun room. Claire's always claimed she was with Kian Egan – as in *with* with? – before he ended up being with Jodi Albert, though, conveniently for her, no one was there to actually *witness* it?

I look over at Erika, roysh, and I notice that she's, like, standing on her own, watching Claire and fock-head dance, literally just staring at them, totally lost in the moment. I tip over to her, still holding Honor, and I go, 'If it's the last thing I do, I'm going to prove that story about her meeting Westlife in Jurys is total horseshit.'

Usually, roysh, you'd expect Erika to at least *try* to top that? She's always hated Claire. But this time she doesn't. She actually goes, 'They're so in love, Ross,' and it's immediately obvious that she's a little bit jorred. 'To think, I used to pity her. And now here I am, weirdly jealous . . .'

'Of *him*?' I go.

'No, not of Garret. I'm jealous of their happiness. Of their certainty . . .'

'Hey, it'll happen for you,' I try to go. 'Just don't go hitting the panic button like a lot of birds do when they stort pushing thirty.'

Half an hour maybe passes. Everyone's pretty mullered even though it's only, like, five o'clock in the day? *I'm* still Hank, so I tip into the kitchen to see if there's any nosebag left. There's, like, a shitload of silver trays from the chinky on the draining board next to the sink, some of them with the odd springroll or wonton in them – focking cold, though I stort milling into them like a freed hostage, feeding the odd one to Honor, while other guests shoot me disgusted looks, although it's impossible to say which of my many crimes today they're pissed off about.

'Ignore the haters,' I make sure to tell Honor, as I pick a bit of beansprout out of her moustache.

I wander over to JP, who's telling Sophie he can't wait for the third season of *Dexter*, while Sophie's telling *him* that in the meantime he *so* should try *In Treatment*. She's just finished the first season and Gabriel Byrne is, like, oh my God in it.

I suddenly decide, okay, now's my moment – cometh the hour and blahdy blahdy blah. I dump Honor into Sophie's orms and go, 'Mind her for a minute or two, will you? Something I've got to do . . .'

Before I get out of the kitchen, though, I just happen, for some reason, to turn my head and catch a glimpse of something outside, through the kitchen window, that turns my – honestly – stomach.

At the same time, roysh, I have to see it up close, just so no one can deny it happened at a later date. I feel like I'm about to hurl.

Erika is *being* with Fionn.

She's more than just being with him as well. He has her sitting up on the coal bunker, her Yo Thai dress hitched up above her knees and he's, like, feeling her bare thighs. At the same time, roysh, *she's* running her hands through his hair and practically eating his face.

I stand there at the door for ages, just staring at them – a little bit mesmerized – until she eventually opens her eyes and notices me. There's not a word of explanation, by the way. She just goes, 'What do *you* want?' and *he's* there, 'Oh, hey, Ross.'

It's him I end up taking it out on. 'I'd say you can't believe you got this lucky,' I go.

She's like, 'Grow up, Ross.'

'You must think all your focking Christmases have come at once.'

Erika's there, 'Fock off, Ross!'

'All that bullshit about that focking painting. This must be the first time that's worked on a bird, I'd say . . .'

'Can you leave us alone?' *he* tries to go. He actually leaves his glasses *on* when he's being with a bird, which is sad *and* hilarious at the same time?

I just shake my head at him. 'She's going to be majorly embarrassed in the morning – you needn't expect a repeat performance.'

'See you later,' he has the actual cheek to go, when all I'm reallly trying to do is, like, save him from hurt down the line?

I walk back into the gaff. The music is for some reason off. The kitchen is full but no one seems to be talking.

'No one go out there,' I tell the room, 'just to warn you – unless you want to see something that'll turn your stomach . . .'

I realize, roysh, with a sudden shiver, that everyone is just, like, staring at *me* – and you can take it I *don't* mean admiringly? I'm straight away thinking, fock! I only took my eyes off Claire for, like, five minutes . . .

Where is she? I manage to pick her out of the sea of angry faces in front of me and – shit – she's crying like a focking refugee, with Sorcha attempting to, I suppose, *comfort* her?

Claire's old dear, I notice, is holding her phone, reading – presumably – the message I sent. People are asking her what it says but obviously no one wants to say the words 'Pixar character in a net curtain', so they just hand the phone around, their faces just dropping as they read it.

I get the sudden feeling that this is yet another porty that's coming to an early end for me. 'Don't ever set foot in Bray again,' Claire's old man just goes, like I'd *ever* make a focking habit of it.

I turn around and look at Garret, who's actually lost for words. He literally *throws* my jacket at me.

'I suppose the silver lining for you,' I try to go, 'is that you know now that I'm definitely *not* in love with her?'

Of course it's no consolation to him. I wouldn't *expect* it to be?

I had, like, seventeen missed calls after I was focked out of the wedding last night. Didn't answer, presuming it was basically other guests, threatening to kick the shit out of me and whatever else. I listen to my messages and there's quite a few of that colour all right. People from Bray have unbelievable imaginations, it has to be said, when it comes to shit like torture. It's all break this and snap that and douse the other in petrol before setting it on fire.

Then, roysh, in the middle of all these threats to my personal safety is a message from one of the all-time greats.

'Hey, Ross, it's Gerry Thornley.'

I laugh. G to the T to the *Irish Times*. It's good to hear the focker's voice. Until, that is, he goes, 'This is one of the most difficult phone calls I've ever had to make . . .'

My blood runs *actually* cold.

I immediately know that unless Michael Cheika has seen

the light in relation to what I could bring to the Leinster team, this is going to be bad news.

'Look,' he goes, 'I've had a tip-off from – let's just say a contact – that you goys are being stripped of your Leinster Schools Senior Cup medals. Anyway, I've had it confirmed by the school. They're saying it was because of the . . .'

He suddenly stops.

'*Methamphetamine*,' he goes, obviously reading it. 'Ross, you and I go back a long, long way, which is why I had to let you know. Dude, we're running with the story tomorrow morning. If you want to give me your side of things . . . Look, you have my number.'

Tomorrow morning is basically now. I check the time on my phone and it's, like, ten o'clock. I'm not even out of bed and the news is probably all over the world at this stage.

I just presumed we'd get a chance to fight this thing before the actual news broke.

I take the medal in the palm of my hand and just stare at it, sitting there, all bright and shiny.

Crede quod habes, et habes.

God, I never got around to even Googling that. I thought I'd all the time in the world.

I get out of bed and make my way over to the window and I stand there for, like, ten minutes, staring down at the traffic on the M50. It's, like, Saturday morning and I'm suddenly thinking, how many of those cors are, like, full of parents bringing their kids to rugby training this morning? And how many of those kids are crying, going, 'Mom, say it's not true! Dad, surely the drugs had very little to do with it and it was mostly down to, like, basic talent and the dude kicking like a focking Ninja Turtle?'

Then – oh shit – Ronan suddenly pops into my head. I'm thinking, what kind of a role model am I to him all of a sudden?

I don't know what I'm going to say to him. All I know is that I have to tell him before he finds out from someone else, even though I know, deep down, that it's going to crush him.

I dial his number, my hand actually shaking. He answers on the third ring and I just take, like, a deep breath. 'Okay,' I go. 'I just wanted to tip you off that there's, like, a story in the *Irish Times* this morning – and it's about me.'

There's, like, silence on the other end of the phone. 'What's it say?' he eventually goes.

I have to tell him, roysh, and there's no nice way of putting it. 'Well, it's a story about me and basically drugs.'

'Thrugs?'

'Exactly. Now, I stand by everything I said about them,' I make sure to go. 'I want you to know that. But what I should have told you – except I was going to wait until you were, like, fourteen or fifteen – is that there's, like, good drugs and there's, like, bad drugs.'

'What kind are you on?'

'Well, I'm not *on* any? What I'm saying is, I *was* on drugs – we're talking ten years ago? And now – even though a lot of people would be of the view that I did nothing wrong – they're trying to take away the most precious thing in the world to me . . .'

I can hear the actual worry in his silence.

'No, not you,' I end up having to go. 'To be honest, that care home is only something your mother threatens you with to stop you drinking her Scrumpy. No, what *I'm* talking about, Ro, is my Leinster Schools Senior Cup medal.'

'Oh,' he goes. 'Are thee gonna send you to jail?'

I laugh. 'I focking hope not! See, that's what I'm trying to tell you, Ro – it's not, like, a criminal thing?'

'Why idn't it?'

'What?'

'Why idn't it? How come the thrugs that Tetty and Laddy do be dealin are illegal and the thrugs that you're on ardent?'

Kids and their questions – you'd have to laugh at the innocence. 'Again,' I go, 'I'm not *on* anything . . .'

'Dudn't that make you a hypocrite but?'

'A hypocrite? That's a pretty big word to be just bandying around.'

'But you tell me, Just Say No. Idn't that what you said?'

Of course he has me twisted in knots at this stage. 'Well, yeah, up to a point. But, like I said earlier, there are different kinds of drugs. Being honest, Just Say No is really only port of the story. What they *actually* mean is, Just Say No . . . to Basically Hord Drugs.'

He tells me I'm full of shit. And even though it's possibly true, I can't tell you how much it hurts. But it makes me even more determined – for my son's sake as much as mine – not to take this thing lying down.

'Terrible,' the old man goes, taking a sudden interest in the John Shanahan's split pea and ham soup stain he's somehow managed to get down the front of his Shred Focking Everything! boilersuit. That's how I know he's trying to, like, avoid the issue. 'Terrible, terrible business.'

I just keep staring at him until he *has* to look at me?

'You've been pretty focking quiet,' I go. 'Two or three years ago, you'd have been on it like a bonnet – threatening legal action, letters from Hennessy, all sorts of shit. Kind of like you did when Erika got mixed up with Toddy Rathfriland. I mean, do you remember how proud you supposedly were when I lifted the actual trophy?'

'Of course,' he goes, still avoiding my eye.

'*Whither Warren Gatland now?* Er, do you remember even shouting that at Mary McAleese?'

'Yes,' he goes, 'during her presentation speech. And I stand by every word of it.'

'Well, you could have fooled me,' I go, 'because it's, like, ten days since I left you that message – no phone call, nothing . . .'

'I *did* ring,' he *tries* to go. 'Went straight to your message recorder. I expect you couldn't hear the thing. I thought, he's listening to some of his world-famous music, I shouldn't wonder. Niggers With Attitude Problems and whatnot.'

Helen suddenly pokes her head around the door of his study. She's like, 'Hello, Ross.'

I'm there, 'Hey, Mrs Joseph.'

'Oh, stop with the Mrs Joseph,' she goes. 'You'll have me feeling my age. Are you staying for dinner?'

'Er, I'd love to,' I go, 'except I've got a lot of work to do. Trying to hang on to this . . .'

I show her the medal.

'Yes,' she goes, 'I was just saying to Fionn, it must be awful to have your name splashed across the newspapers like that.'

I'm there, 'Fionn?'

'Yes, you've just missed him,' it's the old man who goes. 'He's taken Erika out for the night. There was talk of a drink, wasn't there, Dorling?'

Helen's there, 'What a lovely young man. I've always liked him. He's so dependable. So sensible.'

I *could* mention that it's so long since he's had his hole he'll probably need runway lights to guide him. But I don't. They're just happy that this one's not sixty-something and married. So I just go, 'Yeah, he's certainly those things. *If* that's what grinds Erika's gears, which I suspect, deep down, it's not.'

Helen's there, 'I'm going to put a wash on, Charlie. Are you going to give me that suit?'

'Oh, yes,' he goes. 'I shall change right away.'

She turns to me then. 'Can you believe him? Second day in

the new job and he's already got soup on his new suit . . .' She laughs then. 'I don't know how they even let you into Shanahan's dressed like that . . .'

She's actually right. It's, like, a yellow one-piece, with red piping and the name of the company plastered across the back. I hadn't thought what a complete and utter penis he looks.

She wanders off back to the kitchen. I'm thinking, where was I?

'Anyway,' I go, 'if you *were* ringing – and it's still a big if – to tell me that we're going to supposedly fight this thing together, all the way, my answer is that I don't need your help. *I'm* actually handling things this time?'

'Well, good for you,' he just goes, not even seeming that bothered. 'But try to see it in its proper perspective, eh? Nobody's died here.'

I'm wondering did I mishear what he just said. I'm there, '*Excuse* me?'

'Look, I know you're upset. It was a wonderful thing in your life . . .'

'Er, don't you mean *all* of our lives?'

'Yes, of course. But it doesn't define you, Ross. I'd venture there's a lot more to you than just that medal . . .'

I'm waiting, like a focking idiot, for him to stort rhyming off shit. In the end, I have to ask him *what* exactly?

He's there, 'Well, brains for a start . . .'

I laugh, even though I'm technically ripping the piss out of myself. I'm like, 'Brains? Er, *what* brains?'

'Well, maybe you've been hiding your light under a bushel for too long,' he goes. 'But I've seen it in you, Ross. You're a smart one. And what I'm trying to say in regard to the schools cup thing is, yes, we had our fun – wonderful experiences that your mother and I will never forget. But now it's time for you to move on . . .'

'Move on?'

'To new challenges, new triumphs . . .'

I laugh.

'You're talking about me joining your focking ridiculous shredding company, aren't you?'

'Well, why not?'

'Because I don't want to look like you do now – in other words, a prize tit.'

He looks suddenly hurt – at long last.

'I've just come through an anguish something similar to yours,' he tries to go.

'What, that hotel bullshit? Don't even try to say that's the same thing.'

'Well, we've both had to say goodbye to something we worked very hard for . . .'

'Except I'm not saying goodbye to my medal – are you focking deaf or just hord of hearing?'

'The important thing is not to see it as an ending but rather as the start of something else. That's what I've been trying to get across to people in some of my more recent correspondence in the pages of the paper of record. Did you know, the word for crisis, when written in Chinese, is composed of two letters – one represents danger, the other opportunity.'

My eyes automatically wander to his desk. There's one of those how-to-bullshit-your-way-in-business books face down on it. I just shake my head and tell him he's sad.

'Please,' he goes, 'stay for dinner.'

I'm there, 'Er, no thanks. I'm actually *choosy* about the company I keep?'

I'm walking through the corpork of Rosa Parks, looking forward to a Friday night – believe it or not – *in*. After the week I've had – focking up Claire's wedding, seeing my supposed sister scoring one of my best friends, being called a drug cheat in pretty much every newspaper in the country, then getting a letter from the Leinster Branch of the IRFU this morning, telling me, formally, to return my medal without delay – I'm looking forward to just vegging out in front of *Xposé* in my Cantos with the focked elastic.

I call the, I suppose, elevator. The doors open. I step in and hit the button for the top floor, thinking I'm definitely going to order take-out tonight. I've earned it. That's when I suddenly hear the dreaded words.

'Hold de lift!'

Now, I don't know about the rest of you, but those words are usually the cue for me to stort hitting the Close Doors button with the rapid thumb action of a teenage bitch with gossip worth texting.

Which is exactly what I do.

The doors close, nearly the whole way, but then they suddenly stop, no more than a couple of inches aport, and I look down to see a white Lacoste runner jammed in between them.

Of course my hort is suddenly going like a focking express train. I *could* stamp on his foot, then sort of, like, kick it out, but the chances are that he already knows that it's me in here, so I end up *having* to hit the Open Doors button instead?

It's, like, Terry – and then, running behind him, Larry, the brutter.

Terry goes, 'Ah, howiya, Rosser,' just letting me know that he knows Ronan's, I suppose, pet name for me. 'Look, it's fooken Rosser, Laddy.'

I'm just there, 'Yeah, hi, goys,' being civil, roysh, but at the same time trying to keep, like, my distance?

The doors close again and the lift, elevator, whatever you want to call it, slowly groans into life.

'I tink he was hittin de Close Doh-ers buthon,' Terry goes. My face gets suddenly hot – it's obviously red. 'Were you hittin Close Doh-ers, Rosser, were you?'

I'm there, 'No!' the terror obvious in my voice. 'I swear!'

'Feerd nuff,' he goes, like it's suddenly *not* a major deal? 'Ine only aston, so I am.'

There's, like, silence again. I'm looking up at the numbers above the door, thinking how can we only be between the first and second floors? This lift's so slow, they could have a fock-ing Duty Free trolley service on it.

'So how's it goin, Rosser?' is the next thing I hear. 'How's effery little ting?'

It's one of Terry's, like, catchphrases?

'Er, cool,' I just go, making sure to keep staring straight ahead.

At the same time, roysh, I can pretty much feel the weight of them staring at me. This is going to sound racist, but I always imagine working-class people are checking out my orse to see what kind of a drug mule I'd make.

'Any plans for ta weekend?' Larry goes.

'Er, no,' I go. 'Nothing major.'

The two of them stort, like, impersonating me then. '*Nothing meejer.*'

There's, like, silence again. I look up. We're only at, like, the third floor. I'm standing there, listening to the gears grinding away, wondering when will this ever end.

It's amazing, roysh, but back in the day I used to have two or three thousand people in Donnybrook booing me and baying for my blood – and still I never let it faze me. But thirty seconds in a lift with these two yahoos and I'm like an actual jelly.

'Wheat your young fedda in again tutter night, didn't we, Tetty?'

'Young Ronan – we did, Laddy, yeah.'

'He's a fooken smeert one, Rosser. Doatent know where he gets it from. Are ya shewer he's yooers?'

'Er, yeah.'

'I'd two diffordent boords toalt me deed childorden for me – boat a dem lyin. Der hungry bitches for de money, see.'

'Well, you can take it from me – he's definitely mine.'

'Guth for you, Rosser. Ine made up for ya. Smeert kid but. Big future for um in eer line of woork, if he wants it . . .'

I don't answer one way or the other – I know they're only trying to, like, rile me? – and it just hangs there in the air between us.

Fooouuurrr . . . Fiiivvve . . .

'Hee-er, does that lift sounth funny to you?' Terry goes.

Larry's like, 'Imachin it broke dowin. Rosser there'd be stuck wirrus for the night, wha?'

They seem to find the prospect of this focking hilarious.

'Hee-er, don't woody, Rosser,' Terry goes, holding up two shopping bags, 'we've plenthee of foo-it to see us troo,' and they both burst into hysterics, probably because they know – as well as I know – that they'd kill and eat me long before they'd even think of using whatever's in those Lidl bags.

Siiixxx . . . Seeeevvven . . .

'Ronan was tellin us about your thrubbles,' Terry suddenly goes. 'Soddy to hee-er.'

'What did he say exactly?'

'Said you're arthur gettin yourself mixed up in thrugs . . .'

'Er, *hello*? It was, like, *years* ago? And anyway, it wasn't, like, *drugs* drugs?'

Eeeiiight . . .

I'm thinking, *why* did I have to buy a penthouse suite?

'Ronan was sayin it was the sayum stuff yer man Hitler was on . . .'

He's some focking mouth on him, that kid.

I'm there, 'Er, supposedly, yeah.'

Ping.

The doors finally open and I'm out of there like – pardon the pun – but a bullet from a gun. I've just got the key in the door when I hear Larry go, 'Well, just so's ya know, Rosser, your neighbours are all a hunrit percent behoyunt ya,' except he means it in, like, a sarcastic way? 'We know whorrits like to be giffen a bad nayum.'

I ask Fionn how he's getting on with the ringaround and you know *him* – you never get a straight answer. He says it's been a real eye-opener for him. A *real* eye-opener. 'For instance, do you remember Davin Kennedy?'

I tell him, of course I remember Davin Kennedy. He played on the wing for us. He was faster than a skobie with a money-off coupon. Ran the 100 metres in Santry once in ten-point-something seconds, although – famously – he could never reproduce that form in Belfield. The joke was that he just didn't feel the same fear.

I'm wondering, I have to admit, what happened between Fionn and Erika the night they went for that drink, although there's no way I'm going to give him the pleasure of asking. Instead, roysh, I go, 'What *about* Davin Kennedy?'

'Well,' he goes, 'he's working for Anglo-Irish. I'm telling you, Ross, he's got *some* stories about that place . . .'

Of course it's at that point that I should ask him what the fock that's got to do with us trying to hang on to our medals. But it's the usual Jack with me – I can't help being a nice goy, even if people *do* tend to abuse it?

'He says no one in there wants to sit next to the windows – they're all scared a brick is going to come flying through. Or worse. There *is* a lot of anger out there and Anglo-Irish is the focus of it, although I think a lot of people are avoiding asking themselves the difficult questions . . .'

I literally can't listen to any more of this. I'm there, 'Er, where exactly is this going, Fionn?'

He goes, if you can believe this, 'Well, what I hadn't realized until I started to ring our old friends is what a socially inclusive recession this is, in terms of the types of people being affected . . .'

You can imagine me at this stage. 'I don't focking need this, Fionn. How is any of this even relevant?'

'It could well be relevant,' he tries to go. 'That's what I'm trying to tell you – a lot of these guys are struggling, Ross. And not just Davin.'

'So?'

'*So*, I'm not sure how interested they are in this whole thing.'

'*This whole thing?* Dude, I'm presuming they got the same letter as us . . .'

'Yeah.'

'And you're saying they're happy to just give back their medals?'

'All I'm saying is, the impression I'm getting talking to them is that, well, most of them have other things on their minds. I'm just warning you, don't presume that everyone cares about their Leinster Schools Senior Cup medal as much as you do.'

He doesn't realize at first what he's actually said. It's one of those, like, Freudican slips?

I'm there, 'As much as *I* do?'

He doesn't say anything. Busted and disgusted. I'm like, 'What about you, Fionn?'

'Yeah, obviously,' he tries to go. 'I meant to say, as much as *we* do?'

'Are you sure about that?'

'Yeah.'

I don't say anything for ages, roysh, just leave him dangling there in the wind, the focking speckledork.

'Put me out of my misery,' I suddenly hear myself go. 'Did you and Erika have sex?'

'What?' he goes, acting all offended.

'Hey, I'm worried about *you* more than anyone in all of this. You're basically a mate. Has it occurred to you that I don't want to see you get hurt?'

'What happens between me and Erika, Ross, is our business.'

'Whoa, what do you mean by *happens*? Does that mean you're, like, seeing each other?'

'Ross . . .'

'Okay. She's using you – that's my last word on the subject. Nothing else going on for her, so she thinks . . .'

'Thanks very much for that, Ross.'

'Hey, just don't come crying to me when it all goes tits up. And whatever is or isn't going on – sex or whatever – don't forget you've got shit to do. Get the word out there. It's, like, eight o'clock on Saturday night. My gaff in Rosa Parks. I'm going to get a shitload of beer in.'

'Fine,' he goes, like he's *still* not convinced? 'Have you thought about what you're going to say to them yet?'

I'm there, 'I'm going to give them the speech of a focking lifetime, don't you worry about that.'

'Well,' he goes, 'there's six coming so far – they're definites. And I've two or three more still to ring.'

I ask him what he's waiting for . . .

'That school!' the old dear goes. 'When I think about the money that Charles and I handed them over the years.'

See, this is how a normal parent should react.

I only swung out to Foxrock to see if the old man had left any money behind in the safe. He didn't, unfortunately, but

301

there was an incredible smell coming from the kitchen. *She'd* been cooking – all gourmet shit as well – we're talking Madras poussins with pear and rosehip chutney, we're talking Cornish game hens with savoury stuffing balls, we're talking lobster tails in beurre monté with Hasselback potatoes, we're talking veal scallopini with blackberries and Parisienne frites.

It's, like, a reaction, I suppose, to what RTÉ were making her do.

Much as I hate her actual guts, the things the woman can do with a three-ply roaster and a handful of tamarind seeds. So I grab a plate, roysh, and stort helping myself and that's when she says that shit about the school.

I'm there, 'Can I just say, I really appreciate the support. *He* couldn't give a fock, by the way.'

'Who? Your father?'

'So-called. He had Hennessy taking out injunctions left, right and centre when Erika was caught boning that old dude. Yet when it comes to me . . .' I just shake my head. 'He thinks I should just give the medal back, by the way.'

'What?'

She's genuinely horrified, in fairness to her.

'I'm just saying what *he* thinks.'

'Does he even remember heckling Mary McAleese?'

'Says he does. But he reckons those days are in the past now? Thinks I should hand the medal over to some country bumpkin and move on – yeah, this'll give you a laugh – to the *next phase* of my life.'

Her face suddenly hordens. '*I'll* talk to him,' she goes.

I'm there, 'Don't bother. I don't need him. Because *I'm* suddenly handling it. I'm going to fight this thing every step of the way.'

'Well, good for you – have some more frites – you worked too hard for that medal to just hand it over . . .'

'To some village idiot.'

'To anyone, Ross. It's yours – through hard work and sheer talent. And when I saw your name spalshed across the newspapers like that . . .'

I presume she's referring to the DRUGBY LEGEND headline in the *PAYE Daily Monkey*. Foley stitched me up in a major way, even though he did still mention the word 'legend'.

'Disgusting,' the old dear goes.

I nod.

I'm there, 'Yeah, no, the worst thing from my own personal point of view was having to break the news to Ro. I mean, there I am, trying to warn him away from focking Tony Montana and Manny Ribera next door – then *I'm* suddenly busted for drugs.'

'You did explain that they weren't working-class drugs, didn't you?'

'Tried – for all the good it did.'

'That's why you can't afford to give in, Ross. For your son's sake . . .'

Which is a nice thing to hear.

I'm there, 'I know we've had our differences – the whole Trevion thing and blah blah blah – but this is all good shit you're saying to me.'

She smiles at me. 'Well, I can empathize,' she goes, 'because it's very much like my situation. Being told to let go of the past.'

I'm there, 'Okay – because *you've* given *me* a big-up, I have to say, I've watched one or two episodes of the show recently and I think what RTÉ are making you do is basically sick. I don't know how anyone could make another, I don't know, human being suffer like that.'

Her eyes take on a sort of, like, glassy look. 'Do you know what they had me doing today?'

I'm there, 'Don't do it to yourself,' because I can hear her getting all worked up again?

'A three-course dinner, for under a fiver . . .'

'Jesus Christ!'

'Packet soup,' she goes. 'Oxtail, Ross – if such a thing even exists. Followed by pasta shells with Ragù. Ragù! And an ice lolly for dessert.'

I shake my head.

'They used to call us the Singapore of Western Europe,' she goes.

I'm there, 'You wouldn't serve that to a focking dog.'

She nods.

'I told Cathal Goan much the same thing. I'm cooking starvation rations for plane-crash survivors in the Andes. It'll be toothpaste and stagnant water next – you see if it isn't . . .'

She's so upset that *I* end up having to tell *her* that everything's going to be okay, except she looks at me, roysh, her eyes full of tears, and says she's not sure that it is any more.

'And that's the worst thing,' she goes. 'I told you, Ross, that this recession wasn't going to affect people like us. And I was wrong.'

I'm there, 'Hey, I don't want to hear that kind of talk.'

'I can't help it, Ross. It's just this *feeling*. I remember it from the 1980s. This awful, awful negativity. It gets into you. Like cold damp. Like rheumatism.'

I consider reminding her of the words of Harry Connick, Jr – this too will pass – but somehow it just doesn't seem enough.

'Hey,' I go, 'I'm not giving up and neither should you. Even if I'm going to in the end lose, I'm going to go down fighting.'

She sweeps the roads the same way she does everything else. She's, like, a perfectionist?

'You missed a bit,' I shout, from the other side of Dawson Street, just ripping the piss basically. She stops pushing the broom and looks at me. Whether she's pleased to see me or the exact opposite, I'm still not sure. It seems like every time I meet Sorcha these days, I'm studying her boat, trying to answer that basic question. Says a lot, I suppose, about the way I've been living my life.

'Sorry about the whole wedding thing,' I go. 'The text and, well, all the other shit.'

This is outside Louis Mulcahy, by the way. She just shrugs – which is good. 'I actually felt sorry for you on the day,' she goes. 'Everyone ganging up on you like they did.'

'Thanks, Babes.'

'Plus I'm beginning to wonder are you maybe autistic . . .'

I give her, like, a suddenly interested nod, going along with the idea – better than being hated, I can tell you.

'Dad wanted to call the Gords when he saw what you did to Honor's face.'

'We're back to the moustache again, I presume.'

'Then he saw the thing in the *Irish Times* about you being on drugs . . .'

'I wish people would stop saying that.'

'He thinks if we can establish a pattern of this kind of behaviour, we could destroy your claim for unsupervised access when we eventually reactivate the divorce proceedings.'

I'm there, 'We're still doing that, are we?'

She's like, 'Yes,' and she says it firmly. 'We were never *not* doing it. We've only postponed it, Ross.'

I grab the broom from her and stort sweeping a patch that she's already swept, more to avoid the conversation than anything else.

'But the last thing in the world I want is to stop Honor seeing her daddy,' she goes.

I stop sweeping and just nod.

She's there, 'How's Ronan?'

I laugh. 'Don't ask me – ask the two whacks next door. They saw about five times more of him than I did this summer.'

'Oh my God!'

'I know. I know he's always idolized people like them. But I thought it was something he'd eventually grow out of. Now I feel sort of, like, helpless – like I can't *stop* him getting involved?'

Sorcha's always been a glass-half-full kind of a person, which is how she ended up married to me. 'Well,' she goes, 'he's back at school next week, isn't he?'

'True.'

'Starting secondary school. He'll make new friends. Then this thing will just seem like, I don't know, a summer fling . . .'

Her face lights up, like she's been suddenly reminded of something. 'Speaking of which – *what* do you think of Fionn and Erika? Isn't it *so* cute?'

'I don't see what's cute about it.'

'Oh my God, she really likes him, Ross.'

I'm there, 'I doubt that.'

'She does. She's, like, *so* over that whole Toddy Rathfriland thing.'

I'm there, 'Do you know have they done it yet? As in *it*?' and she looks at me like I'm a complete and utter weirdo. I'm there, 'Hey, I'm asking as much out of concern for him as for her. I still think this might be just a sensitive-guy phase she's going through – like a lot of birds do.'

'Oh my God,' Sorcha goes, 'you *so* have issues.'

'I'm just saying, Fionn is an *actual* mate of mine, even though we've had our differences in the past. Is it suddenly wrong for me to not want to see him kicked in the balls?'

Sorcha laughs.

'Ross,' she tries to go, 'who are you jealous of, Erika or Fionn?' and of course I have literally no idea what she's even talking about.

'Being honest,' I go, 'I'd prefer if he just kept his eyes on the prize.'

'Er, *what* are you talking about?'

'I'm talking about his Leinster Schools Senior Cup medal.'

She actually snorts – this coming from the girl who never missed a game. 'I thought you had to hand them back. Ross, you admitted taking drugs.'

'Er, I *know*? But we're still going to, like, fight this thing.'

She doesn't seem at all impressed. 'I don't know why you can't just let it go? It's, like, *so* the nineties, Ross.'

I just shake my head. 'You of all people should know how important this medal is to me.'

She takes the broom back off me. 'Well, I don't think it matters as much to you as you think it does.'

Which is easy for her to say.

I'm there, 'In case you're wondering *how* exactly we're going to fight this thing, let's just say there's a meeting in my gaff tomorrow night – we're talking all the goys back together again. There's going to be a lot of anger, I can tell you that. The plan is to give them a speech that's going to, like, knock them sideways. And that's one of the things that I wanted to talk to you about . . .'

'What?'

I'm there, 'I wanted it to be something along the lines of that dude you're into – Something Obama?'

'*President* Obama?' she goes.

'Yeah. Have you got a copy of that speech he's supposed to have made when he, I don't know, *won* the whole thing?'

'Are you talking about his inauguration speech, Ross?'

I take a punt. 'Er, yeah.'

She just sighs like she's suddenly bored with me, then says if I'm really *that* interested, it's on, like, her Facebook page?

The moment has arrived.

I'm looking around the living room at all the old faces, most of them a lot fuller than they were the last time I saw them. One or two of them are even pretty much bald.

Lot of beer under the bridge and blahdy blahdy blah.

Everyone's, like, catching up. It turns out most of them have got, like, wives and kids and all the focking rest of it. I'm telling you, there's nothing like a ten-year reunion to make you feel your sudden age.

It has to be said, roysh, the first thing that strikes me is that they're a lot more *serious* than I remembered them?

Aodan, just as an example, our old loosehead – you literally couldn't leave your Dubes anywhere near him back in the day in case he took a ten-ounce rump in one of them. But now, roysh, he's wearing the ears off JP, talking about the hypocrisy of the American motor industry. For years, they pulled out of towns like Flint, Michigan, without a backward glance at the tens of thousands they slung on to the dole, saying they were running a business, not a charity. But now they're about to go to the wall, he says, they're on their knees up on Capitol Hill, saying the economic heart will be ripped out of so many communities unless the good people of America bail them out.

Fionn laughs knowingly, then says there's nothing like an economic disaster for turning arch-capitalists into unreconstructed socialists overnight.

There's no way she could be sleeping with him.

Anyway, that's when I suddenly decide to call the meeting to order. 'Okay,' I go, the voice big and commanding like the old days, 'chat's over,' and everyone immediately shuts up.

I'm pretty nervous, it has to be said, especially as I look around the room and see these ten or eleven goys all staring back at me – we're talking Wellies, Melon, Munch, Flash Gorman, Finchy, Foreskin Feta, even the Pocket Rocket – their eyes full of expectation, just like they were back in the day.

But it's very much a case of cometh the hour, cometh the man.

First, roysh, I reach inside my shirt, whip out the medal and just, like, hold it up for everyone to see. I do that for, like, thirty seconds, not saying shit, just letting them drink it in and focus on what's at issue here. 'I won this,' I eventually go, 'through blood, through sweat and through sheer focking talent . . .'

There's, like, one or two nods, though most of them are just sitting there, obviously waiting to see where this is going.

'Okay,' I go, 'the methamphetamine *might* have helped? There's no proof either way. But this I can guarantee you – mostly it was down to me, putting in the hord yords and working my hole like a stripper with the rent due . . .'

I don't get the round of applause I'm expecting for that line. In fact, they all end up just sitting there, staring stupidly at me. That's when Simon, of all people, interrupts.

'To be honest,' he goes, 'I don't know what we're even doing here . . . I mean, fock, how long ago was it – ten years? Does anyone honestly care any more?'

I literally cannot believe what I'm hearing. I even try to laugh it off. 'Does anyone care?' I go. 'Er, history cares, for one.'

Again, no one says shit.

'Look, Ross, no offence,' he goes. 'I can't speak for the rest of these guys, but I've got far more important things to worry about than some focking medal I won back at school. Do you have any idea how much work has dried up for architects?'

I don't know if he honestly expects me to answer that. He insists on telling me anyway.

'Let's just say that what I've brought in in the last ten months doesn't even come close to covering the mortgage. Which means that if things haven't improved by Christmas, Julie and I are going to have to rent out our house – that's if we even can – and move the kids to Abu focking Dhabi.'

The worst thing is, roysh, that that's the cue for them all to stort telling their stories and I suddenly realize, to my total horror, that Fionn was maybe right.

'It's the same for solicitors,' Ultan goes. 'I'm on, like, a three-day week. I'm not putting on the *béal bocht* here – a lot of people have it far worse – but for the last six weeks, I've been putting the weekly grocery shop on my credit card.'

I look at Fionn and JP, expecting back-up, but the two of them just sit there – focking picture, no sound.

Everyone sort of, like, shakes their heads and this – if you can believe it – leads then to a general discussion on the whole, I don't know, bail-out of the banks? 'They behave recklessly,' Aodan goes, 'and it's ordinary people like us who are going to end up paying for it.'

Ordinary people like us? I met that focker in Meadows & Byrne in Malahide last year – he told me he bought three gaffs in the Alliance Gasworks and a cor that he described to me as 'a land-yacht'.

I *could* point that out, but I don't. Instead, I try to show them that the whole current economic thing is affecting me as well.

'I'm not exactly, I don't know, *immune*?' I go. 'I've got cream focking crackers living next door, upstairs, downstairs, every-where. My wife's shop went tits-up. My old dear is cooking pretty much shite on national television . . .'

I even try to draw JP into the conversation then. 'And what about this poor focker? Hook, Lyon and Sinker was practically an institution on the Merrion Road for, what, thirty years, JP? Do you know what it is now? It's an all-you-can-eat Chinese buffet! Er, in Ballsbridge? *Come on!*'

I look around at the faces, roysh, and it's obvious that I'm not reaching them. Most of them haven't even brought their letters with them.

'Look, don't get me wrong,' Simon goes, 'it's been great seeing you guys again – it's brought back one or two memories, I can tell you . . .'

'*Castlerock Über Alles!*' Aodan goes and everyone just laughs, like all it ever was to them was a funny catchphrase.

'But the actual medal,' Simon goes, 'I couldn't even tell you where mine is.'

I give him a serious filthy and tell him it should be round his Jeff Beck. Like focking mine. Like JP's. Like Christian's over in the States, no doubt. Like Oisinn's, I can tell you for a fact, wherever the fock he is in the world.

He actually turns on me then. 'Well, the other thing is,' he goes, totally out of the blue, 'this is all your doing, Ross.'

I'm there, '*Excuse* me?'

'Well, I'm just wondering are you acting out of guilt here? You were the one who was on drugs – not any of us. You were the one who opened his mouth about it in that book . . .'

I notice three or four of the others even nodding their nods.

'Hey,' I go, 'you wouldn't even have that focking medal if it wasn't for me.'

'Well, I don't mind giving it back,' he goes, 'because it doesn't matter a fock compared to what else is going on in my life – like finding schools in the United Arab Emirates.'

He suddenly stands up, roysh, says sorry – to Fionn and JP, but not me – then heads for the actual door. I tell everyone to just let him go – we don't actually need him – but then they *all* stort getting up? Wellies, Munch, even Foreskin Feta.

One or two of them say sorry under their breaths. One or two tell me I should have kept my focking mouth shut. Then the room is suddenly empty except for me, Fionn, JP and Aodan.

The beers have been barely touched.

I'm there, 'Aodan, come on, Dude! What was it that Obama dude said? Can we fix it? Yes we can!'

He just looks at me sadly.

'You've no idea how tight things are with us at the moment,' he goes. 'Look, between ourselves, we haven't been able to pay the twins' school fees. It's only thanks to that prick McGahy that Iollan and Conlaoch are still in the school. What am I supposed to tell him? Thanks, but I'm still not giving back my medal?'

'Jesus!' I go, 'what are the fees for the junior school? Twenty grand a term? I'll give you that myself, out of my own sky rocket.'

He shakes his head and says he's sorry, then off *he* focks as well. Then it's only me, Fionn and JP.

'I used to be able to inspire them,' I just go, then I shake my head. 'You two, by the way, were about as useful as a one-ormed trapeze artist with an itchy focking hole.'

I crack a beer open for myself.

'You have to respect what they say,' Fionn goes, glasses focking galore.

I'm just there, 'Oh, do we? Oh, that's interesting to know,' laying on the sarcasm like it's peanut focking butter.

JP has to throw his two cents in then.

'What Fionn's trying to say is, look, if most of the goys don't even want their medals, what can we do? We're kind of out of options here.'

I tell him he couldn't be more wrong if he tried. The two goys suddenly look at each other, then at me. 'I've got a plan,' I go.

JP sits forward in his seat. In fact they *both* do? Oh, they're all ears now.

'Okay,' I go, 'that secretary of McGahy's? Susan is her name . . .'

Fionn and JP are there, 'Okay . . .'

'What I was going to do is find out where she usually drinks . . .'

'Why?' Fionn goes.

Jesus, for a supposedly intelligent man, he's slower than Calista Flockhart to the focking breakfast buffet.

'Why?' I go. 'Er, the plan eventually being for me to have my sweaty way with her?'

Of course the questions keep on coming. 'To what end, Ross?'

I'm there, 'What end do you think, Fionn? To piss McGahy off.'

It's suddenly JP's turn. 'But how's that going to allow us to keep our medals?'

I end up pretty much losing it with *him* then. 'I don't focking know. But at least I'm coming up with ideas. See, it's all right for you two – I had to ring my son the other day and try to explain all of this to him . . .'

I look at Fionn and I get the impression that he's shaping up to say something. 'Look,' he suddenly goes, 'I might end up *having* to give my medal back.'

I'm there, 'Excuse me?'

'Ross, I *work* in the school. We start back next week.'

'Er, I *know*? Ronan's going, remember. Actually, he wouldn't be if I'd found out about this medal thing sooner. What I'm asking is, what's your point?'

'What's my point? Tom is my boss. He could make life very difficult for me.'

'Well, I'll ask you straight out, then – why don't you quit?'

'Quit my job?'

'Yeah. As a matter of fact, I'm thinking of moving Ro to Blackrock or possibly even – and I know I'll never hear the end of this from focking D'Arcy – but Clongowes after Christmas.'

'Ross, you want me to give up a job I love?'

'To be honest, I don't know why you haven't already. Don't tell me you couldn't get work in the Institute. Er, with *your* brains?'

He has no honest answer to that. But then JP suddenly backs him up.

'Look, the way I see it,' he goes, 'is that one of two things is going to happen next. Either we're going to give our medals back and the Leinster Branch is going to present them to Newbridge College. Or we're going to hang on to them and the Leinster Branch will strike new ones and present them to Newbridge College anyway. Either way, these things don't mean anything to us any more. They're like old fifty-pence pieces. Relics of the nineties. Worthless metal.'

9. The Wire

I ask him again if he's nervous and my voice echoes off the walls along the corridor. Again he says no, except this time it's like he's taken serious offence to being asked – the little hord man face on him.

'Will ya stop aston him dat,' his mother goes – and you can see, roysh, one or two of the other parents checking her out, thinking, yeah, won't be long before she's dropping the kid off here in her focking pyjamas.

'Tina,' I make the mistake of going, 'would you not be more comfortable waiting in the cor?'

She's there, 'Soddy?' like she's about to focking glass me. 'Say dat again.'

'Yeah, no, I'm just saying, I actually *went* to this school? I remember what it was like walking into that very first assembly. I'm just saying, today might be more of a father–son thing . . .'

Ronan laughs. 'Ah, will you give it up ourra dat, Rosser. A fadder–son ting! I'm arthur telling you I'm grand . . .'

'Sure he knows most of de kids in he's class,' Tina goes. 'He's arthur being wit dum in de primary for tree or foe-er years.'

That accent would take the focking face off you. There's no attempt to even, like, tone it down for the day.

I'm there, 'Yeah, but I'm talking about, like, the older kids? I just remember the hell *we* used to give the first years – atomic wedgies and all the rest of it.'

It'll be a brave man who tries to give Ro any kind of wedgie.

I catch him already sizing up this other kid, who must be, like, three or four years older than him. 'There's nothin here's gonna put the wind up me,' he goes. 'It's like Tetty and Laddy says to me last night – you're not gonna be afred of some fooken Tiernan or Tristan, are ya?'

It's always Terry and Larry – still, now he's back at school, I'm hoping it turns out to be like Sorcha said – as in a summer thing?

I immediately get him off the subject. 'I have to say, I really envy you, Ro. It's all ahead of you – oh, take it from someone who's been there and done it. You actually couldn't have picked a better time to finish with Blathin either. She's gonna put the word around Mount Anville – how you treated her and all the rest of it. Means you're an immediate player. They're *all* going to want to be the one to tame you . . .'

Tina gives me a filthy – presumably for bringing up Bla's name. He obviously still feels secretly bad. All I'm trying to do, though, is let him know that there's, like, an exciting new world about to open up to him. 'Do you want money for Wesley?' I go, whipping a wad of notes out of my pocket.

He looks at Tina. 'I'm, er, too young,' he goes.

I actually laugh. 'Hey, we were *all* too young,' I go, peeling off a couple of fifties. 'Crouching Cider, Hidden Naggin.'

Tina snatches the money out of my hand. 'He's twelve!' she goes – er, this from the woman who lets him smoke?

She doesn't give me the fifties back either.

'In anyhow,' Ro suddenly goes, 'I'm not gonna have time for boords. I'm gonna be stuttying – tree, tree and a half hours a night.'

I'm obviously in shock. I'm there, 'Studying? What's all this about, Ro?'

'He's arthur deciding,' Tina goes, 'he wants to be a solicithor.'

'A solicitor? Ro, I thought you hated the law. What was it

you shouted at the jury when Buckets of Blood got sent down that first time? *You've signed yisser own death woddunts?*'

He just shrugs. 'I'm gonna be like that fedda Levy offa *The Wire* . . .'

'Levy? We're talking the crooked lawyer dude who's always getting Stringer and Morlo off?'

Of course there's no need to even ask who his first clients are going to be.

The next thing, roysh, out of the corner of my eye, I cop McGahy, walking with his orms behind his back and his head in the air, like a focking sorgent-major inspecting a parade. I already have my medal hanging *outside* my shirt? Just to let him know that I still have it and that I'm never giving it back, whatever Fionn, JP and the rest of them decide to do.

Tina has to let me down, of course. She's there, 'Howiya, Mr Moogahy!' at the top of her voice.

It has to be said, roysh, I'm not ready for what happens next. *He* practically runs over to where we're standing and the two of them are suddenly all over each other – I swear to fock – like bezzy focking mates, we're talking airkisses, the lot. He even goes, 'It's Tom, Tina. Call me Tom.'

And she's there, all, 'How's your mudder?' and that's when I suddenly cop it – his old dear must have been in, like, Beaumont?

'On the mend now,' he goes, 'thanks to you and the other nurses. I just dread to think what would have happened if you hadn't got her blood pressure down that night . . .'

Of course I'm standing there, sort of, like, adjusting the angle of my medal, trying to catch the sun on it and blind the focker. He cracks on not to notice – makes a big point of it, in fact. 'It's getting more and more difficult to manage her diabetes,' he tries to go.

Tina smiles at him – she's letting me down big-time here. 'Tanks again for de flowers.'

He waves his hand at her. 'It was nothing. I just wish, as a society, we valued the work you do more.'

I'm actually on the point of focking borfing here.

He turns to me then, suddenly all serious, gives me, like, a nod and goes, 'Hello, Ross,' *trying* to be professional, even though he's obviously bulling that I've still got this baby hanging around my neck.

Then he looks at Ro. 'Well,' he goes, 'how are you feeling, young man? Excited?'

Ro's like, 'Er, yeah, I am a bit.'

'Well, we're excited about having you here. We've had nothing but glowing reports from the junior school. In fact, just between ourselves, two teachers from the maths department have already fallen out over who's going to be teaching you!'

Ro looks at Tina, both of them delighted, while I just throw my shoulders, not so easily impressed by that kind of shit.

'Come,' McGahy goes, 'I'm about to start assembly,' then he moves off and we follow him, Ronan at his heels like a little focking terrier, me and Tina walking five or six feet behind.

'You're focking unbelievable,' I go to *her*, out of the corner of my mouth. 'Saving his mother's life – where's your focking loyalty?'

She doesn't say anything. She's just speechless. It's called a guilty conscience.

We're about to take the turn, roysh, into the corridor that leads to the actual assembly hall. The Walk of Legends, it was always called, because they have photos of all the great Castlerock College teams of the past lining the walls on both sides. *We're* up there, the famous Dream Team – as is my old man, even though *they* lost in the first round to, like, Pres Bray of all focking schools.

I shout ahead, 'Hey, Ro, when you turn this corner, the important thing is not to be intimidated . . .'

So he takes the corner, then *we* take it a few seconds later. Except it's me who ends up just stunned into silence. The pictures have all been taken down and the walls have just been, like, whitewashed?

I actually stop, dead in my tracks, like some focking madman, running my hand over the bare brickwork, going, 'Used to be . . . Used to be . . . All pictures . . .'

'Gut luck, Ro,' I hear Tina go and he's there, 'Tanks, Ma. See ya later, Rosser . . .' but I can't even get it together to answer him.

McGahy opens the door and the noise suddenly hits us like the heat from an oven. Ronan walks in there, chin up, shoulders back, not a care in the basic world.

McGahy has a last look back at me. I could be, like, imagining it, but I'm almost sure I can see, like, the trace of a smile on his lips.

I've heard watching the Magners League described as like having sex while wearing a condom – in other words, you'd be better off staying home and burping your worm.

And after already winning the Heineken Cup this year, I admit there *is* a touch of anti-climax about playing the Newport Gwent Dragons at the RDS on a rainy September Saturday.

But what can I say? We're your die-hord Leinster fans. We've followed this team through thick and thin – on and off – for the past ten years. It's not just an honour to be here – it's, like, our duty?

Even *though* it's pretty focking boring.

I spend most of the first half shouting kicking advice at Johnny Sexton, none of which he needs unfortunately, then grilling Fionn about his latest supposed date with Erika last night. 'Ross,' he goes, suddenly thinking he's hot shit, 'I'm trying to watch the rugby here.'

I'm just, like, staring him out of it. The focker honestly doesn't know how lucky he is. 'All I'm asking is, where did you take her?'

He just, like, rolls his eyes and says One Pico. I'm thinking, One Pico? That's pretty smooth for a goy who spent practically his entire teenage years pulling his plum to *Countdown*.

'See,' I go, 'that wasn't hord. It's actually a nice restaurant. And again – am I allowed to ask? – what did you do afterwards – as in, did anything happen?'

'For fock's sake!' he practically roars at me – and Fionn pretty much *never* swears?

'You don't have to tell me whether you'd Ant and Decs with the girl. Just answer me this, did she go back to yours even?'

'Look, Ross, it really isn't any of your business.'

'Oh, isn't it? I was the one who focking told you to try and meet someone. I didn't think it was going to end up being my sister.'

'Hey!' JP goes to us. 'Why don't you get oiled up and wrestle?' which a good few people in the Anglesea Stand seem to find hilarious.

'Well,' I go, 'I'm just trying to make sure the dude stays focused on what's important. Birds are all very well, but we've still got a battle on our hands. I know you two have pretty much already given up. I told you about the pictures, didn't I?'

'Yes,' Fionn goes, 'several times.'

'Gone from the walls. It's like we're being, I don't know, airbrushed out of history. So just bear that in mind. You as well, JP. Ask yourselves what's more important – that or your, suddenly, girlfriends.'

JP goes, 'Hey, Ross, maybe I'll bring Danuta to the next game – sit her between the two of you . . .'

Of course that immediately shuts me up.

Anyway, it ends up being half-time. I check my phone and

it turns out I've got, like, a text message from my old dear, which is an actual first. She says thanks for the chat that day in the gaff and blahdy blahdy blah. She's decided to quit *FO'CK on a Budget* and make sure to watch her final show next Friday. Doesn't know what she's going to cook yet but she's going to make it one to definitely remember.

I'm actually trying to work out what she means when all of a sudden the stadium announcer storts going, 'Ladies and gentlemen, can I have your attention please . . .'

It's weird, roysh, because I instantly know that something *not* cool is about to go down here?

'Ladies and gentlemen,' he goes, 'we have a special half-time presentation to make on the pitch today. Ten years ago . . .'

It's as soon as he mentions ten years, roysh, that I suddenly turn to look at Fionn, then JP.

'Newbridge College were beaten in the final of the Leinster Schools Senior Cup competition. Castlerock College, the victors that day, have since been stripped of their title due to revelations regarding the use of performance-enhancing drugs . . .'

Everyone storts booing, if you can believe that – these are so-called Leinster supporters.

'So today,' the announcer goes, 'we are going to finally correct a sporting injustice by presenting the medals to their rightful winners. Ladies and gentlemen, please be generous in your applause for the Newbridge College team of 1999.'

Out they morch. Right into the middle of the RDS pitch. Blue blazers. Cream chinos. White shirts. We used to say Newbridge were like Tori Spelling – focking talentless, but they dressed well. The crowd storts getting behind them, as in really cheering them. I turn around to Fionn. I'm like, 'What the fock?'

For once, he doesn't seem to *have* an answer.

I look down. Mocky – we're talking *Mocky* – is being presented with the cup. The only way to describe how I'm suddenly feeling is to say it feels like I've died inside. I watch him accept it from . . . fock, it's Mary *actual* McAleese, the same woman who presented it to *me*. I just shake my head. *She's* changed her focking tune.

'Ladies and gentleman,' the announcer goes, 'the 1999 Leinster Schools Senior Cup champions – Newbridge College!'

Mocky takes the cup in both hands, then just thrusts it up to the sky and practically the whole RDS goes ballistic.

Fionn and JP are both unbelievably quiet. JP, being honest, looks actually ill, obviously suddenly regretting being all *Weekend at Bernie's* that night in my gaff.

The players stort doing, like, a lap of honour with the cup. A few of them are just, like, staring at their medals, almost studying them, obviously thinking, 'Devil a lie but my heart is pounding with joy this very night! I'm as happy as if I'd been presented with a cow!'

It's when I see one of them suddenly kiss his – in exactly the same way that I kissed mine a million times before – that I end up totally losing it. It's literally like watching a bird you're still in love with swapping spits with some dude who isn't even in your league. I fly into a sudden rage. I throw my leg over Fionn and hop into the centre aisle, then stort running down the steps towards the pitch.

'Ross!' the two goys are going, 'don't do it,' but I just keep going.

One or two stewards make a grab for me but I ride the tackles – unbelievably well, a neutral would have to say – and the next thing I know I'm suddenly pitchside, with the Newbridge players parading right in front of me, loving the attention, loving themselves, so I end up letting this sudden roar out of me, giving them everything I've pretty much got.

'You Cooley-waltzing, donkey-punching, Frances Black-loving muck-savages!'

The entire stadium, it's fair to say, is suddenly stunned into silence. If it's true that places like Kilkenny and Carlow *are* in Leinster, I suppose I'm touching a fair few bases with a line like that.

The stewards suddenly catch up with me, grabbing me and pinning both my orms behind my back. They're just about to haul me off, roysh, when one of the players – I'm pretty sure he was their number eight – goes, 'The Lord between us and harm! Would you look who it is!'

'You're making basic tits of yourselves,' I scream at him. 'Everyone knows who the *real* 1999 Leinster Schools Senior Cup champions are!'

The dude has the actual balls to laugh in my face. 'My word but you're a polished trickster! To lay eyes on you, you'd take the oath there wasn't a crooked bone in your body! But you were on the drugs – *sha*, 'tis belled throughout the country. You put the roguery across on us all. And we owe you no discourse.'

I struggle against the stewards' grip, going, 'Focking Kildare!'

It's then, roysh, that Mocky emerges from the little huddle of players. Seeing him hold the trophy that I worked so hord to lift suddenly in *his* dirty farm hands makes me mad enough to pretty much kill. I'm there, 'You give me that actual trophy! If these two goons weren't holding me back, you could consider yourself *already* decked?'

Mocky's there, 'Quit your tip-of-the-reel and your hullaba-loo!' obviously loving it. 'I can't hear my ears!'

I'm there, 'Hey, we hammered you on the day – beat you like a cross-eyed stepkid. I've got a gold medal still hanging around my neck to prove it.'

'The dickens sweep you,' he goes, 'your mittle and goat's wool would make good stockings!'

Everyone in the crowd laughs, even though I haven't a clue what he's talking about. 'Small blame to you,' someone even shouts at Mocky. ''Tis only fair, the cup is yours. 'Tis fairer than Niamh the Comely at the death of Talc Mac Trone! And the curse of Mushera Mountain down on top of that other fella!'

It's true – the Leinster crowd is definitely changing.

Mocky's there, 'You heard the man. We worked for it – we ate no easy bread. But ye thought all we were good for was cutting furze on the brow of Coum. Well, 'tis ours now – and ye'll be lighter for the road without it!'

'You focking bogger!'

'Oh, you're a man with curses to burn! And you're none too thankful for your bargain now! But you'd be as well getting reconciled to it!'

'You're focking loving this.'

'*Sha*, 'tis true. I've never had a happier day since I was christened Seamaisin Ruadh. And I wouldn't prefer a present of the whole parish this particular night! Even better that it's put a scowl on you. I'll not give you a pennorth of sympathy. I don't care if you're found wandering demented around Baile an Fheirtéaraigh!'

He goes to, like, walk away then. 'You give me that actual trophy!' I end up going, then two or three more stewards have to come and help restrain me, because I end up totally losing it, kicking and thrashing and threatening all sorts.

This – honestly – chubamungous focker with a huge rack and a head like Shrek steps forward then. 'By the heavens but you've notions,' he goes, in a real threatening way. 'Look at you, you're blue-moulded for the want of a baiting!'

'Knock his two eyes into one!' one of the other players shouts.

Then someone else goes, 'He'll not leave this spot tonight without the taste of blood on his teeth!'

See, they're all very brave when I'm being held back.

He's getting ready, roysh, to throw a dig at me, when all of a sudden I hear a voice go, 'You're going to have to go through me first.'

It's Fionn. I can't tell you how focking humiliating it is to have *him* riding to my rescue but I appreciate the back-up anyway.

'And me,' I hear another voice go.

JP.

I'm on the point of being focking milled here and they're ready to be milled with me. That's friendship. I could also say that's rugby.

The focker suddenly thinks better of it. Mocky actually puts his hand on the dude's chest and goes, 'Let's not stand here swapping every second angry word with him. Let him cool the skin he heated in. For this is the best day we ever stood in the prime of our manhood. Tonight, I may tell you, there'll be capering and dancing and music. I own to God, we'll be going clean out of our minds with the singing. Let *them* cut their own sticks now – the whole clutch of them . . .'

Then off they walk, laughing and lepping and whatever else it is that people from Kildare do, while the three of us are dragged outside and literally, I don't know, *deposited* out on to Anglesea Road.

Helen answers the door. She gives me what would have to be described as a sympathetic smile, then says she heard what happened at the RDS. She's sorry.

'Thanks,' I go. 'Again, no phone call from *him*, though.'

She's like, 'Ross, don't just run in there shouting at him. Promise me you'll listen to what he has to say, will you?'

All these people are just, like, suckers for his whole routine. I'm there, 'Where is he – the study?'

She nods. 'Hennessy's with him.'

'Are they hammered?'

'They played nine holes this morning.'

I just shake my head. I'm serious, she could do, like, *way*, *way* better. But I head for the study, roysh, fully intending to hear the tosser out, as Helen suggested, but it's as I'm pushing the door that I hear a snatch of conversation that pulls me up short. It's actually some shit Hennessy says, about how he phoned Regina last night and told her the money would be in her account by eleven o'clock Monday morning.

'Ross!' the old man goes when he sees me standing at the door, cracking on to be delighted, out of obvious guilt more than anything else.

I'm there, 'No, no, please continue.'

He waves his hand at me. 'Just some bit of business,' he tries to go. 'Not important.'

Now I might be as thick as a focking brick on Batch, but I immediately know what's going down here. 'Regina?' I go. 'You wouldn't happen to be talking about Regina Rathfriland would you? As in, wife of Toddy?'

Neither of them answers, which *I* take as a yes. I'm there, 'So how much?'

'What are you talking about?' the old man goes, trying to take advantage of my legendary slowness off the mork.

I end up just roaring at him. 'How much did you pay her to drop Erika's name from the basically divorce proceedings?'

The old man looks at Hennessy and Hennessy sort of, like, nods. The game is up and he knows it.

'One point seven million,' the old man goes.

At first, roysh, I think I must have heard him wrong. 'Sorry, for a second there, I thought you said . . .'

'One point seven million, Ross.'

'You're pulling my focking wire.'

'No. Unfortuately, I'm not. See, the injunction was just a temporary one. It was going to get out. Regina was going to see to that. Unless, of course, she could be persuaded – by fair means or foul – to drop poor Erika's name from the proceedings altogether . . .'

'So you focking paid her one point seven million snots?'

'I just didn't want to see her life ruined, Ross. Which it undoubtedly would have been had it hit the papers.'

That's when I *really* end up losing it? '*Her* life?' I go. 'What about mine? You heard what happened at the match last night?'

'Yes.'

'But you don't *give* two focks – you've already told me that.'

'I care that you're upset – of course I do.'

'No, you don't. Because you're too busy these days with all this new shit you've got going on. You've even stopped calling me Kicker – have you even *thought* about that?'

'Well, I thought it rather annoyed you,' he tries to go.

'Focking everything about you annoys me! But it was still nice to get the recognition every so often. I mean, you *used* to say the real scandal in this country that needed investigating was the fact that I was never called up to the Ireland rugby squad. You even asked a question from the audience about it on *Questions and Answers* . . .'

'The night they were debating the Hepatitis C business. I haven't forgotten.'

'Haven't you? Well, you could have fooled me. Because while you've been throwing your money around supporting Erika, you haven't supported me one little bit. Telling me to move on and find something new. It's like you're almost *glad* it happened?'

Something happens to his face then, which I'm definitely not imagining. It's, like, a sudden change of expression, like he's on the point of saying something, though he's still not sure whether he should or not.

'Whoa!' I go. 'This is a turn-up. You *are* glad. Come on, out with it!'

He looks at Hennessy. 'Wouldn't mind giving us a moment, would you, old chap?'

'Charlie,' he goes on his way out of the room, 'we been friends a long, long time. But I've got to tell you this. I want to beat that boy's eyes into the back of his head.'

I just give him the finger. Then off he focks.

'Of course I'm not glad,' the old man goes. He says it with a bit of a focking tone as well. 'I'm ashamed!'

I'm stunned into almost silence. 'Ashamed? Ashamed of *me*, you mean?'

'No, Ross, ashamed of *me* . . .'

I'm thinking, okay, this I'm prepared to hear. 'Continue.'

He takes, like, a deep breath. 'Ross, I know I haven't been much of a father . . .'

'Agreed.'

'But then my father wasn't much of one either. What I mean is, I didn't have a very good role model when it came to, inverted commas, parenting . . .'

'Cue the focking violins.'

'It seems I disappointed him in everything I did. Well, I've told you this before. When you were born, I remember saying, this little chap is going to make me proud as I failed to make *my* father proud! What a crazy thing to even think . . .'

'Sorry, am I being really stupid here? What the fock are you talking about?'

'I'm talking about living our dreams vicariously through our children. Except it was worse in my case, because it wasn't even *my* dream I had you living out – it was my father's . . .'

'That's not true.'

'It is, Ross. Sadly, it is. I put pressure on you from the first moment I put that bloody Gilbert in your hands. Telling you all those famous stories about Campbell and Slats and, oh, the whole bloody lot of them – asking you to measure up . . .'

I'm suddenly, I don't know, *confused*? 'I'm sorry to disappoint you,' I go, 'but it had fock-all to do with you. I played rugby because it was the one thing in life that I was actually amazing at.'

'No,' he goes, 'I sent you to a school where I knew you'd do nothing but eat, drink and sleep it. Once old Denis got a hold of you, I knew you didn't stand a chance. Did I know he was giving you drugs? No. Would I have objected *had* I known? As I said to Helen, probably not . . .'

He's on the point of actual tears. He nearly has me nearly feeling sorry for him, the sap.

'I was blinded by it, Ross. I expect other parents felt the same. I wanted that medal, whatever the cost. But now I'm looking at you, having to pay that cost. And that's why I'm ashamed, Ross. That's why I think about that piece of metal and I say good riddance to it, let's just move on with our lives . . .'

'Good riddance? You mean, just let some random rabbit-lamper have it?'

'I'm not saying it's right, Ross . . .'

'Of course it's not focking right. Jesus, when I think of Mocky – you remember how he bottled it on the big day – walking up and down the main street of whatever focking town he's from with that medal around his neck, showing it off at the local dance, I get an actual pain in my chest . . .'

He doesn't say anything for, like, ten seconds. Then he goes, 'Okay,' and he nods, like he's decided on some, I don't know, course of action?

I'm there, 'What do you mean, okay?'

'If you *really* want to fight this thing . . .'

'Er, I do?'

'Okay, well, according to your godfather – who, as we know, is an expert in these matters – you do have some legal recourse . . .'

'Okay, break that down for me – words I can understand.'

'Hennessy says you're entitled to a hearing under the Constitution.'

'The what?'

'Have you ever heard of the Constitution of Ireland?'

'No, but move on . . .'

'Well, according to our learned friend, irrespective of the school's wish to forfeit the match after the fact, you're still entitled to present a defence to an independent jury before any sentence is pronounced on you. Oh, it's enshrined, by all accounts.'

'So what happens now?'

'Well, presumably, if so instructed, Hennessy will go and seek interlocutory relief.'

'That sounds filthy.'

'Oh, it's not filthy, Ross. Not at all. It's another of his world-famous injunctions – preventing Newbridge College from calling themselves Leinster Schools Senior Cup champions until after you've put your case.'

I actually punch the air. I'm like, 'Yes!' and then I go, 'See, this is you being a proper father again.'

He sort of, like, smiles. 'I shall instruct our friend accordingly. And *you* might do one thing for *me*, Ross . . .'

I can't actually believe him. 'Er, I don't think you're in any position to ask for favours . . .'

'Just hear me out. Will you come and work for Shred Focking Everything!?'

I laugh – no even choice.

'Please,' he goes. 'Just two weeks. If you don't like it, well, I'll never bring it up again.'

Seven o'clock on Sunday night and there's, like, another porty in full swing next door. Some mate of Terry and Larry's called Shavo got out of prison relatively recently and he's moved into one of the vacants on the third floor. I know this because I met him in the lift, a Calor Kosangas bottle in either hand.

Naturally, roysh, I presumed he had a couple of Supersers, which are still very popular among the working classes. But when he copped me looking at them, he went, 'For fooken protection, so thee are,' and then, when I suddenly tried to look away, he went, 'Fooken law come for me again, these two are goin over the bleaten balcony, so thee are!'

Another great addition to the neighbourhood.

Anyway, Sunday night's porty seems to have been thrown in his honour, given the number of times I hear people congratulating him on keeping his mouth shut.

I'm just sitting there, doing a bit of work on the old laptop. All right, that's actual horseshit. In fact, I'm on, like, YouTube, watching chav women fighting in the street – as you do when you're bored.

That's when my phone all of a sudden rings. It turns out to be, like, Christian.

'May the Force be with you!' I instantly go. 'How are things in Vegas?'

But Christian says fock-all back. He might be on the other side of the, I don't know, *world*, but there *is* no shitting him. 'Why didn't you tell me?' he just goes.

I'm there, 'Who told you?'

'I got the letter from the school,' he goes. 'My old pair forward all my post to me . . .'

I hit pause on a clip of these two Geordie birds slapping the fock out of each other on a hen night.

'You should have told me,' he just goes.

I'm there, 'Dude, I just figured you'd enough on your plate, with, like, the baby and shit? How *is* little Ross anyway?'

'He's fine. Getting huge.'

'That's good. Well, there was that – plus the fact that . . . ah, I don't know . . .'

'What?'

'It just something Simon said – and he's possibly right. I mean, it's all my fault, isn't it?'

'Don't even think like that.'

'But I do, Dude. I mean, *I* was the one who was on drugs – even though it wasn't, like, *drugs* drugs? In a weird way, I feel like I've let you all down . . .'

'Hey, we wouldn't have these medals if it wasn't for you.'

'Okay, I'll allow you that one. Look, I'm sorry I didn't tell you. I just figured, I don't know, if I could stop you finding out about it, I could maybe buy myself some time to make this shit right. We could all end up hanging on to our medals and you need never have known how close we came to actually losing them.'

'Ross,' he just goes, really *firmly* this time? 'What did we always used to say? We're stronger together.'

It's an amazing thing to suddenly hear. I'm there, 'I haven't forgotten.'

'Haven't you? Well, you could have fooled me.'

'I just thought . . .'

'Ross, we won those medals as a team. And, if it comes to it, we'll lose them as a team. How are Fionn and JP taking it? Not well, I presume.'

'You'd presume wrong, then. I think they're actually resigned to it.'

'What?'

'Fionn's still working for McGahy.'

'He hasn't quit?'

'No. Look, in fairness to them, they did seem in pretty much shock when Newbridge were presented with the trophy.'

'Newbridge were presented with the trophy?'

'At half-time in the Newport Dragons match. But, deep down, I think they're like, fock it, whatever. See, they're both loved up at the moment. JP's with some Russian bird – focking lunatic, hates me, by the way. And Fionn's with . . .'

'Who?'

I don't know *why* I don't tell him? Maybe because I know it's not going anywhere. 'Ah, just someone. Suffice it to say, their priorities seem to have changed. I mean, I was the only one who tried to get on the pitch to deck Mocky . . .'

'Mocky! That's a name from the past. He had a lashback.'

'He still focking has it.'

'Jesus. The idea of *him* having a Leinster Schools Senior Cup medal.'

'Well, rest easy, my friend, because he's not going to have one for much longer – you don't have to worry on that score.'

He sounds delighted to hear it. 'Are you saying there's a plan of action?'

'Oh, you better believe there's a plan of action!'

He laughs then, seriously relieved. 'I had a feeling your old man wouldn't sit idly by and just let it happen.'

I'm pretty offended by that, it has to be said. 'Why do people *always* presume it's him?' I go. 'Er, maybe it's down to me this time.'

'I'm sorry, Ross.'

'Look, it's cool, Christian – I just hate when people assume. Anyway, as it happens, it *is* down to my old man – he's sending Hennessy into the High Court tomorrow to get, like, an injunction.'

'This sounds very much to me like fighting talk.'

'It's very much fighting talk.'

'Do you mind me saying, you suddenly sound like the *old* Ross O'Carroll-Kelly – from, like, ten years ago?'

That immediately stirs something in me. I'm not being crude here but I've suddenly got half a focking teacake in my chinos – *and* there's nobody here.

'Christian, I'm not blowing smoke up your hole,' I turn around and go, 'but the way you're talking there is giving me an unbelievable urge to, well, definitely fight this thing every inch of the way.'

He's there, 'Well, if anyone can, you can.'

And I'm like, 'Dude, you better believe it.'

'You know,' the old man goes, 'I'm almost certain it was *me* who once famously said, "In business, as in life, keep three things with you always – patience, courage and good friends – and you'll never know the cold of a recession." And that's a lesson, Ross, that everyone would do well to heed in these, inverted commas, changed times – from your senior executives at the top of the tree, all the way down to your lowly commercial property lawyer.'

I cast the old mince pies skyward. I can't believe it's come to this – sitting in a white Gloria Este with the old man, facing into a day of, believe it or not, work. I might as well have said yes to JP's old man's offer. I'm just about to tell him that I've changed my mind when he suddenly hands me what turns out to be a business cord.

In big red letters, it's got, like, the name of the company on it – obviously SHRED FOCKING EVERYTHING! – then underneath, in black type, it's like, *Ross O'Carroll-Kelly – Managing Partner*, and even though every muscle in my body is screaming at me to go back to bed and watch *The Morning Show with*

336

Sybil and Martin, it's actually the job title that appeals to that little bit of – I suppose you'd have to say – ego in me?

'I do like this,' I go, waving it at him, so he hands me the rest – a big focking brick of about five hundred of them and I'm staring at them, thinking, I can't focking wait to stort flooding the likes of Krystle and Residence with these – let the birds out there know that, just because the country's focked, it doesn't mean we're *all* eating the Bentley's early bird and using public focking transport.

'Before we enter the, inverted commas, breach,' he goes, 'I thought I might outline for you your areas of responsibility.'

Of course that brings me back to earth with a bump. 'Responsibility?' I go, my hand instantly reaching for the handle of the door. 'There's *always* a focking catch with you, isn't there?'

He has, like, a quick look at his watch. 'Eleven o'clock. Hennessy will be in court about now.'

Subtle as a kick in the knackers. I let go of the handle.

'Now, don't go worrying your head,' he tries to go. 'When I say responsibility, I only mean overseeing the overall business practice of the company, supervising in the areas of marketing and business development . . .'

'Something tells me that a giant neon *and* is about to light up this conversation.'

'And, well, yes, collecting sacks of documents from offices and feeding them into the shredding machine in the back of the van there . . .'

I'm there, 'Manual focking labour? Me? Erika's right – you *have* been working too hord.'

'Just two weeks,' he goes and there's nothing I can do, of course, except shake my head and tell him he has balls like focking churchbells.

He changes the subject then, asks me how Ronan's getting

on in his new school. I tell him the first couple of weeks seemed to go fine, though I'd much prefer if he was going to a place that still played actual rugby. 'Either way,' I go, 'once he's out of the clutches of those two next door . . .'

He smiles at me, then he delivers this unbelievable compliment. 'You know, I wish *I'd* been more like you as a father . . .'

It's, like, a major boost for the old confidence, even coming from him. I'm there, 'Do you actually mean that?'

'Well, naturally I mean it. Because it's true. I mean, look at you. You're never done worrying about that little chap of yours. And as for Honor – well, I *know* the reason you ended up living where you do was to keep a roof over *her* head . . .'

I *could* mention the whole supposed UCD dormitory angle to the story, though I don't, probably because I'm enjoying him bulling me *up* for a change?

'I look at you when you're around your children,' he goes, 'and I think, what kind of a bloody miracle is that? What, with the father *he* had?'

I'm there, 'You weren't that bad,' probably getting carried away by the moment.

'It's very kind of you to say so,' he goes, 'but we both know that's a lie. To you *and* Erika, I was a colossal failure. I'm just happy that you won't end up like me – a silly old man trying to live with his regrets . . .'

He has me all of a sudden feeling sorry for him. 'Dude,' I end up going, 'the past is the past.'

He's like, 'You know, Helen's taught me that, in her kind, patient way. The past is yesterday's snow, her mother used to say. One thing I *can* still do is to make sure my children are provided for. That's the reason I started Cheeses Merrion Joseph. I'm hoping Erika will take over when Helen and I retire . . .'

I laugh. 'Er, I think you're going to have some focking job persuading her.'

338

He even laughs then.

Something suddenly occurs to me. 'Hang on a minute – are you saying this van is *my* focking inheritance?'

'Well, it won't always be just a van, if this country's need to purge its guilty conscience is even half what I suspect it is. It'll be a fleet of vans, operating out of a great big shining corporate headquarters, with the words O'CARROLL-KELLY & SON over the door.'

I'm there, 'Of course you have to get *your* name in there first, don't you?'

'No,' he just goes, '*you're* O'Carroll-Kelly, Ross. And Ronan is the Son.'

The focker knows exactly what strings to pull. I don't say anything for ages. I actually *can't*?

'Are you crying?' he eventually goes.

I tell him let's just do this focking thing – stort the engine, which he does, then we're off to our first pick-up of the day, which he says is a bank. I could tell you which bank except it's supposed to be, like, a confidential shredding service?

'My brains and your brains,' the old man goes, as we pull up outside.

I'm staring at my business cord again when I suddenly realize something. 'Is portner not spelt with an *o*?'

He doesn't answer – probably too busy thinking, this goy is going to keep me on my serious toes.

This is cosy. This is very focking cosy. I'm talking about the four of them being out for dinner, we're talking Fionn and Erika, we're talking JP and that focking mentalist of his, all of them in Mint – probably among the last few to eat here, because the word is that *it's* also focked, Michelin stor or not.

'This is focking cosy,' I go.

They all look up from their langoustines and whatever else

– not a bit guilty, by the way. 'What are *you* doing here?' Erika even goes.

I'm there, looking around me, going, 'They don't do tables for six, no?' letting them know, in no uncertain terms, how I feel about being left out of their exclusive little club.

Fionn goes, 'Who would you have brought, Ross?' and I'm thinking, the focking cheek of him – years without his Nat King Cole and now he suddenly thinks he's me.

I don't take the bait, though. I just wave my iPhone at him and go, 'Any one of a thousand, my friend. Any one of a thousand.'

Danuta, by the way, is just glowering at me, like even the *idea* of me makes her angry?

'Zees fugging eediot again,' she goes, not even under her breath, which is the reason I decide to, like, cut it short here.

'Okay,' I go, 'the reason I'm here is just to tell you that Hennessy *got* the injunction . . .'

The two goys just nod. I might as well have told them that I had an incredible shit in the toilet on my way in here. Which I did, by the way.

I'm there, 'Er, preventing the Leinster Branch from declaring Newbridge College champions until *after* I've been formally chorged and offered the opportunity to speak in my own defence?'

They both nod again – at least *trying* to seem more enthusiastic this time?

'And I'm going to do that, don't you worry. Get ready for the trial of the focking century, goys.'

I hear Danuta sort of, like, tutting loudly, so I decide to, like, speed shit up.

'One last thing I probably should tell you – more good news – is that Christian went into the Wikipedia entry for the Leinster Schools Senior Cup and stuck us back in as the 1999 champions, with, like, an asterisk beside it, then underneath it's just like, pending a disciplinary hearing. In other words, bring it on, baby! Bring it focking on!'

'When is the, er, date for the hearing?' is all JP can think to say.

'They said they'd be in touch,' I go, 'over the next, like, week or so? Sorry, goys, pordon me for saying it, but I thought it'd be, like, high-fives all round here tonight.'

I look at Fionn. I actually stare him out of it because he seems to have something he wants to say. 'Ross,' he goes, 'you've already admitted your guilt, in that stupid book you did.'

'Your point being?'

'My point being – they're going to give you your hearing, you're going to admit what you did and then we're going to be stripped of our medals anyway. Does it not just seem like a colossal waste of energy to you?'

'And money,' Erika suddenly pipes up.

One point seven million yoyos for a fling with Toddy Rath-friland – er, *she* can afford to talk?

'Why don't you giff zees fugging medal back?' it's Danuta who suddenly goes. 'Zees ees problem wiz people now. Zey want to keep what ees not zares any more. Like woman today – she ees sprawled on bonnet of Porsche Cayenne, saying, let me keep, let me keep! I say, no, ees not yours – ees finance company's. Now you poot Rimmel foundation on windscreen, fugging beetch . . .'

I should know better than to answer her back. But she wasn't there to see the mess we made of Newbridge College that day, which means she has no right to say this medal doesn't belong to me. 'Don't worry, I know what's eating you,' I go. 'You're just bulling because it was the same drugs that your man Heil Hitler was on when he invaded your actual country?'

Her mouth just drops open. She turns to JP, roysh, wondering has she, like, misunderstood. *He* just goes, 'Ross, I'm about to translate what you just said for Danuta,' and then he nods in the direction of the door. 'Why don't you get a good head start?'

My first full week of work turned out to be not half as bad as I *thought* it was going to be?

He's a focking dope – you'll get no orguments from me on that score – but, like I've often said, he can actually be all right when he doesn't try too hord.

The other thing is – and I can't believe I'm even thinking these words – but there ended up being something weirdly satisfying about doing an honest week's work – *if* you can call destroying documents before the Fraud Squad get their hands on them honest.

'God's work,' the old man called it as we were getting ready to break for lunch on Friday. He put his hand on my shoulder, picked up a random bank statement that I was about to feed into the machine and gave it the quick left to right. 'If people knew the half of this, they'd be rioting in the bloody streets . . .'

He shook his head.

'As I said at my trial, *this* is what your economic miracle was built on. Greed, avarice and corruption. And they thought it was hilarious, do you remember that?'

I went, 'You *did* make a tit of yourself, though.'

He even laughed. 'Yes, I expect I did . . .'

Then he said I could knock off early. The weird thing was, roysh, I didn't even *want* to? But we'd already done our final collection of the week.

So anyway, roysh, I'm on the Stillorgan dualler, on my way out of town, when I suddenly remember that today is the last ever episode of *FO'CK Cooking* and that the old dear said she was going to make it one to remember.

I check the time and I realize it's about to stort. There's no way I'd make it out to Ticknock in time, so I decide to swing into, like, RTÉ itself to watch it in reception. I'm thinking, I might even ask that Shanna Moakler one for her digits – about time she got a shot at the title.

When I walk through the revolving door, I immediately notice that she's dabbing at her eyes with a tissue.

I'm like, 'Hey, what's the story?' because I still don't know her name.

She's there, 'Oh, we're all a bit teary in here today. Chico passed away this morning.'

'Who?'

'Do you watch *Fair City*?'

I laugh. 'Er, I don't need to. I can just stick my focking ear up against the wall.'

Except I say it in, like, a flirty way?

'Well,' she goes, 'Chico was Bela Doyle's cat. Ah, he was just a stray who used to hang around the lot. Then they decided to write him into the show. He was only in it for six or seven episodes. They said he'd heartworm.'

I haven't a bog what that is but it sounds focking revolting. 'That's, er, sad,' I go, trying to soften her up. You've got to make sure to give them plenty of sympathy. That's a fact.

'God, I focking love animals,' I go.

She nods and dabs at her eyes again. She's there, 'They're having a wake for him in McCoys.'

'Well, I'll certainly pop in – pay my respects and blah blah blah.'

'Oh, that's nice.'

'Well, it's the least I can do. And, by the way, if you fancy grabbing a drink after you knock off, maybe talk about the whole thing – the cat being dead and blah blah blah – I can cancel my plans for tonight . . .'

She smiles at me. She's actually on the point of saying yes, roysh, when the reception area is suddenly filled with these angry voices. I turn around, roysh, and all these people are suddenly coming through the revolving door, shouting at the same time.

They're dressed like the queue for the 77 bus and it doesn't take me long to work out that it's the cast of *Fair City*.

'He's gone!' I hear one of the women shout in what I have to say is a surprisingly posh accent. It's more like, 'He's gawn!' and then I remember hearing somewhere that the entire cast was made up of Southsiders *pretending* to be skobies? 'He's gawn! He's simply gawn!'

Of course the obvious question is, 'Who the fock?'

'Chico!' she goes. 'We had him laid out – *beautifully!* – in the pub. Someone's taken him!'

It's weird, roysh, but it's another of those moments when you don't know but at the same time you somehow *do*?

I sort of, like, instinctively turn to the huge TV they have in the waiting area. The old dear's face is filling the screen, smiling away, which she hasn't done for weeks on the show. Maybe that's why everyone's attention is suddenly drawn to it.

'Now,' she goes, 'recently, I showed you how to prepare a vaguely edible three-course meal from the scraps that most of us discard every day as rubbish. Today, I'll be showing you how to cook a beautiful Morrocan-style tagine – and don't fret, those of you out there who are watching every cent right now, because it's not only very simple but also very, very cheap to make.

'Now, many of us are familiar with the heartache and sadness that come from losing a family pet . . .'

I'm thinking, no way – no *focking* way!

'Some of us – myself included – have buried faithful old dogs in the back garden, marking the spot with a stone that will serve as a permanent reminder of a loving and fulfilling relationship. However, *in* the current economic climate, with money scarce, we can no longer afford to ignore the fact that our once-loved pets, even after death, still contain good meat . . .'

The camera pans back.

It feels like I'm dreaming but she's holding – I swear to fock! – a dead cat by the tail. And I could be wrong but that looks very much to me like a Spanish onion shoved into its dead mouth.

There's all of a sudden, like, screams from the *Fair City* cast – and they're definitely not acting.

'It's Chico!' one or two are going.

Others are just there, 'Nooo!'

Not only that, roysh, but you can hear, like, screaming coming from the floors above us as well.

'What . . . what's she doing?' Shanna Moakler goes.

'I'm pretty sure she said a Morrocan-style tagine,' I go, equally in shock.

'After the break,' the old dear continues, 'I'm going to show you how to bring a bit of post-mortem cheer to the house by turning a once-loved pet into a delicious nomadic stew. All you need for this is an onion, two carrots, a turnip, a dead cat and a country that thinks that an economic downturn is an excuse for us all to return to the Middle Ages.'

Someone must pull the plug on her then, roysh, because the screen goes blank, then up comes a message saying there's been, like, a breakdown in transmission, which is obvious horseshit.

I look around me. Everyone looks like they've been pulled from the focking North Sea. They're all, like, hugging each other and shivering and crying.

I look at Shanna Moakler. She's, like, totally distraught. It's definitely not the time to bring it up. But I do. 'Again, we can talk about *all* of this over that drink . . .'

Except she just stares straight through me.

The next thing, the doors into the studio open and the old dear breezes through reception, as if nothing ever happened, going, 'Oh, hello, Ross, dorling! Shall we get a late lunch?'

This woman – she's a real Yummy Mummy If She Wasn't So Tonney – she hands me a sack of, like, documents and you'd honestly swear she was handing me her focking first-born. 'You'll look after it, won't you?' she goes. 'I can trust you . . .'

I end up having to pretty much wrestle it from her. I'm there, 'Look, I'll pour it into the shredder right now,' and she finally lets go.

She goes, 'There's things in there . . . My husband and I would go to prison.'

This is, like, Killiney we're talking, so they probably wouldn't, although the old man was right about a lot of people having a lot of shit to suddenly hide.

I shred it anyway, while *he* drives on to the next pick-up. When we stop again, I hop out. We're porked on, like, Castle Street in Dalkey. The old man, I notice, is talking to someone through the driver's window.

It turns out to be Sorcha – she's pushing Honor in the stroller. 'Hello!' she goes when she sees me. You'd never think divorce was even *on* the cords. 'Very smart,' she goes, checking out my yellow jumpsuit.

'Shreeed,' Honor goes, trying to read the lettering on it, 'fff . . . fffock . . .' and what can me, Sorcha and the old man do other than laugh?

'You'll know that word soon enough,' Sorcha goes to her, 'if you spend enough time around your daddy.'

Sorcha looks unbelievable, I don't know if I mentioned. 'I was just saying,' the old man goes to me, 'that you haven't had a break this afternoon . . .'

Then Sorcha smiles at me. 'Do you fancy a coffee?'

It's like – er, does Pinocchio have a hickory dick?

So we end up hitting the new Buckys, just me and her and Honor. 'Do you mind me saying,' I go, as she eats the froth off her skinny cappuccino, 'that this is the best I've seen you looking for a long, long time?'

She loves that I've said it. She's like, 'Thanks, Ross. I'm finished with my communty service next week, you know?'

I'm there, 'Cool,' and then I ask her, what then? She says she still has no idea, except she sounds sort of, like, happy about that. 'I'm going to spend some time with my daughter,' she goes, 'and just *be*, if that makes any sense.'

I tell her it makes perfect sense – she means just sit on her hole for a few months.

She laughs. It's the jumpsuit again. She obviously can't believe I'm back *working* for a living.

'It's actually been pretty cool,' I go, 'even though it was originally supposed to be only for, like, a week or two? See, the old man's actually all right, deep down. Did I tell you he's backing me now on the whole medal front? We managed to get an injunction.'

'That's good. Look, I know how much it still means to you.'

'Big-time. Plus, I don't know, he *knows* loads of shit, the old man. I possibly should listen to him the odd time. He's putting this whole recession thing into definite perspective for me. He says we all got, I don't know, lazy and complacent. No offence, by the way . . .'

'No, he's right, Ross – certainly in the case of my shop. I mean, I grew up knowing nothing *but* prosperity. I just didn't have the skills-set to cope with this changed world we've all woken up to. You heard Nu Blue Eriu's gone, did you?'

'I certainly heard it was in trouble . . .'

'Everything's in trouble. That's what my dad said to me. He was like, "Sorcha, *you* haven't failed – your country has failed *you*!" Which was *so* an amazing thing to hear.'

I tell her I can only imagine. I give Honor a sip of her organic apple juice.

'Yeah, no,' I go, 'I don't see this as being, like, a long-term thing for me – as in, work? What I'll probably do is carry on helping the old man build the business up, then flog it for, like, millions – hopefully get out of that squatter camp I'm living in.'

She's there, 'I still feel bad about that. I mean, I *know* you did it for us.'

Except I'm like, 'Hey, I can't think of a better reason for doing it,' and the thing is, roysh, I actually mean it. 'By the way, I'm earning pretty all right money doing this – I can afford to up your, er . . . maintenance?'

I nearly called it vagimoney – force of habit.

'What you give me is enough,' she goes, 'despite what my dad says.'

I don't argue with her. I'll hit the old Hilary tomorrow and change, like, the standing order. There's like, a lull in the conversation then.

'Did you hear about my old dear trying to cook the *Fair City* cat,' I go, for the want of something more interesting to say.

She smiles at me, except sadly. 'Who am I to judge your mum?' she goes. 'I cracked under the pressure as well. Like I said, no one could have seen this thing coming.'

'I suppose.'

'The only thing I *would* say is that Honor saw it. She ended up having terrible nightmares. I just couldn't get her settled.'

I laugh. 'Speaking of settling,' I go, 'Erika and Fionn seem to be getting on very well.'

She's there, 'Ross!' even though I know she secretly considers it a cracking line. 'They're actually really, really happy.'

'*She* couldn't be. She's into, like, rich and powerful men. Fionn hordly fits that bill.'

'Well, she's changed, Ross. In fact, she thinks she might even be in love.'

I laugh again.

'Yeah, roysh. Just leave the two of them to it, would be my basic attitude now. When it all goes to hell on a jetski, they needn't come running to me expecting me to listen to all the juicy details . . .'

That's when, all of a sudden, Sorcha puts her head down and storts using her hand to, like, shield her face. I ask her what's suddenly wrong and she says that Corrine Wilson just walked past the window – as in, Corrine Wilson who she was in school with?

I'm there, 'Er, are you ashamed to be seen with me or something?'

'No,' she goes, 'I just don't want to see her.'

I'm like, 'Hang on – I thought you two were friends?'

'Only on Facebook,' she goes. 'If I met her in, like, real life, I honestly wouldn't know what to say to her.'

It's then that I realize that I'm still in love with Sorcha and probably always will be.

So there I am, roysh, in the cor, on the way out of town, with the seat right back, the sunnies on and *The Blue Corpet Treatment* on full blast, watching Donnybrook just zip by.

It's as I'm hitting the red light outside Bang & Olufsen that I happen to look in the old rear-view and cop this unbelievable-looking bird – Françoise Boufhal would *not* be an exaggeration? – sitting in a white-chocolate Clearcoat Lincoln Navigator. She's singing away to whatever song she's got on, really giving it loads, which *is* pretty cute, it must be said, so *I* end up flicking on the radio then and stort lashing through the presets, trying to find whatever song it is.

Turns out it's, like, 'Push the Button' on Today FM.

Of course I'm too busy ogling her in my mirror to notice that the lights have turned green and she ends up giving me a blast of her horn, telling me to shift it.

One thing I love about birds is attitude – non-menstrual obviously.

So suddenly, roysh, I'm driving with one hand while digging out a pen with the other. By the time we've hit the the next red light outside Donnybrook stadium, she's pulled into the bus lane and I've written my mobile number down on the back of an old speeding ticket. As moves go, I have to admit, it's as smooth as an otter in a tux – and it *actually* works, because when I take away the piece of paper, she's laughing, shaking her head and keying my number into her iPhone.

The next thing, my phone rings and I answer it going, 'Hey, Babes – what's the Bill Murray?'

She laughs. She's like, 'The what?'

I'm there, 'Er, *beeping* me like that? Are you in, like, a rush somewhere?' but I'm saying it while giving her the big-time come-on.

She goes, 'You were on another planet,' and I'm there, 'Oh, I'm on another planet all right! I see you're, like, a Sugababes fan.'

She laughs. 'So, what, you read lips?'

I laugh then. 'I do a lot of things to lips!'

She's there, 'Oh my God, this is, like, *so* random,' obviously delighted with herself. 'So what's your name?'

I'm there, 'You genuinely don't know?' Must be the Oakley Doakleys. 'I'm, like, Ross O'Carroll-Kelly? In other words, *the*?'

The lights turn green again and I give it some serious lead, inviting her to, like, chase me, which she does. 'Oh my God,' she's shouting down the phone, 'come back!'

I give it some brake when I hit the bridge at UCD, just to let her catch up. I look at her across the lane. 'I'm Branna,' she goes. 'Branna O'Neill?'

I'm there, 'So what are you doing later, Gator?' which is a famous line of mine.

She's there, 'I don't know,' all giggly – a serious wide-on for me, I can tell. 'Stuff!'

'Stuff? That sounds exciting. Well, do you fancy going for a drink?'

'I don't know,' she goes.

'Maybe Blackrock?'

'This is like, Oh! My God!'

'You say *that* like it's a bad thing.'

'I'm not saying it's, like, a bad thing? It's just, well, I don't even *know* you?'

'You're *interested*, though.'

'Oh my God, you *so* have tickets on yourself, don't you?'

'Hey, I know women well enough to know the signs.'

This kind of shit continues, back and forth, for the next, like, ten minutes, with me patiently going through the phases, edging ever closer to the line.

It's just after we pass my old gaff – the old Spirit of Negative Equity – that I spot something out of the corner of my eye which forces me to slam on the actual brakes. I notice Erika, roysh, walking into the Galloping Green – which is weird enough by itself – except, roysh, she's in the company of a man old enough to be her actual grandfather.

It's funny, roysh, it's another one of those times when you immediately *know* the Jack?

I suddenly swing the wheel left and watch Branna disappear in the direction of White's Cross. 'Where have you gone?' she goes and I'm there, 'I'll bell you later,' and I hang up on her.

I pull up outside the boozer, then give them a minute or two to get, like, *settled* in there? At the same time, roysh, I'm thinking, okay, what's my play here?

I know what I'm *tempted* to do is to ring Fionn and tell him I told you so. I knew he'd an almighty kick in the knackers on the way. When it comes to, like, men, Erika's only ever been interested in one thing and that thing happens to be moo. She'll never change.

At the same time, I *am* thinking, poor Fionn. In fairness, the dude was never in her league. He was writng cheques he couldn't honour and I'm saying that as his friend.

I can't wait to see the look on his face when I tell him she's back with Toddy.

I push the door of the lounge and the first thing I hear is *her* voice. They're obviously sat to my immediate left, behind the partition, because I can hear her, like, talking? I don't know what she's saying but I can tell from her tone that she's giving him plenty of tude.

The place is empty. There's, like, a TV in the corner with, believe it or not, soccer on it? Manchester Something Or Other against some other random flecks. See, there's no chance she'd run into anyone who knows her in here.

Or so she thinks.

I lean against the partition and have a closer listen. I'm still trying to decide whether to just, like, spring out in front of them, when I all of a sudden hear *her* go, 'No!'

He's there, 'Please. Come away with me – tonight.'

'Toddy . . .'

'We could go to Val-d'Isère. The jet's here – at Dublin Airport. We could be there by midnight.'

'It's over. I told you that months ago.'

'You'd love it there. I *always* said that, didn't I?'

'You said a lot of things.'

'But we could talk there – properly talk.'

'Talking to you bores me, Toddy. It always did.'

'Look, I know things are a mess. But we're *getting* that divorce now. This is what we talked about, isn't it?'

'It's what *you* talked about. It was only ever a fling for me. Er, get *over* it?'

'Erika . . .'

'I've met someone.'

He's like, 'What?' and you can tell straight away that he doesn't believe her. 'Who?'

The funny thing is, roysh, I still think she's going to mention someone *other* than Fionn? 'You don't need to know,' she goes. 'You're not, like, *in* my life any more.'

He's there, 'What does he do?' big-time Scooby Dubious.

'He's a teacher.'

'A teacher? Come on, Erika – someone like that can't make you happy.'

Well, you know how *I* feel about that.

'He *makes* me happy,' she goes.

I hear, then, a crack in his voice – we're talking actual emotion here? He's focking deluded if he thinks *that's* going to get him anywhere. He's like, 'Erika, I already stand to lose everything. That's fine. It's a recession. But, well, what I *can't* stand to lose is you.'

'I think I'm about to throw my lunch up,' she goes, taking the words right out of my mouth. 'Do you think being pathetic is going to make me suddenly want you?'

It's, like, refreshing to see that her being with Fionn hasn't stopped her being an out and out bitch. I'd, like, *miss* that?

'All I was ever interested in was your money,' she goes. 'I never made any secret of that and you didn't particularly mind. But now you don't have any money . . .'

'That's not entirely true. There're two or three of the restaurants, I think I can get them back from the receiver. I mean, they're still profitable . . .'

'Having sex with you was like being trapped under rubble.'

'But there's actual money there as well. You're not listening to me. A lot of money. Okay, Regina's going to take a lot of it, but there's still more than enough for us to . . .'

She's there, 'Toddy, you're going to need to start getting your head around this. I don't want you. Even the idea of touching you makes me sick to my stomach. It was a fleeting thing. It was never going to last. Now, live with it.'

I take that, roysh, as my cue to step out from behind the partition. I'm just there, 'You heard the lady.'

Erika's in, like, total shock seeing *me* suddenly stood in front of her. *He* is as well? Of course he hasn't a breeze who I even am. 'Is this *him*?' he tries to go. 'Your teacher man?'

I feel like actually decking him. I don't even *care* how old he is. He's sat there, roysh, thinking he's hot shit in his beige chinos and his pink shirt and his blue Ralph Lauren jacket, which are all, like, thirty years too young for him, by the way. One of those old fockers who can't act or dress his age. And the hair still dyed off his head.

I go, 'No, actually. I happen to be her brother. And, before you ask, the answer is yes, I probably do have some feelings for her as well.'

From his reaction, I don't think he *was* going to ask. 'Ross,' *she* goes, 'I can handle this. Go away.'

I'm like, 'I'm not going anywhere. Not until *he's* out of here.'

He laughs. He's some balls, I'll give him that.

I can't get that whole sorbet episode out of my head. I fix him, roysh, with this seriously threatening look and I go, 'Dude, do yourself a favour – get in your little plane and fock off to your little makey-up place, whatever the fock it's called. If I hear that you're ever giving my sister Hasselhoff again, you can consider yourself already decked. Now hit the bricks, old boy.'

There's no doubt, roysh, that I've put the serious shits up him. He stares at me, then he looks at Erika, presumably for back-up, though none comes.

'Don't ever call me again,' she just goes.

He stands up, roysh, knocks back what's left of his Cabernet Sauvignon, straightens his jacket, then walks out, stopping once and obviously considering saying something nasty to her.

'Don't even think about insulting the lady,' I go. He thinks better of it, then disappears out the door.

Erika just fixes me with a look and tells me I'm a wanker. She's like, 'Sad *and* a wanker.'

The old man says he's never seen anyone work so fast. If this were a unionized operation, he says, I could expect a tap on the shoulder, then a polite word from one of these, inverted commas, *shop stewards*, telling me to slow down – that's the work of two men you're doing there, Comrade.

'Of course there'll *be* no unions,' he goes. 'I merely mentioned it to illustrate my point that you're a hard worker, Ross . . .'

I do have to admit, roysh, I find the actual shredding sort of, like, calming – even therapeutic? 'Every document I put in there,' I go, 'I picture it as McGahy's focking head,' except what he says in reply actually surprises me.

'That's a common trait in people, Ross, and it's more and

more in evidence in the current economic whatnot – people always seek to find a human form for their unhappiness. Not so long ago it was your mother, you'll remember. What's she earning? What's she spending? Or it was poor old Seanie Fitz. Oh, it'll be Fingers Fingleton next, you see if it isn't. Of course, nobody cared a jot who any of these people even were while the tills were ringing like the bells of St Mary's.'

He puts what's left of his sandwich back in the Tupperware box it came in. '*Cottage* cheese,' he goes, like we're suddenly sharing a joke, presumably about Helen. 'On about my – inverted commas – cholesterol again.' He stands up. 'Now, are you absolutely sure you don't mind me leaving you on your own?'

I'm there, 'Dude, I know how to drive this thing. It's cool. Take the afternoon off.'

'Oh, I shan't be taking the afternoon off, Ross. No, no, I've discovered the identity of the chap supplying Sheridans with their famous Comté Marcel Petite. I'm going to take a spill down to Wexford to see if I can't get me some. These are the lengths to which we must go if we're to remain successful in business.'

He focks off. I finish shredding the three bags that are left, then I climb over the back of the driver's seat and stick the key in the engine. I've only got, like, two more pick-ups scheduled for the afternoon. I might even give JP or Fionn a ring, maybe go for a few early scoops.

I'm putting Old Amnesia into reverse, roysh, when a cor suddenly pulls up behind me, instantly blocking me in, then I end up nearly shitting seven colours because it turns out to be, like, the Gords?

I'm immediately telling myself to calm down – as the old man said, anything incriminating back there is good for fock-all now except confetti.

Then I watch in the rear-view as two – get this – *lady* cops get out and I relax a bit. They're both suddenly stood at my window. I wind it down and go, 'What can I do you for, ladies?' and that's when I get my second sudden shock. I *know* one of them? And yeah, I *do* mean in that way.

She's there, 'Hellaw, Ross,' and I'm like, 'Er, hey, Breege,' the events of the night coming back to me fast.

'So,' she goes, 'this is what you're doing now, is it?' taking in what it says on the side of the van.

'That's right,' I go, 'this country's dirty little secrets aren't going to shred themselves,' at the same time hating myself for using one of my old man's lines.

There's this, like, awkward silence then and I decide that there's something I should possibly say. 'I'm, er, sorry again about that night – well, morning. Like I said to you, I was never one for the big *Grey's Anatomy* goodbyes.'

She actually laughs. I think country birds *are* more forgiving – possibly grateful they're getting any.

The other one pipes up then. The only reason I haven't gone into any detail about her, by the way, is because she's one of the ugliest life forms I've ever set eyes on. I wouldn't touch her with asbestos focking gloves.

'Is this the fella?' she goes. 'Ah, lads!'

Ugly or not, I've always been weirdly aroused by the way country women call each other lads.

Breege says yeah, it's him all right, then ends up going through the entire focking story again, even though most of, like, Harcourt Terrace has probably already heard it. 'He was trying to sneak out without saying goodbye,' she goes. 'He says, "I'm not into the old post-match chat." I says, "That's fair enough, Ross – but this is your apartment!"'

'I think I might have been sleepwalking that morning,' I end up going, which makes them laugh even more.

I notice Breege then cop a sly look at my tax and insurance – they can't focking help themselves, can they? So I go, '*Anyhoo*,' trying to hurry the conversation along, 'what is this, just a catch-up?'

They both get suddenly serious. 'I hear you've moved apartment,' Breege goes, 'since that night.'

I'm there, 'Don't even focking stort me – I got stitched like a quilt. I rang your crowd by the way. They'd no focking interest.'

She doesn't look like she has either – at least in *my* side of the story. She's there, 'It sounds to me like a civil matter.'

Which are the exact same words they used in, like, Kill of the Grange? Being a Gord must be like working in a focking call centre, where there's, like, a set answer to every complaint people make.

'You're living next door to a couple of dangerous characters,' the wreck goes.

I'm there, 'Yeah, that's not the kind of thing you could fail to focking notice, you know.'

She smiles and says she supposes not.

'My sister works in the Special Branch,' Breege goes and I'm presuming it's the sister she was with in Kehoes that night, the one who drinks like a focking sieve. 'They're trying to build a case against them . . .'

I suddenly cut in.

'Oh and let me guess,' I go, 'she wants access to my aportment so they can plant, like, a listening device in the wall?'

The thing is, roysh, I'm only, like, ripping the piss saying it, but it turns out that's what they *actually* want? I can immediately tell from the way they exchange, I suppose, glances. I'm there, 'You've got to be shitting me! Someone's watched too many episodes of *The Wire*. The answer, I'm afraid, is no.'

She nods, pretty much accepting my answer. 'You probably

should tell your son to stay away from them,' the other one goes and I'm left in sudden shock.

I'm there, 'You . . . You know about Ronan calling in there?'

Breege goes, 'Like I said, they've been building a case. Have a think about it. I know you've been getting a hard time from them. It might be a way to get them out of your life, once and for all . . .'

Fionn rings and the first thing he says to me is, like, thanks. 'Erika told me,' he goes, 'about, well, the scene with Toddy? She said you handled it very well.'

Has to be said, it's nice to get the big-up.

'I, er, don't think she actually needed my help,' I go. 'She was doing a pretty good job of telling him to go fock himself before I even *arrived* on the scene?'

'Well, she said he was being quite insistent. And she doesn't know what would have happened had you not been there.'

She'd never say that straight to me, of course – wouldn't give me the pleasure of knowing.

'Look,' I go, 'I have to say, I'm still struggling with the whole idea of you two, you know, doing whatever you're doing together. Still freaks me out a bit . . .'

'I know.'

'Plus, I still think you're going to end up getting kicked in the mebs. Enjoy it while it lasts is the best advice I can give you.'

He laughs and goes, 'Again, thanks, Ross. You really are a good friend.'

The old dear has decided to skip town, just until the whole, I don't know, controversy over her trying to cook the *Fair City* cat on live television has died down.

She's got, like, the paparazzi outside the gate – day *and* night

– and then there's, like, the death threats? One or two so-called animal rights heads have been on, promising to do this, that and the other to her. Of course there's no telling them that the cat was already dead when she seasoned it and shoved that onion in its mouth.

I suppose that's why they *call* them extremists?

I tell her she can't let these people drive her out of her home.

'Can I remind you of something that happened when I was a little kid?' I go, the two of us sitting in the kitchen in Foxrock.

She looks suddenly worried.

'No, it's not actually *bad*?' I end up having to go. 'No, there was this one day – I was, like, eight, maybe nine – and we were coming out of Sydney Vard, do you remember that?'

'On South Anne Street . . .'

'Yeah, when that bird with the dreadlocks shouted, "Murderer!" and threw a bucket of red paint over you?'

'Oh,' she goes and puts the back of her hand against her forehead, a bit Emma focking Thompson with the dramatics. 'My brand-new mink shawl jacket!'

I'm there, 'But do you remember what you did next?'

She suddenly smiles.

'Yes, I turned around, walked back into the shop and bought another one.'

'And do you remember what you said to the bird on the way out the door the second time?'

'If I keep buying them, they'll keep killing them!'

I laugh. 'God, I was so proud of you that day.'

'Were you, Ross?'

'Big-time. I mean, yeah, I probably called you a sad sack and told you to stop focking embarrassing me, but deep down I would have been thinking fair focks. I might have even learned a lesson from you that day – might explain why I'm not prepared to just hand over my Leinster Schools Senior Cup medal. Because you stood up for yourself. You didn't allow yourself to be intimidated . . .'

She says she's not being intimidated now. She just needs a break, which is why she's booked a week in the Corinthia Grand in Budapest.

I stort flicking through the brochure.

'They *call* it a luxury hotel,' she goes, 'though it's more of a monarchial residence. Oh, it totally invokes the atmosphere of the Austro-Hungarian Empire,' which she obviously means as a good thing. 'Which it just what I need, with the country going the way it's going. Here's an idea, Ross! Why don't you come with me?'

'Come with you?'

'Yes! You need a holiday as much as I do. With all *you've* been through this year? Do you a power of good to get away from that bloody juvenile detention facility you've found yourself living in.'

I laugh. 'No,' I go, 'I've got, er, well, *work* . . .'

She smiles. I still stand by what I've always said – she looks focking revolting when she does that.

'Work!' she goes, genuinely amazed. 'Your father, by the way, thinks you've a real gift for it.'

I'm there, 'I wouldn't get too carried away. I'll do it for a little while longer, get a deposit together, maybe finally get out of – like you say – Wheatfield.'

She smiles, then says she'd better get on the road or she'll miss her flight. 'You know what the M50 is like,' she goes, 'and I expect I'll have my bloody photographer friends on their motorcycles with me the entire way.'

It's, like, Saturday afternoon, roysh, and I'm sitting in, watching TV, knocking back a few Richard Geres and generally chillaxing after my first full month on the job. That's when I go and do something that I immediately end up regretting.

It's probably a mixture of Heineken and curiosity that gets the better of me but I end up putting a pint glass to the wall and having a bit of a listen to whatever shenanigans are going on next door.

I'd seen it done on, like, TV and shit but I had no idea that it actually worked.

Larry and Terry have company and I can tell you this – *they're* not watching the E! channel's special on the feud between Lindsay Lohan and Hilary Duff.

'Will yast me bollix – a Walther!' this voice goes. It's not Terry or Larry talking. It's, like, whoever their visitor is? 'Do ye know fooken athin? The fooken ninety-nine's a rip-off *of* the bleatin seventeen . . .'

'Worra bout the XD?'

That's Larry.

'The XD?' the original dude goes. 'Monta fock ourra dat, will ye, witcher XD! It's MA1s next and M and fooken Ps . . .'

It continues like that for the next, I don't know, five minutes or so. Loads of letters, loads of numbers and loads of telling each other to go and fock yourself. I'm thinking it must be like teaching algebra to kids in Clondalkin.

'Just point it, Tetty, and puddle the fooken trigger – don't woody, it's not loated – then teddle me what ye tink . . .'

'Hee-er, stall the ball – are ye asthin me or telling me?'

'Tetty, just puddle the fooken trigger . . .'

There's, like, silence for maybe ten seconds, roysh, then I hear this sudden click. Terry cracks his hole laughing, then the other two join in. 'I fooken luff it,' Terry goes.

The other dude's like, 'I told ye – why wooten ye? The orichinal Glock is stiddle the best – noyin millimether, high-power, semi-authormathic. It's veddy loigh. It's made ourra advaddenced syntetic polymers – plastic to the loikes of youden I. It's small, easy to conceal and veddy easy to hughes – veddy few pieces, see. I moigh also add that it's the most redliable piece there is – neffer, ever jaddems . . .'

'We'll take all torty,' Larry instantly goes, 'if dats what ye have.'

The dude laughs. He's like, 'Mister Van Voorden will be veddy happy to heerd it.'

In my mind, roysh, I imagine them shaking hands to – I suppose – *seal* the deal? Again, that might be *me* watching too much TV. Then I hear Terry ask him if he fancies a drink.

He's like, 'Nah, I bethor split . . .'

It's at that exact point, roysh, that there's a sudden knock on the door. As in *their* door?

You can tell that they all nearly shit themselves. 'Who the fook is that?' the – obviously – orms dealer goes.

Terry's like, 'I haffent a fooken clue.'

'I swear to fook, Tetty, if that's the law . . .'

'Do ye tink the fooken law would knock?'

He probably has a point. 'Joost ansod it,' Larry goes.

The next thing I hear is Terry turning the key in the lock and I'm, like, picturing him at the same time holding the gun behind his back. I hear him pull down the handle and slowly open the door. Then I hear three words that end up giving me a pretty much hort attack.

'Ah, howiya, Ronan.'

I feel like automatically screaming out, telling him to get the fock out of there. But then, I don't know, *reason* takes over and I'm thinking that any sudden noise or movement could be actually *fatal* here? 'I brought this back,' I hear his little voice go.

'What is it?' Terry goes. 'Ah, the Burden It Dunne tee-fee-tee . . .'

Ro did mention that they lent him, like, a boxing DVD.

'Shuren that was a gift, Ro.'

'Was it?'

'Yeah, from Laddy and me . . .'

'Oh. Tanks, Tetty.'

'Not a bodder . . .'

There's, like, silence then. Ronan's obviously waiting for an invite in.

'Er, *we're* in the mithel of something he-eer, Ro – I'm goin to haff to go . . .'

'Er, okay.'

Except he's obviously *not* okay? He actually sounds a bit hurt.

'Birra business – yunderstand?'

Then the door suddenly closes.

I take the glass away from the wall, roysh, and I stand there in total silence. I suppose I'm waiting for him to knock on *my* door. He must be thinking about it because I don't hear him move for, like, twenty or thirty seconds.

I've got, like, my eyes closed, thinking, *I'll* watch Bernard Dunne with you. I'll watch Bernard Dunne with you day and focking night. Just knock, Ro. Please just knock.

The next thing I hear is him walking away. Then the elevator doors open and he's suddenly gone.

I storm back into the living room – in a bit of a rage, to be fair – and I whip out my phone. I scroll down and find Breege's number. I end up just staring at it for maybe even a minute, even though, deep down, I know what I'm going to do.

I hit dial.

'Hellaw,' she goes. That accent – wherever the fock Mullingor even is.

'Hey,' I hear myself go. 'You can tell your sister I'll do it.'

*

She's getting drenched – and we're talking totally. I open up the umbrella and just hold it over her. She doesn't say a word, just looks up at me – big blue eyes – then gives me a smile, as if to say, my hero!

'Thought I'd come and keep you company,' I go. 'It's your last hour, isn't it?' and she goes, 'Oh my God, yeah,' thrilled, of course, that I remembered.

She's back scraping old posters, by the way, this time down by Pearse Street Dort Station.

I stand there holding the umbrella, just watching her work. Then I end up having to laugh. 'The Dubai Overseas Property and Resorts Show!' I go. 'We were too busy buying up other people's countries to realize that we didn't even own this one. We've some stones, us, don't we – as, like, a nation?'

Then I just shake my head.

'By the way, do you know what's going to be announced any day now?' I go, making a grab for my medal out of, like, instinct. 'A date for my own hearing, slash, trial, slash, whatever you want to call it.'

'That's great,' she just goes, then continues working the scraper, then just when I think she's not going to say anything more on the subject, she actually does. 'Look, I'm, like, a hundred percent behind you, Ross? But just remember – ask yourself, what is it about you that people love? And I'm talkng about the people who actually matter, Ross. Is it that medal? Or is it you?'

And I'm left just thinking about that while she scratches off the last corner of the poster.

'Done!' she goes, with a real – I know it's *not* a word? – but *finality*? I tell her that's her debt to society paid and she ends up just giving me this, like, long, lingering hug. Then I go, 'Come on, I'll drop you home.'

Half an hour later, we're pulling up outside the gaff on

Newtownpork Avenue. She asks me in but I cop her old dear's Renault Koleos in the driveway and I sort of, like, *hesitate*?

'It's honestly fine,' she goes. 'Really.'

Which it actually turns *out* to be? Her old dear greets me at the door with – believe it or not – a kiss on either cheek, then Honor comes running out of the kitchen going, 'Mommy!' followed by a gasp when she cops me standing there in the hall. 'Daddy!'

I can't help but think that this is what it'd be like every day if I hadn't focked things up in a major way.

Old too soon, wise too late. Another of Fehily's favourites.

Sorcha hops into the old Jack Bauer. While she's in there, roysh, her old dear smiles at me and goes, 'I should say thank you, Ross.'

I'm like, 'Er, as in?'

She's there, 'Well, you'll never hear this from Edmund, but Sorcha would never have made it through this year without you . . .'

That leaves me almost literally speechless. 'I can't tell you,' I go, 'how amazing it feels to get that kind of a boost.'

'Well, like I said, you've been so good to her.'

She heads off just after Sorcha gets out of the shower. She's all, 'See you tomorrow, Dorling,' because they're hitting Roly's, as a family, to celebrate.

When she's gone, I make a big show of checking my watch, except Sorcha – in only her dressing-gown – goes, 'Why don't you put Honor to bed, Ross? I'll phone for a Chinese . . .'

It's funny because I know exactly what's going to happen here. And I *mean* exactly?

I read Honor her favourite book. It's kind of, like, a cheat for me because it's, like, a pop-up book – as in, *My Fairy Princess Palace*? – and every time I turn a page to reveal a new room in Honeysuckle Hall, Honor goes, 'Oh my God!' and I end up having to laugh because she says it exactly the same way as her mother.

It doesn't take long – maybe fifteen minutes – before she's out like a light. Then I tip downstairs.

'You know,' I go, 'I think that moustache is actually storting to wear off.'

Sorcha even laughs, finally seeing the funny side of it. Then there's a sudden ring at the door and it's, like, the delivery dude.

Sorcha dishes it up. The mixed vegetable satay for her and the deep-fried squid with chilli and salt for me. It was always our Saturday night thing – on the rare Saturday nights she could get me to stay home.

I open a bottle of the old Château les Hauts de Pez and we take everything through to the living room.

I stick on the TV, except I put it on mute, and we end up just talking while we eat, which is amazing.

When we've finished our dinner, I take the plates through to the kitchen and I rinse them off before stacking them in the dishwasher. When I turn around, she's stood right behind me – as in *right* behind me – looking up at me, those eyes again.

I kiss her. Well, we kiss each other. A long, just amazing kiss that tastes of, like, peanuts and you'd have to say Bordeaux.

She pulls away then, takes my fingers in her hand, turns and leads me upstairs to the bedroom – *our* bedroom.

She undresses me slowly. I pull the belt on her dressing-gown, then I peel it off her shoulders and let it fall to the floor.

And then we make – believe it or not – love. And I'm not giving you any more details than that.

When we're finished, we end just up lying there, spooning, for an hour, maybe two, drifting in and out of sleep, listening to the rain batter away on the window.

'I think I'm ready now,' I suddenly hear her little voice go in the dorkness of the room. 'I'm ready to go through with the divorce.'

I tell her I know she is, already calculating where she dropped my clothes.

10. Only Metal . . .

I get a letter in the post – it's only, like, a couple of lines long. I've been called to, like, a hearing on Friday, 30 October 2009, in the Gresham Hotel of all places – to answer chorges that I used a prohibited substance, contrary to the rules of the Leinster Schools Senior Cup, and that I brought the game of rugby into, like, disrepute.

I punch the air. 'Yes!' I just go. 'Can't come quick enough.'

I celebrate the news by hitting the town – we're talking Thursday night, on the old Tobler.

Fionn and JP got the exact same letter but they were both doing other shit. Fionn was hitting the flicks with my sister, while JP and Danuta – or Dani, as JP's taken to calling her – are repossessing a Ford Territory Ghia somewhere in focking Lucan.

Still, when it comes to the hunt, I've always been a lone wolf.

Anyway, to cut a long story short, I end up pulling this bird called Alaia, who works in, like, Renords. If you can imagine this, roysh, she's sort of, like, a cross between Karina Smirnoff and Gretchen Rossi?

In other words, bathe her and bring her to me!

I was *on* fire, by the way. I gave her one or two lines while she was collecting glasses off the bor in front of me. 'Well, you're very cute,' I went, 'there's certainly no getting away from that,' and I could see her, like, looking at me, thinking, that's at least different from the usual lines I hear in this place.

Anyway, roysh, her shift finished at one and I took her back to Rosa Parks, where I proceeded to give her what I call the all-inclusive package – a little bit of listening, a little bit of kissing, a little bit of foreplay, then the full treatment. And far be it from me to write my own reviews but there'll be no heaven for her if God really *is* that sensitive about having his name taken in vain.

Anyway, we both wake up the following morning after an, I don't know, *contented* sleep? That's when there's an all of a sudden ring at the door. This is, like, ten o'clock on a Friday *morning* we're talking? At first, roysh, I presume it's just the old man, wondering why I never made it in to work today. 'Are you not going to answer that?' Alaia goes.

I stort kissing her neck and her shoulders, going, 'I'd *prefer* to talk you through the breakfast specials . . .'

She loves it like pudding, of course, while *I've* got a dick on me like a focking cistern handle. Except the ringing just continues. 'You'd *better* answer it,' she goes. 'Whoever it is, they seem pretty insistent.'

I throw back the sheets in a bit of a snot, then I go out to the hall in just my boxer shorts. I pick up the phone and then, without even looking at the little screen, I go, 'I'm pulling a focking sicky – get over it, will you?'

Except, roysh, it ends up *not* being the old man at all, but these three dudes in, like, fluorescent-yellow jackets. 'Howiya,' one of them goes. 'We're from, er, Earcom?'

I'm like, 'Eircom?'

He's like, 'Yeah. Believe you're having one or two problems with your, er, your line?'

He's, like, winking into the little camera.

I'm there going, 'No, the phone's working fine.'

'You were, er, talking to one of our engineers,' he goes. 'Breege?'

Of course, I'm focking slower than . . . well, focking Eircom. It's, like, the Feds.

I buzz them in, then about, like, a minute later they come out of the lift – three of them.

'Come in,' I suddenly go. 'Sorry, you even had me totally fooled there. *Howiya!* That's good undercover work, it'd have to be said.'

In they come, Cavan's finest.

The main dude introduces himself, although the name goes in one ear and out the other. He says, though, that it's a state-of-the-ort eavesdropping device – as used by the Feds in the *actual* States? – and that they're going to disguise it to make it look like a standard telephone connection point. They'll even plug, like, a phone into it, though it obviously won't work. It'll be, like, a decoy?

You can tell, roysh, that I'm suddenly getting into it here.

The other two boys are straight down to work. They find a point in, like, the adjoining wall that they're happy with, then they stort drilling.

I'm there going, 'It *is* actually just like *The Wire*, isn't it?'

The dude's like, 'Well, we're just engineers . . .'

I'm there, 'I don't *give* a fock, as long as you get rid of them. Focking gangland knackers . . .'

'Ross?' a voice behind me suddenly goes.

I turn around and it's Alaia – fully dressed as well. I'm thinking, fock, I forgot about her. You can see the three dudes looking at her, roysh, thinking, this boy's obviously a serious player. I'm there, 'Are you not staying? Not even for . . .' and of course I don't want to say it in front of them, so I go, 'Ham and eggs?' which is, like, a secret code I have for it.

'No,' she goes, putting clips in her hair. 'I have a job interview at lunchtime.'

I follow her out to the front door. I'm there, 'A job interview? Er, why would anyone want to leave Renords?'

No amount of shit that I've been through since this whole recession storted can prepare me for the shock of what she says next.

'Did you not hear?' she goes. 'Renords is closing down.'

He answers his phone like I'm suddenly interrupting something. I'm there, 'Hey, Ro, what are you up to?'

'I'm studying the multiplication of matrices using complex numbers,' he goes.

I'm like, 'Jesus, it was just a figure of speech, Ro – I didn't ask for your focking life story.'

Of course then I feel instantly bad. But it *is*, like, Sunday night, and he's sat at home with his nose in his focking books, which can't be right.

'So you're, like, well into the swing of things with school,' I go.

'Er, yeah.'

I sort of, like, chuckle to myself then. 'Sunday night was always my time for doing house calls. Usually, I'd been a bad boy all weekend – been with one bird on Friday, another on Saturday, maybe even another on Sunday afternoon. Then Sunday night, I'd have to call out to Sorcha or whoever I happened to be going out with at the time and try to, like, sweet-talk them around. Have they told you what musical you're doing yet?'

'*Carousel.*'

'With what school?'

'Eader Rathdowin or Alex.'

'Okay, pray that it's Alex. We used to always say that Rathdown was like the Irish summer – you get one decent year out of every ten. What about games, have you learned any yet? Do they still play Loreto bingo?'

'What?'

'Every player gets a cord with all the different Loretos on it. Foxrock. Green. Dalkey. Beaufort. Bray. Then Swords and Balbriggan, just to make it interesting. The – and you can tell me if this is a word or not – *objective* is to end up being with a bird from each. And obviously the quickest wins.'

'Haffn't heerd of it.'

'Plenty of time.'

'In anyhow,' he suddenly goes, 'I've a gut bit to get troo here, Rosser,' obviously trying to get rid of me.

They say the teenage years are the most difficult for a parent – it's all ahead of me.

I'm there, 'Okay, just before you go, I need to ask you for a favour.'

'A favour?'

'Yeah, I know I've said it to you before, but I want you to stay out of Terry and Larry's gaff for the next couple of weeks.'

'Why?'

'Don't ask me why. I just have a funny feeling that they're about to be, I suppose, *busted*?'

'Boosted?' he goes, sounding suddenly concerned. 'You're not fooken snitchin on them, are you, Rosser?'

I'm like, 'No!' possibly a bit *too* eager? 'Yeah, no, like I said, it's just a feeling I have – you'd be probably well advised to stay away from them over the next while.'

Eimhear Huet was one of those, I suppose, colourful characters who helped make Renords what it basically was. She was known to have a thing for, like, Good On Paper goys. You could have a face like a bag of water and it wouldn't matter a fock to her – it was your career prospects that she was only ever interested in.

JP's telling the famous joke about the time she supposedly

walked in here and shouted, 'Is there a doctor in the house?' When some focker's hand went up – the story goes – she sat down beside him and went, 'Buy me a Bellini?'

We've heard it, like, a hundred times before but we still all crack our holes laughing. We're going to miss these walls. We all practically grew up in Renords – or at least we spent the years of our lives when we *should* have been growing up in here.

I give Robbie Fox a nod, just to thank him for the bottle of Moët he sent over.

Who would have ever seen Renords going tits-up? This is where I scored the likes of Glenda and Roseanna and Caroline Morohan and where I got a slap across the face from Pippa O'Connor. In other words, it was *the* place. If you thought about it, it'd actually get you down.

Fionn tries to keep it cheerful by remembering all the times that Oisinn was borred over the years – supposedly for life.

The funniest, I have to admit, was the night he ended up on a really shit date with Jade Slyne, who was a friend of, like, Fionn's from the Institute? Fionn had, like, a major thing for her – thinking about it now, I don't think she was *that* unlike Jenna Dewan – although he was never going to close the deal, so Oisinn ended up getting in there like swimwear.

Anyway, she made it clear to the old Ois Monster beforehand that there was going to be none of the old nasty-nasty at the end of the night – wasn't that kind of girl and blah blah blah. Which was the reason he cancelled the table he'd booked at La Mère Zou and took her instead to a place up the road where they give you a glass of crayons and let you draw on the focking tablecloth.

She was *not* a happy hippo, by all accounts, although it didn't stop her eating her chicken enchilada, then insisting on following Oisinn to Renords, where he'd decided to come to meet up with the rest of us, having already written the night off as, like, a dead loss.

After being stung for *two* glasses of Sancerre, he came up with what even *I* thought was a focking genius idea to basically burn her off. He went to the jacks, whipped off his boxers, ran them under the tap, then wrung them out. Then he went back to the table – commando, remember – hung them over the back of her chair and went, 'Better let them air out for a while.'

The bouncers ran him through the doors like a focking battering ram.

I'm, like, cracking my hole laughing at the memory of it. We all are, roysh, and it's amazing to be sitting here like this, just us – no girlfriends – like old times.

But then the laughter suddenly stops and we're all just sat there, you could possibly say deep in thought.

'I quit my job,' Fionn suddenly goes.

You can imagine me, roysh, I'm in total shock. I'm like, 'What?'

'I told Tom I wouldn't be coming back after mid-term.'

I look at JP, then back at Fionn, and I feel instantly guilty. I'm there, 'You loved that job . . .'

He's like, 'No, I love *teaching*, Ross. Like you said, there *are* other schools.'

'But, I don't know, it *is* only a medal, isn't it?'

'No, you were right, Ross. It represents something – a very special part of the past, for each and every one of us. And Tom wants to take that away from us. And I don't want to work for a man like that.'

'Are you sure this isn't just the bubbly talking?'

'It's not.'

JP pipes up then. 'I'd like to, well, second everything that Fionn has just said. I'm sorry, Ross, for not being more supportive.'

'This is actually getting a bit gay.'

'It's not gay, Ross. I'm just saying, I should have been more appreciative of your efforts to get us to hang on to our medals.'

'What's brought this on?'

The funny thing is, roysh, I know the answer before he even says it. 'Christian rang.'

'Christian?'

Fionn looks at JP. 'Told us both a few home truths. Things we needed to hear.'

Good old Christian.

I'm there, 'But, Fionn, even so – your focking job. There's supposedly loads of unemployment out there all of a sudden.'

He's like, 'Forget about it. I'll ring the Institute in the morning.'

They're both gee-eyed but I can't tell you what an unbelievable feeling it is to have them fully on my side again. That might even *be* the reason I end up having one of *the* most inspirational ideas I've ever had in my life.

I'm up at the bor, roysh, handing over my credit cord for the next round, when it all of a sudden hits me. I go back to the table actually laughing, because I can't believe it didn't occur to me before. 'I know how to find Oisinn,' I suddenly go.

Hammered or not, I have their immediate attention. I'm there, 'Er, the Gords?'

They just look at each other then, as if to say, do *you* know what he's banging on about?

I'm there, 'The Gords find people, don't they? It's, like, port of their job?'

Fionn pushes his glasses up on his nose – he goes, 'I suppose it is.'

I'm there, 'Well, I happen to know one – a woman as well – who owes me a favour.'

JP's there, 'What kind of favour?'

'Okay, being honest, I told her she could put, like, a listening device in my wall cavity so they can keep tabs on focking Skobie O'Gill and the Lidl people.'

They both look at me, roysh, like I've just whipped out a mangina and changed my name to Rosalyn.

'Ross,' Fionn goes, 'tell me you're joking.'

I'm there, 'Hey, I didn't know you cared so much, Fionn,' but JP doesn't laugh along with me like I expected him to.

He just goes, 'Fionn's right, Ross. These people don't fock around when it comes to snitches.'

I'm there, 'Snitches? Fock, you're worse than Ronan, the pair of you. I'm hordly snitching. The Feds *have* an actual warrant. I'm just allowing them to use my wall space to basically eavesdrop on them. Er, *big* difference?'

JP just shakes his head and says he hopes I know what I'm doing. I tell him of course I focking know. Then I just raise my glass.

'Hey,' I go. 'To Renords!'

They both smile and return the toast. Fionn says porting is such sweet sorrow.

No, I haven't a focking clue either.

She answers on, like, the third ring.

'Hey,' I go, 'it's Ross.'

She's there, 'I know who it is,' sort of, like, losing the actual *rag* with me? 'You can't keep ringing me up every two days, Ross, asking me why they're not gone. I keep telling you, they're trying to build a case against them, which takes time.'

I'm there, 'Hey, chillax, Breege, that's not why I'm even ringing.'

'Well, why *are* you ringing?'

I give her a few seconds of silence, then I hit her with it. 'It's just I've been, er, thinking about our little arrangement . . .'

'And?'

'Yeah, no, it just strikes me that I'm putting my pretty face on the line here and there's nothing actually in it for me . . .'

'Apart from your apartment going back up in value.'

I laugh. 'Sure, who the fock's going to buy it? According to a mate of mine – in other words, JP – there's, like, three hundred and fifty thousand vacant gaffs in Ireland. Who's going to pay good money to live in a shithole like this?'

She's like, 'So what *are* you asking me for, Ross?'

See, she's no fool. They don't just let any old fuckwit with two passes in the Leaving into the Gords

'Good question,' I go, loving the sudden power, maybe even a little bit *too* much? 'What could I possibly want from you?'

'Well, if it's *that*,' she goes, 'you can forget about it. I've already told you, I'm back with Malachy now and we're talking about getting engaged.'

I laugh.

'Don't worry, it's not that – even though I'd definitely take it if you put it in front of me. Yeah, no, what it is, roysh, is this – you've got people in your place who investigate, like, credit cord fraud, don't you?'

'Oh, for the love of God,' she goes and she says it with a tone that suggests it's a ridiculous question.

I'm there, 'Okay, I'll take that as a yes. So if I gave you, like, a credit cord number – as in, *any* number? – you could find out if that cord has been used recently.'

'Well, *I* couldn't. It's not my department. But Malachy has a brother in Fraud.'

Fock, they certainly stick to their own kind, don't they?

'Okay,' I go, 'my question stands. If I gave you, like, a friend of mine's credit cord number, you could tell me if he's using it . . .'

'Yeah.'

'And more importantly where.'

'In theory.'

'Cool,' I go. 'I'm going to ring you back in two minutes. Have, like, a pen ready,' and then I hang up and scroll through my contacts, looking for Oisinn's old dear's number.

My old dear is back in the country. I only know because she's on the front page of pretty much all of this morning's newspapers, breezing through the arrivals gate at Dublin Airport in a pair of glasses that make her look like a sort of vagrant Gok Wan.

It has to be said, roysh, the headline in the *Indo* is the best of the lot. It's like, PURRR-FECT STORM! and then, underneath, it's like, STUNNING AUTHOR AND TV CHEF RETURNS TO FACE ANIMAL CRUELTY RAP.

I'm sitting in the front of the van with it laid across my lap. 'I don't know if I mentioned,' I suddenly go, 'but I actually feel sorry for her. I mean, you know how I feel about her in general – hate her focking guts, same as I hate yours – but I still don't think she deserves the shit that's been thrown at her.'

The old man just smiles. 'What a lovely thing to say,' he goes. 'You're a humanist, Ross. I've always said it.'

'Well, I wouldn't go that far. I'd probably just sum it up by saying, they've been on her case for, like, months now – er, *enough* already?'

He nods like I've made a good point.

'I think the mistake too many people are making,' he goes, 'is to take this recession personally. It's nothing personal. It's simply the way of things. People thought the good times were going to last for ever. But nothing is permanent, Ross. Not even us. We're loath to admit it but we're really no different to any of nature's creatures. We build our little kingdoms, then the winds and the rains and the tides come and they wash them away. From Babel to Ballsbridge, it was ever thus!'

My phone suddenly rings. I notice straight away that it's, like, Breege, so I answer it – *actually* excited.

I'm there, 'Hey.'

'It's bad news,' she instantly goes, bursting my balloon.

'*Bad* news?'

'Yeah, that credit card number you gave me, it hasn't been used since the 14th of November last year . . .'

The 14th of November was the day Oisinn pegged it.

'As a matter of fact,' she goes, 'it's been cancelled.'

'Fock!'

'Are you happy now?'

I'm suddenly staring again at that shot of the old dear, emerging through the automatic doors, in her focking Lainey Keogh cordigan-coat, with this – I don't know – *hunted* expression in her eyes. 'Ross?' Breege is going. 'Are you still there?'

I've suddenly had another idea.

I'm there, 'Yeah, I'm still here. I need you to run just one more number for me . . .'

She holds up a petit fours between her thumb and forefinger and says aren't they unctuous little things?

Focking *unctuous*! Your guess is as good as mine.

This is us in the Terrace Lounge in the Westbury, by the way. She looks actually all right – certainly not the screaming mess she looked in the papers the other day.

I ask her about Budapest – as in, how was it? She sweeps cake crumbs off the cover of the Smythson brown leather-bound notebook on the table in front of her and says wonderful, at the same time, roysh, smiling, sort of, like, inwardly, like she's enjoying some private joke or trade secret.

I don't even *want* to know? I only focking asked because it's nice to be nice.

I end up just blurting out the reason I asked her here.

'I've found Trevion,' I go.

I don't *get* the reaction I'm expecting? She basically ignores what I said. 'What a dainty little strainer,' she just goes, then pours herself another cup of Darjeeling.

I'm there, 'Are you even listening to me? I said I found Trevion.'

This time it seems to, like, register. She just sits back, staring into space, saying fock-all, although obviously doing a lot of thinking. 'He's staying in a Comfort Inn,' I go, 'in a place called Minnesota. I know it *sounds* like I've made that name up? But it exists, believe you me.'

I hand her the piece of paper with, like, the *number* of the hotel on it? Except she doesn't even look at it. 'How did you find him?' is all she can go. It's obvious I've impressed her.

'It's a long story. Suffice it to say that he gave me his credit cord one night when he sent me out on a date with one of his actress clients . . .'

I laugh.

'Jesus Christ, she was like a focking basketball with eyes. Anyway, I wrote the number down, with the intention – and this is going to *sound* bad? – of robbing the focker blind by putting all sorts of shit on it, concert tickets, blah blah blah.'

'But how did you *locate* him?'

'Er, I'm *getting* to that bit? Okay, so there's this bird who I had a one-night thing with. She's, like, a lady Gorda, but actually *good-looking* if you can believe that? I won't go into the ins and outs of it but she owed me a favour – a big-time one. Turns out she knows someone who works in, like, Credit Cord Fraud. He agreed to run the number. And that hotel is where it was used last. I rang, like, an hour ago. He's still there. Asleep, actually. The receptionist said it was, like, five o'clock in the morning or some shit.'

She thinks about this for, like, twenty or thirty seconds. From her face, it's impossible to tell *what's* going through her mind. And I'm not talking about the Botox.

Then, without even looking at it, she rips the piece of paper in half, then in half again, then in half again – then just throws it there, next to the napkin she used to mop up the coffee that I spilled earlier. 'Er, what are you doing?' I go. 'I don't have a copy of that, just to let you know.'

'That part of my life is over,' she just goes.

'Over? Er, you were going to, like, *marry* that dude?'

'That all seems like such a long time ago now.'

'Yeah. And you could end up being with him again – as in *with* with. You could get out of this country. It's a tip. Like you said, we're going to be eating our own shit soon enough.'

'I can't leave – not now.'

'Why not?'

'I have too many people relying on me.'

'As in who?'

'Well, my readers for one . . .'

I just laugh.

'Readers? I thought you'd, like, dried up.'

'Well, that's *why* Budapest was so wonderful,' she goes, grinning from ear to ear, like she's about to pass a focking gallstone. 'I've rediscovered my mojo.'

She sort of, like, indicates the Smythson notebook with her eyes. I pick it up, obviously fearing the worst.

'It returned, just like that, Ross, while I was enjoying a Kaffee mit Schlag by the infinity pool one morning. A moment of pure inspiration. I was thinking, okay, what kind of fiction *is* commercially successful these days? I thought, of course! Misery memoirs!'

'Er, *misery* memoirs?'

'Yes, absolutely. Look at all the ones already out there. *Ma, This is After Happening to Me* and *Ma, That's After Happening to Me* and *Ma, You'll Never Guess What's After Happening to Me Now.* I thought, look how miserable *I've* been these past six months – why not make this unhappiness my new métier?'

I open the cover. On the first page, in big letters, it's, *Mommy, They Said They'd Never Heard of Sundried Tomatoes.*

'That the title?' I go.

She nods, smiling. She seems especially pleased with herself. 'The story is told in the voice of a little girl – I've based her on Honor, I hope Sorcha won't mind – growing up in an Ireland where a baked potato with an EasiSingle stuffed inside it suddenly constitutes a meal.'

I just nod. It *is* a pretty good title, in fairness to her.

'Read!' she goes. 'Read!'

Which I do.

It's like:

My mommy looked at the clock and she gasped with the fright: 'Look at the time! Where does the day go?' My daddy would be home from work in four hours and she still hadn't started work on dinner.

'Better make it something simple today,' she said. 'Perhaps my minted sprouts and chestnut roast, gratin potatoes with pancetta and pousses d'épinards, and a scarlet runner, tomato and orzo salad. No point in overcomplicating matters this late in the day.'

My mommy was very, very pretty and there was nothing in the world that made her happier than cooking. My daddy would eat the delicious meals she prepared, rub his tummy and say, 'Who needs to go out to restaurants with Michelin stars when this keeps coming up at you, night after night?'

It always made my mommy very happy to hear that.

I was lying on the floor, reading my Diego Márquez adventure, when she asked if I would like to help her today.

'Yes, please!' I said, because I wanted to grow up to be a wonderful cook too.

She took out all the pots and dishes, all the plates and bowls, all the chopping knives and salad forks she would need. Then she took out the ingredients – the feta and the pinenuts and the balsamic vinegar and the oregano lemon vinaigrette.

'Oh, no!' she suddenly exclaimed.

I asked her what was wrong and she said we had somehow run out of heirloom beans and pousses d'épinards!

'Never mind,' she said. 'Pop next door – there's a darling – and ask the neighbours for some, just until I get to Superquinn tomorrow.'

I was very scared because I had never met the neighbours before. They were only new but I had seen them once through the window and they looked to me to be very poor. My mommy said I mustn't look down on them because the man had lost his job in a motor dealership in the recession and the family had been forced to trade down.

I knocked on the door but I was still very scared. A woman answered. She wasn't as pretty as my mommy. She talked like she was always angry, even though she wasn't angry.

I said, 'My mommy wants to know can we please borrow some heirloom beans and some pousses d'épinards?'

She just stared at me with her mouth open. So I repeated what I said. 'My mommy wants to know can we please borrow some heirloom beans and some pousses d'épinards?'

'Wait there!' the woman said, then she went back into the house. She returned a few seconds later, not with heirloom beans or pousses d'épinards, but with her husband.

'See can you work out what language she's speaking,' she said to him.

He looked at me. 'Go on,' he said, 'give it another go.'

So I said it again. 'My mommy wants to know can we please borrow some heirloom beans and some pousses d'épinards?'

He shook his head. 'Could be French for all I know.'

Then he shut the door in my face.
I went home and told my mommy. I was very, very scared.

'Well?' the old dear goes – big, I don't know, expectant face on her. She's looking for my actual opinion. The thing is, roysh, I still feel sorry for her, so I decide to say something actually *supportive*?

'People bought your other shit,' I go. 'I suppose there's no reason why they won't also buy this.'

'Stop!' I suddenly shout.

For a few seconds the old man hasn't a clue what I'm even talking about.

I'm there going, 'Pull over! Pull over!' the reason being that I've just copped JP's old man's flatbed truck porked on Shrewsbury Road.

So he pulls in, roysh, immediately behind it, then he suddenly realizes what I'm talking about.

He's there, 'This is Oisinn's place, isn't it?'

And I'm like, 'Was. Is. I don't know – but yeah.'

We both get out, then approach the truck – the old man on the driver's side, me on the passenger's. They're, like, sat in the front, the three of them – we're talking JP, Danuta, then, behind the wheel, JP's old man.

They've obviously seen us coming, roysh, because JP already has the window down and, without even looking at me, he goes, 'I didn't know, Ross. The order just had the house number on it. It didn't mention Perineum Manor.'

Oisinn named it that because he'd a dick on one side of him and an arsehole the other.

I'm there, 'So what are you actually here for?'

He gives the paperwork the old left to right – not that he

even *needs* to? 'All electrical,' he goes. 'His music system. TVs. The home cinema.'

Meaning the home cinema where we used to watch the DVD of the 1999 Leinster Schools Senior Cup final – we're talking pretty much every Paddy's Day without fail.

I don't even *need* to remind him? I can tell he's thinking the exact same shit.

'Is just anusser job,' Danuta tries to go. 'Forget he ees your friend. Is just anusser man who cannot pay for his lifestyle, yes?'

I can tell from the expression on his face whose side JP's old man is immediately on. Still, he decides to give his son a moment to get his shit together. He just, like, turns to the old man, at the other window. 'A flatbed truck and a Hiace van on Shrewsbury Road,' he goes. 'One with *Last Resort Asset Reclaim* written on it, the other with *Shred Focking Everything!.* Ever think you'd see the day, Charles?'

The old man sort of, like, *laughs* to himself? 'Maybe not on this road, no. Still, it's the way of things, is it not?'

I look at JP and try to find some words of, I suppose, *comfort* for the dude? I'm like, 'Oisinn's gone, Dude. Even if he's still alive . . .'

'Don't say that, Ross.'

'Even *if* he's still alive, we're possibly never going to see him again. He's already said goodbye to this port of his life.'

JP's there, 'Still doesn't feel right.'

I must have actually learned a fair few things since this whole recession storted, roysh, because suddenly I'm having deeper thoughts that I've possibly *ever* had?

'Look,' I go, 'it's like the whole, I don't know, Michael Jackson being dead thing? As in, look at all the stuff *he* had. All sorts of shit – a lot of it really cool, in fairness to him. But what happened when he died? It all still went into a focking skip, didn't it? It's going to be the same for all of us, Dude.'

He looks at me, roysh, like he's surprised by my sudden wisdom.

I suppose *I* even am?

'Your eediot friend is right,' Danuta goes. 'And eef we do not do thees theeng, lot of others wheel do instead.'

JP takes, like, a deep breath, then just nods. He suddenly unclips his seatbelt, then Danuta does the same, while his old man smiles at me, as if to say thanks.

I take an instant step backwards, then JP opens the door and walks around the back of the truck to, I suppose, *retrieve* the sledgehammer? Danuta hops out, as does JP's old man.

'Come on, Ross,' *my* old man goes, but, before I go, I tell JP not to sweat it. We both know how cool Oisinn is – there's, like, no way he'd even blame him. He high-fives me, roysh, as if to say, 'You're actually a really, really incredible friend,' then I just leave them to it.

For some reason, roysh, as we're walking back to the van, I happen to look over my shoulder, in time to see JP's old man give Danuta – get this – three shorp little pats on the orse. It's the kind of thing I've seen him do to female employees maybe a thousand times over the years. Habit, as much as anything, and he wouldn't have meant anything by it, except just, 'Trip along now!' and possibly even, 'By the way, nice hoop!'

Because it's Danuta, though, I'm immediately thinking, ohhh – fock!

It's honestly like the world has suddenly stopped, when *actually* it's only Danuta who's stopped. She's stood there, roysh, frozen still. At first I presume she's in, like, shock, trying to make up her mind what to do. Except she knows exactly what she's going to do. Her movement is so quick that it happens in an actual flash. With one hand, she grabs his wrist;

with the other she snaps his fingers four focking ways – north, then east, then south, then west.

We can hear the cracks from where we're standing. Bones basically breaking. The dude lets a roar out of him that has the Venetians twitching up and down the road.

He's, like, seriously howling and holding his wrist. His hand suddenly looks like those focking cheese strings that Sorcha buys for Honor as a so-called treat. The poor focker's got four fingers and a thumb all pointing in different directions.

JP's in as much shock as the rest of us.

'Get back een the truck,' Danuta tells his old man calmly, like this kind of shit happens to her twenty times a day. 'JP and I wheel get the equipment. Then we wheel tek you to the hospeetal to get feengers reset, yes?'

Sophie says she's thinking of giving up Facebook. Which I already know from her post yesterday on, funnily enough, Facebook.

She says she was in, like, Empty Pockets the other night and she had the chicken tenders for the first time in – oh my God – years? Anyway, she'd only eaten, like, two of them when she found herself suddenly whipping out her iPhone and writing about how she'd forgotten how *actually* good they were? Anyway, by the time she'd updated her status, replied to three messages, added yoga and *30 Rock* to her list of interests, joined the groups 'I Love My Bed!', 'RIP Jade Goody!' and 'My Sister Said If I Get One Million Fans She Will Name Her Baby Megatron!', sent a sad face – then a cocktail – to Alesta Mannion for changing her relationship status from engaged to single, put a block on some goy who's been – oh my God! – *stalking* her, then approved seven new friend requests, well, her tenders had gone *actually* cold.

'Oh my God,' she goes, 'it, like, *so* takes over your life?'

Actually, she said *that* on Facebook as well?

Chloe says there are, like, *way* too many ads on TV these days. 'Although,' she goes, 'this really, really good friend of mine from when I was in college – she's got *loads* of problems, she's had, like, two nervous breakdowns and *I* actually think she might be an alcoholic? – she was telling me that you can burn, like, ninety calories by actually exercising during the seventeen minutes of ads during the average hour-long TV show?'

Sophie goes, 'That's, like, Oh! My God!'

'I know!' Chloe goes. 'She's also the one who told me about this whole recession sex thing?'

'Oh, *her*? Oh my God, I am *so* going to try that!'

I don't know what the two of them are even doing here, other than horsing through *my* Pringles and talking all the way through the final episode in the fourth series of, like, *Prison Break*.

'Oh my God!' Sophie suddenly goes. 'You know who I saw on, like, Grafton Street the other day? Claire and Garret. Oh my God, Ross, they still haven't forgiven you for ruining their day!'

I'm about to go, whatever, when all of a sudden Chloe leaps to my defence. 'I think it was actually cool what you did. *Someone* had to show that girl up for what she was.'

She's being unusually nice for Chloe. I could be wrong but I think she's actually flirting with me.

What happens next, you'd nearly want to see it in slow motion, it happens that quickly. First, roysh, she yawns, then she asks Sophie if she's still going to Ashtanga in the morning. Sophie immediately takes this as a hint that they should be, like, hitting the road – as in both of them? – and she stands up.

But Chloe actually stays sitting.

'I think *I'll* stay,' she goes. 'I don't think I've got enough suppleness back after my operation to go back to yoga yet,' except of course Sophie's already storted to make a move. 'I'll text you tomorrow.'

Sophie suddenly stops and turns around, fixing Chloe with a look, then me. She knows what's going down here – of course she's suddenly spitting like a focking rotisserie chicken.

'Oh, you're going to let me walk down to the corpork by myself?' she goes, although we all know the real reason she's bulling is that her mate's about to get some and she's not. 'Oh, thanks *very* much . . .'

Chloe rolls her eyes at me, then we both wait for the sound of the door slamming.

She stands up then and storts whipping off her threads. I watch her first kick off her ballet flats, then pull off her cordigan, then unzip her dress and pull it over her head until she's basically standing there in her Biggie Smalls – and this, by the way, without a single word passing between us.

I'm suddenly remembering her mentioning, like, recession sex? It must be sex where the actual pleasantries are cut back to the bare minimum.

Anyway, you know me, I'd get up on a barbershop floor if it had enough hair on it.

'Here or in there?' she goes, flicking her thumb in the direction of the bedroom.

'Er, let's do it here,' I end up going, portly because bringing her to bed means she'll want to stay the night and portly because I really want to find out what happens to Michael and Lincoln in the end of this.

Luckily, another ad break comes on.

I get undressed without even getting up off the sofa and she comes over and sits – I think the word is, like, *astride* me?

I'm suddenly horder than a bailiff's knock.

After maybe thirty seconds of preliminaries, we move all of our – let's just say – bits and pieces into position and she throws out a few oh my Gods, just to get the ball rolling.

I'm thinking how I'd better be quick here. There *are* a lot of ad breaks but they're actually quite *short*?

She puts her hands on my shoulders and – I swear to God – storts bouncing up and down on me like this is for the focking Aga Khan Trophy.

Chloe has been an occasional mount of mine over the years, but I've never known her to be this, I don't know, *vigorous*?

That's when the shouting all of a sudden storts. 'Friday!' she goes. 'I swear!'

I'm there, 'What?'

She's there, 'I'll have it for you Friday. That's not an excuse.'

I'm like, 'Chloe, what the fock are you talking about?' obviously totally clueless but at the same time struggling to keep my stroke.

'It's been a slow month. Just a few more days, that's all I'm asking . . .'

It's suddenly obvious that the girl is, like, role-playing without actually telling me?

I'm there, 'Chloe, what the fock is going on here?'

Now, I've been in some situations over the years. I've bedded a lot of women and I've heard all sorts of shit shouted in the heat of battle. I thought there were, like, no surprises left for me in that deportment.

I was obviously wrong, because Chloe all of a sudden goes, 'Shut up! Just fock me like I owe you money!'

I'm actually mid thrust, roysh, when she shouts it and – to be honest – it ends up giving me a bit of a jolt. Whatever way I move, roysh, Chloe ends up letting a sudden scream out of her – the kind that'd strip the focking enamel off your teeth.

I'm there going, 'What? What?'

393

She's like, '*Aaarrrggghhh!!!*'

'Chloe, what?'

'Stop focking moving!'

'What's wrong?'

'My focking hip has popped out.'

Like I said, I *thought* I'd seen it all before.

Her nails suddenly dig into my shoulders, pretty much tearing the muscles from my bones. 'Chloe,' I manage to go, even though the pain is actually blinding, '*please* let go! My trapezius muscles are pretty much focked from my rugby days and my levator scapulae aren't the best either.'

'Stop focking moving, then!'

'I'm only moving because you're digging into my . . . aaarrrggghhh!'

'*Aaarrrggghhh!*'

'Aaarrrggghhh!'

'*Aaarrrggghhh!*'

I'm there, 'Jesus Christ – that's actual torture! What do you mean, your hip has popped out anyway?'

'Exactly what I focking said, Ross. The doctor told me to avoid anything too . . . *aaarrrggghhh!!!*'

I'm like, 'Hey, just bear with me, Chloe. I'm going to reach down and try to pop it back in. I've seen it done before on the rugby field . . . aaarrrggghhh!!!'

'Don't focking move another inch!' she goes. 'Or I will tear a chunk out of you, I swear to fock!'

I'm there, 'Chloe, we're going to have to do something here – we can't stay like this for ever!'

She's like, 'Ring for an ambulance!'

'With what? My mobile's in the bedroom, basically chorging.'

'Then we're going to have to shout through the wall to the neighbours.'

'Do not!' I go. 'You haven't met them, remember. I'd prefer to be found like this by focking archaeologists than have them see us. I'd never hear the focking end of it.'

'You have exactly ten seconds, Ross, to think of something else . . .'

Of course the irony is that I wasn't even that much in the mood for it tonight. I'd a quick Anglo Irish during the *Afternoon Show* earlier and would have considered myself wankrupt until *she* storted coming on to me.

'Ten seconds are up,' she suddenly goes, then she storts screaming the actual wall down. '*Aaarrrggghhh!!! Aaarrrggghhh!!! Aaarrrggghhh!!!*'

Of course sixty seconds later, roysh, Larry and Terry are at the door, going, 'Hee-er, what's goin odden in dayer?'

I'm like, 'Don't sweat it, goys – go back to whatever you're doing?'

But Chloe's going, 'Kick the door down!'

You can hear the two of them going, 'Is she arthur sayin kick the doe-ur dowin?'

'I tink tats what she said.'

'Kick the focking door down!' she goes again.

Which is what they end up doing. From my position on the sofa, I can see, basically, just an explosion of splinters, then in they chorge, the dynamic focking duo.

Of course at first, roysh, all they can do is just stare. It takes, like, a while for it to register with them.

I'm there, 'Come on, let's get the jokes out of the way first, even though they're all going to be obvious.'

They're just like, 'Doorty . . . fooken . . . adimal . . .'

'I've popped my hip out,' Chloe goes – no focking embarrassment by the way, just, I suppose, agonizing pain.

Larry's there, 'Your hip?'

'Yeah, I had it replaced earlier this year.'

'Alreet,' it's Terry who goes, 'foorst tings foorst. Laddy, you pho-in for an ambiddance,' and then he's like, 'What's your nayum, luff?'

She's like, 'Chloe.'

'Alreet, Callowie, I'm goin to go get you a doressedin-gowun – cuffer yerself up and dat.'

He disappears out of the room.

Larry, I notice with a sudden focking terror, has picked up the fake phone, the one that's plugged into the socket with, like, the listening device behind it? He's holding it to his ear, hammering away on the little button, trying to get a line.

'Er, that phone's actually focked?' I go.

Chloe's there, 'Ross, if you move again, I swear to God, I'm taking flesh off.'

'It's probley only yisser wirin,' Larry goes.

Then – oh fock! – he suddenly gets down on his hands and knees and storts checking out the little connection box that the Feds attached to the wall. My hort's suddenly thumping like a focking Opel Corsa with the bass on full.

'Who de fook put this in for ya?' he goes.

I'm there trying to keep my cool, going, 'Er, Eircom?'

'It waddent fooken Earcom, I can tell ya dat for a fact. Electrics is one of de tings I know a birra bout . . .'

I'm a focking dead man here.

'Have ya a screwderiver?'

A sudden pain shoots through my body. 'Aaarrrggghhh!' I go. I heard a definite tear that time.

Chloe's like, 'I'll do it focking horder if you move again!'

'Larry,' I go, 'just use my focking mobile – it's on the table there.'

Which, to my temporary relief, is what he decides to do.

Terry arrives back with *my* dressing-gown, the one I got the time me and Sorcha stayed in, like, Ashford Castle. I catch him checking out the embroidered logo on it, then having a little smirk to himself before he drapes it over Chloe's shoulders – gently, in all fairness to him – and she pulls it around her, then ties the belt.

Chloe says thanks and Terry says no botter luff.

The wait for the ambulance seems to go on for ever, mainly because Larry won't let the phone thing go. He's suddenly down on his knees again, back fiddling with the connection. He's there, 'Did it effer woork?'

I'm there, 'Er, believe it or not, I don't *actually* remember?'

Terry's like, 'Hee-er, ders anutter pho-in oafer hee-er, so der is,' and he holds up the Philips cordless that JP bought me as, like, a moving-in present? He checks it then. 'This one woorks foyin, Laddy.'

Chloe has to get in on the act then. She's like, 'Why have you got two phone points in one room, Ross?' still straddling me, remember.

I'm there, 'Chloe, honestly, stay the fock out of it.'

'Veddy odd,' Larry's going, with his ear to the wall, tapping it with two fingers. 'Der shuttent even be a point on dis wall. Dats de mayin junction box oafer dare. But der *is* somethin behoyunt hee-er – ya can heerd it, listen . . .'

I'm actually about to just blurt it out – as in just tell them the truth and beg for forgiveness – when all of a sudden the ambulance crew arrives. The first thing I go is, 'You took your focking time, didn't you?' more out of relief than anything else.

You can tell from the smiles on their faces that this is going to become one of those stories they're going to tell every focker – like the stories that every nurse who's ever worked in A&E has, involving broom handles and ketchup bottles and blahdy blahdy blah blah.

To cut a long story short, they basically winch Chloe off

me, *while* supporting her hip, of course. I wouldn't say it's *entirely* painless if the noises coming from her are anything to go by, though she does stop howling long enough to tell them to take her to Blackrock Clinic, just as they're strapping her on to the trolley, and also what Vhi plan she's on.

The next thing, roysh, she's suddenly gone and I'm left sitting there, stork-bollock-in-the-raw, my shoulders feeling like two wrung-out dish towels, with two of Ireland's most dangerous criminals just staring at me.

I'm suddenly very aware of my, I suppose, *vulnerability*? I grab the *Sunday Independent* magazine off the coffee table and use it to protect my, I don't know, dignity, genitals, whatever you want to say.

'Hee-er, Larry,' Terry goes, a sudden smile on his face, 'go and get Rooney.'

Now it's *me* who's suddenly screaming.

'Goys,' I go, 'I know we've had, like, our differences and shit? But please – in the name of all that is focking holy – do *not* let that dog in here! Please! Please!'

I've got, like, my eyes clamped shut while I'm saying this and the next thing I hear is the two of them cracking their holes laughing.

I open my eyes. 'We're only fooken wit ye,' Terry goes, then he throws me my clothes. 'You're some tulip, ya know dat?'

I laugh – again, it's just relief. 'That's what Ro always says about me – it'd be one of his lines.'

'He definitely needs a thrink,' Larry goes. 'Look at de fooken colour of um. Haff yeddy whiskey, Ross – spidits, athin like dat?'

I'm there, 'No, I'd be, er, mainly a Heineken man,' a bit weirded out, to be honest, by the way they're being suddenly nice to me.

'Ders a bottle of Patty in eer press,' Terry goes, 'Go and grab it, Laddy. I tink we all neeth one.'

I apologize for the whole Mary Kennedy mix-up. Terry tells me I'm mustard but I still feel like I owe them, like, an explanation? 'I was possibly only showing off,' I go. 'I've got a major thing for her. Always have. I make no apologies for saying it.'

Larry pours me another two fingers. 'Ah,' he goes, '*we* were de ones winethin you up . . .'

I actually laugh, happy to let it go if they are. I'm there, 'Do you mind me asking, do you even *like* Leo Sayer?'

They laugh then.

'We do,' Larry goes. 'See, eer fadder was a fan, Lort have meercy on um.'

I *did* wonder about their old man. But I somehow know not to ask what happened to him. I knock back another gutful and Larry tops me up again.

This is us sitting at my breakfast bor, by the way.

I notice, roysh, that Terry is suddenly smiling at me – why, I don't know. 'Do you moyunt me aston ya,' he goes, 'who in Jaysus's nayum soalt dis place to ya?'

I laugh. It's a fair enough question. 'A bird called Ailish,' I go. 'She stitched me up in a major way.'

'A *boord* did?'

I sort of, like, nod. 'It's generally *always* a bird with me. That shit with Chloe tonight, that'd be pretty much por for the course. Since I hit puberty I've just been following my dick around from crisis to crisis . . .'

The two boys crack their holes laughing. I *can* be very, very funny, even I have to admit.

I'm there, 'I'll never change of course . . .'

'Ine tellin ya sometin elts yill never do,' Larry goes, 'and dats sell dis place – not wirrus liffin next doh-er! Who'd want da like of us as neighbours? *I* ceertainly wootunt!'

We *all* crack out laughing at that one. Funny because it's true.

More whiskey, more calling it like it bascially is. Hours must pass. The weirdest thing is, roysh, I actually like them. I suddenly don't *care* what they do for a living?

'Dat young fedda of yours,' Terry goes at some point in the early hours. 'Smeertest kid I ever fooken meth . . .'

I nod. 'You know he's only, like, two or three IQ points away from being considered officially gifted. That'd be, like, a major thing over this side of the city.'

'Me, I left skewill at torteen. Laddy'd be de sayum.'

Larry's there, 'Torteen as well, yeah.'

Thirteen is the next age that Ronan's going to be.

'I worry about him,' I all of a sudden hear myself go. 'He's, like, totally besotted with – no offence – but *your* whole world? I mean, *I've* probably encouraged it – buying him the *Sunday Wurdled*, helping him make that replica pipe bomb for ort class . . .'

'Ah, he's a clever one, but,' it's Larry who goes. 'Too smeert to get mixed up in athin . . .'

'I don't know about that. He's talking about becoming a solicitor.'

'What koyunt?'

'I think basically *your* personal solicitor.'

They both laugh.

'We'll be fooken gone,' Terry goes, 'long befower he ever sees coddidge . . .'

At first, roysh, I presume he means retired. 'Are you talking about buying a pub in Alicante – or is that just, like, a stereotype?'

'No,' he goes, 'we'll be dead,' and he says it, roysh, so matter-of-factly that I'm pretty much stunned into silence. 'It's a showurt career, Rosser – and no one ever retires ourrof it.'

There's just, like, silence then. I listen to the kitchen clock ticking for a minute or two. I don't *know* why but I get the impression they're both thinking about their old man.

'So why do you do it?' I go.

It seems like an obvious question.

Larry goes, 'What elts are we gonna do? It's like aston Leo Sayer why he sings . . .'

He suddenly bursts into song then – one I immediately recognize as 'Living in a Fantasy'.

Terry joins in. And – being honest? – so do I.

'What's this?' the old man goes, spotting the envelope sticking out of my jacket pocket. It's got, like, the world-famous horp on the front of it and he cops it immediately.

'Is it from the Leinster Branch?' he goes.

I just, like, hand it to him and tell him it arrived last week. So he opens the envelope, whips out the letter and gives it the old left to right.

'The Gresham!' the old man tries to go, shaking his head in absolute disgust. 'Why in hell are they making you cross over to O'Connell Street? Part of the overall scheme, no doubt, to try to bring rugby to the, quote-unquote, common man.'

'Hey,' I go, 'you don't have to say that,' because I know he's only doing it, roysh, to try to make me feel better. 'It's honestly cool.'

He storts nervously picking random sheets of A4 paper off the floor of the van then and feeding them into the mouth of the machine.

I'm there, 'Look, I know how hord this must be for you – given that you think it's *your* actual fault? But it's something I still feel I have to do – even for future generations who go into Wikipedia and say, "Hey, I wonder who won the Leinster Schools Senior Cup in 1999."'

He sort of, like, smiles to himself then. 'We're all so obsessed with our legacies,' he goes. 'I know *I* was. Lot of other big names I could mention too. *What will future generations say about me?*'

He laughs.

'Hubris,' he goes. 'Purblind bloody hubris. To think that history will remember any of us. You know who *will* remember us? Our wives, our children, our friends. And our grandchildren, Ross, if we're lucky. But to *their* children, we'll just be an old photograph. And to theirs, not even that. Maybe one day, out of curiosity, one of them will go to the National Library and find your birth date, and the date you died, but know nothing of all the wonderful glories, all the desperate reverses, that came in between . . .'

He laughs, then apologizes.

'Ross, all I'm saying is, by all means, get your medal back – *if* it's what you want. Just don't think that some little piece of metal defines you. Because it's not who you are.'

'That was what Sorcha said.'

'Well, Sorcha's right. Who you are, Ross, is the chap who parked his own happiness for a moment to try to keep a roof over the heads of his wife and daughter. Who you are is the chap who's been worrying himself sick over his son becoming a teenager. Who you are is the chap who I watched try to change his mother's life the other day with a single act of kindness . . .'

'Who I am,' I go, 'is also *this* – as in, me and you? And that's not an invitation, by the way, for us to suddenly have a focking moment here. I'm just saying it. Surprisingly, I've enjoyed it – as in, us working together? End of.'

'I've enjoyed it too.'

'That's the focking mushy bit over, then. See, that's the weirdest thing about this whole recession – I've been learning an awful lot.'

'Oh?'

'I'm talking, like, actual lessons. You know, I think I was wrong about those two next door.'

'Were you, indeed?'

'Ah, something happened the other night – I'll spare you the sweaty details of it. They surprised me, is all, with how decent they actually are. I suppose I was just too focused on the kilos of heroin and the semi-automatic weapons to see it.'

'We're all only people,' he goes.

That was one of Father Fehily's sayings – actually, it's always been one of my favourites and the old man knows it.

He tells me then that our four o'clock has cancelled – turns out the Criminal Assets crowd got there before us. 'You may as well take the rest of the day,' he goes, and it's like, job's a good 'un, because I *am* pretty shattered.

He's there, 'By the way, do you think you could manage by yourself next week?'

I'm like, 'Er, yeah – why, what's the Jack?'

He seems a bit – if you can believe this of him – embarrassed. 'Actually,' he goes, 'it's an, em, anniversary of sorts for Helen and me. Forty-seven years since our first date, Ross! *Escape from Zahrain* in the Deluxe on Camden Street. Yul Brynner, if you don't mind!'

'I'm going to say fair focks . . .'

'Well, Helen's been at me for some considerable time to visit the South of France with her – so that's where we're bound!'

'*I'll* manage.'

'Don't worry, I shall be back for your hearing. Good old Michael O'Leary can have me in and out in a day, you know . . .'

'No,' I automatically go, 'stay there with Helen. You goys need a break. And if this whole current economic blahdy blah has proved anything, it's that I might have to stort fighting some of my own battles.'

He smiles at me. I don't think he's ever looked prouder – even on that famous day.

I head for the hills, happy to get out of town before the traffic gets mental. I throw the beast into the corpork, then call the lift, except I realize, roysh, after five minutes of waiting that it must be, like, out of order, so I end up having to take the stairs.

Eight flights later, I'm back cursing that focking Ailish again, thinking she'll hopefully get her reward in hell. I'm practically out on my focking feet when I take the last flight. I push the door that leads from the stairwell to the landing, then I all of a sudden stop.

Because I can hear Ronan's voice.

I let it close again to just a crack, which I can just about see through. He's at, like, Terry and Larry's door.

I notice, by the way, that the reason the lift's not working is that Ro has jammed the door using his schoolbag, presumably so he won't have to wait for it when he's going back down. Which is unbelievably clever. See, that's what it means to be very nearly gifted.

I listen. I hear Larry go, 'De ting is, we're veddy busy at de moment, Ro – dis, dat and deutter.'

They're obviously not letting him in.

'Er, fair nuff,' Ronan goes, even though he sounds majorly disappointed. 'I'm only aston did you want to hang out. What about tomorrow?'

'Look, de ting is,' it's Terry who goes this time, 'we don't want ya calden rowint hee-er addy mower.'

Ro sounds literally crushed. He's like, 'Why? Why not?'

'Ro,' Terry goes, 'ya know who we eer and ya know what

we're about. Dis is no place for a young fedda to be hangin arowint . . .'

Larry's like, 'Especially one like you, wit brayins to burden. Why doatunt yast yer oul fella if he wants to hang out?'

'Because I want to hang out with the both of *yous*.'

'Lookit,' Terry goes, 'we're serdious, Ro. Doatunt call hee-er again. Because we woatunt be ansorden de doh-er . . .'

Then I hear it suddenly slam.

Of course all I want to do at that moment, roysh, is rush out there and give him a hug, because I know how badly his hort will be broken. But at the same time I know he has his pride and he won't want me to have heard the two boys red-cord him like that?

So I don't move. I just stay watching him.

He just, like, trudges back to the lift, gives his schoolbag a kick, then disappears inside.

The first thing I do, roysh, when I get back into the aport-ment is grab, like, a paring knife – because I don't actually *own* a screwdriver? – and I undo the four screws on the fake phone point. Then I grab the box, give it a hord yank and it comes off in my hand, broken wires spilling out of it everywhere.

An hour later, I'm watching actually *Malcolm in the Middle* when my mobile suddenly rings. I don't even need to check to know who it is.

It's Breege.

'My sister just rang me . . .' she goes.

I don't give her a chance to ask what happened.

I'm just there, 'Yeah, I pulled it out of the focking wall. The deal is off.'

'Do you mind me asking why?'

She *is* entitled to ask, I suppose. 'It's a long story – and I don't have the time to go into it.'

'I did you a favour . . .'

'I know. And I *am* grateful? But I'm afraid you're going to have to find yourself another Bubbs.'

Why does *he* have to be here?

JP tells me to keep the head.

'I'm *going* to keep the head,' I go. 'It's just, why is he here?'

McGahy hears me – not that I *give* a fock?

'I'm here,' he tries to go, this is in front of the entire foyer of the Gresham, bear in mind, 'to offer my testimony.'

I'm like, 'Your *testimony*? Er, as in?'

He's wearing his best tweed sports coat with the leather patches on the sleeves. Are they, like, *compulsory* for teachers or some shit? I must ask Fionn.

'We found quite a lot of supporting evidence among Father Fehily's things,' he goes, loving the sound of his own voice. 'For instance a schedule of the drugs you were given – with your name on it and the dosages on different days. Just in case your earlier admission that you took banned performance-enhancing drugs isn't considered sufficient evidence . . .'

I'm there, 'Don't get me wrong – I'm actually *glad* you're here?' which totally throws him. 'See you inside, Dude.'

He nods at Fionn then. He's like, 'Hello,' obviously bulling that the dude's going to be storting in the Institute when the schools go back next week. Then he disappears into the room to take his seat.

A crowd suddenly storts appearing through the revolving doors. It's the entire Newbridge team. I *could* make a sheep or a cow noise but I don't, though JP *does* laugh.

'Look at them,' he goes. 'Who'd even believe they were *ever* a rugby team?'

Even the staff are looking them up and down – and this is the Gresham, remember, which is far from the focking Merrion.

'There you are, you devil,' Mocky goes, when he cops me

sort of, like, sneering at him across the foyer. 'Oh, you're some kind of plucky and no mistake!'

He walks over to where we're standing, then looks the three of us up and down. 'This is it, is it?' he goes, grinning like a cat eating shit out of a hairbrush. 'Just the three of ye?'

I just shrug.

He's there, 'As I love God, it's a fine clutch ye make. The scrapings of the skillet! Well, I'd put a lie on my soul if I said I haven't longed to see this day!'

I smile back at him. 'You know, you might get an actual surprise in there.'

'Ah, would you forget it for a story! Your wits are scattered to God and the world!'

Three or four other players wander over to where we're standing then. One of them is Something Óg. 'In the presence of my maker,' he goes, 'I'll knock smoke out of this fella,' meaning *me*? 'I'm only waiting on the wind of the word!'

'Warm his shins!' one of the others goes.

But Mocky's there, 'Let him be. His main stock-in-trade is soft talk with very little to beck it up.'

Suddenly, JP, out of the blue, goes, 'I didn't know Lois were still *making* jeans,' which immediately prompts a bit of pushing and shoving and I end up having to drag JP away before he decks Something Óg.

I'm going, 'No! Not like that, my friend! *Not* like that!'

'Yerrah,' Mocky shouts after us, 'we'll not listen to another bar of your tongue. 'Tis all about to come beck at you, like shit on a trampoline. The cup will be ours by the end of this very night – and you may die a death for the want of it.'

We go into the room – me, Fionn and JP – yeah, just the three of us from the original fifteen, but that's all we need.

Fionn suddenly whips out his phone. I ask him who he's ringing.

He's there, 'Christian. Even if he can't be here, he said he wants to hear every word of what's said.'

I smile. I want him to hear it as well.

There's, like, a long table with five suits sitting at it – obviously the men who are sitting in, like, judgement of me.

McGahy's sitting on his own in the crowd, ready for his big moment.

I spot One F as well. *And* Gerry Thornley. They were there ten years ago at the stort of this crazy journey – it's only right that they should be here today.

I'm told to suddenly stand up.

I instantly think about Sorcha, standing in the box in that courtroom during the summer, on her focking Tobler – and that's where I suddenly get my strength from.

'The charge,' the suit in the middle goes, 'is that you knowingly and wilfully used a substance that was prohibited under the rules of the competition in order to gain an advantage . . .'

I'm just there, 'Can I just say something here?'

'In due course,' he goes. 'We have procedures that have to be . . .'

'Believe me,' I go, 'we'll all be out of here a lot quicker . . .'

The five of them all turn to each other. I look at McGahy and it's obvious he's bulling, suddenly worried he's going to be denied his big moment in the limelight.

'Okay,' the dude in the middle goes. 'What do you have, some kind of personal statement you want to make?'

I just stand up and, like, clear my throat.

'Well,' I stort by going, 'I had this plan in my head of all the shit I was going to say here today. Oh, *I* can make pretty speeches, don't you worry about that. Just ask those two goys over there – they'd have walked through walls after one of my world-famous pep-talks . . .'

Fionn and JP both laugh.

'I was going to give you all the full, I don't know, Something Obama treatment. *All this we can do, all this we will do and blahdy blahdy blah blah* . . . But I'm not going to. Oh, no. Not today.'

The atmosphere is electric and I'm not just saying that because it's me who's doing the talking here.

'I used to think my Leinster Schools Senior Cup medal was the most important thing in the world. There was something, I don't know, reassuring about the feel of it under my shirt. For ten years, I actually never took it off. I showered with it. I slept with it. I even made love with it. Oh, it got many a spit and polish, don't you worry about that . . .'

There's, like, roars of laughter from One F and one or two others. See, with speeches, you have to throw in a little something for everyone.

'The last few months, we've all been waking up to reality – that's what everyone keeps saying, isn't it? Well, without actually knowing it, I've done a fair bit of waking up myself. And what I've realized is this . . .'

I look at Fionn and JP. They have no actual idea what's coming. I take the medal in my hand. 'This is only focking metal.'

There's one or two, honestly, gasps from the Newbridge players. It's all, 'Man dear!' and, 'God save the hearer!'

I'm there, 'Oh, you heard me right. The medal itself, it's basically worthless. Which is why I've decided to plead guilty to the chorge and to tell you, here and now, that I don't want it any more . . .'

I take it off, like I said, for the first time since 1999. Then I just drop it on the floor. I look at Fionn and JP. They're, like, smiling – almost as if they're proud of me.

And maybe they are.

'Oh, sure,' I go, 'a lot of people are going to be disappointed. A lot of people who grew up worshipping me are going to be very sad tonight, asking is this the end of Ross O'Carroll-Kelly? But my message to them is, hey, just pick a favourite moment from my career and remember me that way . . .'

I walk the length of the top table, looking each of the five, I suppose, judges dead in the eye.

'What I say to you five is – you can expunge the record books. Reverse the result of the match. Write us out of history for ever. You can take away our medals. But you can't take away the memories of what we actually shared together . . .'

'Well said!' JP just shouts.

Then I turn and, I suppose, address the Newbridge players. 'As for you lot, I bear you no grudges – certainly no more than the usual. Tonight, you can take your medals back to your villages, your townlands, your homesteads. They might even light a bonfire for you in whatever inbred backwater you're unfortunate enough to call home. Enjoy every minute of it. Because I know *I* did.'

Then I look at Fionn and JP again. 'To you goys, I want to apologize, for basically letting you down . . .'

'Nothing to apologize for,' it's Fionn who actually shouts and for a split second, roysh, I don't care if he *does* end up being my brother-in-law.

JP goes, 'You didn't let anyone down, Ross. Far from it.'

I'm there, 'That's actually nice to hear . . . I already feel, I don't know, naked without that thing hanging around my neck. I know that every so often I'm going to keep reaching for my chest, expecting to feel it there. When I take off my top at night, I'll expect to see the glint of it in the bathroom mirror. But I won't miss it, because I'll remember the wise words on it . . . *Crede quod habes, et habes . . .*'

That gets everyone's immediate attention. One F and Gerry Thornley are suddenly scribbling like lunatics. It's like, er, *Ross* talking Latin? I know it's going to make *all* the papers tomorrow.

'You know,' I go, 'I looked at those words every day for ten years but I never knew what they actually meant. Never even stopped to think about it. But I actually Googled them last night, when I made up my mind to give back my medal. They could be, like, a motto for our times . . .'

I look around at the crowd – they're all dying to know what it means.

I'm there, '*Believe that you have it . . .*' and then I pause, roysh, just for dramatic effect. '. . . *and you have it!*'

JP is the first one to stort clapping, then obviously Fionn. Then a few others join in – One F, GT and a couple of other journos at first, then it sort of, like, spreads throughout the room, like a ripple effect, until suddenly even the Newbridge College players are on their feet, clapping, Mocky included.

'Legend!' JP just shouts at me. 'Legend!' as I turn around and walk out of there, with possibly the last applause I'll ever hear just ringing in my ears.

I hand him the Saturday-night edition of the *Sunday Wurdled* – another hero of his, found face down in the Royal Canal – but he doesn't even take it, just says he'll look at it later. He's on the PlayStation.

'What one is this?' I go and he honestly can't take his eyes off the screen.

He's there, 'Er, the new *Grand Theft Auto*,' he goes, '*Chinatown Wars* . . .'

I'm there, 'Wow!' taking an actual interest, see. 'How many cop cors have you disabled so far?'

'Eighteen.'

'Eighteen?' I just laugh. 'Fair focks, Ro. It has to be said . . . Whoa, shoot that CCTV camera!'

Which he straight away does. Actually, he throws a petrol bomb at it and I'm suddenly getting into it as much as him. 'Er, why are you stealing *that* cor? Would you not get something more, I don't know, high performance and shit?'

'Nah, the high-performance ones you have to hack the fooken immobilizer. I prefer to hotwire them. I'm old school, see . . .'

He suddenly pauses the game. 'Do you want to play?'

I'm a bit, I don't know, taken aback. 'Er, yeah . . .'

He throws me the other controller. It's then that I notice it on the side of his neck – a dirty big hickey.

I actually *laugh*? 'Who gave you that?' I go.

He immediately puts his hand on it, like he thinks he can suddenly hide it from me. 'Don't make a big deal of it, Rosser.'

'I'm asking out of genuine interest – who gave it you?'

'Shadden Tuite.'

'Who the fock is Sharon Tuite?'

'A boord off me road, is all.'

I'm looking at him, roysh, so unbelievably proud. It's like when Honor got her first tooth. These are the moments. And, dare I say it, it looks like he might end up being a chip off the old block.

He's there, 'Leave it, Rosser.'

I hear the door suddenly slam. It's, like, Tina, home from her shift at the hospital. She comes in, flops down on the couch, wrecked.

'Athin in the peeper?' she goes, picking up the *Wurdled*.

I don't *mention* the dude in the canal?

'Unemployment's supposedly worse than the dorkest days of the eighties,' I go. 'Half of Cork's under water. And that swine flu's apparently becoming, like, an epidemic. That's famine, floods and a plague. I wonder will God give us a heads-up before he sends the focking locusts.'

Tina and Ro both crack their holes laughing. See, that's what I mean when I say I can be very funny.

'Are ya stayin oafer?' she goes.

Ronan's like, 'Say yeah, Rosser,' without even looking at me, so I end up going, 'Er, yeah,' then Tina says she'll go and make up the spare room so.

It's at that point, roysh, that my phone suddenly rings. It's, like, my old man's number? I'm thinking, er, midnight on a Saturday from the South of France? He's almost certainly wankered drunk. But I answer it anyway.

I'm like, 'So, go on, how many have you had?'

'A bottle with dinner,' he goes, 'and three brandies to help it down. We're in Monaco, Ross – in the famous Casino de Monte Carlo . . .'

I'm like, 'Yeah? Thanks for that, Craig focking Doyle – how exactly does this affect me?'

And he goes, 'Because Oisinn is here, Ross. I'm looking at him right now.'

Epilogue

'Twist!' I go.

He doesn't even turn around in his seat. He just stops – his cords held out in a fan – and stares straight ahead for, like, ten seconds. You can even see the dealer thinking, what the fock?

Then he turns around.

'This is poker,' he goes. 'You don't twist in poker.'

I'm there, 'Well, you know me, Oisinn. I was never one to play by the rules.'

A smile suddenly breaks out across his face. 'How did you find me?' he goes.

I'm there, 'The old man spotted you in here last night.'

He nods, like it suddenly makes sense. 'I *thought* I saw Helen on the Avenue des Castelans . . .'

'Er, is that all you can say?'

He gathers up his chips with one hand and gives the dealer the nod to say he's calling it a night. The dude says *au revoir*.

'What do you want me to say?' Oisinn goes and he tries to walk away – he *actually* tries to walk away – until I step in front of him pretty smortly.

'You just take off like that? Leave your cor in the airport? All your shit still in it?'

People are suddenly looking up from their tables.

He goes, 'Ross, do you have any idea the kind of trouble I'm in?'

And I'm there, 'Er, yeah, I have actually. I read the papers like everyone else.'

He lets that one go. 'Then you'll know how much money I owe – more than I could pay in this life.'

'So what, you decided to just get yourself another life?'

'Something like that.'

'And no phone call to anyone? You know your old dear's going off her nut?'

He finally looks at least guilty.

'Oh, yeah,' I go. 'Tears in Marian Gale, the works.'

Then I regret it, roysh, because I suddenly see *him* filling up.

'Hey, Big Man,' I go. 'I'm sorry. I didn't mean . . .'

He grabs me then – without any warning – in, like, a bear hug. His chips go flying across the floor but he doesn't seem to *give* a fock about them? He stands there just crushing the life out of me and crying on my shoulder, while I'm just patting him on the back, telling him it's okay – it's *going* to be okay.

He releases his grip on me and I take a step backwards, so I can see his face. I'm trying to think have I ever seen Oisinn cry. I actually don't *think* so?

'She used to be so focking proud of me,' he goes.

I'm there, 'Dude, they're our parents. They're *going* to love us, whether we like it or not – for all our fock-ups . . .'

This sort of, like, waiter dude has gathered up Oisinn's chips and he hands them to him, going, '*Voilà*,' and Oisinn's there, '*Merci, monsieur.*'

I laugh. Listen to him – he's picked up the lingo and everything. 'Okay,' I go, 'what's Monte Carloan for let's hit the focking bor!'

He smiles and says it's the same as in English.

'By the way, my name's not Oisinn any more,' he goes at some point in the, I suppose, foggy hours that follow.

I'm there, 'You changed your name?'

He nods, then shouts for *deux* more JDs. 'It's Johnny Keith,' he goes.

415

'Johnny Keith?'

After Hayes and Wood, I realize as soon as I say it – his two heroes.

I tell him he doesn't look like a Johnny Keith. He says I can keep calling him Oisinn, then. It's actually a nice moment between us.

The thing I *don't* get, I tell him, is how he ended up here. He says he flew to London – which we all knew – took the Eurostar to Paris, then the old *bualadh* from Paris to Monaco.

What I'm trying to say, I suppose, is that I didn't expect to find him looking so well. He's wearing, like, chinos and a pretty smort blazer, it has to be said, whereas I thought he'd be, I don't know, sleeping *rough* somewhere?

'I did have ninety grand with me when I left Dublin,' he goes. Then he leans in close, as if to, like, confide something in me.

'You can do anything in this town once you've got money,' which I take to mean open a bank account under a different name.

'Johnny Keith,' I go, just shaking my head.

He says he got my messages about Ireland winning the Triple Crown, roysh, and Leinster winning the Heineken Cup, which is nice to hear. He says he used to phone his voicemail once a day to listen to his messages – until he couldn't take the sound of his old dear crying any more. Then the account got cut off anyway.

'Fionn really did a streak?' he goes.

I'm there, '*And* JP . . . Dude, it was hilarious.'

He laughs. 'We always said we'd do it if Leinster won.'

'We did.'

'Thanks for the messages anyway.'

I tell him it's not a thing – which it isn't.

'So,' he goes, 'what's been happening back home?'

I just shake my head. It's, like, where to even begin? 'You honestly wouldn't recognize it as the same, I suppose, country. You know Renords has gone?'

'What?'

'Dude, that's only the tip of the iceberg. Cocoon. Mint. Yo Thai. Town Bor and Grill is supposed to be in trouble now. As is Residence, by the way . . .'

'Shit! The bed!'

'Even Sorcha's shop went.'

'Hey, Dude, I'm sorry.'

'Forget about it. See, it's like the old man says, there's, like, a time for everything – she'll find something else.'

I hate to bring the subject up, roysh, but I end up going, 'I see you're still gambling,' because he *had* a major problem – with internet poker especially. Of course it's only a major problem when you're not very good at it.

'Yeah, I'm still gambling.'

'What about . . .' and I make, like, a sniffing sound.

He shakes his head and I have to believe him.

'You know,' he goes then, 'we all had a gambling problem when you thnk about it . . .'

He's obviously talking about the Celtic Tiger – another one dissing it.

'See, that's why I haven't been able to face my old dear. She used to say to me, how much will be enough, Oisinn? How much before you make do with what you've got?'

I order two more JDs.

'Speaking of making do,' I go, 'did you hear Erika's with Fionn – as in *with* with?'

'No! Focking! Way!'

'Way.'

'That's great, isn't it?'

'Well, I still think he's heading for a kick in the balls – a serious one. But what can you do, except be there for the focker when she crushes him into the basic dirt?'

'Fionn and Erika,' he just goes, shaking his head – as in *delighted* for them?

There's, like, silence between us then.

I go, 'Dude, remind me to tell you something when you're pissed.'

He looks at me, half-eyed.

'I'm pissed now,' he goes.

I'm there, 'Okay. We've been stripped of our Leinster Schools Senior Cup medals . . .'

I don't get the reaction I'm expecting. He just kind of, like, nods, except it's like he's still – I don't know – *digesting* it?

'It's because I was on – let's be honest – drugs,' I go. 'I shouldn't have opened my mouth, but I did and now . . .'

'You know,' he suddenly goes, 'I don't actually care.'

I'm there, 'Are you serious?'

'What happiness did it ever bring us?'

I actually think he's bang out of order there but I don't say it.

'Hey, let's get out of here,' he goes; 'I need some air.'

We stagger down to the harbour, which is an incredible sight, by the way – we're talking thousands of yachts, some of them the size of actual hotels.

We stop and lean over a rail, looking down at, I don't know, whatever focking sea it is below us. We're both mullered. Of course I'm thinking, so what happens now, Johnny Keith? 'Are you coming home with me?'

He laughs.

'Home? You're joking, aren't you? Home to what, Ross? Ten years of court cases, watching everything I had repossessed, closed down, wound up? And at the end of it, what, bankruptcy?'

'Come on,' I go, 'you can dig yourself out of it. I've actually got a business idea for you.'

'A business idea? *You?*'

I laugh.

'I know, I'm actually pretty surprised at myself. Okay, there's, like, tens of thousands of vacant aportments in Dublin at the moment, which they haven't a hope of focking selling. I mean, who wants to end up being practically the only person living in a focking tower block.'

'Not many.'

'Exactly. So what these property developers have to do is convince people – potential buyers basically – that the block is actually occupied . . .'

'Okay.'

'Now, we've just had yet another shitty summer in Ireland – focking third in a row.'

'Rain?'

'Like you wouldn't believe. So I'm thinking, Woodie's and all that crowd, they've got to be thinking about cutting their losses and flogging off their gorden furniture cheap. So what *you* could do, roysh, is buy it from them, then lease it out to these developers for, I don't know, a certan amount every week, to stick on their balconies and make it look like someone's actually living there.'

He doesn't say anything for ages, just stares out to sea. Eventually, he goes, 'You'd *give* me that idea?'

I'm there, 'Yeah – are you saying it's good?'

'No, it's terrible.'

'Oh.'

'No, it's not terrible. But it's not going to raise the seventy-five million I owe.'

I'm there, 'But I'll come up with more for you,' and I realize all of a sudden – very embarrassing this – that I'm suddenly crying. 'See, all I need is a bit of time and space to think, Dude. I mean, that idea just came to me literally on the flight over here. I honestly think my old man was right. This recession could end up being the making of people like me.'

He puts his orm around my shoulder.

'Ross,' he goes, 'forget the idea. It's enough for me to know that you'd give that to me . . .'

'Well,' I go, 'that's friendship, Oisinn. You can't focking drug test it, man. Or put it in front of a jury. Or take it from one of the greatest rugby players of his generation and give it to some random focking livestock-worrier . . .'

He takes his orm from around my shoulder, reaches inside his shirt and pulls out his medal. Somehow I knew he'd be wearing his. He takes it from around his neck and, like, stares at it there in his hand. He's there, 'Of course, the cinematic thing to do would be to throw it out into the Mediterranean . . .'

The Mediterranean. See, I knew it was either that or the Pacific.

'But I'm not going to, Ross.'

He grabs my wrist, roysh, turns my hand over and presses the medal into my palm.

He's there, 'I want you to have it . . . Captain.'

Then he staggers on up the road. I don't even hesitate. I reach out over the rail, open my hand and drop it into the water.

It's just as I'm catching Oisinn up again that my phone suddenly rings. Because I'm banjoed, it takes me a good few seconds to answer it, though when I do I instantly sober up.

It's Helen.

She's screaming down the phone at me, to the point where I can't make any sense of what she's saying, until she finally blurts out the words I instantly understand. 'Your father's had a heart attack.'

I just stop, roysh, dead in my tracks.

I'm like, 'What?'

Oisinn must hear something in my voice because he stops too. 'My old man's in hospital,' I tell him. 'He's had a . . .'

He takes immediate chorge. He takes the phone out of my hand and asks Helen what hospital, while at the same time hailing a Jo.

I get into it. I don't even remember *getting* into it. I just know that I do, because the two of us – as in, me and Oisinn – are suddenly sat in the back, me feeling that everything's happening a hundred times slower than usual. I'm like, 'What if . . .'

Oisinn doesn't even let me finish my sentence. But I *do* finish the thought.

What if he . . .

Then it suddenly pops into my head that the old man's father went the same way.

Is it in the family?

We pull up outside the hospital. Oisinn pays the driver and screams at me to go on ahead. I peg it into the building, although I can't actually feel my legs moving. I'm looking around for some kind of reception desk but, before I find it, I spot Helen running towards me.

She's lost it.

'Your mother told me,' she goes, between sobs, 'she told me to watch his heart, Ross, and I didn't . . .'

Then she buries her head in my chest and I automatically hold her. She mentions that Erika's on her way – she's trying to get a flight, which means it mustn't look good for him.

She's there, 'You'd better go and see him . . .'

She leads me down this corridor and points out the ward. For about a minute, I don't even go in. I stand in, like, the frame of the doorway, looking at him, laid out on the bed, tubes and wires going in and out of him, this machine at his bedside beeping every second or two, measuring presumably his hort rate.

I walk closer. I don't *know* why, but I'm suddenly on, like, my tiptoes? His face is pale and he has a bruise on the side of his head. I'm presuming he must have fallen.

So I touch his hand and he turns his head, slowly, towards me. His voice is just a whisper, which I suppose could be the meds. 'Well, Kicker,' he just goes, 'this is a fine how-do-you-do, isn't it?'

And I don't remember what I say to him after that and I don't remember what he says to me – because all I can think about is that he called me Kicker.

He just wanted a decent book to read ...

Not too much to ask, is it? It was in 1935 when Allen Lane, Managing Director of Bodley Head Publishers, stood on a platform at Exeter railway station looking for something good to read on his journey back to London. His choice was limited to popular magazines and poor-quality paperbacks – the same choice faced every day by the vast majority of readers, few of whom could afford hardbacks. Lane's disappointment and subsequent anger at the range of books generally available led him to found a company – and change the world.

'We believed in the existence in this country of a vast reading public for intelligent books at a low price, and staked everything on it'
Sir Allen Lane, 1902–1970, founder of Penguin Books

The quality paperback had arrived – and not just in bookshops. Lane was adamant that his Penguins should appear in chain stores and tobacconists, and should cost no more than a packet of cigarettes.

Reading habits (and cigarette prices) have changed since 1935, but Penguin still believes in publishing the best books for everybody to enjoy. We still believe that good design costs no more than bad design, and we still believe that quality books published passionately and responsibly make the world a better place.

So wherever you see the little bird – whether it's on a piece of prize-winning literary fiction or a celebrity autobiography, political tour de force or historical masterpiece, a serial-killer thriller, reference book, world classic or a piece of pure escapism – you can bet that it represents the very best that the genre has to offer.

Whatever you like to read – trust Penguin.